OF STONE & MIST

BY DONNA HAWK

ISBN-10: 0985339004
ISBN-13: 978-0-9853390-0-5

Printed in the United States of America

To my family with love.

CONTENTS

CHAPTER ONE
ZEROS FOR ONE

Maria looked down at her torn dress as if seeing it for the first time, and thought absently that the dirt stains would never come out of it. The hysterical laugh that bubbled up in her throat was too near madness to care about the dress, though. This night was blacker than she had ever remembered night being. No moon. No stars. No lights of any kind. A heavy, wet mist had settled over the ground and had stubbornly gotten thicker and wetter. Too many things could be hidden in the mist.

She peered around the corner of the stone building to see if the way was clear across the length of the driveway. She could see her car, so near, yet her heart was sinking because she knew she couldn't be exposed for that long and expect to survive. It... he was sure to see her.

As madness set in, her heart, pumping so frantically before, was slowing into a heavy thud, sinking into a tar pit of black despair. She could feel it behind her. She could smell it: its cold, acrid scent of death.

In slow motion movement, she pushed her body away from the stone mansion. Her once-white evening dress fluttered away from her like a cloud. Her pumping arms flailed around trying to force her body to pick up speed. Her legs, leaden with fear and madness, could barely propel her body forward.

Maria looked behind her. That was her fatal error. She could see it coming for her. Slowly. Taking its time. Steady. Strong.

She tripped and fell to the ground, then turned over to her back and watched as it approached her. Like a spider, she tried to back away. It was ugly, but she couldn't take her eyes away from it.

Finally, she stopped thrashing about. She could feel her future shorten to the length of the driveway. It hovered over her and her eyes fluttered shut. As her fingers uncurled in acceptance, a small, gold object rolled away from her and hid in the grass at the edge of the driveway. Her last deep breath was of the cloying stench of it.

A wispy, dark mass settled over Maria's stiff body, then coalesced into a solid shape, consuming the young woman. It stood upright and turned back to where it had come. The now black-cloaked figure of

a man eyed the imposing structure that was the stone building and smiled.
He walked toward it, never glancing back to where Maria once laid.

Present day...

Jessa flipped through the pages of *National Geographic* and sighed heavily. Her wistful expression masked the absolute conviction that her photographs were just as good, if not better, than the ones displayed here. The thousands of dollars and the thousands of hours she spent on her passion danced frivolously through her brain. She was good... damn good, and she should have her photos spread across this magazine. She sighed again and put the magazine down.

Bills, bills bills! Jessa pushed the envelopes unopened away from her across the table. Her dream of working for a great magazine as a leading photographer seemed so far off despite the fact that she had won numerous awards and had been hired by top paying clients for her work. Still, she had bills to pay and needed some way of making ends meet until her big break.

Living so far from her dad was a definite disadvantage. Raised on a farm in Kansas, she moved north to go to college and he retired to southern Texas for the weather. However, even if he lived next door, there was no way she could bring herself to ask him for a loan. He had not been pleased with her choice of professions, and she did not want an "I told you so" lecture. Anyway, he was enjoying a warm cruise in the Bahamas with Margaret, her stepmother. She wasn't about to interrupt their fun.

Looking out of her small front window, she could see the beautiful fall day unfold. Though it was still early, the sun had already been up for a time, and the air had warmed to the ideal temperature for a nature walk. Today, though, she couldn't afford to spend her day seeking the perfect wildlife pictures in the hills of southern Wisconsin, nor could she visit her favorite winery as she often did in her free time. Today, she had to find a way to pay the bills and feed the enormous appetite that was her passion: her beloved photography.

With a bowl of oatmeal in her belly and a travel mug full of hot coffee in her hand, Jessa grabbed her jacket and practically skipped out to her car. Little in the world could keep her mood down for long; she was eternally optimistic and ceaselessly exuberant. Quick to smile, she had an equally quick tongue that had a tendency to be sharp. This often got her into trouble, but more often than not, her sunny disposition was just as quick to get her out of her difficulties. She was a little woman, but with a stalwart disposition.

Though she resisted, she was tempted for a moment to roll the car window down to let the warm air tug on her short, spiked hair. The dark chestnut color of it sparkled with golden highlights as the sun hit it.

Heading toward the state's capitol, Jessa found herself staring in awe at the bright white, imposing structure. The entire city of Madison seemed to revolve around this beautiful centerpiece. She parked her car in one of the parking garages, located in the downtown area of the city, and crossed the Capitol Square to a restaurant that resided in the shadows of the great capitol building.

With her camera slung over her shoulder and her precious photo portfolio tucked under her arm, she entered the restaurant where a friend worked as a waitress. She had confided to Jessa that the restaurant's manager might be interested in some advertising and needed updated photos. Jessa decided she'd take a look at the place and see if there was a job here.

Jessa spoke quickly to the hostess in hopes of speaking to the manager. Then, she took a chair near the door and waited. Patience was not strong in her character, so she thrummed her fingers on the seat beside her and looked around with interest at the restaurant's décor. Mentally taking notes on angles and positions to show the restaurant off at its best, she became distracted by voices being raised in anger and distress. She craned her neck around a column and listened closely.

The voices, between a man and a woman, raised and lowered in volume. The woman, obviously upset, was near tears. The man was stern, but sympathetic. As Jessa listened closer to catch their conversation, it became clear they thought they were alone in the room.

"I can't! I can't let it go! David, it's only been three years. How can I let our baby go?" The woman's voice caught in her throat as she became choked with tears.

"This isn't healthy." Jessa caught the sound of a cloth napkin being slapped against the table. David sighed loudly. "Honey, she's gone. We still have people keeping their ears and eyes open for her, but damn it, it's been three years. Don't you think she would come back if she was still alive? She was such a momma's girl." He sighed again, but when he spoke, his voice was full of unshed tears as well. "This is killing me. Losing my daughter; hell, no trace, no body… but now I feel like I'm losing you, too." He waited silently for his wife to get her voice back.

Finally, she spoke quietly, "I'm sorry. It's just… it's just that I need to know what happened to her. Just for my own peace of mind. My baby… my baby!" The woman dissolved into tears and Jessa could hear the clinking sound of silverware being pushed across the table. After a few silent, anguishing minutes, she spoke again. This time, however, her voice was harsh and angry. "I think *he* did it. *He* murdered our little girl and disposed of her body. Son of a bitch got away with murder and what happens? He is elected to public office. Death is too good for him!"

Another sigh. "You don't know that." The distraught woman mumbled something Jessa couldn't hear, then David continued, "I have to admit, though, it sounds fishy. He didn't have much of an alibi."

The next moment, a tall, young man dressed in tasteful black dress pants and a crisp, white shirt interrupted Jessa's rapt attention to the grief-stricken couple. The little red bow tie looked quaint and old-fashioned, but somehow appropriate for the modern/rustic setting of the restaurant.

The young manager raised a disapproving eyebrow as he realized Jessa had been listening to the couple on the other side of the column. Jessa dropped her gaze, ashamed that she had been caught so blatantly eavesdropping. Then, grinning, she looked up and said, "Is it always so quiet in here?" She thought to herself that some background music would be a nice touch to fill up the empty ambiance.

The manager smiled slightly, as if put off by her criticism to justify listening to the couple. "May I help you, or are you just here for the... atmosphere?" The sarcasm was not lost on Jessa.

Jessa didn't lose the smile, but the challenge had been accepted. "Atmosphere?" she repeated. "Oh, *that!* A little mood music would take care of that, you know." She watched as the young manager simply raised an eyebrow, so she hurried on, "Do you know Jeanette Wilson who works here on the weekends?" She waited for his nod. "She told me you were considering new advertising and I wanted to offer my services as a photographer... my prices are very reasonable. I have my portfolio with me." She lifted it from the floor beside her chair. "May I show you some of my previous work?"

The young man held up his hand in front of him to stop her from talking. "I'm sorry, that won't be necessary. I manage, I don't decide. That will have to be taken up with the owner. Let me give you his card." He walked over to the bar and reached around the counter. When he came back, he put the card on the table in front of her. Then, he looked pointedly at her and then the door and said, "Good day, then."

Knowing she'd been dismissed, Jessa stared up at him, then slid her gaze to the column which hid the now silent couple from her sight. She knew now would be a good time to retreat, so she reluctantly got up and headed for the door. Disappointed, she wished she could hear more about the missing daughter. The story intrigued her. Just inside the door, she hesitated. Studying the phone number on the card from the restaurant, she carefully tapped the numbers on her cell phone. Her phone was against her ear and she could hear the phone ring on the other end. Jessa glanced up as she heard a phone ring in tandem with hers at what must have been David and his wife's table.

"Good morning, David Escher speaking."

Jessa gasped as she heard David's voice in the receiver of her phone, as well as only a few feet from where she was standing. In a surprised panic, she whispered, "Sorry, wrong number!" and snapped her phone shut. She was too embarrassed at her eavesdropping to speak to David with the missing daughter.

Outside in the sunshine, Jessa hesitated and looked around. She could feel a groan of despair form in the pit of her stomach. *God, please don't make me go back to waiting tables!* she hissed under her breath.

She headed back toward her car. Her mind wandered in disappointment as she made a mental list of options. The bills had to be paid and she was the one to do it. She had to get a job.

Her reverie was interrupted by a woman's voice calling, "Miss? Oh, Miss!"

Jessa turned around to see a woman approach her. She was tall and thin, fifty-ish, very stylish and obviously wealthy. Following her was a man of like description, but less enthusiastic and falling farther behind.

"Yes?" Jessa eyed the woman as she approached. She recognized the voice from the restaurant, and wondered what she could possibly want from her.

For a moment, the woman looked ashamed as she smiled. "I…" A hint of tears welled up in the woman's eyes. It was evident she had been crying, but through the tears, the woman laughed self-consciously. "I have to apologize for eavesdropping, but I have to admit I overheard you talking to

Peter, the manager of our restaurant. You are a photographer?"

Jessa nodded, now that it was clear why the woman had sought her out. Jessa smiled encouragingly. Maybe there was a job here after all.

The woman nervously brushed her hair back away from her face. "I'm sorry; I forgot to introduce myself. My name is Norma Escher. My husband, David, and I own the restaurant." She swept her hand to her right, indicating the storefront. Then she looked at Jessa with a stern expression that was hard to read. "You do advertising." It was a statement. "You do just advertising or do you do other photographic projects?"

Jessa couldn't help but grin. "I do all kinds of photographs. Portrait, nature, advertising, children… what kind did you have in mind?"

In an effort to keep from drawing attention to their conversation, Norma beckoned Jessa back inside the restaurant. She followed, suppressing giddy excitement. David followed silently behind.

When they were seated, with cups of steaming latte in front of them, Norma leaned on her elbows toward Jessa and looked seriously into her face. "Would you be willing to take pictures for us? Nothing illegal, of course, but highly unconventional."

The question took Jessa by surprise. Thinking quickly, she could feel a story here and wondered if it had anything to do with the missing daughter. Nevertheless, to play it safe, she hesitated. "Define unconventional."

David and Norma exchanged a look that said they'd had this conversation before. "We want pictures of a man, where he lives, what he does…"

"But that's stalking. Isn't that illegal?" Jessa frowned.

"Oh no," Norma was quick to reassure her. "Not stalking. This man is a public official, a member of the city council. His home is on the register of historic sites and is open to public tours. You'd have every right to be there. And if you happen to take pictures of, well, other things, then you'd have the perfect excuse." Norma's eyes started to water again.

"You mean," Jessa pondered what Norma had told her, "a snoop job? You want me to spy on this man?"

Again, David and Norma exchanged a familiar look. Norma spoke, "We don't have to use that term, do we? We are just interested in his daily activities."

Jessa was silently thoughtful for a minute. "So, basically you want me to check this man out and see if he does anything out of the ordinary, take pictures of his activities, and report back to you? Any particular reason why him?"

A tear silently rolled down Norma's cheek. David was in little better shape. "He murdered our daughter," Norma said. "We need some little bit of evidence that will reopen the case. Anything out of the ordinary. Anything about his house that could conceal her body. Any piece of paper that would question his innocence. We need to know why our daughter was murdered!"

Jessa could feel her face flush with excitement at the challenge and the anger at the shameless audacity of a man who could be so careless with the life of another. "What is this man's name?"

A small triumphant smile passed between husband and wife. "His name is Mitch Connor."

"Mitch Connor!" Jessa almost choked. She didn't know much about the man, but what she did know made him seem like a saint. He was terribly handsome, obscenely wealthy, and was probably the most eligible bachelor in the entire city. He had recently been elected to the city council, though why he needed a job was anyone's guess. He was an accomplished scuba diver and loved sailing on the lakes. His public image was spotless, but his private life was carefully concealed.

"So, do you think you'd be interested in the job?"

David spoke up for the first time.

Jessa shrugged. She had bills to pay, and it sounded like this would be a full-time job that would last for a while. "I have to make a living."

David smiled, though without humor. "Money is not a problem." He wrote a figure on a napkin, and then pushed it over to her. When she saw the numbers written there, she almost choked again.

"Are you kidding?" She had never seen so many zeros willing to be hers.

"That number will be yours every week you bring us information, no matter how trivial you think it is." David tossed his pen down onto the table in exclamation.

Jessa's eyes glazed over. "Yes, I think that will do fine. Where and when?"

Norma reached over the table and clasped David's hand. "Now!" The word was emphatic. "Do you know where the Maple Bluff area is? You may need to drive several blocks before you see the historic register sign, but when you do, turn left down a lane that looks not much larger than a one-car path. It's groomed, of course, but there are so many trees around that the lawn is somewhat obscured. There is an old mansion there with a stone foundation. The Bristol House. He has an apartment on the top floor, but he also has an apartment downtown. So… sometimes he's not there." There was great meaning in her last comment.

Jessa nodded with understanding. "What makes you think that Mr. Connor is guilty of murder?"

Norma was silent a moment, and Jessa was afraid the woman would start crying again, but the expression hardened on her face. "Because she was engaged to Mitch when she disappeared. They were supposed to be at a party together, an engagement party for a friend of theirs. Something happened, though. He claims he left the mansion without her; she was to meet up with him later as she was busy doing… something. But when he showed up to the party, he was drunk and upset.

He didn't seem in the least surprised that our daughter never showed up to the party. At least, according to his friends."

Jessa could feel her heart breaking for this couple. "What was your daughter's name?"

Norma smiled, genuinely, for the first time. "Her name is Maria."

WHEN JESSA LEFT THE RESTAURANT, she felt the weight of the check with many zeros in her pocket. Her first course of action would be to deposit the check and keep her bill payments from overdrafting her checking account. Then she would see if she could find out something about the Bristol House and its mysterious owner, Mr. Mitch Connor.

Nearly at the garage where she'd left her car, Jessa found her attention diverted to a curio shop that had one of everything. What caught her eye was a stand of postcards. As a photographer, she often eyed the cards critically. As if led to it, she picked up the nearest card and studied it. "The Bristol House" it claimed and showed the photograph of an old stone and wood mansion with an imposing Victorian tower jutting out from the top level. On a whim, she ambled up to the counter, purchased the postcard and stuck it in her camera bag. Outside, as if foreshadowing the days to come, gray clouds covered the once-blue sky and a streak of lightning flashed brightly.

CHAPTER TWO
JESSA MEETS BRISTOL HOUSE

A dark, misty rain settled over the city of Madison. Though it was still early in the fall, the air took on a chill as it often did when the sun was out of sight. This did not deter Jessa from settling her current debts, then heading her car toward the Maple Bluff area where Bristol House was located.

As she drove through the isthmus, she carefully skirted the Capitol Square's one-way streets and headed northeast on Johnson Street before turning straight north to residential Maple Bluff. If she had hoped the rain would let up, she was disappointed. If anything, the day darkened until the middle of the afternoon resembled late evening.

The woods in this area were thick and tall. Tangles of overgrown foliage covered the ground, obscuring buildings and houses. Occasionally, Jessa got a glimpse of Lake Mendota through the branches and trunks as she drove. The lake water today was as gray as the sky.

Except for the general location of Maple Bluff, she was unfamiliar with the area. She drove slowly, looking for the billboard the Bristol House would surely display. Set away from the other houses in the area, she finally saw the sign. It was built of stone and wood, like the house, and was elegantly simple. On the front a sign advertised: The Bristol House, circa 1860: THIS SITE POSSESSES NATIONAL SIGNIFICANCE IN COMMEMORATING THE HISTORY OF THE UNITED STATES OF AMERICA.

Turning in the driveway, she sincerely hoped she did not meet another car on the narrow strip of pavement.

When Bristol House finally came into sight, Jessa drew in a surprised breath—the postcard had not done the structure justice. It was a beautiful Victorian home that made her think of pictures from a historical periodical! It was elegant and grand but with a touch of mystery about it. The main story was gray stone with a wide stone porch, or veranda, that ran nearly the entire length of the house. A great bay window, facing the lawn, stared blankly out at the gray day. The second story, also the same gray stone, had two visible balconies: one facing the road and one looking out over the woods. There was also a large, square room that covered the corner and hid, what Jessa suspected, was a third balcony, invisibly facing the direction of Lake Mendota. The third story of the structure was wooden, as was the quaint, round tower that jutted out of the corner nearest the driveway.

The wooden portion of the house, in the dark daylight, appeared to be off-white, eggshell color, but the trim and gables were a dusty shade of mauve. Gingerbread arches and curlicues adorned every corner, window, doorway, and rail post. Its immaculate condition spoke of generations of care. A parking area had been designated for tours. However, today was, apparently, not one of those days as the lot was now empty.

Jessa parked near the house, turned off her car, and stared up at the house. It was a magnificent structure with good lines, preserved as it would have been when it was new. As she was about to turn away, a movement in an upper story window caught her eye, but when she looked again, she decided it must be the reflection of a breeze blowing woodland branches around.

She donned her raincoat before she left her car, covered her camera with a plastic casing to protect it from the moisture, and shut the door as quietly as possible. In her mind, she composed a justification for being here on a day that was obviously not set aside for tourists. She would say she was taking photos for the Historical Society since this was on the register of historic sites of Wisconsin. How could the owner argue with that? That is, she raised an eyebrow in contemplation, unless he checked with the curator of the Historical Society!

Jessa was a tiny figure against the monumental size of the house. Barely reaching five-foot-four, she could scarcely claim one hundred fifteen pounds. However, what she lacked in stature, she made up for in courage. She stood brazenly in the middle of the lawn and shot a straight-on picture in front of the house. Then she went to the corners and snapped some more photos. Birds chittered noisily in accompaniment to the shutter clicks from her camera.

Today the house was not the only thing she was interested in photographing. She also took careful pictures of the foundation, as well as the shrubbery and other foliage that surrounded it. She took several quick photos at the upper floor windows and considered climbing onto the porch to look in the first floor windows that were low enough for her to reach. First, she decided to finish her scan of the outside perimeter.

Walking around the lake side of the house, she saw the architecture was just as interesting and the design just as intricate as the front. The care of the house wasn't just a public façade, but seemed to be genuine throughout. In the back by the woods, she found an outdoor cellar. There was a padlock on the heavy wooden door to keep away any intruders. The paint near the lock looked fresh and shinier than that around it, indicating it had recently been painted in just that area. Jessa cocked her head to one side to contemplate the meaning of that.

Finally, she turned in the direction of the only side of the house she had not yet photographed: the side nearest the road and parking lot. As she walked, she became aware of the sound, or rather, the lack of it. It was suddenly as if God had pushed the mute button on the world's remote. Just as that thought crossed her mind, she could hear a faint creaking of a door, and then a "click" as the door shut. Her heart hammered in her chest. If the owner caught her here on this back side of the house, it would be obvious that she was not taking ordinary pictures.

She hurried to the road and looked up into the windows on the upper floors. They remained dark and empty. The house looked vacant but the sound of the shutting door had said otherwise, and as Jessa headed for her car, her ears were assaulted once again by the noisy birds that roosted in the woods.

She could hardly wait to get her photos loaded onto her computer. Her bank account now made her excited to share whatever pictures her new clients wanted. However, as she stepped into the parking lot, she looked up to see another car was parked there. Because the lot was large and empty, she found herself annoyed that this person would park in the only space that bordered hers.

The car beside her little Honda was a sleek, black BMW convertible, though with the top up. It oozed taste and wealth, much like the driver sitting quietly behind the wheel studying her. *Yikes!* she thought as her heart raced guiltily. *Busted!*

She stopped short in her tracks and stared back at him. She reminded herself that this was, in some ways, public domain and she had a right to be here. All the same, she swallowed hard.

The man in the car got out and shut the door quietly, never taking his eyes off her. He was very good-looking, dark, expensively dressed… and furious. Taller than most men she knew, she wondered how a man with the perfect high cheekbones and just enough five o'clock shadow to look rakish could glower so attractively. Jessa knew that if she waited for him to yell at her, she would sound guilty and no words would come into her brain that would make her appear otherwise. So, she opted for sarcasm.

"Really, dude? Seriously?" she chastised, "could you park a little closer, please? Jeez, I wouldn't want your pretty little car to get sideswiped!"

The surprised look on his face said her words did exactly as she had hoped. While he was still off guard, she quickly unlocked the door to her Honda and slid behind the wheel. However, she was prevented from shutting the door when the man pulled the door open farther away from Jessa. She stared at him straight in the eye and declared, "Look, maybe you don't care, or maybe you have a whole fleet of pretty little cars at your disposal, but this is my only car and it's getting wet in here. If it gets wet, I get wet. If I get wet, I get pissed. Now, shut the damn door!"

"What the hell are you doing around my home?" His voice was pleasantly low, but his handsome face was scrunched up into such a furious scowl that Jessa considered laughing out loud... see how he'd react to that!

"Oh! I'm sorry," she mocked, "aren't they giving tours today?" She looked around her quickly, as if assessing the empty parking lot. "Well, dang, I must have gotten my days mixed up. Sorry, mister. I guess I'll study the schedule a little more carefully next time." She finally managed to wrest the door away from the man and slammed it shut. An instant later, her engine roared to life, and she wasted no time backing out of the parking space and accelerating down the driveway. The man from the BMW stood still in the rain and watched her car drive away.

Jessa's heart was still thumping loudly in the silent car as she drifted deep in thought along the Beltline. That was the first time she'd seen Mitch Connor up close and personal. He was even more handsome than the photos she'd seen, with his dark brown hair and intense green eyes. He was tall without the long, lanky look many tall people had, and was perfectly proportioned. What she had remembered most about their brief meeting was the absolute fury in his expression when he caught her there. Sure, her sarcasm hadn't won her his undying affection, but what could she expect? She smiled slightly at the memory.

Her apartment was a little stuffy after the fresh, albeit rainy, afternoon. Jessa opened her kitchen window several inches to let the cool autumn air waft in. Moments later, the apartment smelled like fresh coffee.

Popping open her laptop on the kitchen table, she inserted the media card from her camera and began to load the photos she'd taken at Bristol House. She grinned conspiratorially, trying to devise a way to get into the house to take some pictures there. With all those zeros waiting for her, she didn't want to end her snoop job too soon.

However, the pictures were very disappointing. The first few at the front of the house were the best. Clear. The color was excellent. Focus sharp.

The others, however, and getting progressively worse as she had stayed there, had become foggy and the color faded. At the very end, the images were nearly black and white, perhaps cast a little on the yellow side.

Dust orbs, or perhaps raindrops, danced in some of the photos as they were caught by the camera's flash. Mist smudges kept appearing in the top, right corner of her screen. Even the windows, though the house had been observably empty, had smudges in them.

Perhaps she'd forgotten to clean her camera lens, but then negated that idea. She always cleaned her lenses.

Well, her camera was due for a sensor cleaning, apparently. She couldn't make money with a dirty camera. She got out her phone book and was searching the yellow pages for the name of a camera repair shop that cleaned sensors when she stopped suddenly and chucked to herself.

The house had not been empty. She had distinctly heard the creak and closing of a door. She wondered briefly who the handsome owner's visitor was. Still, manmade window smudges or not, it wouldn't hurt to have her camera sensors cleaned.

A short while later, after she'd dropped her camera off at Hanson's camera repair shop, she returned to her apartment and dug her old camera out of its storage in the back of the coat closet. It had been cleaned before being stored, and though it was a little out of date, she loved the pictures it took. She spent the evening re-familiarizing herself with the older camera and thinking about Mitch Connor.

He was definitely a looker, but in no way did this sway her opinion of him... which was getting lower by the hour. In fact, she decided, he was a low-down scum. Even if he hadn't done away with poor Maria (though Jessa was convinced he was guilty,) he had clearly not expected Maria to show up to the party, as well as arriving drunk and upset. This did not speak well for a would-be murder suspect.

If he hadn't murdered Maria, what did he know? If it wasn't him, did he know who it was? Was he trying to protect someone? Something didn't add up, and Jessa was absolutely determined to find out what was going on. At some point, perhaps, she could go to the library to look at the archived films of newspapers from the time of Maria's disappearance.

It was late when Jessa shut her computer off. The only accounts she could find on the Internet about Maria Escher were of a missing persons report and her parents' plea to return her unharmed. As the months passed, though, the pleas for return became pleas for the location of her body. Still, no one came forward, no one had seen her, and Mitch Connor was not talking. Suspicion had automatically turned to him, but the fact that he came from one of the wealthiest families in the state and that his reputation for decency and kindness preceded him, little suspicion actually formed into fact. It was a fact that he was engaged to Maria. It was a fact that he was at the engagement party alone... and drunk. It was also a fact that he had been sailing in his new boat on Lake Mendota with friends, drinking themselves stupid, when poor Maria was supposed to have disappeared. As money talked, Jessa suspected, little damaging information got out into the public eye. Something in this story didn't add up for Jessa. In fact, it stunk.

Despite the coolness of the rainy afternoon, the evening was warmer by far, so Jessa left the kitchen window open slightly and started to turn out the light. Just as she was reaching for the wall switch, she remembered the postcard she had stuck inside her camera bag. It was the one with the photo of Bristol House on it.

She pulled the card out of the bag and studied the photo closely. Coincidentally, this photograph was taken on a day comparable with this rainy afternoon. The photo was dark, as were the windows of the house and the cloud-laden sky. The colors of the house itself had been super-saturated, probably in a photo-editing program. The eggshell color of the siding was too bright, the mauve too pink, and the gray stone on the first story was nearly black. The photo had a strange, almost 3-D quality to it, as if it was a window where a person could walk right up to the house.

Jessa set the postcard on a shelf near the kitchen doorway and reached up to the wall switch to turn the light off. She had been afraid that the day's extraordinary events would keep her brain from allowing her to fall asleep, but to her pleasant surprise, that was not the case. She fell asleep easily and slept hard.

As sunlight greeted her sleepy eyes the next morning, her first thoughts were of going back to Bristol House to do some more snooping. This time, she would try to get inside the house. The main change she'd make, she decided firmly, would be to hide her car. She didn't think two days of sarcastic innocence would sit too well with the wealthy Mitch Connor.

As was her custom, Jessa showered, then headed to the kitchen for coffee and cereal. Just inside the kitchen door, the postcard of Bristol House fluttered to the floor and landed by her feet. She picked up the card and studied it once more. The house, which had started to appear ominous the night before, now looked like an ordinary mansion... or as ordinary as a mansion could look.

She set the card back up on the shelf in a position that would keep it from falling off again. She looked up and shivered at the breeze coming in from the open kitchen window. Reaching up to shut it, she saw the bright orange breast of a robin as it flitted by. Smiling, she ran for her camera, but by the time she got back to the window, the bird was gone. Disappointed, she made herself a small pot of coffee, and while it was brewing, she ate a bowl of oatmeal. She loved this part of her day.

It was a lovely, sunny day without a cloud in the sky. She hoped it would stay this way, especially after getting soaked in yesterday's rain. Besides, she wanted to see Bristol House in the sunlight. Without knowing why, she had the thought that the house seemed moody. For a while she pondered that thought, then dismissed it with a frown. Only a fantasy freak would give that much credence to a manmade structure. She was after facts.

When she entered the Maple Bluff area, she looked critically at the sky. It was still bright blue and cloudless. The sunshine gave her confidence for what she was about to do. Then, just as she was approaching the driveway of Bristol House, a sleek BMW convertible came blasting out of the small lane. Jessa swerved to keep her Honda from being hit. When she pulled off the road and came to a stop, she held her hand over her heart to calm her shaken nerves. Her first reaction would normally be to jump out of her car and yell and stamp her foot and pump her arms in rage at the dim-witted driver in the other car. Today, she attempted to temper her road-rage enthusiasm. Mitch Connor had not been looking where he was driving. He had not noticed that he nearly ran over her, had not even seen her. Today, that was probably a good thing.

CHAPTER THREE
TOURIST DAY

Since he was gone, Jessa happily decided to take the easy route and park her car in the parking lot again. She was surprised, when she got there, to see the lot nearly full. This must be a tourist day. Instead of being disappointed, she was glad to be able to get inside the house without worrying about being arrested.

Armed with her old, but trusty, camera, Jessa headed across the veranda for the front door of Bristol House. In today's sunshine, the house appeared calm and innocuous. The gingerbread ornamentation gave the house the appearance of a fairy tale. Jessa took her place in a line of smiling sightseers and purchased a ticket.

As she entered the house, she could feel a surge of excitement. She was tantalized by the story this old mansion would tell her. The walls seemed alive: what secrets would they reveal? A shudder of electricity raised the hair along her arms. Jessa grinned in giddy anticipation, made even more thrilling by the job she was here to do.

Just inside the front door, she entered a long, narrow hall made narrower by a flight of stairs on the left. To the right was the parlor, or living room in today's homes. At the end of the hall, a tidy young woman waited for a group of tourists to assemble. She had a no-nonsense way about her that said she would like to be somewhere else, probably enjoying the last warm days of the year. Then, as the crowd came together for their tour, the young woman's demeanor changed. She smiled and started her spiel about the house lore.

Motioning for the group to gather closer, she spoke loudly, "Hello everyone, my name is Debbie. I'll be your tour guide for Bristol House today." The crowd stopped talking and waited patiently for Debbie to resume. When she had their attention, she continued, "Welcome to Bristol House, home of city council member Mitch Connor, one of our most prominent citizens. Now, S. J. Hubert and his lovely wife, Virginia, built Bristol House somewhere between 1860 and 1863. The exact date is in question because they say that Virginia, who was very particular about the way the carpenters were handling the original floor plan, insisted they redo a great part of the first floor. Because she was unhappy with the arrangement of the kitchen, she spent a great deal of money to have them rearrange it to suit her. But like a lot of women these days…" she winked at a middle-aged man standing near her "…she changed her mind yet again and had the carpenters tear the new kitchen out and replace it with…" Debbie paused for effect "…the original floor plan kitchen!" Debbie grinned and waited until the assembled crowd finished tittering. Then she moved into the parlor and the group followed. "The parlor was seldom used except for entertaining clients of S. J., who was an attorney for the city of Madison."

The parlor, with its antique oak woodwork, was connected to a hall by sliding doors and had a front window of plate and stained glass. From the parlor, they toured the dining room, which was large and light and opened out to the front veranda. It had a large bay window looking out on the lawn. Across the hall was a beautiful and sizeable sitting room, or family room, that had a tiny children's bedroom annex. The hall had a second set of stairs leading to the second floor, and finally, the kitchen was at the back of the house, and opened to a covered porch. At the time it was built, the kitchen would have been the newest, nicest thing. A lovely, ornate water pump adorned a clawfoot sink. There was an unbelievable amount of cabinets, unusual for the time, and a large pantry.

Though practical, the kitchen seemed plain in comparison to the outside of the house. Jessa ran her hands along the counters and felt the smooth woodwork. She could imagine a young woman being very happy and pleased with this kitchen, especially in that long ago era.

Jessa listened to Debbie talk and point out details of the house. She was a very good tour guide, but it seemed to Jessa that some information was either missing or incomplete. So, at the end of the tour, which sadly didn't involve any of the remainder of the house, only the first floor, Jessa raised her hand to ask a question. "Why did they name the mansion Bristol House? I figured that a man named Bristol built it." Jessa asked.

A pleased looked crossed Debbie's face as she smiled hugely at Jessa. "Yes, that seems like it should be right, but in fact, Bristol House was named after S. J.'s in-laws. Bristol was Virginia's maiden name. Her family lived on the east coast near Boston. When Virginia and S. J. got married, they came out "west" and fell in love with the area. As far as anyone knows, she never returned to Boston. Not even to visit."

Jessa thought about that answer. "Did the Bristols ever get to see the house that carried their name?"

Again an expression of pleased surprise crossed Debbie's pretty features. Jessa suppressed a grin; though she must be messing up Debbie's carefully practiced delivery, the young woman probably didn't get too many questions from her captive audience. "No, unfortunately they never came to Wisconsin. It isn't clear if they didn't want to come, couldn't afford it, or if Virginia didn't want them to come."

"Doesn't it seem odd, though," Jessa considered, "that they would go to the trouble of naming the house after the Bristols and then not want them to come see it?"

Debbie laughed slightly, though her expression was becoming weary. "Then perhaps the answer is that they couldn't afford the trip. It would have been a very expensive trip, as well as long and tiring. Or perhaps one of them had taken ill. Any number of things could have happened that would have prevented the Bristols from visiting. Like I said, the reason they didn't visit here isn't clear. The only thing known for certain is that they didn't." Debbie stopped talking and, looking pointedly at Jessa, waited for any other questions.

"Okay, thanks." What she'd learned about the Bristol family didn't make sense to her. The house was obviously expensive, so money was probably not an issue. It was doubtful that estrangement was an issue either, or why would Virginia have named the house after her parents? Something else was afoot, Jessa suspected, because a visit to their daughter's home would have been very important. Perhaps, Jessa mused, it was illness as Debbie offered as an option or even a fear of traveling "west".

Speculating about their motives, Jessa also couldn't help but wonder why a young woman wouldn't want to return home, even if it was just for a visit. Perhaps S. J. hadn't been inclined to spend the money for a train ticket back to the east coast. Then another thought popped into her mind: if money was no object in building Virginia the perfect house, maybe it was S. J. himself who stopped her from going home. Was he insecure enough to force her to stay close by? To prevent her family from seeing her?

It wasn't until the tour was over and Jessa's group was leaving that she realized she'd been so involved in the history of Bristol House that she hadn't taken one photograph. She cursed herself silently. With an expression of chagrin, she stepped up to Debbie and another tour guide and asked, "I would love to take some photos. If I promise to stay out of everyone's way, could I stick around and get some?" She smiled her brightest smile. Plus, a little flattery couldn't hurt. "It's just that your speech on the history was so fascinating I forgot I even had my camera!" Debbie blushed with pleasure.

"Oh, sure, I don't think that would be a problem. Just… stay on the first floor." Debbie glanced quickly at her coworker, and then back at Jessa. "Rules, you know?"

"No problem!" In her mind, though, Jessa had already dismissed the two guides and was devising a plan that would get her upstairs without being noticed.

For half an hour, Jessa stayed on the first floor, out of the way of the tour guides, and took pictures of every nook and cranny. Doors, closets, strange little recesses, the children's bedroom annex… nothing was left alone. She made sure she caught the eye of Debbie occasionally in the hopes that she became comfortable with Jessa's presence and would ultimately ignore her. With that (hopefully) accomplished, she stepped lightly and quickly up the stairs two at a time, using the stairway in the hall just off the kitchen. It was out of the way, obviously less used, and out of sight for most of the time. At the top of the steps, she heard a loud creak, and cursed the loose boards of the stairs. Looking behind her down the steps, no one had come to investigate, so she quickly hopped away from direct sight.

She found herself in an upstairs hall almost identical to the one downstairs. This stairwell entry opened to a long hallway that divided the upstairs into two halves. There were several bedrooms up here. The one in the back was where the servants might have stayed at one time. Since the Huberts had only one heir, a boy, the other bedrooms were probably either used for guests or a study for S. J. or his son. The front hall stairwell was wide and opened to the tower, which in turn opened onto the balcony. The windows of the tower were curved to match the curve of the walls. Jessa was fascinated as she ran her fingers along the windowsill. The woodwork and wainscot on the second story, unlike the oak parlor, was probably ash. The patina on the wood had darkened with age, but was remarkably well preserved.

Each bedroom had an ample closet, but there was only one bath in the entire house located at the back of the second story across from the servants' bedroom. When Jessa had taken all the pictures she needed at this point, she started to tiptoe her way downstairs again, but then was caught by the notion that this house had three stories. Yet, she had not seen another set of stairs leading up to it.

So, she retraced her steps through the second story. This time, as she explored every bedroom, she examined the inside of each of the closets. She found that the largest bedroom, probably the master owing to the fireplace in the corner, had a door recessed into the wall of its closet. Dressed to look like the wallpapered surface, she discovered the practically invisible knob to open it, and exposed another set of stairs leading to the third floor. This, she reasoned, is where the mysterious Mitch Connor lived when he stayed here at Bristol House.

It was odd, she pondered, that the door to the third floor was located inside the master bedroom closet. Unless the Huberts were secretive about the third floor, some obvious reconstruction had been done to the house. The question was: was it done before Mitch Connor had taken possession of the house, or did he have the reconstruction done himself? If he did it, was it done before or after the disappearance of Maria Escher? If it was after, what was he hiding in the reconstruction?

Jessa took pictures of the doorway and the stairs leading up. For a moment, she tried to decide whether or not to take a chance on going to the third floor. The door, however, opened easily when she turned the knob. Since the lack of confidence and audacity had never been her problem, she took a deep breath and stepped onto the stairs.

The stairway was narrow and the steps were short as if they were made for a child. As she slowly went up in elevation, she considered that the top floor might have been used as a playroom for their child. However, with that in mind, it seemed an unlikely location for the stairway. These steps, unlike anywhere else in the house, were covered with carpet.

Jessa stepped out of the stairwell and into another world. A modern world. Wall-to-wall carpet covered the entire floor in pale tan. The walls were painted tastefully in shades of pastel gold with taupe accents. Every modern state-of-the-art convenience dotted the entire third floor. Though a small apartment, there was no lack of amenities here.

One entire wall was dedicated to entertainment with a huge flat screen television and a top-of-the-line stereo system. Jessa found herself lured to the titles of Mitch Connor's CD collection. Ella Fitzgerald... Van Halen... Frank Sinatra... Buddy Holly... Taylor Swift... Nine Inch Nails... was there no end to his eclectic taste in music?

Similarly, she was drawn to his massive collection of book titles. *Beowulf* to a compilation of sailing manuals... this man was certainly amazingly well rounded. Plus, the whole apartment was immaculate. That probably meant he had a cleaning woman, which meant someone Jessa needed to talk to.

She figured she had all the pictures she needed for the time being, and so turned to sneak back down to the first floor. So far, so good. She seemed to be pretty good at snooping. She smiled to herself at her clever ways.

Apparently, she had congratulated herself too soon. It was only luck and good hearing that she heard heavy, measured steps ascending the stairs. As the stepping sound reached the door to the apartment, they turned around and slowly descended as if they had changed their mind about entering. Then, she heard the soft scrape of the door to the third floor and the almost silent "click" of that door being shut. The footfalls ascending suddenly did so at an alarming rate. In a panic, she looked around the beautiful apartment for someplace to hide. *Damn*! She cursed her luck.

With little time to plan, she dashed toward the kitchen end of the room and hid under the bar. Though it effectively concealed her, she could see around the granite-molded edge to the top of the stairs. She waited. Several minutes passed. Just to be certain, she waited longer.

Then, almost out loud, she laughed at her panic. Someone must have come up to the second floor and saw that she had left the stairway door open. They had checked the stairway, but not knowing she was up here, they had shut it. No one had come up the stairs at all. Well, she berated herself, next time she would be more careful. A snoop could not be careful enough—this was her new rule number one.

For posterity (and to remind herself of this close call) she propped herself up against the kitchen cabinet, still sitting on the floor, and took a photograph of the bar and stairway. She giggled wildly in relief.

She was not all the way to her feet when she heard the stairway door open again and the unmistakable sound of hurried footfalls taking the steps at least two at a time. Her heart jumped in her throat and pumped so loudly that her hearing suddenly went numb. *Oh, my god*, she wailed silently.

She ducked behind the counter just in time for someone to appear in the room. She only got a cursory glance, but she suspected it was the inexplicable Councilman Connor. With one eye, she peeked around the bar, lightheaded with her good luck, that the structure was solid. A man dressed in sleek, black slacks and a tweed jacket had his back to her and was looking out of a set of glass doors that led out onto a balcony. His mood seemed to be pensive as he stood in thought and stared. Then, with the quickness of a predatory cat, he turned around and faced the bar, then walked to the kitchen where Jessa sat, without breathing, on the floor, under the bar.

Jessa closed her eyes and said a little prayer. She could almost feel a noose around her neck. No amount of sarcasm could get her out of this fix.

The "chink" of keys and change rolling around on the granite top of the bar was way too near for comfort. Jessa could imagine the man coming around to her side of the bar to get something out of the refrigerator and discover her there. Oh, man, that would be bad!

However, to her relief, quiet footsteps took him away from the kitchen area into what she could only assume was the bedroom. At odds with her current situation, she found herself disappointed that she hadn't thought to check out the bedroom and bathroom while she was here. Well, that could wait for another trip. She knew, just as she knew she would not be caught this day, that she would return to this third floor apartment. Mitch Connor was way too interesting, and she was getting paid way too much to leave him alone.

As soon as she heard him shut the bathroom door, she popped up off the floor and made a silent dash to the stairway. Down the steps by twos, she stopped at the bottom and, as quietly as possible, opened the door and left the stairwell. This time, she made sure she closed the door behind her.

She didn't breathe until she was safely in her car and headed down the narrow driveway that led away from Bristol House. Her nervous laughter was as much from adrenalin as fright. Her only thought now was to get the pictures off her camera.

On her way back to her apartment, she stopped at Hanson's Camera Repair Shop and picked up her other camera. It was clean now, so there shouldn't be any problems with smudgy photos.

By early afternoon, Jessa had her new photos loaded onto her computer, and had repacked the old camera in its box, returning it to its place in her coat closet. She didn't bother to peruse her photos as a cursory glance told her the color was bright and the clarity was perfect.

The beautiful, sunny day lured her outside. It was uncommonly warm for autumn, but cold weather was inevitably around the corner. Jessa spent every possible moment outside to soak up enough warmth to last until April.

Wollersheim Winery in Prairie du Sac was one of the many wineries that Wisconsin could boast, and it was Jessa's favorite to visit. Located on top of a hill, the rock building had originally been a huge barn, but was converted to a winery a couple of generations ago. Grape vines, now withering with the onset of winter, spread across the nearby hills.

Sitting among the many visitors, she listened to and watched the film provided by the winery's owners on their history.

Then when the tour guide opened a door to lead them to another part of the winemaking operation, Jessa was stunned to see that a certain city council member was staring directly at her. Had Mitch Connor followed her here?

CHAPTER FOUR
TRAPPED!

So, Jessa did the only thing she could think of: she tipped her nose fractionally higher and ignored him.

Unfortunately, the theory behind this was easier to manage than the actual practice. The group she toured with was small, and she could not help but physically bump elbows with him. Each time this happened, she withdrew her arm as if she had gotten burned and moved away. However, "away" wasn't nearly far enough to make her happy. By the end of the tour she was on edge, angry, and felt in desperate need of the wine samples that were sure to be forthcoming.

What really aggravated her was that Mitch Connor remained coolly detached and seemingly oblivious to her discomfiture. She didn't even bother to smell the pinot noir or let it roll around her tongue to taste the black currant, or the hint of bay leaves and eucalyptus. Much to the consternation of the tour guide, she tipped her head back and swilled the small glass of wine like a drunken sailor.

Not surprisingly, this earned her the attention of the entire group, Mitch Connor included, and all she could do to defend herself was smile and declare, "Damn fine pinot noir. My favorite… could I have another glass?"

She didn't end up with another glass of the excellent pinot noir, but instead a bottle, which she purchased at the gift shop when she wasn't allowed to continue sampling with the tour group.

Outside, sitting on a bench in the warm sun, she pouted and wished for many horrible things to happen to Mitch Connor. She was tempted to open her magnum of wine and drink directly from the bottle, but she suspected this might get her kicked off the property forever and, well, that would be a shame considering how much she enjoyed visiting here.

Bright sun and warm temps lulled her to a sleepy state, so she closed her eyes and started to relax. She pointedly ignored the subject of Mr. Connor in her mind, since all he seemed to do is make her angry, and without any effort at all. All too soon, her peaceful lull was shattered when a pleasant, low voice pierced the silent afternoon.

"Do you enjoy making a fool of yourself?" It was a statement disguised as a question.

Jessa opened one eye and found herself staring into the frank gaze of Mitch Connor. She was suddenly wide-awake, and sat up from her sleepy slouch. "Love it," she countered. "Keeps me young. So, what's your story?"

"My story?" He frowned. "What makes you think I have *a story?*"

Jessa smiled knowingly, and replied, "Everyone has a story. Some just hide them better than others. We can use you as an example." Jessa paused to make him wonder what she might know. "Let's talk about a missing girl named Maria Escher."

The look Mitch Connor gave her was pure loathing. "This conversation is over." He stood and turned away from her, walking stiffly back to the gift shop.

Jessa couldn't help calling to his retreating back, "That's what all the guilty say!" It wasn't until she had returned to her apartment hours later that she realized she didn't know why he'd approached her in the first place.

IT WASN'T THAT SHE WAS DISAPPOINTED in her photographs as much as she was confused. The hour was late, and she was fighting sleep. She wanted to have a look at the pictures she'd taken at Bristol House before morning to decide if she needed to go back again tomorrow.

The first few were clear and bright as was usual for a camera of this caliber. Though it was the older of the two cameras, she'd spent a small fortune on it when it was new. But in Bristol House's kitchen, and the interior back hall, the fog was back with a vengeance. It was, perhaps, the result of someone smoking in the house, though she didn't remember smelling cigarette or cigar smoke anywhere. She fought annoyance that she would have to take this camera into Hanson's to have its sensors cleaned as well. She was thankful that Mr. Hanson had already cleaned her other camera so, at least, she had one to use.

Frame by frame, she studied the photos. As the fogginess thickened in every picture, Jessa became concerned that it was beginning to take the shape of a person. If she squinted and concentrated hard, she could almost make out the head and arms of a ghostly apparition. She grinned and felt the adrenalin pump through her as she began to frighten herself. Though she didn't believe in ghosts, she loved to watch spooky movies and often scared herself silly with them.

When she got to the photo she'd taken for posterity inside the kitchen of Mitch Connor's apartment, she dropped her smile abruptly. What she'd seen and photographed was the bar and across the room to the stairwell opening. What she got was nothing like that. Close to her—so close that it was a little out of focus—was a figure dressed in black from head to toe. The bearing and dress indicated it was a man, heavy-set, and standing directly in front of her camera. The face was obscured by the countertop of the bar, and she could still see the stairwell opening *through* him!

Her heart raced pathetically and she felt suddenly faint. She did *not* believe in ghosts, which made her wonder: could digital cameras accidentally take double exposures? That would be the only explanation she could think of that would produce the dark figure. At some point, either before or after she'd taken that photo, she must have accidentally taken a photo of the heavy-set man, which, somehow, must have been superimposed over the apartment photo.

Suddenly, she didn't feel like perusing the rest of the photos. Maybe tomorrow, in the bright light of day, she would finally understand what had happened with the silly old camera. She didn't bother to shut her kitchen window after she snapped her laptop shut.

She flipped the wall-switch kitchen light off and hurried into bed. However, relief was not to be had. While it was fortunate she fell asleep immediately, it was unfortunate that her night was crammed with crazy dreams of a lone young girl running away from the ghost that haunted Bristol House.

With bleary eyes and a foul mood, Jessa stomped into her kitchen the next morning. Just inside the kitchen doorway, the postcard of Bristol House fluttered to the floor and landed at her feet. She picked it up and studied the photograph of the house. Its dark windows remained dark, but today she noticed a whitish smudge in an upper floor window. Strange she had not noticed that before. Perhaps the photographer who took the picture was having trouble with his camera, too.

She set the card back up on the shelf in a position that would keep it from falling off again. She looked up and shivered at the breeze coming in from the open kitchen window. She reached up to shut it, and as she did so, she saw the bright orange breast of a robin as it flitted by. Smiling, she almost ran for her camera, but knew that the bird would be gone before she could get back to the window. She made herself a small pot of coffee, and while it was brewing, she ate a bowl of oatmeal. Then she stopped and looked around. Why was it that her morning had seemed predictable? She shrugged.

Before leaving her apartment for Bristol House, she took the time to take a few quick pictures inside her living room and then outside in the yard. She loaded them onto her computer to be certain how her camera was operating. She was taking no chances with a faulty camera today if she was to get any positive results for the Eschers. Before leaving her apartment, she grabbed her jacket as today promised to be much cooler than yesterday.

The busy Beltline did not improve her mood as she made her way to Hanson's Camera Repair Shop to drop off the old camera. She had not wanted to dig it out of the coat closet and spend the money having the sensors cleaned, but she knew she would wish she had when it came time to use it again.

Finally, Maple Bluff came into view. The sun, probably because the day was much colder, didn't seem to penetrate the gloom that hung over Jessa's head. Her foggy photos, so far, had been a bust and she was afraid if she took them to David and Norma Escher, they would take all those zeros away from her. She had to get some good photos and hopefully this time they would include Mr. Connor.

It was with a mixture of gladness and trepidation that Jessa approached the empty parking lot. This was not a tourist day. That meant that Mitch Connor may or may not be home. She would have to be careful.

There were several outbuildings around the property. Behind what was probably once a carriage shelter, Jessa parked her car. It was close to the road and the parking lot without being visible from the house. With her camera loaded with fresh batteries and a clean media card, she headed for the house in what she hoped was a path invisible to anyone looking out of a window. Hiding behind the various buildings, the only place she could possibly be seen was between the wooded areas at the back where she'd attempt her entrance via the screened-in porch behind the kitchen. With any luck at all, no one would be near the old-fashioned kitchen and she would be able to enter unseen.

Standing near the screened-in porch, she realized the doors to the house were locked. Checking the windows, she found they were likewise unable to be opened. She frowned, trying to find a way inside the house without breaking in. In a last ditch effort, she jogged to the cellar door. The padlock was firmly in place and no amount of tugging would jar it lose. She was nearly ready to scream, when a tiny window at the corner of the house caught her eye. It was barely open, maybe an inch, but that was all she needed.

Jessa gingerly eased the screenless window open and wondered how in the world she had missed seeing the gap a moment ago. Lucky she was small, she eased her body up and into the opening, landing quietly on her feet inside the screened porch.

Once she was indoors, the quiet told her that no one was home and so she was free to roam the house alone. The lack of sunshine made the house seem lonely in its emptiness. Dust motes danced energetically in the shaft of light coming through the filmy sheer curtains on the windows. With no lights on in the house, it took on the diffused colors of a bygone era.

Once again, Jessa could feel static electricity making the hair on her arms and scalp rise. Her adrenalin was high, and her heart pumped wildly. Slowly and carefully, she took pictures of the old place. Doorways. Corners. Closets. Anywhere with an opening where something could be hidden…

The chill of the day pervaded the old house with a vengeance. Jessa shivered as a draft wafted around her, clinging to her like a scarf. She wished she had brought a heavier jacket. Looking out of a window, she thought to check the parking lot to insure she was still alone before heading up to the third floor to where Mitch Connor often lived. Then, as she stood at the window looking out on the lawn, a cool hand brushed her arm, then pushed slightly on her shoulder.

She groaned out loud… *busted… again*! She turned on her heel, expecting to see the angry face of the owner, but…

She was alone. Her heart stopped for a moment before thunderously starting up again in her chest. The curtain beside her was not moving, yet a breeze through the window was the only logical explanation she could find for the tender touch.

Suddenly, she was not sure she wanted to continue to

explore the old house alone. Well, perhaps she would take one quick look upstairs before she got the heck out of this depressing place.

Only then did she hear the front door opening. Peeking around the corner, she saw Mr. Connor walk purposefully into the front hall. Jessa scrambled to get to a closet to hide, and shut the door quietly behind her. She was surprised when he didn't continue on up to his third floor apartment, and instead walked into the old kitchen. The closet she was in was close by and, opening the door a crack, she could see him prowling back and forth across the floor.

The old house was very quiet. Mitch leaned against the kitchen windowsill and stared outside toward the woods. Jessa scarcely breathed in her effort to stay quiet, though it was hard to imagine he couldn't hear the furious beating of her heart. She jumped fiercely at the unexpected sound of his cell phone ringing. She closed her eyes for a moment, praying she hadn't made any noise. When she opened them, he was speaking into his phone. She strained to hear what he was saying.

The fluctuating strength of his voice made only bits of his words discernible. "...kill it... don't need them any more... I'll be crucified if that happens. No, get rid of her... now!" Terrified by his words, Jessa backed farther into the closet, but she couldn't take her eyes off the man. Then he moved away from her line of sight and the kitchen became quiet. Jessa decided she'd heard enough anyway; his cryptic words somehow condemned him in her mind. Hoping he had gone on upstairs, she left the relative safety of her closet and attempted her escape. She only made it as far as the front hall. Mitch was walking swiftly out of the old kitchen. Only luck kept him from seeing her scurry to her only available escape route: up the stairs to the second floor.

She was frantic to find another hiding place, but the sound of his steps indicated he was directly behind her. She had no choice but to enter the nearest bedroom, the master, and dashed into the closet just in time to keep Mitch from discovering her. She couldn't see him, but she could hear that he stopped walking. She was trying to decide what had made him stop—perhaps to look out of the window? An instant later, she got her answer.

He sniffed the air. It was a long, inquiring sound. Silently, she cursed herself. It had not occurred to her that the fragrant body lotion she always wore would get her into trouble. He could smell her. He knew she was here, but he hadn't found her. Yet.

She knew that the instant he walked into the closet to go upstairs, he'd find her. Ever so gently, she slipped off her shoes and tiptoed silently up the stairs to the third floor apartment. In her mind, she cursed herself. She knew she was going the wrong way. She knew the only safe thing was to leave the house, but getting cornered at every turn forced her to do the one dumbest thing ever. She was trapped in his private apartment.

Inside the third floor apartment, she quickly hid again behind the granite bar, hoping beyond hope that he didn't head straight for the kitchen. Jessa barely made it to the floor before Mitch entered the apartment. When he headed to the bedroom, she looked around the bar cabinet with plans to make a dash for the stairway. Luck deserted her, though, as she stepped away from the kitchen and into the living room. Only feet away from the door, plainly out in the open, she could only stare in horror as he left the bedroom and stepped into the kitchen where she'd just been standing. If he had looked up, he would have seen her standing in the middle of his living room; she could almost have touched him. With the refrigerator door open, she could not get to the door without being seen and had barely enough time to slip in his bedroom closet and shut the door behind her. Unable to turn the light on to alleviate the dark interior, she was at least thankful of the louvered doors that allowed her to see into the room.

By now she was nearly in tears. Terrified of getting

caught, she could only stay quiet and still until he either left his apartment, or he fell asleep. She was determined that she would return home undiscovered. At least, that was her hope.

He never left his apartment. As the hours passed, she dozed fitfully. She was afraid to take any photos, or even look at the ones she'd already taken, for fear the sound of the camera mechanism would be loud enough for him to hear. It was unfortunate that she was here alone: no one knew she was here, no one waited for her, no one would care if she went missing for several days.

Later in the afternoon, her stomach rumbled noisily, making her grab her middle and hold her breath. Her throat felt like sawdust and she had to pee. Snooping was way more fun yesterday.

She must have fallen asleep because she woke with a start. Immediately, she wondered what had woke her. It was much later than she realized. A cold draft wafted irritatingly inside the closet, almost like frosty hands caressing her.

The apartment was silent and dark. All evening, Mitch had the television going and had silently sat through sitcom after sitcom. She found it odd that he never laughed at the stupid antics, but maybe he wasn't actually watching them.

Now, she peered through the louvered doors and saw Mitch's prone figure sprawled out on the bed. Without a sound, she pushed the closet doors open. Right at the very end, there was a muffled creak from the hinge. Jessa stopped moving immediately and waited until he turned restlessly over in his sleep. When he didn't move for a full minute, she crept away from the bedroom and into the living room. She didn't bother to shut the closet door; she was only too glad to get out of there and away from Mitch Connor.

While the house may have been still and dark, it wasn't quiet. Creaks and groans pushed her quickly down the stairs. Ghostly hands brushed by her as she ran. White phantasms motioned for her to hurry. She fumbled clumsily at the lock on the front door, making too much noise, trying to get outside. As the minutes ticked by, her fear of getting caught mounted, and she felt the panic threaten to strangle her.

She didn't care. All she wanted was to be gone. Visions of poor Maria thrashed about her brain as she rushed. She didn't want to end up like Maria.

Her car was a welcome sight after she ran across the lawn and through the maze of buildings. Only after she opened the door and slid behind the wheel did the likelihood occur to her that her car might have been spotted and moved. She revved up the motor a little too loudly and cringed. Taking a deep breath, she gunned the engine again and raced down the empty driveway and onto the streets of Maple Bluff.

She was thankful to be going home on this particular night. It was a close call not to have been murdered and buried in the cellar beside the beautiful, dead Maria Escher.

Inside her own apartment, she checked to see that her kitchen window was closed against the night's chill, and without taking off her clothes, fell into bed in an exhausted sleep. As slumber claimed her, she promised herself that her snooping days were over and all those zeros would have to belong to someone else.

CHAPTER FIVE
SILENT INVITATION

Morning brought yet another day of sunshine and the promise that all was not lost. Jessa woke with a new determination to discover what Mitch Connor's real story was. Having survived the skirmish yesterday, she was ready to continue the war today.

After a long, hot shower, she rebelliously slathered her body with the fragrant body lotion that almost got her into trouble the day before. She toweled her spiky, chestnut brown hair nearly dry before heading to the kitchen. As she passed the small shelf in the kitchen, the postcard of Bristol House fell off the shelf and fluttered to the floor by Jessa's feet. She picked it up off the floor and studied the house, wondering what secrets the house held.

She set the card back up on the shelf in a position that would keep it from falling off. Again. She looked up and shivered at the breeze coming in from the open kitchen window. She reached up to shut it, and as she did so, she saw the bright orange breast of a robin as it flitted by. She considered running for her camera, but the bird was gone before she could turn away from the window. She frowned. Had she seen a robin yesterday by the window? She made herself a small pot of coffee, and while it was brewing, she ate a bowl of oatmeal. She didn't taste the oatmeal as she stared at the now shut kitchen window. Why did she have to shut it this morning if she'd shut it last night before bed?

An unsettled feeling suddenly gripped her. Not sure where it was coming from, she quickly shoved her laptop into its carrying case and tossed the strap over her shoulder. Then, grabbing her jacket and camera, she rushed out the door.

It was a good day to sit in a coffee bar with her computer out in front of her and surf the Internet and people watch all at the same place. Her apartment was just too lonely today, and after yesterday's imprisonment, she needed a little people time.

She hadn't gotten as many pictures as she would have liked, but under the circumstances, she felt lucky to have any at all to show for her snooping around. Once loaded, she was not surprised to see the misty fog was back in the photos, and she was beginning to realize what it must mean. Nothing at all was wrong with either of her cameras. The fault was in Bristol House itself. Though here in the daylight, it seemed so unlikely and so childishly ridiculous, but the conclusion would not change... Bristol House appeared to be haunted.

As soon as that thought solidified in her mind, an icy cold draft wafted across the room. She shivered and looked around her. No one else acted as if they noticed the chill at all. She slipped on her jacket and turned her attention back to the pictures on her computer's screen. To say she was a little spooked would have been an understatement.

She was practically sloshing with coffee, but she refused to leave the cheery confines of the coffee bar. Instead, she decided to take advantage of their wi-fi and surf the Internet for any information on Mitch Connor. Most of what she found was the same boring information she would be able to find on any public official. His birth date (he was a bare three years older than she was), his parents' names, grandparents, schools attended... She learned that he was not raised at Bristol House. Instead, he had been reared in a lovely new home inside of town near the University. His family owned Bristol House, having been handed down to him through his mother's side, but rarely had anyone actually lived there since S. J. and Virginia Hubert passed away all those years ago. The ones who had lived there hadn't stayed long, and Jessa suddenly suspected she knew why. Who wanted to live in a haunted house?

Mitch spent many summers of his childhood in Canada fishing and hunting with his father. Then, abruptly when he was in junior high, he was sent off to a military school in Missouri for three years, returning to finish high school at Madison. No reason was given for the sudden change of venue, but whatever had happened, it had been a hasty decision. He had already started attending his seventh grade classes, but by the middle of October, he was being boarded in Missouri. *Odd*, Jessa thought. Digging deeper did not come up with any explanation as to the reason for the sudden change of schools.

Another strange fact, Jessa noted, was that after the change of schools, there were no more hunting or fishing trips to Canada or anywhere else. They just stopped. There were no siblings. No cousins, no aunts or uncles. Jessa discovered that his parents were still alive, but living in south Florida enjoying the year-round summertime: a big change from the harsh winters of Wisconsin.

She felt deep inside that there was information about Mitch that was somehow missing. Internet searches did not come up with anything that satisfied her curiosity. Then she had an idea: a family with the kind of money they had must have had servants. Hadn't she thought, herself, that Mitch had someone come to his apartment to clean? If she could find that person, she could interview her. Surely someone who worked for the family would have information not normally found through Internet searches.

Next, she searched the employment agency listings until she found a maid service that was used by the city's wealthier families. Then, she got out her phone and made a number of phone calls, pretending to be a top-notch housekeeper. She finally discovered the company that was indeed used by the Connor family. Using her cell phone, she found out that the head housemaid was now retired, but yes, she'd love to speak to Jessa if it would help out the family she'd loved for so many years.

Jessa quickly wrote down the address and hopped in her car. She hoped she knew enough about housekeeping to keep the old woman from being suspicious about her motives.

Olivia Weller. That was her name. The old woman had worked for the Connor family long before Mr. Mitch was born, and continued working there until she retired fifteen years ago. Jessa had to bite her lip to keep from jumping with joy at the information that was sure to be forthcoming.

Mrs. Weller was a lovely old woman. She had a sweet demeanor and an efficiency about her that would have been appreciated in a household used to being in the public eye. When asked about the child Mitch had been, Mrs. Weller could not say enough nice things. Jessa began to think that he had been born with a halo hovering above his head.

Mrs. Weller's smile faltered somewhat, though, when Jessa asked about the years Mitch had spent in the military school in Missouri. "Well," Mrs. Weller wrung her hands nervously, "Ms. Connor never was much to comment about that. I don't suppose she would want me to comment about it now."

Jessa was persuasive. "But I must know all about him or I can't take the job working for him. Mrs. Weller, I need the money bad. So, I gotta know."

Finally, Mrs. Weller sighed. The story was more telling than poor Mrs. Weller would ever know. As a child, Mitch Connor was gregarious and lively, almost naughty, though Mrs. Weller refused to see him as anything but angelic. Mitch and his next-door neighbor were best friends and inseparable through most of their childhood. This boy (Mrs. Weller could not remember his name) would go on camping trips to Canada with Mitch and his father. Mr. Connor treated the young neighbor as another son. However, at the beginning of their seventh grade year, the friendship turned suddenly sour, and the boys parted ways. One evening, young Mitch had been outside playing in the neighborhood, and had been seen several blocks from home in the company of his former best friend. He came home late that night to very worried parents; they had been frantically searching for him. Mitch refused to talk about his activities, and had cried himself to sleep.

The next morning, the young boy who had been Mitch's childhood confidante was found dead in a nearby park: beaten to death with a stout piece of lumber. In short, to keep suspicion from falling on their son, he was shipped off to military school, and then allowed to return when it was clear there would be no trouble. The boy who returned, however, was not the same happy boy who had left. The world assumed that military school had calmed him down.

In contrast, Jessa's conclusion was much more sinister. Perhaps the military school had not had the calming effect that was so evident in the minds of the world. Maybe the boy who returned was saddled with the guilt of murder! Jessa shivered. People seemed to have a habit of disappearing from Mitch Connor's life.

Armed with this new information, Jessa was now convinced the man was guilty. The cards were stacked against him. The Eschers *believed* it. Circumstantial, sure, but the coincidence was too great to ignore. With greater determination, Jessa decided to plan another infiltration of Bristol House. This time her search would be different… and in many ways, much more dangerous.

On her way back to her apartment, Jessa stopped by the mall at Dick's Sporting Goods to purchase a pair of binoculars. Waterproof and lightweight, it was amazing that something so small could be so expensive. They were powerful and fit snugly in the left-hand pocket of her raincoat. The right-hand pocket carried a small, palm-sized instamatic camera; the first camera she'd ever owned. The pictures would not be as good of quality as the SLR cameras she was used to using, but the size made it more convenient for her new plans.

It was late in the afternoon before she set out for Bristol House. Ideally, she wanted to get in, then out, before Mitch came home. The binoculars would allow her to spy on him if he was home, so either way was a win for her. The only glitch in her plans would be if the window she'd crawled in yesterday was locked.

Parking her car well away from the residence was an absolute must, so she walked the last few blocks through the brush, and along property lines near Lake Mendota. Finally, Bristol House came into view, looking as imposing as ever in the waning light. Her first impression of the place was that it was angry, but this new mood was probably a reflection of her own mood and her new resolve to see Mitch Connor behind bars for the murder of Maria Escher.

Staying just inside the woods, she pulled the binoculars out of her pocket and studied the house. There was a light on in the upstairs apartment. Mitch was home. Pocketing the binoculars, she looked around for some way to elevate herself enough to see inside the windows of the third floor.

Pretty good as a kid, she found her tree-climbing skills were not lacking as she hoisted herself up the sticky branches of a pine tree. It was not a huge tree, but she was able to peer into the window of his bedroom with the aide of the binoculars. This was not the view she had wanted, but the bedroom door opened to the front living room. The straight shot allowed her to see at least part of it.

For a while, no one appeared in her view. Then, coming from the area of the kitchen, Jessa saw Mitch's figure walk by the doorway, and then he sat on a couch in full view. Long minutes passed as she watched him flip through television channels with his remote. Finally, he got up, and then came back a short time later. When he sat back down, he had a magazine in his hands. He stood up, then sat again. He looked restless.

Jessa lowered the binoculars slowly and frowned with her face turned up to the window. It was almost as if he could sense her watching him: he looked directly at her out of his window. She knew there was no way it was possible that he could actually see her, though. The darkening light and her dark clothing would hide her in the branches of the tree.

A moment later, Mitch stood up and walked sharply into the bedroom, returning to the lighted living room with a jacket on. He disappeared from her sight as he descended the stairs to the lower levels of the house. An instant later, she could hear the slam of the front door and the rattle of the knob as he yanked it to make sure it was secure. He could be seen, then, walking to the detached garage. The engine of his sleek, black BMW roared powerfully. Moments later, he backed it out of the building and squealed its tires sharply as he pealed quickly down the driveway.

Jessa couldn't believe her luck. The house was hers!

She fell more than climbed down the pine tree in her haste to get to the house. Her hands were sticky with pinesap, which she tried to rub off onto her jeans. Just to be on the safe side, she waited a few more agonizing minutes before dashing across the lawn to the back of the house. Like yesterday, the doors and windows were locked here. Even more disappointing was the little window she'd crawled in before was also locked.

Nervously, she circled the house, trying to open each window. Just as she was about to give up, she eyed the front door. Could it be…? She walked slowly across the veranda and stood in front of the main entrance. Her hand reached out to touch the old-fashioned crystal knob. Turning it slightly to the right, she heard the "click" as the latch released the door. She pulled it open effortlessly.

Mitch had forgotten to lock the front door!

She slipped silently inside the house. Here, alone at dusk, the house seemed to welcome her, but she couldn't shake the impression of anger she'd had when she first arrived. Static electricity ran up and down her arms. She rubbed them as if she were cold, hoping to stop the sensation. Uneasily, she fingered the camera inside her pocket.

Her goal: the third floor apartment. She crept quietly up the stairs. Though there was no particular reason for her stealth, she somehow felt that silence was vital. It was not until she reached the master bedroom on the second floor that she caught a faint pungent puff of something foul. She stopped moving for a moment and sniffed the air. Dead animal? Rotting vegetation?

Oh, god! Could it be a body? Her heart raced furiously until the pounding filled her ears and burned her eyes. Could that explain his nervous restlessness? With an inexplicable nudge to her shoulders, she was propelled forward toward the stairs leading to the top floor.

Walking carefully through the threshold, she saw the apartment was neat and clean. This time she didn't bother looking through the stacks of CDs or volumes of books. She headed to the bedroom and found what she was looking for: his desk.

Unlike the rest of the apartment, it was a disaster. Stacks of papers lay aimlessly about. Several drawers were left open. The contents were an erratic jumble of journals, reports, stationery, and other random documents. Jessa knelt on the soft carpet and pulled out her camera.

Taking care to return each sheet of paper to its original place, she carefully sifted through the documents, first on the desktop. There was nothing particularly incriminating there, but to be on the safe side, she took photos of the most important-looking ones. Next, she began to sift through the topmost drawer. It housed mostly pens, pencils, paper clips, and an odd assortment of office necessities. She moved quickly on to the next drawer.

She had her hands deep inside the drawer in the process of pulling a handful of papers out when a noise caught her attention. She stopped stone cold and listened. The unmistakable sound of laughter floated up to her from directly below her on the second floor. It was the husky voice of a man. A foul odor seeped up from under her feet.

Gulping nervously, Jessa pulled her arm away from the drawer as quickly and silently as she could. Mitch's laughter sounded odd to her and quite unlike his voice, which was smoother, and more refined. He would not be laughing long if he caught her at his desk.

Walking as hastily as she dared, she crept her way to the stairway, hoping to make it down before he headed up. Then, as she passed the window, she glanced outside. To her surprise, she couldn't see Mitch's car inside the garage's open door. She frowned in confusion.

Stepping quietly down to the second floor, Jessa decided to take a look at the room that would be located directly below Mitch's bedroom. She walked down the long hallway, turning her head and looking in as she passed each door. Most of them were shut, but the ones that were open were fairly empty except for an old-fashioned bed and dresser.

Cautiously, Jessa stood just outside the door to the room from where the laughter came. With her back against the wall, she strained to listen. No sound came from the room. Daring to peek, she turned her head around the corner of the door frame just enough to see inside. Like the other bedrooms, the old bed was in the middle of the wall on the far side with an antique dresser beside it—but no one was in the room.

However, the foul odor was stronger in here than in the master bedroom earlier. A macabre sense of curiosity lured her into the room farther. She stood in the center of the room, and turned a complete circle. The room was empty except for the bed and dresser.

The closet door was slightly ajar.

Jessa could feel fearful adrenalin coursing through her veins. She was utterly powerless to stop her feet from stepping nearer to the closet. Almost detachedly, she could see her hand reach for the doorknob, grab it, and pull it open. It was as black as ink inside. She stepped through the door and took a deep breath.

The fetor was oppressive. With one hand over her

nose, she reached with the other toward the center of the little room in hopes of finding the chain to the light switch before she realized that this part of the house had not been built with electricity. Just as that thought crossed her mind, however, her fingers found the pull chain, and the room was flooded with electric light.

Almost blind after walking around in the dark, she backed away from the light defensively. When she could focus, she saw the room was larger than she had thought and was filled with a huge amount of cardboard boxes. Some were old, others not so much. Closer to the door, most of the boxes seemed to be filled with papers and other documents. Her eyes widened with this new-found treasure trove of information. She itched to dive into the boxes. Maybe this would contain the information she would need that would open Maria's missing persons case.

She did not hear the soft footsteps behind her, but the words spoken chilled her to the bone: "What the hell are you looking for?"

CHAPTER SIX
TRIP TO THE CELLAR

Jessa used the only weapon she had with her: her sarcasm. "What the hell am *I* looking for? You're freakin' kidding me! Besides, you about scared the ever-lovin' crap outta me!" Reaching up to turn the light off with a snap, she pushed Mitch away with a hand to his chest, and stormed passed him. "Move!" she demanded.

She had barely gone two steps away from him when his fingers curled around her arm like a vice, and jerked her to a stop. "Have you ever heard of breaking and entering?" he sneered furiously. "This is private property, princess. I could shoot you for trespassing and the law would not only allow it, they'd welcome it!"

She yanked her arm away from his grip, and pulled back like she'd been burnt. "Oooooh, aren't you the big man; I'm soooooo scared! You like this, trying to scare women? Well it won't work on me, big guy. I might be little, but I'm tough. Your teeth aren't strong enough to break through my skin, honey. Go scare someone else." Jessa belligerently moved away from him and headed determinedly for the bedroom door.

His face turned red and, if possible, angrier. Suddenly, he was barring the doorway with his body so she could not pass. With his arms folded tightly across his chest and his legs wide and firm, she would not be able to muscle her way around him. So she mimicked his stance and folded her arms across her chest and stared back at him.

When he said nothing, or didn't trust himself to speak, she started tapping her foot impatiently. "What?"

Mitch took a deep breath and shook his head in exasperation. The anger was still there, but it was tempered with confusion. "What the hell are you doing in my house?" This time the question was just that. He simply wanted to know.

Just breathing lifted and dropped Jessa's chest as she fought for oxygen. "I'm searching for something that was lost. But if it's any consolation, I haven't found it yet."

For only a brief moment, it looked like he wanted to smile. "Well, can I help you find it so I can continue with my evening alone?"

Jessa sneered, and put another dark look on Mitch's face. "Let's put it this way, buster: what I'm looking for, you will most certainly help me find, but you won't be helping me look for it. That, I'll do by myself. Thanks anyway." The cryptic answer, she knew, would make him angrier, but she couldn't seem to hold her tongue.

Goddammit! he mumbled harshly under his breath. Jessa cringed slightly when he grabbed her shoulders and shook her sharply. "Look, princess, my name is Mitch Connor. You have, perhaps, heard of me? You have entered my home without my knowledge or permission. Breaking. And. Entering. Period. If you don't tell me what you're doing here, I will not even hesitate to call the police. Not kidding. Not even close. Now *talk!*"

In answer, Jessa clamped her lips together and lifted her nose away from him. This seemed to kick his anger up another notch, and it made her wonder how many notches Maria had kicked it up before he murdered her. In the next moment, she found herself being dragged by the arm out of the room and down the long hallway. She suspected that he would either drag her all the way to the front door and kick her bodily out, or murder her where she stood and bury her body in various-sized pieces out in the woods behind the house.

In the end, he did neither. Traveling down the long, dark hallway, Jessa didn't voice the sudden fear the gripped her throat. Wafts of ice-cold air were tangibly thick, like vines of gossamer webs that brushed her face and pushed at the short strands of her hair. By the time he yanked her into the second story master, she knew they were headed for his apartment. At least, with the exception of the odd, superimposed man in the photograph she'd taken by the kitchen, it was a less scary place to be.

In the end, they didn't make it there either.

As they headed for the stairs leading up, an abrupt, cacophonic rumble exploded loudly beneath their feet. Coming from a lower level, they both looked down, then back up at each other. Mitch turned and headed for the bedroom door with Jessa right on his heels.

Immediately, he turned around and barked at her, "No! You stay here. I'll go by myself. I don't know who is down there, but if someone has broken in…" Suddenly, he stopped talking. Then, gripping her arms again, tight enough that Jessa could feel the blood to her hands slow, Mitch snarled savagely and lowered his face to within an inch of hers. "Unless you have a breaking and entering buddy waiting to bash my head in…"

A little frightened by the intense rage that consumed him, Jessa shook her head immediately and said in a fierce, resentful voice, "No, I do all my breaking and entering alone."

"Then stay." It was not a request. It was an order.

Jessa, who was ordinarily a rule-follower for the most part, was immediately consumed with contempt that Mitch thought he could order her to stay. Here. Alone. *Not on a bet!* she seethed. "Go to hell," she retorted with a calmness that surprised herself, and him. She was right on his heels.

So rather than argue with her, he rolled his eyes scornfully, and let his words float behind him as he moved, "I'm on my way there now."

They moved across the old house, and down the stairs as hastily and as quietly as they could. They stopped in the front stairwell hall to listen for another noise. Standing absolutely still, Jessa found that she had reached up and laid her hand on Mitch's forearm. Likewise, he had a hand cupping her shoulder protectively. As they listened, they became aware of their protective stances, and pulled away from each other suddenly as if they'd been scorched.

Jessa's face burned with the knowledge that her subconscious must have needed his protective nearness. She vowed to be entirely aware of any proximity to him from now on. She would not be charmed by his wealth and good looks, as it appeared others had been.

Another noise below them made them start suddenly, though it was not the same noise. This time, it belonged to the voice that had laughingly lured Jessa to the second floor to discover the old boxes of documents.

"Where?" Jessa whispered, looking around them.

"Cellar," he responded, equally low.

She looked up at him in question. The only entrance to the cellar was outside. Did they have to leave the house? By the same token, why would anyone break into the cellar if there were no access to the house? It made no sense.

Mitch read her expression and nodded wordlessly for her to follow him. They crept slowly down the hall and across the parlor, the other hall and into the huge kitchen. Every few steps, he would stop and silently point to various floorboards, wagging his forefinger to make her understand she was not to step on that board. The house creaked with age.

He led her into the pantry that was just off the kitchen. It was a large room with enough space for two or three people to stand comfortably. Then he reached over and gripped the side of one of the many floor to ceiling shelves and gingerly pulled it away from the wall. It swung out easily, making a soft, scraping sound as it moved over the floorboards. They cringed in unison, afraid the intruder in the cellar would be able to hear their approach.

When Jessa peered around the hidden door, the musty smell of earth and disuse assaulted her olfactory senses. With that was the rotting smell she'd encountered in the master bedroom, and again in the bedroom at the end of the second story hallway.

Her head reeled with malodorous overload. She felt faint and nauseated. The static electricity was back with a vengeance, running painfully up and down her arms and across her scalp. The cellar was a well of inky blackness. The narrow, uneven stairs leading down disappeared in an ebony void.

Even Mitch, who probably knew the house as well as anyone else alive, hesitated at the threshold. Jessa's liquid gaze studied his face. *What now?* she mouthed wordlessly.

After a moment's hesitation, Mitch reached in his jeans pocket and fished out a small set of keys with a miniature flashlight key fob. The tiny blue light gave them only enough luminosity to see a couple of steps ahead, but that was all they needed.

Jessa's pledge to keep a careful distance between herself and Mitch vanished in the dark confines of the cellar. With him leading the way, she practically glued herself to his backside and crushed his shoulders in a death grip as she followed him down.

A second laugh, though it was farther away than before, resonated softly in the dark recesses. Whoever it was, taunted them to come farther into the gloomy substructure. She tried to get the sudden thought out of her head that this could become a tomb. *Their* tomb. Jessa felt faint.

Mitch turned his head slightly and breathed almost silently in Jessa's ear: "There is a pull chain light switch just to my right. I'm going to turn the light on suddenly. When I do, I will scan to the right, I want you to scan to the left. If there is anyone down here, we should see them, unless they have moved to one of the little storage rooms down here. Ready?"

Jessa's nod was almost imperceptible. Then, with a tiny "click", the cellar was abruptly filled with yellow electric light. Shadows swayed back and forth as the bare bulb swung wildly on its wire cable. Jessa blinked blindly and looked frantically about, but there was no one in the cellar. A look in Mitch's direction said the same.

However, the cellar was far from empty. There were more boxes down here, stacked haphazardly in untidy groups. Old furniture, much of it broken, was stacked up and propped against the walls. A dressmaker's mannequin stood partially dressed in a corner. A child's wooden rocking horse sat forlornly among other odds and ends of junk. The shiny head, which at one time had probably been furry, was rubbed to slickness by the hours of pleasure from many little hands. It was missing an eye, and the tail was gone.

An old wooden checkers game had broken open from the box; its contents were strewn across the floor. Marbles were scattered and had rolled and rested in the cracks of the floor and against some boxes. Several kitchen chairs were broken and lying in shredded fragments and piles. One large wooden crate had been shattered, littering the floor with papers, ribbons, and other mementos. Jessa felt disgust that the cellar was in such a sorry state of disarray. It looked like someone had been involved in a fistfight recently.

"Holy cow!" she whispered. "What a mess. Don't you guys clean down here?"

When Mitch didn't answer, she looked up at him. He was also staring at the mess in the cellar, but his expression was quite different from hers. He was furious!

Without answering, he walked to one of the old broken chairs and picked up a piece of the old lumber. It looked to be one of the chair legs. Examining the end, he then brought it to his nose and sniffed it carefully. Jessa could see that the break was recent; that the varnish on the rest of it was a darker patina that spoke of age. The break was very fresh.

"Someone has been fighting down here," he said quietly. He looked up and met Jessa's stare.

Jessa rolled her eyes. "Oh? Ya think?" she murmured sarcastically. Then she carefully slipped her little camera out of her pocket. She held the viewfinder up to her eye to take a picture, but stopped and looked at him. "May I?"

Mitch nodded faintly, frowning as he watched her

snap picture after picture. "What are the pictures for?" he asked quietly.

She hesitated a moment, then replied flippantly, "Research."

"Research?" he repeated. Then as meaning dawned on him, his face darkened with anger yet again. "Oh, hell no!" He took a swipe at her and almost grabbed the camera away, but he missed, and she danced away from him.

"What?" she piped innocently, the smug feeling falling from her expression.

"You're spying on me, aren't you? Who the hell hired you to spy on me?" Mitch was angry, and rightly so, but Jessa was not going to cave.

"You are out of your flippin' mind, Mitch Connor!" She backed away from him and toward the stairs leading upward. "I'm a photographer not a spy." However, the lie sounded sour in her ears.

Mitch snorted angrily as he watched her retreat. "Who *are* you?"

She was too afraid not tell him anything that was at least close to the truth. "I'm a researcher. I am looking for the truth. Trust me, I'll find the truth if it is the last thing I do."

She hoped her words did not foreshadow her future. The closer to the stairs she retreated, the more he matched her step for step. His voice was soft and melodious as he followed. "What kind of truth are you looking for?" There was a sinister tone to his words.

"Well, I'd like to know who was fighting down here." Behind her, she could feel the first step. She raised the heel of her foot and slid it to the level top.

"I've no idea. I'm just as surprised as you are. Do you have any ideas?" His eyes never left hers. His handsome good looks masked a tumultuous fury just below the surface.

Jessa laughed, but it was not a pleasant sound. "Let me take a guess… you?"

His returning laugh matched hers. There was nothing

of humor in it. "Me? Who the hell would I be fighting with? Myself? I live alone here, in case you didn't know."

Then Jessa threw caution to the winds. "Of course you live alone here." Her voice dripped with mockery. "If you get tired of someone, you don't ask them to leave, you get rid of them!"

"What are you talking about?" His voice sounded innocent enough, but there was something in his eyes that made Jessa think he already knew.

"My business here is over, Mr. Connor." At least for now, she qualified to herself. "I will get out of your hair." She felt the second step and hoisted herself up.

With his lightning quick reflexes, he reached out and grabbed her arm, effectively preventing her from ascending the stairs. "Not until I know your name."

"Why?" was her whispered response.

"'Know thy self, know thy enemy.' If you are going to accuse me of something, I should be allowed to know who you are and why you are doing this." His grip tightened.

Jessa gasped with pain as his fingers dug into her skin. "If I tell you my name, will you let me go?" He nodded reluctantly. "My name is Jessa Bennett. I'm a photographer. That's all I can tell you right now... please, you're hurting me."

Mitch let go suddenly, compelling Jessa to step away from him. She rubbed her arm resentfully, but was careful not to let her emotion show in her face. "Don't come back. Ever. Do you understand?"

She nodded vigorously. No, she thought to herself, she wouldn't come back—as long as he was home. Now, she was more determined than ever to figure out the mystery behind the man. There was nothing in her wildest imagination that would convince her he was not guilty of doing away with Maria Escher. Likewise, he was likely guilty of the death of the unnamed boy who had been his childhood friend.

Before he could change his mind, Jessa turned and ran

up the stairs and away from the dark, rotting stench in the cellar. As she ran, she could hear his heavy footsteps in pursuit of her. Terrified that he had changed his mind, she didn't take the time or energy to look back until she came to the front door. As she threw it open, she tossed a cursory glance over her shoulder.

As she did so, the sound of footsteps stopped and Jessa found herself staring into an empty room. Mitch had not followed her. She was alone, shaking with terror.

She jerked the front door open, banged it against the wall, and did not bother to shut it. Catapulting her body across the veranda and onto the front lawn, she ran the length of the driveway and did not stop until she arrived at her car several blocks away.

Even in her car, she could feel the sinister malevolence that had been in the cellar. She shuddered with revulsion. She would return to do the job she was hired for, but there was no way she'd ever live in a house like that!

She forced her heart to slow down and her brain to clear as she drove back to her apartment. Her camera, with a wealth of new photos in it, weighed heavily in her pocket. What a waste, she mused, that Mitch was involved on some level with the disappearance or murder of Maria Escher. He wasn't particularly pleasant, though with wealth like his, he probably didn't need to be. Charming or not, though, he was extremely easy on the eyes.

Not that anything about him would stop her from finding the truth about what had happened. If the truth came out and he was not guilty, then she'd most certainly apologize to him. But it was looking bad for the rising political star.

CHAPTER SEVEN
THE TERRACE

He wished he could erase the day, or at least start over and give it another go. There had been other times in his life he'd wished the same thing. Mitch watched Jessa sprint up the cellar steps, and listened as she stomped angrily across the house. The stomping stopped in the middle of the parlor, then he heard the front door being jerked open and hitting the wall, followed by silence.

For a little woman with tiny feet, she sure could stomp!

It did no good for him to get angry, though it was an emotion close to the surface. That girl had more brass than anyone he'd ever known. Didn't she realize *who* he was, for crissake? No living person had ever treated him with such disrespect.

He took one last look around the ruined cellar and decided to wait until morning to tackle the mess. Fighting always made him disagreeable. The worst part was cleaning up the debris. He disregarded the noises that brought them down here. He knew they were one of the many odd things connected with old houses. Disjointed noises, laughter, scraping and shutting doors... all that could be explained away in the bright light of day.

There was no one in the cellar.

Something would have to be done about the smell down here, though, he realized. If it continued to be bad, or get worse, the tours would have to stop. The last thing he needed was a professional cleaning crew to come in and sanitize this place. They'd most definitely make him get rid of all the old contents. While it was probably a fire hazard of some kind, the stores of ancient documents he'd found begged to be looked at. Some of the aged papers were written in old fashioned handwriting. Besides, the foul smell seemed to come and go.

He tugged on the chain that turned the light off, and headed back upstairs. Shoving the shelves against the wall, he effectively closed the secret doorway and stepped into the kitchen. He ignored the hint of static electricity he often felt when he walked through the house alone.

Jessa Bennett was on his mind—and that annoyed him.

Forcing himself to think about Maria instead, he climbed to the top of the house, into his apartment, and shut the door, where he could pretend he was not living here in this old house alone.

The deal he had made with his parents still stood, though as time passed, he found that he disliked their agreement more and more. Bristol House had belonged in his family for a long time. It was one of the oldest houses in the city that was still privately owned, but open to the public for tours. And, in a manner of speaking, he was its sole owner and caretaker.

That was the problem he wrestled with. The deed still read that it was his mother who was the actual owner, but since their move to Florida, she had decided to give him a chance to acquire it from her. She didn't need the money; neither did he. It was not a money issue. It was about ownership.

To gain ownership, he had agreed to live in the mansion for five years. That time was already almost up. In a few months time, the Bristol House would wholly belong to him. Why he wanted it was a mystery even to him. He hated this house. He had hated the house since he was a child. It always felt as if it had an illness to it that had seeped into the very woodwork. That said, however, he felt as if it needed his protection. Or, perhaps it was he who needed protection from the house.

He sat back on his couch and closed his eyes. Maria's face floated through his mind. He had loved her very much and they'd made plans to get married. Though she was several years younger than he was, she was perfectly suited to be the wife of an up and coming city leader. At the time, he'd had lofty political goals in his mind. After Maria disappeared, those same goals seemed pointless to him. Now trouble seemed to follow him.

His consciousness turned away from the night that Maria disappeared. Too many emotions were tied to that night and he did not want to deal with that now. Nevertheless, her face refused to leave him.

Tall and willowy, Maria had the elegant presence of a supermodel, and had been brought up to assume an important role in society. She was graceful and soft-spoken, but her word was law: there was no arguing with her once her mind was made. Plus, she was a beautiful woman.

She also had a dark side... a private life that was hidden from the public eye. For a long time now, Maria was an avid believer in necromancy and used the mysteries of a psychic to determine or influence many of the decisions of her daily life. She believed fervently that her ancestors, who were the objects of her necromantic desires, helped her with these decisions.

This part of Maria's life had remained unknown to Mitch for a long time. When he accidentally ran across a check for a huge amount of money she'd written to the psychic, he had questioned her about her activities. At first, she'd denied there was anything to it. As time lengthened, however, and she continued to supply the psychic with regular checks of like amounts, Mitch found himself turning his head the other way. If that made her happy, who was he to take it from her?

She was kind. She loved. She would make an excellent wife, but she would have to keep that part of herself away from the eye of the world.

Furthermore, he hated it. Its very idea tore at his heart. With great guilt, a part deep inside of him was glad that there would be no more ghostly sojourns from Maria's dead ancestors. Instead, he brought to his mind a vision of Jessa

Bennett. She infuriated him. She intrigued him.

After all this time of being alone and worrying about Maria, Jessa breezed in and ripped open the careful cocoon he'd constructed around himself. As annoying as she was, he actually smiled at her daring. Her sarcasm was outrageous. Her attitude was provoking. Her timing was frustrating... and he wanted to know more about her!

BY THE TIME JESSA GOT HOME, her mood had improved. She took a mental step back and tried to look at her evening activities rationally. First, it was just a house. She'd been jittery when she entered because she knew she wasn't supposed to be there. Her adrenalin and senses were heightened from the start. Second, knowing that Mitch was probably involved with the disappearance of two different people elevated her mental spook-o-meter. She'd felt like she was taking a huge gamble. Third, add all that to an old creaky house, and the result was a recipe for a haunted house deluxe.

It was still early in the evening when Jessa took the time to unload the pictures from her camera. She was particularly interested in the ones from Mitch's desk. Though the little instamatic did not have the high quality photos her bigger cameras had, she was still able to study the documents she'd photographed. Bank statements... correspondence from city offices... a letter from his mother... She stopped and read that one.

The letter wasn't entirely comprehensible, also incomplete due to lens blur, but it seemed to be talking to him about a "deal" he'd made with his mother. Whatever the deal entailed, the result would be that he would own Bristol House.

Other photos waited for her perusal. She had a lot of them to go through. She needed to spend time on them and also go through the ones from the last couple of days. However, she couldn't bring herself to admit that that was the fourth, and most confusing, ingredient of her haunted house deluxe recipe. Any abnormalities on the photos were so much more physical than any "feelings" or "emotions". Though her head was clear and she was away from Bristol House and its peculiarities, she didn't think she could handle looking at what the pictures might contain.

An hour later, she had showered and changed into tight black pants and a sparkly silver halter-top. She wore her short-cropped hair spiked up and rhinestone earrings that hung down.

Jeanette Wilson, her friend from the restaurant, was more than happy to spend the evening with Jessa. While they both had many casual friends, they had become close during college before Jeanette decided school was not for her. They remained close, spending many of their dateless evenings together. At the Terrace, Jeanette waved her over and gave her a quick hug before they found a seat. Sipping beer, watching people, and listening to the live band by the edge of Lake Mendota was a favorite pastime of everyone in Madison. For a while, the girls kept their conversation to mundane daily activities. Who was dating whom was always a hot topic, and that always led to checking out the different men around the Terrace and guessing (or just making up) what job he might have and how much money he might be making.

As Jeanette was laughingly relating an anecdote about something that happened at work, Jessa was swept up suddenly in a silent rush of emotion. The loud world at the Terrace had abruptly gone mute and she could feel the icy fingers of static electricity crawl up her arms, making the hairs stand up in agitation. Jeanette laughed and talked, but Jessa could hear nothing. She looked around in a panic. No one else seemed to be having this same awareness. Then, across the lake, where Bristol House would be located, she could feel a dark presence. There was nothing to see; there was nothing to hear. Just the same, the sensation called to her.

Her heart tripped frantically as she tried to pull her mind away from the direction of the house. She closed her eyes to break the almost physical contact. Nausea welled up in her chest. *Stop it!* she pleaded silently. She put her hands up against her ears to block out the deathly stillness.

Jeanette had just started to look at Jessa with concern when a loud *pop!* snapped inside Jessa's head. Her hearing returned with such a rush that for a moment she couldn't discern one sound from another. Then, thankfully, the sounds returned to normal and the world righted itself. Her friend looked away suddenly, as if she had not just been concerned about Jessa, and started chattering again.

It all happened so suddenly, and ended so quickly, that Jessa could almost convince herself that it had not happened at all. She frowned and committed the experience to memory. Forewarned would be forearmed. She could not afford, at this point, to be lulled into a false sense of security by the dark forces that lingered around Bristol House.

She forced herself to smile and concentrated on Jeanette's story. A part of her felt foolish to let her imagination run wild at what was probably just an old creaky house. Somehow, though, she didn't think her fears and feelings were unfounded. Something was wrong there. Like it or not, she had become involved and she suspected that she would not be able to ignore or resist the pull now that it had become aware of her.

Then, just as she was finally able to put thoughts of Bristol House to the back of her mind, her eye caught a glimpse of a handsome dark-haired man leaning against the Terrace's rail that overlooked the water. Staring in the direction of Bristol House, was Mitch Connor. In the evening gloaming, the planes of his cheeks seemed to be chiseled from granite. He looked like a perfect, beautiful, statue.

At first she dropped her gaze to her cup of beer. Watching the bubbles float around, she tried to listen to Jeanette, who obviously never expected any particular response as she prattled on. Jessa, though, could not keep her eyes from straying to Mitch. He was alone, and looked somehow sad and empty.

Jessa put her hand on Jeanette's arm and patted it gently. "Give me a minute, okay?"

Jeanette nodded questioningly, then when she saw who Jessa was looking at, she smiled. "Go for it, girlfriend!"

Jessa smiled back at Jeanette and rose from her seat. She walked over to the rail near Mitch and leaned on it with her elbows. She looked out over the water. The sun had been down for some time, but the lights from the Terrace and the houses on the far side of the lake shined and bobbed with the water currants. A cool breeze wafted softly across her face. She shivered slightly.

"Hello." Her voice was soft, but just the same, the sound startled him. "May I call you Mitch? Or are you a 'Mr. Connor' kind of guy?" She knew her voice was full of sarcasm, but somehow her soft tone reduce its bite.

He lifted one brow in question and surprise. "I'm Mitch if you're Jessa. Fair enough?"

Jessa nodded, grinning. "Deal." A companionable silence settled over them as they stared across the water. Finally, she pointed at a dark spot that could be felt more than seen. "That about where Bristol House is?"

Mitch nodded, then he looked down at the rail he was leaning on. He sighed. "I wasn't fighting in the basement, you know. There must have been an intruder. I know you don't believe that, but it doesn't really matter if you believe it or not."

Jessa knew it was just a statement, but she felt that there was an apology in there of some kind. She wasn't sure why he might be apologizing, unless he was guilty of something. Once more, she was struck by the feeling that he *was* guilty... but she was not sure of what. Still, her heart went out to him.

"Want to talk about it?" Jessa questioned.

He looked up sharply and frowned. "Talk about what? I have nothing to say to you." There was an edge to his voice now that had not been there a moment ago.

She put her hands in front of her chest defensively. "Sorry. Just thought I'd ask. You looked like a man with a confession."

He snorted. "Go to hell," he said quietly. Then he laughed softly. "I know you are trying to get me to admit something. Thing is, I'm not sure what it is." He turned his body so he faced her. "What do you want from me, Jessa Bennett?"

It was her turn to look away in confusion. His green eyes glowed with an intense light that drilled into her head, trying to captivate her. His smile caused faint laugh lines to fan out attractively from his eyes. His features, perfectly symmetrical, were rugged, yet refined. His melodious voice soothed almost musically… everything seemed to lure her in to him. He was a very charming man. Even so, the evidence said he could be very deadly, too. Still, here on the Terrace, what could happen?

In the end, she could not help but smile back at him. "Right now, all I want is a fresh beer."

So, she was not surprised that a moment later, he took her hand and together they left the Terrace for the union building and into the Ratskeller to buy the beer. There were students and older patrons alike roaming around the halls with plastic cups of beer and soft drinks. Mitch led Jessa away from the crowd and to a quiet seat away from the Terrace railing, away from the band still playing some lively tunes.

Here it was quieter. And darker. Though Jessa was not exactly afraid—after all there were probably close to a thousand people in and around the Terrace area—the idea of being alone with Mitch intimidated her. Yet, she could not ignore the thrill of excitement that buzzed through her head and chest when he looked at her. It wasn't just that he was strikingly beautiful. There was definitely some kind of chemistry here… possibly volatile, crazy, scary chemistry.

An unspoken truce settled over them. Bristol House

became a taboo subject for the evening. They talked about their favorite music; his list seemed unending. Hers was shorter, but when she listened to his vast knowledge of music, she promised herself to open her mind to a larger variety of genres. He seemed to be fascinated by her understanding of photography, though he was not without expertise himself. They both had some background in composition, hers in art and his in architecture, and both had an eye for color.

He was an avid reader. Almost every book title Jessa could think of, he'd already read or already had in his library. Their tastes in literature were strikingly similar. Jessa found herself wishing she'd never heard of Maria Escher.

Time passed quickly. With a hasty glance at her watch, she knew she needed to get back to Jeanette. So, she thanked him for the beer and smiled to ease her abrupt departure. He nodded quietly at her and watched her walk away. As she weaved her way around the crowds of people, she thought about how he never asked to see her again.

One part of her was disappointed. Another part of her knew that this was as safe as it was going to get; it would be insane to get involved any more than she already was. Still, another part of her knew without a doubt that this was not the last she'd seen of Mitch Connor.

Jeanette seemed to take Jessa's absence in stride. Though she was interested in Jessa's run-in with Mitch Connor, she had the presence of mind not to ask about it. They didn't stay long afterwards. For Jessa, the evening had become dull and tiresome. As she waved good-bye to Jeanette and started her car up, her thoughts stayed with Mitch's seductive face.

CHAPTER EIGHT
GHOSTLY SHADOWS

Only when she'd been lying in bed for forty-five minutes did Jessa realize that sleep was not going to come easy. Though she yawned almost continuously, her eyes stayed stubbornly open. Finally, she tossed back the covers on her bed and got up.

Throwing on her robe, she padded quietly into the kitchen to get her laptop. Then she returned to her bedroom, propped herself up against the pillows, and opened the computer.

Her bedroom, finished in cheery shades of pink and white, was her favorite place in the apartment. Surely, nothing scary could break through this protective barrier. Cautiously, she opened the folder with the pictures she'd taken of Bristol House.

She looked at each picture carefully starting from the first day. The smudges were wispy, like smoke. There was no shape to them. No substance. On to the second day: the pictures from the old camera were, like the first day, clearer and brighter at the beginning. As the time passed, the color got duller and the edges started showing the strange smudges. Oddly, the smudges began to take on the appearance of a person... well, part of a person. A torso with a head and arms... surely that was a mistake. What kind of nonsense was she trying to dream up?

Finally, she took a deep breath and opened the photo taken from the floor of Mitch's kitchen. As big as day, there was a heavy-set man standing between her and the stairway door. She knew, as well as she knew her name, that she had been alone in the apartment at the time. Who the hell was this man? Even though the question of a double exposure bounced around in her head, she knew it was not a possibility. With film, yes, she'd done it on purpose a million times for effect. But digital? She could not think of how that would be possible.

So, the big question lingering in her mind was this: who was he? Another big question: how did he get into her picture? His black suit looked terribly old-fashioned, unless this man was into steampunk dress. Somehow she thought not: it was too conservative without the accessories associated with that style of costume.

Jessa closed that photo carefully. Keeping her mind open, and trying very hard not to spook herself, she opened the last set of photos she'd taken just that afternoon. Today had by far been the scariest time she'd spent at Bristol House. That place officially gave her the creeps. She shivered.

She could immediately tell that the pictures were not right. The color was not bright. A haze permeated each frame. Odd smudges, or perhaps the light bouncing off dust particles, showed up randomly throughout each photo. As she came to the pictures that coincided with the foul odor in the master bedroom, she could see a dark shadow begin to form in a corner of the room. The more she looked at it, the more shape the shadow took. Then, as she had gone up to the apartment on the third floor, the pictures cleared and the color returned. This is where she took the photos of the documents on Mitch's desk.

Those pictures, she stopped and studied. There was nothing there that was even remotely incriminating, but she had to admit to herself that she had not gone through the desk thoroughly. It would definitely require another trip.

Her heart rate had almost returned to normal while she perused the desk pictures. The next ones were taken in the smaller bedroom on the second floor.

Remembering what had lured her down there, almost made her snap the top of her laptop shut. Sooner or later she would have to examine those pictures, too. She would not be able to ignore them for long. So, she took a deep breath and forced herself to look.

Right away, she knew there would be something important in those boxes she'd photographed. Documents practically oozed out of them. From the looks of the boxes, she guessed the contents were pretty old. These were not cardboard or plastic boxes that a person could pick up at Wal-Mart and store their items in. They were much older than that: they were old wooden crates. On the sides, she could make out the faint hint of paint that said these were apple and peach crates.

Her heart suddenly jumped in her throat. In the darkest, shadowed recess of the closet, she could barely make out the black figure of a man, heavy-set, looking directly at her. Of course, the figure was not clear, but she could see that he was a white man and probably older than her by twenty or more years. Though the dress was right, he was not a steampunker.

Jessa quickly looked through the other photos to see if she could see the man in any other pictures. She was desperate to get a clear enough view of his face that she might recognize him or a picture of him. As far as she could see, though, there were no other pictures of the strange black-clad man. Opening the closet picture again, she frowned in confusion as he now seemed to fade slightly into the shadows of the tiny room. The harder she looked, the more he faded. Then, blinking in disbelief, she could see that he was only a dark-shaped shadow far back into the recess of the closet and not a man shape at all. She could *just about* imagine that she'd made him up: that there had been no one in the photo at all. Her eyes were seeing things… in a photo!

She almost didn't want to look at the pictures from the cellar. Only because she had not been there alone was she able to finally work up the nerve to open them. Gooseflesh raised the hairs on her arms. There, standing in the shadows behind the ruined furniture, was the same man in black. Here, his face was a little clearer. Though still too blurry to recognize, she could see a scowl mar his face. A wide, thick mustache was a charcoal slash above his lips. Nothing was as frightening as the anger radiating wildly from his eyes.

Then, as soon as that thought was completely formed, the man faded and became just another dark shadow that lined the boxes and other broken debris. Still, there was no doubt about what she saw... she just wouldn't be able to prove it.

Jessa sat back and closed her eyes for a minute. Her heart hammered noisily in her chest. Her brain felt numb. What was it she saw in the photos: ghost or man? It was late: had her imagination taken a turn to the macabre? Was Bristol House haunted? Or was she going insane?

Of all the pictures she'd taken, these ones with the strange specters were not the ones she'd been particularly interested in at the time. She'd been looking for odd or convenient places a person could hide a body, perhaps a telltale splash of blood on the floor. She had hoped to come across a document that would incriminate Mitch, or maybe a tearful confession...but the pictures that were the most interesting were the ones taken in the open.

She groaned and snapped the lid of her laptop shut. What had she done? Was there some evil spirit haunting Bristol House that was now aware of her? It seemed to her that the ghostly figure followed her, tried to get her attention. If that was so, then why?

Why did it want her attention? She groaned again and scrunched down in her bed, flinging the covers up over her head.

At some point during the night, she fell asleep. She was so exhausted that she slept straight through her alarm the next morning. When she finally woke, she sat up with a start and looked wildly around her. The sun was not where it normally was when she rose and a cursory glance at her watch told her why.

She quickly showered and hurried into the kitchen. As she entered, the postcard of Bristol House fell from the shelf near the door, fluttered to the floor, and landed at her feet. She stood still for a second and stared at the card. Strange emotions surged through the arteries of her heart. She picked up the card and stared at the photo of Bristol House. It almost seemed to her that some of the vibrant color had drained from the picture. The misty fog in the top floor window had congealed into a thicker, more pronounced mass. Jessa's heart trip-hammered in her rib cage.

She set the card back up on the shelf in a position that would keep it from falling off again. She looked up and shivered at the breeze coming in from the open kitchen window. She reached up to shut it and as she did so she had the feeling she'd done this very action before. She saw the bright orange breast of a robin as it flitted by. Distracted, she didn't give her camera more than a moment's thought. It would make a nice photo, but she knew that the bird would be gone long before she got back to the window. Her actions were slow as she made herself a small pot of coffee. While it was brewing, she ate a bowl of oatmeal and wondered why her morning seemed like it had already happened.

Since her camera media was cleared of all photos, she decided to attend an informal political rally at the Terrace and take some pictures of the candidates or any other public personalities who might also be attending. She hated lowering herself to scandal sheets, but in desperate situations (and fortunately she was not too desperate at the moment) sometimes she could sell photos of this type to the tabloids. Also, though all those zeros were currently residing in her bank account, there was no guarantee they'd remain there.

Jessa was one of many photographers there, hoping to get a good photograph. Some, like the ones from the newspaper, came with an attitude of superiority. Their meal ticket was already paid for. Jessa ignored them and concentrated on what she knew she had to do. She leaned against the railing with her back to the water and watched as the crowd thickened.

Then, like needles in the back of her neck, she could not ignore the feeling of being watched. She turned ever so slightly and looked out across the water. It suddenly occurred to her that this was the very spot she'd stood with Mitch the night before when they'd considered and spoken of Bristol House. It was too far across the lake to make out the house, but she instinctively knew the spot where it stood. If she used her imagination at all, she could almost feel it calling her name.

Jessa...

The whispered word reverberated in her head and quickened the speed of her heart.

Jessa...

She turned her head swiftly away from the water and the way her name was whispered on the wind, but the soft sound of her name didn't end there. "Jessa..." It was a man's voice. "Are you alright?"

Raising her eyes, she looked directly into the handsome face of Mitch Connor. Suddenly, the world became very real. Bristol House was not calling her. This was real life. There were no such things as ghosts.

Furthermore, in her eyes, Mitch Connor was still guilty of the murder of Maria Escher.

"Yes, I'm fine, thanks very much. You?" She met his frank gaze with one of her own, and for the first time in a long time, she couldn't think of any sarcastic remark to make.

Mitch seemed to take this as a truce of some kind. He shrugged and grinned slightly. "Okay, I guess. I used to love this kind of thing. Now, not so much."

Her old, confident self was coming back to her. She grinned back at him. "Makes it hard to be out in the public when you can't be yourself, doesn't it? You know, when you are worried about questions they might ask and you can't answer? Or you don't want to answer? Let me ask you something... have you ever wanted to say something so outrageous, so shocking, so true, that no one would actually believe you?"

Mitch slowly lost the smile from his face. "Lady, I don't know what the hell you are talking about. Do you have a twin sister or something? You see, I met this really nice girl last night. Here. On the Terrace. She looks like you. She sounds like you. But she isn't you because your tongue is as sharp as a knife and the girl who was here last night was nice."

Jessa laughed, but it didn't quite reach her eyes. "I think you know exactly what I'm talking about. But like all politicians, you know how to answer the question without answering the question."

Mitch shook his head in exasperation. "I don't know what question you want me to answer. Shoot. In English this time. I'll answer anything."

"Okay," she said smugly. "Why don't you like these political rallies?"

"Crowds are too big. The older I get, the less I like crowds, but they come with the job so here I am. What else?" Mitch folded his arms over his chest.

Jessa lifted an eyebrow. "Is there a particular reason you don't like crowds? Are you afraid they will ask you questions you can't or won't answer?"

He considered before answering. "There is no particular reason I don't like crowds except that I just don't. I have never had anyone ask me a question I was unable or unwilling to answer. Now if you'll excuse me, I need to be standing near… someone else." He turned away from Jessa.

Instantly, she called after him, keeping her voice low enough so that he was the only one who could hear her. "This is what I was talking about. When the questions get hot, you and everyone else of your ilk run away like scared puppies."

He stopped short, furiously facing her. "You have a particular question in mind?"

There was a part of Jessa that cheered with the win of this verbal assault, but there was a part of her that felt sorry for him. Only because he was an elected official was his life an open book. If not for that, he would be able to tell her to take a hike, but she couldn't back down now. "What happened to Maria Escher?"

Dark fury crumpled any remaining congeniality that had remained on his face. "I don't know what happened to Maria. No one does. Maybe she ran away. Maybe she joined a cult. I don't know!" He stomped away from her.

Jessa was not proud of herself as she watched Mitch leave. If only they had met under other circumstances. If only there had been no Maria. If only … if only he hadn't committed murder, as the Eschers believed.

She had little enthusiasm for the pictures she took. While there were not official speeches, there was light bantering and introducing of various people in the city's hierarchy. Several hundred people stood by watching the city leaders, shouting questions, and listening to answers.

No way would she return to Bristol House today, so she decided to go through her photos once more and see if there was anything to report to David and Norma Escher. After calling and making an appointment with them, Jessa spent the next couple of hours writing notes and filling a digital file folder with various photos of the house. For some reason, she didn't include the photos she'd taken of the contents of Mitch's desk, nor did she include the one of the heavy-set man in Mitch's apartment. That was just too weird to explain.

The other photos could be explained with the bounce of a flash, or perhaps the fact that she'd had to get her sensors cleaned. Nothing in any photo was conclusively spectral in nature, so her best attack at this point was to gloss over her fears.

She gathered her notes, burned a CD, and left her apartment. More than twenty minutes later, she was finally standing nervously in front of David and Norma's restaurant. Peter, the disapproving manager, was there to greet her. With absolutely no recognition whatsoever, he led her into a private room in the back where the older couple waited beside a running computer.

They looked over every word she wrote. They asked her over and over about what she saw and how Mitch had taken her intrusion. They wanted to know if she'd mentioned them by name.

They poured over the pictures, pointing to certain spots in some, and practically ignoring others. Jessa couldn't tell what it was, exactly, that they were looking for. There seemed to be neither rhyme nor reason to their visual search. She hoped the confusion she felt didn't show in her face.

In the end, the zeros remained in her bank account. David and Norma seemed pleased with what she'd done so far, though it was obvious to Jessa that she had not found what they were hoping for. Of course, she had known it would not be an easy job. If the police investigators had not been able to find enough evidence to bring Mitch Conner to trial, then why would she think she could find more evidence? However, the answer to that was easy: the police investigators were not allowed to have the power of all those zeros! They had no incentive.

As soon as she returned to her apartment later that afternoon, Jessa began to feel dirty. After this snoop job was over, she knew she'd never take another. It wasn't the snooping she didn't like; it was what it did to the person being snooped. Guilty or not, she felt bad about what she was trying to do to Mitch Connor.

The light was fading from the day, and the cool evening set in. Jessa closed the kitchen window and locked it. She shivered and pulled on a cardigan sweater to keep warm. Curling up on her couch, she flipped the switches on the television until she found an old movie. It was a love story about a man and a woman. Normal people. No ghosts. They fell in love, got married, and had kids. Normal.

CHAPTER NINE
A DATE WITH MITCH

Rain pattered depressingly on Jessa's bedroom window. She'd been awake for quite some time, but had found neither the inclination nor energy to rise. There was a chill in the air that spoke of the nearness of winter. All too soon, she'd be dragging out jackets and long stockings.

The clock on her bedside table refused to stay still, so as the minutes ticked by, she finally found the resolve to drag her body into the shower. She felt better after emerging from the hot water, and walked softly into the tiny kitchen. She had her eye on the shelf just inside the door and watched as the postcard of Bristol House fluttered to the floor and land at her feet. She frowned at it for a moment, then she slowly bent to pick it up. This seemed to be a habit she had recently acquired: the positioning of the card on the shelf and the puff of air currents she created with the movement of her body must make the card unstable.

She gave the photo only a quick glance before replacing it on the shelf in, what she hoped, was a more stable position. She looked up and shivered at the breeze coming in from the open kitchen window. She reached up to shut it with a shaking hand, certain that she'd shut and locked it the night before. As she did so, she looked up and, as expected, she saw the bright orange breast of a robin as it flitted by. She resisted the impulse to reach for her camera; somehow the appearance of the bird didn't seem right. She made herself a small pot of coffee, and while it was brewing, she ate a bowl of oatmeal.

In the middle of a spoonful of oatmeal, she stopped cold and glanced up at the window. She had not been paying too much attention, but she swore that a moment ago when she'd seen the robin outside, it was bright and sunny. Now, the kitchen window was shut against the rain that pattered softly against it.

She swallowed, then silence. The animated world was suspended in a moment of time. There was no breeze; the ticking clock was unexpressed. The soft thrumming of the rain was extinguished. An oppressive hush strangled the room. Jessa's eyes darted around nervously. This felt like it had when she'd been on the Terrace with Jeanette. Finally, her eyes landed on the postcard of Bristol House. As she studied it from across the room, the photo, which had darkened perceptibly, lightened suddenly to normal. Along with that, the rain pattered gently on her window once again and the soft breeze could be heard outside.

Then suddenly, her phone rang shrilly. She jumped, startled and spooked. As she reached for the phone, she dropped her spoon into the oatmeal, sending globs of hot cereal across the table. She swore miserably under her breath as she flipped her phone open.

"What!" she barked.

"Good morning to you, too, sunshine." A melodious male voice greeted her. Jessa could feel a hint of mockery in the tone. Mitch Connor continued, "I think it would be a good idea for us to talk. Would you consider having lunch with me?"

Jessa's breath quickened at the sound of the voice, which seemed, like the house he owned, to haunt her at every turn. Besides feasting her eyes on the sexy way his hair curled and the clear green of his eyes, his voice caressed her ears and lulled her brain into a security that was almost hypnotic. She could not stop the sudden flutter of her heart. With no will to stop herself, she replied, "I guess that would be okay. Um, what did you have in mind?"

He mentioned a time and the name of a café uptown on Capitol Square, just down the block from the restaurant owned by Eschers. It was famed for its outdoor tables from late spring to almost winter. Today, Jessa could not imagine them sitting outside, but it was just as lovely inside. She agreed in brief, then made her excuses and hung up quickly. Mitch seemed to cloud her usually good judgment, and she needed to clear her head before she met with him.

This morning there were errands to run. First, there was makeup to carefully apply, there was the decision of what to wear (not that she was trying to impress him), and of course, she had to decide what fragrance to put on… not too seductive, but definitely feminine.

By the time she'd arrived at the appointed time and place, she was so nervous she could hardly speak. She had almost convinced herself that her nervousness was due to Mitch's questionable activities and not the fact that this was beginning to seem like a real date. She could be walking into the trap of a murderer. Yet, she was drawn to him like a bee to honeysuckle.

The rain had stopped and though the day was still dark, all the outside tables and chairs had dried off. The temperature warmed up enough that Mitch waited for her outside. He stood as he watched her approach.

Jessa smiled and sat across the little table from him. She was glad a waiter showed up immediately because she was without anything clever to say. Though, with a glass of wine under her belt, she could finally feel her tongue loosen.

"Okay, Mitch. What did you want to talk to me about?" Yeah, Jessa thought, throw the ball into his court.

His short laugh sounded a little like a snort. "You took me by surprise yesterday, Jessa. I guess I was expecting the girl from the night before. Instead, I got the prickly girl from Bristol House. I know you are trying to snoop me out, but what I can't figure out is why and for whom?" He looked at her expectantly.

Jessa almost caved under the intense stare. She licked her lips, hoping the action didn't look as sensuous as it felt. Blood heated her face as she dropped her gaze to his lips, then forced it back up to his eyes. She mentally reached for her solid shield of sarcasm. "So I have to be working for someone to satisfy my own curiosity?"

Mitch laughed. "Normally I would say no, but pictures? Come on! If it was your own curiosity you were trying to satisfy, then there would be no need for them. Is it me you are spying on, or are you trying to discover why Bristol House is haunted?"

The admission came as a shock and Jessa lifted her brows in question. "So Bristol House is haunted. Who is the ghost?"

Mitch studied her for a moment without the smile he had been wearing. "You never heard any rumors about it being haunted?"

Jessa shook her head slowly and frowned. "No, I haven't. Is it true, then? That could bring in some more tourism. I would think your girls would mention it during the tours."

"Most of them don't know. In fact, when anyone becomes suspicious, they are let go... with a nice departing fee, of course."

"Of course," Jessa agreed with a roll of her eyes. "Why don't you want anyone to know about a ghost?"

Mitch shrugged. "Not too sure it really exists. There have been some strange things that have happened, though. Sometimes the ghostly actions seem... slightly... violent. That wouldn't draw a crowd, as I'm sure you'd agree."

She nodded. "I see what you mean."

Leaning back in his chair, Mitch studied her face again. "You didn't know about the ghost... why is it that you don't seem particularly surprised about it then?"

Jessa leaned on her elbows, smiling brightly. "Why should I tell you?"

"Because it's my house and I asked so nicely." He grinned back, stealing the breath from Jessa's lungs.

She swallowed hard before she could come up with an answer that didn't sound like gibberish. "I've taken some pictures that are, for the lack of a more appropriate word, weird. Not only that, but some of the photos have actually changed in appearance right before my eyes." She sat back and folded her arms across her chest, daring him to believe her.

The surprise in his face was quite obvious. "Wow, I never thought of that. It didn't occur to me to take pictures. Cool. Could I see them?"

Jessa almost lost her breath again, but this time it was from fear. If she showed him the pictures, he'd know why she'd been taking them. It was obvious, to her at least, that she was photographing secret hiding places. So she went for an ambiguous answer, "We can see what can be arranged. In the meantime, do you know who the ghost is?"

Mitch shook his head. "No idea. Although I suspect it is probably a relative of mine. My relatives are the only ones who have ever lived in the house."

Then a thought occurred to Jessa. "You don't think it could be Maria's ghost?"

The dark look on Mitch's face was back. "No, it is not Maria's ghost. First, there is no proof that she is dead. Second, the ghost has definite male qualities. What do your photos tell you?"

It was Jessa's turn to shrug. "Male," she admitted. "But just thought it didn't hurt to ask in case there were two of them."

There was silence for a moment; strangely tense. Finally, Mitch spoke in a very low voice, "What are you going to do with the photos?"

"Ha!" Jessa erupted a little too loudly. Then she looked around and noticed she'd acquired the attention of patrons from the other tables. She waited until their attention was elsewhere before she could look at Mitch and answer his question. "The photos are mine. I'm keeping them."

"Is that all, or are you planning on sharing them before you keep them?" Mitch agitatedly thrummed his fingers on the table.

For an instant, Jessa imagined that he knew all about

the proposition David and Norma had made. That was silly, wasn't it? There was no way he could know unless they'd told him, and there was no way they'd tell him. Stubbornly, she refused to elaborate. "I will keep them. Right now, I have no plans to show them to anyone." She was telling a partial truth, she realized. Though she had already had a meeting with the Eschers, they had not seen the odd photos.

"I have no choice but to trust you. I hope you won't share this information with the tabloids. It could cause me quite a bit of trouble." He looked up and held her gaze. "If I said please, would you tell me before sharing them with anyone?"

Her heart trip-hammered again. He was looking at her so intently that she thought she'd drown in the depths of his appeal. "The photos are safe for the time being. That's all I can guarantee."

He sighed. "Then that's all I can ask for. But I do have another question for you."

"Shoot," she said.

"Who are you working for?"

"I thought we'd already been over that question. You have no reason to think I'm working for anyone." She looked away from him.

"You and I both know that isn't true. What I want to know is: which tabloid sent you over to take the photos?"

Jessa could feel laughter bubble up in her chest and throat. "I can tell you without any doubt that I am not working for a tabloid." Then, because he raised a doubtful eyebrow, she qualified, "Yes, I was there for the tabloids yesterday, but that is not why I was at Bristol House the day before. I just want to know what happened to poor Maria."

Once again, Mitch snorted in disgust. "Well, when you find out, please let me know. I've been wondering for years."

In silent agreement, they spoke no more of Bristol House. Taboo, also, was the subject of wayward photos. That subject, too peculiar and strange, could not find a place in their attempt at a normal conversation. Now, it seemed that Mitch turned her emotions another way entirely. She studied the way he tilted his head when he told a funny story. She admired the way his chest rumbled when he laughed. She caught a cloudy look in his eyes when he spoke of anything sad. She'd never been so drawn to anyone as Mitch drew her now.

Even knowing she should be wary of his every move, his every motive, every word that could have a double meaning, she could not quell the way her heart reacted when he was charming. Charming was something he was very good at.

No more than an hour later, Mitch walked Jessa to her car. She stood awkwardly by, not knowing if she should just get in the car and go or if he would expect a friendly handshake. Neither happened.

She smiled slightly, and said, "Thanks for lunch, Mitch. I'll probably be seeing you around." She hesitated slightly. Go or stay?

"Sure." Then, before she could turn away from him, he clasped her shoulders and leaned his head in to give her a light kiss on her lips. She stood there, a little startled, with her eyes shut and her mouth slightly opened. When she finally opened her eyes, she couldn't make out the expression on his face. For a moment, she wondered if he was testing the waters; would she prove to be an easy mark for his effortless charms? There were probably few women who could resist his wealth and good looks.

An amused look softened the features of his face. He seemed to be stunned, pleased. She certainly was. Perhaps he hadn't planned on kissing her? Then, with no control over her own actions, Jessa leaned slightly toward him and kissed him as he had kissed her. She had meant the kiss to be slightly challenging, she was not a pawn in his romantic quests, but passion exploded in her body. Her arms wound around his neck, fingers threaded through his hair, just as his arms circled her waist. His solid body pressed eagerly against hers.

Her body became liquid. She melted and swayed against him. The little control she had dropped away as the world around her faded. She opened her mouth and felt his tongue caress her lips. Pleasurable moans seeped out of her throat, and even if she was aware of them, she could not stop them. His arms lifted and tightened around her shoulders, fingers caressing the bumps of her spine, lowering until his hands rested just above her bottom.

Then, just as suddenly as the kisses started, Mitch drew away abruptly. He stood back from her with a foot of air between them, and a puzzled expression on his face. Pink embarrassment flooded Jessa's features as she tried to figure out what had just happened. What had she done wrong? Or perhaps more accurately, were her kisses more than he had bargained for?

He left her abruptly, as she stood and watched his retreating back.

With his black, shiny BMW parked nearby, she could see him revved the engine, then shot off down the road like a rocket. After barely a moment's hesitation, Jessa hopped behind the wheel of her Honda. It roared to life, and she jerked the car into the street, following behind Mitch at a distance where she wouldn't be noticed.

Her thoughts were singular: what does a man like Mitch do on a free afternoon like today? It was apparent he wasn't going to the office to work. He was not headed for Bristol House. Where would he go? What would he do?

The fact that she found Mitch interesting and attractive had nothing to do with this surreptitious chase, she told herself firmly. She had a job to do. This was it.

Jessa followed Mitch as he drove southwest. She could not begin to guess where he was leading her, but she was certainly curious. When they arrived at the University's Arboretum, the answer she was seeking wasn't any nearer.

The parking lot was nearly full of vehicles. As the

weather had warmed and the sun began to make periodic appearances, hikers and runners were likely to make use of the many trails that crisscrossed the lush green prairie meadows, as well as the woods and wetlands. Few types of weather actually stopped a true Madisonian from this outdoor wilderness during any season.

Today Jessa parked several spaces from the familiar black BMW, then waited until Mitch had left the lot for a path that struck out toward a hillside overlooking the Arboretum. She followed far enough behind him that it was unlikely he would see her. It was only when they got to a clearing that she had to let the distance between them lengthen. When that happened, she dashed behind well-placed evergreens to keep him in sight.

At length, he stopped by a young tree, an oak sapling about three or four feet tall. Beside it was an ornate, white, wrought iron bench, big enough for two people. He sat there and leaned toward the tree with his elbows on his knees and his head hanging down. At first Jessa thought he might be praying, though that didn't seem likely because he occasionally raised his eyes to the tree. He would mumble something, then stop as if waiting for an answer.

Jessa frowned, but could not get any closer without being seen. She could just barely hear his voice, low and melodious. A warm breeze carried his words away from her.

She studied him. His posture told her he was saying something very emotional. Were there tears in his eyes? She squinted her eyes and strained to listen. One word came to her very clearly before fading away with the rest of his words: Maria! Jessa pulled back as if she'd been burned. What was this emotion she could see? Sorrow? More likely, it was guilt! He looked like a man with a lot on his mind: a guilty mind that was trying to find some peace from what he'd done.

After a time, Mitch stood and stared down at the sapling, fingering its smooth leaves gently. Then he turned and continued on the trail for a short distance, but away from the forest and back toward the parking lot. Jessa watched him go and was torn between following him and examining the bench by the tree. After he had walked away, she could see that the bench had a plaque, and she was curious to see what was engraved there.

CHAPTER TEN
REMEMBERING MARIA

In Loving Memory of Maria Escher
May you find happiness wherever you are.
Your devoted parents, David and Norma Escher

Jessa read the plaque several times very slowly. As many times as she'd been to the Arboretum, she'd never noticed this bench or plaque before now. A moment of overwhelming sadness gripped her as she thought about what the Eschers must be going through. The loss of their daughter... nothing would make that okay.

She scanned the area but could not see any sign of Mitch. She walked around for a while before the soggy ground forced her to head back to her car. She wasn't dressed for hiking and the sky had clouded back up.

She didn't want to go back to her apartment just yet, so she drove slowly toward the shops near campus and parked her car in a garage. Though the clouds gathered thickly in the sky, it looked like the rain would hold off for a while. She walked along the streets, and watched the university students milling around. She heard the strumming guitar of a man playing and singing softly, so she dropped a dollar in his open guitar case as she walked by.

The pungent scent of brats and beer filled her head as she walked by a sports bar. She wasn't hungry, but the vision of eating a hot brat was almost more than she could resist. She walked on.

She was nearly out of the shops that lined the streets, so she turned back and headed down the sidewalk on the opposite side of the road. A bright advertisement in front of one of the shops caught her attention: *If you can't find what you're looking for, keep looking!*

Jessa thought about the sign and somewhere inside

her, she laughed grimly. Well, she certainly had not found what she'd been looking for regarding the Eschers and poor Maria. She walked on slower still, wishing for the hundredth time that there were no connection between Mitch and the missing girl. He would be so easy to fall for, yet she was most certainly not his type under normal circumstances.

As she got ready to pick up her pace, another sign distracted her and stopped her in her tracks. *Come check out Maria's place. It's where all the action is!* Jessa gulped noisily. She looked up at the entryway where someone had tacked up a homemade banner over the usual storefront sign: Maria's Flea Market.

Jessa turned hastily and marched quickly away from the flea market sign with her heart in her throat. Yikes! she thought nervously. She was in a weird, creepy mood, apparently. However, a couple of blocks later, a movie marquee loomed largely. It was a theater that showed out-of-date movies on the big screen again: *Ghost* was being advertised. She stopped and stared, as the word seemed to pop into her brain. Then when she turned her head slightly, she read: *Paranormal!*

Tears filled her eyes. The titles seemed to want to tell her something. She ran to her car blinded by panic. She had not wanted to return to Bristol House: not today, not ever! Even so, she could feel its pull. She knew she had to go back there.

Maria needed her.

Jessa found her car and headed as quickly as possible to her apartment. She shimmied out of her little skirt and ballerina shoes, and slipped on her comfiest pair of black jeans and a black hoodie sweatshirt. Even the shoes she chose were dark.

She grabbed her camera and headed out the door. Like the last time she sneaked into Bristol House, she parked a couple of blocks away. She doubted Mitch was there now; he seemed to have other things on his mind when he left the

Arboretum, but she wasn't about to take a chance on his return with her car parked in the lot.

With the return of darkness came the return of the rain. The wind that came with it caused the black-silhouetted trees to sway and rustle. Jessa tiptoed down the driveway, her eyes darting in every direction, expecting to see someone follow her or waiting ahead for her. The night was oppressively shadowy.

Finally, the house loomed ahead like a silent and angry sentry. Jessa looked up through the fine, misty rain at the huge mansion, and she could feel its baleful glare bear down on her. It watched and waited. She could sense its breath moving imperceptibly, swirling malignantly through the windows and doors.

She hesitated on the edge of the lawn and continued to stare up at the house. A deep, slow thrumming kept time with the heavy beat of her heart. Her jittery breath was quick and sharp. Closing her eyes, she mentally tried to find the strength it would take to enter the house once again.

All the strange photos, memories, sounds, and stories began to flood her brain. Her hands shook, though she tried to hold them still in her pockets. Her instincts told her the house resisted her. It did not want her there—and she did not want to be there.

She almost turned away, but the sudden image of the signs she'd seen uptown flashed across her eyes. Maria! Jessa stepped toward Bristol House.

Giving the house a wide berth, she stepped into the back where the cellar door was. No way would she enter in that dark hole, but she'd been lucky once to find an unlocked window. It was a good place to start.

The house, inside, was alive with audible activity. A groan whined inarticulately. A door latched with a soft click. Rustles and shuffling steps seemed to travel up and down the halls; near, then far; loud, then soft. Jessa's hands shook as she tried to open each window and door at the back, but they were all locked. Though she needed to get inside, she wasn't entirely disappointed nothing would open.

She looked up at the looming structure once again. It towered mysteriously over her. She had the feeling it was taunting her, amused because she couldn't enter. The strange man's laugh, the one she had heard on the second floor and again in the cellar, swirled eerily around the air above her head.

She jogged swiftly along the side of the house nearest the lake. There were no windows close enough to reach to test the locks, so she kept jogging. The rain began to come down in earnest and, with that, Jessa decided to head back home. This was a crappy night to be sneaking into such a creepy, old house anyway.

Then, just as she jogged passed the veranda, she heard the slight creaking of another door; except this time the sound was close enough she could have spit on it. She turned her head quickly toward the front door and watched it swing slowly on its hinges. It stopped when it was pointing at her. An invitation had been issued.

Jessa swallowed hard and stared at the door. Even the wind, pushing and puffing against the old wood, didn't budge the position of the door. She leaned toward the veranda, helplessly following her feet as they stepped slowly toward it. Then all too soon, she reached out and lightly touched the door with icy fingers.

Invisible hands pushed her and prodded her until she had no choice but to step through the door: the invitation was accepted.

Jessa's hand groped for the camera still slung over her shoulder. She wasn't sure why the camera's presence gave her a small amount of comfort, except that it was something familiar with happy memories attached to it. When she was inside, she straightened and looked around the dark room. The house was very still.

Yet, it wasn't quiet. Little scuffling footsteps, like

those of a busy rodent, came from the corners of the rooms and doors leading to various closets and other spaces. If Jessa let her imagination get crazy, she could think she heard the moans of a long dead individual. She could almost imagine that she could hear the husky laughter of a man. The sound of doors opening and shutting on the second floor was almost recognizable as such. She shivered.

Stepping farther into the house, Jessa ached to turn on a light, but she didn't want to alert a neighbor, or possibly even Mitch. He had told her not to return, and she was not sure what he'd do if he caught her again. Then, as she was standing in the center of the parlor in the dark, she realized she had no clear idea of what she was looking for.

She walked slowly around the parlor using a small flashlight that was hanging from her belt. The room was sparsely furnished with beautiful period pieces. What the room lacked in volume was made up for by an abundance of ornate designs. Curlicues, elegantly bright fabric patterns, curvy backs and arms; all the furniture was stunning. This was probably not the original furnishing of the time when S. J. and Virginia lived: the wood was too new, the fabric too vivid, but they were excellent reproductions.

Jessa ran her fingers lightly across the back of a chair, feeling the slight tingle of static electricity crackle at her fingertips. She headed for the hall between the parlor and kitchen. As she passed through, she looked up the stairs, but they ascended into darkness and Jessa wasn't even tempted to explore that direction. Not yet.

She walked into the kitchen and shined her little flashlight around the room. The hair on her scalp prickled, but the room was empty. Her heart thrummed in her chest like a fistful of hummingbirds. In confusion, and without conscious decision, she felt herself turning off the tiny flashlight, pitching the room into sudden darkness. Only, it wasn't really dark. She could make out the shapes and sizes of the tall kitchen cupboards. At the end of the counter, she could barely see the big ornate water pump.

At the same moment that she realized the room was not black, she raised her camera to her face and peered through the viewfinder. The kitchen was dark enough that little of it could actually be seen through the camera lens. She started to lower the camera again, but just as she did so, a brilliant flash of white skittered across her LCD screen. She drew in a surprised, sudden breath and put her eye against the viewfinder again. Slowly, she scanned the dark room through her camera lens. Finally, seeing nothing, she lowered it again.

Only then did she think to take a picture. Hadn't there been weird stuff in the photos that she had not seen in the room at the time they were taken? Perhaps there was something here that she could only see in photos. Carefully she raised the camera again.

Time and again, Jessa aimed the camera and felt the almost physical shock of the flash as it lit up the room to take a photograph. Standing in the center of the room, she turned a full circle, snapping close to thirty pictures. Theoretically, she could make a 360 degree panoramic composite of the room.

Then, just as she finished her camera sweep of the room, she knew it was time for her to go. She didn't stop to question herself why this thought was pushing its way forward. She didn't test the thought, nor was she tempted to. It *was* time to go. She was not going to take any chances tonight.

She walked to the front door in as straight a line as the floor plan would allow. The front door loomed ahead, open, and when Jessa walked through it, she hadn't realized she'd been breathing so shallowly. She took a deep breath of fresh, rainy air.

Hopping off the veranda, she looked back at the house. As she watched, the front door closed slowly and clicked shut. She had the distinct feeling that if she tried to open it, she would find it locked. She turned away from the huge old house and sprinted across the marshy lawn toward her parked car.

Her drive home was a dark, damp, frantic journey of chaotic rationalization. The thoughts in her brain were spinning so crazily that she had no memory of the actual drive. She just knew she stopped safely in front of her apartment building.

Her heart thudded in her chest. She leaned her head against the steering wheel and closed her eyes. She was so exhausted. If she hadn't been so uncomfortably wet, she might have been tempted to allow herself to fall asleep in her car. Instead, she pried her eyes open and forced her body to get out of the car with her camera in her hand.

She didn't know what she'd find in the photos on her camera, but she knew with absolute conviction that she'd find something. Once inside her apartment, though, she lost her courage and set the camera aside for the lure of a hot shower.

Later, armed with a huge cup of steaming hot cocoa, she loaded the pictures onto her computer. One by one, she let the pictures load. One by one, she stared as they filled the screen. One by one, she gasped in horror and panic.

MITCH COULD NOT DO IT. There was no way he could return to that big house tonight. Screw it; the folks could have the damn thing back. Even as he thought this, he knew that would not happen. The Bristol House was his burden, but he would not go there tonight.

He stood on the balcony of his apartment in a high-rise building looking over Madison's city center. It was a night with heavy clouds, yet the city was not dark by any means. Lights twinkled all over the city, giving it an electric glow, somehow alleviating the depressing darkness that a stormy night brings.

He had always been a person who needed sunshine. Light. Winters were long here, but rarely dark due to all the electric lights bouncing off the snow and clouds and back and forth until the night often resembled the day.

His life hadn't always felt this dark. There had been a time when he was a carefree young boy with childish dreams and hopes. In an instant, a horrible and deadly accident had changed all that.

He had a fight with his best friend, Jacob, and they had parted ways in anger. Weeks went by. Finally, when he couldn't stand it any longer, he went to see Jacob and they had mended their differences. It was only a temporary fix; Jacob was still angry. So Mitch turned his back and stomped away.

Too far away. He could hear the boy's screams. Mitch knew Jacob was in trouble, so he retraced his steps, but it was too late. His buddy had fallen after climbing on frail wooden scaffolding. A huge thick piece of lumber broke Jacob's fall, and his back. At first all Jacob could do was look up at his friend and gulp for air he could not get. With his body broken, skin ripped, face distorted with pain, Jacob stopped gulping for the much-needed air. Mitch knew he was dead, but he reached to his friend and with his little boy hands, tried to stop the blood that flowed over the wood and onto the ground. He cried and shook Jacob's shoulders. He apologized and promised to be his friend forever if he would just wake up. If Jacob would just not fall, as if it could be taken back and undone, maybe they'd be friends yet. If only....

His parents had not believed it was an accident. Or, that's what he had thought, because the next day, he was on an airplane to military school. That year, he never smiled. It seemed to be okay, though, because they never expected him to. A good soldier, they told him. An ideal student, his teachers praised, but his heart was bent, almost broken.

Mitch's eyes blurred for a moment as he forced himself back to the present. That was a long time ago. It was a terrible, tragic accident. It had almost ruined his parents; had almost ruined him. Not a day went by that Mitch didn't miss Jacob.

Then, Maria disappeared. First she was there, then she wasn't. It was his fault, he reasoned. He should have stopped her flirtation with her dead ancestors, but the dark practice enticed her and she loved the thrill of it. It seemed to be the only time she was truly happy, so he turned a blind eye. It didn't appear to be doing any harm. Then hell broke loose. Literally.

He had decided not to fall in love again. It was a risky process, this idea of giving away his heart. If he didn't love, he couldn't get his heart broken.

But damn, he was lonely! He returned inside to the plush furnishings of a huge living room. A wet bar beckoned, and he filled a glass with whiskey. He pitched it down his throat with one toss of his head, and poured another of the same.

When Jessa Bennett's face floated into his memory, he slapped the glass down hard on the counter, sloshing the amber liquid over the rim. He sank into the plush comfort of a recliner and leaned back, closing his eyes. He concentrated on Jessa's face.

That girl... she had a lot of nerve, that was for sure. He was surprised at the fire in her eyes when she was obviously in the wrong. It seemed that every time he saw her, every time he caught her snooping around, she lashed out when she should have been groveling for his forgiveness. He smiled, still with his eyes shut.

She had the most amazing eyes. She had the most amazing kiss. He had not planned to kiss her there at the restaurant, but had to help himself to a taste of those luscious, pink lips. He had thought it would spark a firestorm of anger and sarcasm, but no, she had responded to him. That had completely taken him off guard.

If that wasn't enough, while he was trying to decide his next step, she had leaned in and kissed him! Oh man, what kisses they were! He could still feel her softness, and her sweetness. He could hear the delicate moan in her throat when his tongue explored her lips. He wanted nothing more than to taste her sweetness again. And again. And again.

CHAPTER ELEVEN
DÉJÀ VU...AGAIN

Jessa's hand shook as she lifted the mug of hot cocoa to her lips. The steaming liquid sloshed over the sides and dripped on her robe, and then onto the table as she hurriedly set the mug back down.

The pictures she'd loaded from her camera were amazing, but not what she had expected at all. In fact, had they not come from her camera, she wouldn't have been able to identify them at all. With her digital photo folder open on her computer, she randomly chose a picture to open and study. As she did so, she had to take a mental step back. Too much emotion was tied up in them, and she couldn't afford that right now.

Though her flash had tripped, the background of the photos was almost pitch black. Only the smallest amount of detail could be seen of the kitchen. That, she ignored completely. Directly in front of her camera lens was the faint ghostly face of a young woman. The face was not white, as she might have expected a ghostly image to be. This young woman was blue, light and transparent. She was perfect in every detail. Jessa would have guessed the figure's eyes to be black holes, as in the ghost stories she had read as a child, but these eyes were bright and large and quite striking. Beautiful eyes. Ordinary eyes.

In life, this woman would be stunningly gorgeous, but who was she? In Jessa's mind there were only two choices: this was either the original owner, Virginia Hubert, or it was the missing Maria. Jessa couldn't remember if anyone had said how old Virginia was when she died, but she had thought she was older than this ghost appeared to be. She quickly closed that photo and opened another. If the young ghost would back up a little, she could see what the apparition was wearing and see if it was a period costume or something a little more modern.

In each photo she opened, the style of the costume was inconclusive. The most opaque part of the apparition seemed to start from the middle of her face and fade as it fanned outward. Long hair radiated around the face like it was floating in water. The woman wore some kind of gown with a vee so deep, it often appeared as if she were wearing nothing, if not for the thin straps randomly appearing on her shoulders. An evening gown, perhaps? A nightgown?

The young woman was faint, and so transparent, that the dark kitchen could be seen beyond, but Jessa could not stop looking at her beautiful features. She didn't seem threatening at all. In each photo, she was staring directly into Jessa's eyes, entreating her.

So, the big question: what was she doing in Jessa's camera? Was this Maria, who had lured her there with the signs uptown? Suddenly, Jessa slapped her forehead with the heel of her hand. There had been pictures on the walls of Bristol House. Why hadn't she thought to look at them? Surely, there would be at least one of S. J. and Virginia! Chances were good that she could find one of Maria, too. Or, if not at Bristol House, she would return to David and Norma Escher and get a picture to take a look at their only daughter. She shook her head in disgust. Why hadn't she thought of that before? Even as that thought pummeled her brain, she knew the answer: the ghosts of Bristol House were a closely held secret. The Eschers would not know, would not think, that Maria would still be walking around those halls.

Then, as Jessa studied the photos randomly, she noticed that in some of the photos the woman's mouth was slightly open. In others, closed. If she had been looking at a strip of movie film, she'd think that the actress was speaking. Then understanding came to her suddenly. Perhaps this young woman *was* trying to speak.

Jessa carefully selected all of the photos together, then clicked on "slideshow" and watched the photos streaming on her computer. What she saw shocked her. The stunning face floated around inside the photo frames as if trying to stay steady. The mouth opened and closed, pursed and stretched; she was trying to make contact.

Jessa played the slide show several times, trying to decipher what the words might be. What was this young woman trying to say? Not able to read lips, Jessa could feel the frustration mount. She had to know. There had to be a reason the ghostly specter had wanted her to return to Bristol House. Jessa wracked her brain, searching for a reason. Perhaps she was a ghost with unfinished business? Perhaps she was angry that she'd been murdered? Perhaps she wanted to explain why she'd committed suicide? There was a reason she had not gone on to what God had intended; Jessa just needed to figure out what it was.

She would be going nowhere at this late hour, so she closed her laptop gently and allowed her mind to wonder about the young woman. What had happened to someone so young and so beautiful? What fate had led her to this end? Was it something of her own doing or was it because of foul play? Absently, she shut and locked the kitchen window against the cool nighttime breeze.

Jessa lay in bed staring at the ceiling. Rain pounded against her window and occasionally she could see a flash of lightning, and then hear the accompanying crash of thunder. The tumultuous weather outside was no match for the turbulent emotions roiling inside her head. Besides finding the identity of the ghostly girl, she now had absolute proof that Bristol House was haunted. Though the ghost was real, she couldn't bring herself to share those photos with the Eschers, nor any tabloid; there was too much heartache and emotion tied up with the strange specter. Would she want images of her own dead loved one posted all over the world? No!

Should she tell anyone about the photos? Before she finally allowed sleep to claim her, she decided she would show the photos to Mitch; they were, after all, his ghosts.

The next morning came earlier than Jessa would have liked. She had tossed and turned restlessly most of the night, ducking out of the way of the ghosts who wanted her to join them. So early the next day, she padded sleepily to the kitchen.

Just before entering the kitchen doorway, Jessa looked up at the shelf just inside the door and could see the postcard of Bristol House propped there. Somewhere in her brain, she had the thought that she knew what was going to happen. Perhaps she was having a déjà vu moment, if she stepped a little closer...

She took each step carefully and slowly. The moment she was within a couple of feet of the shelf, she stared in amazement as the postcard of Bristol House suddenly fluttered off the shelf and landed on the floor at her feet. She bent to pick the card up and stared at the photo. It didn't look any different: except for the odd shaped whitish smudges in the windows on the upper floor—and the fact that she'd never noticed the front door of the house was slightly ajar—Jessa swallowed hard.

She set the card back up on the shelf in a position that would keep it from falling off again. She looked up and shivered at the breeze coming in from the open kitchen window. Reaching up, she snapped it shut angrily. She was not surprised to see the bright orange breast of a robin as it flitted by. If she ran for her camera, it would only be to throw it through the closed window at the stupid bird. She made herself a small pot of coffee, extra strong, and while it was brewing, she ate a bowl of oatmeal.

And then she froze. She looked at the window again, knowing she'd shut and locked it the night before. She couldn't believe the window was open. Yet, she hadn't been surprised to find it open. The robin she'd seen a moment ago was gone, but he showed up this morning as he had for several mornings. That in itself wasn't odd, but it was odd that it was always the same moment of shutting the window when the bird flew by. She felt as if she was caught in an unending cycle of déjà vu. From across the room, she eyed the photo of Bristol House, but couldn't keep her eyes there. She quickly finished her breakfast, grabbed her coffee and left the kitchen with her heart in her throat.

She left the apartment shortly thereafter. Her first stop would be to see David and Norma and get a photo of Maria. She would start her search by eliminating the most probable suspect. However, they were not home and when she drove by the restaurant, they were not there either. Disappointed, Jessa realized she needed to talk to Mitch.

She didn't want to return to Bristol House, especially if he was not home. So she searched through her phone log until his number popped up. With a deep breath, she pressed the "send" button.

His sleepy "Hello?" told her she'd woken him up.

Smiling, she said in her perkiest voice, "Hey there, Mitch. Jessa here. Need to talk. You up to it?" She grinned and let the question dangle, knowing he was filtering through the webs of sleep and trying to collect a coherent reply.

Jessa stifled a laugh as she heard the unmistakable sound of Mitch's hands rubbing his face as he tried to surface from sleep. Nevertheless, his voice was strong and sure when he replied, "Sure. Where and when?"

"Why don't I just come to you? There is something I'd like to see at Bristol House anyway." As she spoke, she shuddered. Entering Bristol House again would take a lot of courage. That place got creepier every time she went in, but it would be less so if Mitch were there with her.

"Hmmm, I'm not there. I'm at my apartment uptown. Give me fifteen or twenty minutes and I'll meet you there."

After a quick agreement, Jessa closed her cell phone. Guys! Jessa smiled, knowing there was no way she'd ever be able to get ready to meet someone in fifteen or twenty minutes, let alone taking the time to get there if she wasn't already on her way.

Fifteen minutes later, Jessa sat on the veranda of Bristol House and waited for the black BMW to appear in the driveway. It was another ten minutes before that happened. When Mitch got out of the car, he held up two Styrofoam cups of hot coffee. Jessa smiled and smelled the hot brew appreciatively.

Sitting beside her, he didn't appear to be in any more of a hurry to go inside than she had. This made her stop to wonder: did the place creep him out as much as it creeped her out? If so, why did he continue to live there?

"So, Jessa," he drawled slowly, "what brings you out here so bright and early this morning?"

"You know," she laughed out loud, "I guess it is pretty early. It's early enough I can't think of one sarcastic thing to say!"

Mitch rolled his eyes, though it was tempered by the smile on his lips. "So, are you going to make me guess, or is this surprise visit the surprise?"

Jessa cleared her throat, suddenly nervous. "Do you have any pictures of S. J. and Virginia?"

Stopping in mid-sip, Mitch frowned. "What do you know about them?"

"Only what I heard at the tour the other day. Or was I not allowed to pay money and go on the tour? Isn't that, you know, income for you? Don't you need the money or something?" Sarcasm dripped off of every word.

"Okay, Miss Bennett, no more coffee for you! I liked you better before you woke up." Then he laughed at her embarrassed expression. Jessa couldn't suppress a smile after that: he had an infectious chuckle. "Why do you want to see S. J. and Virginia?"

Jessa's head started to spin. It was almost as if Mitch was flirting with her. She tried to compose her face into a serious expression, then said, "I want to see their faces; Virginia's actually. I want to know what she looked like."

This time, Mitch was genuinely puzzled and frowned

at her. "Why?"

Then it dawned on her that she'd have to admit she'd been to Bristol House yesterday. Alone. When no one else was there. Snooping.

Her mouth dropped in confusion and embarrassment. How much detail should she admit? She leaned her face in close to his and spoke in almost a whisper, "The last time I was in the house, I saw something. Remember when you were telling me about the ghost? I think I saw it. I just thought if I saw a picture of Virginia, I'd know whether or not it was her. And if not, I thought maybe Maria…"

Mitch's face darkened with anger. "Good lord! You are a piece of work, Jessa Bennett. You have this morbid curiosity about Maria and you just won't let go, will you? You want to know what she looks like? Hunt down her parents. I'm sure they'll be happy to show you every picture they took of her from birth until she went missing. Why come to me? My life with Maria is over, and it will remain over forever. Now get the hell off my property!" Mitch stood with his arms tightly at his sides.

Jessa looked down at her feet in shame. "I stopped by their home and their restaurant, but they weren't there," she said in a small voice. "I'm truly sorry, Mitch. It didn't occur to me that asking about her would hurt you so much. I didn't think…"

"No, you didn't think." He ran a hand through his hair. "Just when I think I can get on with my life, someone brings this up, or something happens to remind me. Who put you up to this?"

"No one put me up to this!" It was Jessa's turn to get angry. She'd apologized, what more could she do? How many times did she need to apologize? "Look, I'm really, really sorry about Maria. Please, I truly do need to know what she looks like. I swear, Mitch, I have something that will creep you out. I've never seen anything like it."

Despite himself, he sat back down, then looked up at

her with interest. "What are you talking about?"

"I think there are at least two ghosts in Bristol House. A man *and* a woman."

He was quiet for a few minutes and studied her face for sincerity. "And what makes you think this? There have been a lot of people who say they think they've seen something in there. You know, stories go around. Old houses creak, and suddenly, you have ghosts. The stories of Bristol House aren't always pretty, but that doesn't mean there is anything wrong here. It seems like a good place for a ghost to reside, and to be honest, I've thought I've seen something myself. Or more like smelled something. However, there is no real evidence, unless, of course, you can produce a photograph." He laughed without humor. "How can anyone tell if a certain ghost is a man or woman? Just a feeling, but no picture of the dead will help you. I'm sorry."

"What if," she said carefully, "there was evidence of a ghost? Not just dust orbs, or a scary sounds, or a medium who feels something. What if the evidence was real? Truly real?"

Mitch laughed again, but there was no humor in it. "What the hell are you talking about? What evidence? Nothing you have can possibly surprise me. I've seen it all."

"Have you seen a photograph of a ghost so real that you feel like you can touch the contours of its face? Pictures so genuine that you believe, you actually know, the ghost is trying to tell you something?" Mitch did not answer her. Instead, he continued to stare. "I have that photo, Mitch. I just need her to be identified. I don't know what Maria looked like... but you do."

She expected him to get angry again. However, he was not just angry, he was furious! "You are not expecting me to believe that you have a photograph of a female ghost taken in Bristol House?" His body stiffened, and he pulled back away from her.

"I most certainly am. At least, I'd like to show you and

let you tell me who it is, if you know."

"Anyone can Photoshop a ghostly image. I've seen tutorials on how to do that myself." Mitch stood and walked a few feet away from the veranda. He stood with his back to her.

"I am really good at Photoshop, Mitch, I am. Truthfully, I swear to you, I did not Photoshop the images of the ghost." Jessa stood beside him, though he still had his back to her.

"Images?" He finally looked at her, his frown still in place.

"Yeah," she nodded. "About thirty. It's the craziest thing I've ever seen."

"No Photoshop?"

"Oh my god, Mitch, I swear! No Photoshop." Jessa found her fingers gripping his shirt, but she didn't let go. The contact made her feel as if she could make her point a little clearer.

"Just a woman? Why did you say there was a man too?" His eyes held hers.

"Because I got a photo of him, too. Not as good, to be honest. And that's the one who kept changing. I think I already told you about it."

Mitch nodded, still frowning. "I guess it won't hurt to take a look. I think you'd better come up with some good evidence. I'm tired of this game."

Jessa nodded vigorously. "Deal," she said simply.

As Mitch headed for the front door, Jessa fell into step just behind him. He unlocked it, making her remember the feeling of the door locking behind her when she left the house the night before. Before they entered, he turned around and faced her. "I know I should be furious at you. Actually I am, but I will be less so if you can actually come up with some decent evidence. Tell me how, exactly, did you come up with these photos? Unless you have been breaking and entering again, you seem to have a lot of verification for the short time you've spent in the house."

Taking a chance on his good humor returning at some point, she grinned at him with her most enticing expression. "Guilty."

CHAPTER TWELVE
MEETING S.J. AND VIRGINIA

Bristol House was nothing more or less than an old house as the two stepped through the front door and into the hall. New paint and lemon furniture spray masked the musty smell usually associated with older places. Mitch led Jessa into the parlor, stopping in front of an old fashioned loveseat with curved wooden legs and a circular curved back. The subtle flowers on the fabric were too modern to be very old, but fit the style of the old mansion.

Above the loveseat, Jessa found herself staring at the images of two adults: a man and a woman. The pictures were oil on canvas. Except for the faces, the portraits were painted with dark colors, mostly blacks and dark blues. S. J. was a gray-haired man, rail-thin, in a pinstriped, three-piece suit. The chain of his pocket watch draped fashionably out of his vest pocket, looping around the front button, allowing the watch to dangle over his stomach. He looked stern, though with laugh lines visible, and his eyes were very dark brown.

Virginia looked as though she was tall, very thin, and also stern. Her skin had a grayish tint that S. J. lacked, and Jessa wondered if she'd been that odd color in real life, or if this was the artist's touch. Without make-up, her eyes appeared small and round, and her cheekbones were prominent in her thin face. Her hair, drawn back tight against her scalp and twisted into intricate braids and loops, was fashionable for the time. She would have been considered a very pretty lady. However, the one thing that struck Jessa as an absolute fact, as she stood there gazing at the long dead woman: this was not the woman in her camera.

Mitch raised his eyebrows at her in a silent question. Without turning to see his expression, Jessa could feel it; she shook her head and sighed. Together, they turned around and sat on the little couch.

For a long time, they said nothing. The silence of the house settled around them. Finally, Jessa sighed deeply, splitting the calm, and spoke just above a whisper: "I suppose if you had other pictures of her, maybe when she was younger, I could take a look at them. I have to be honest with you, though, I don't think that's my gal at all. She's older by several years."

Mitch shrugged, his agreement in the look of his eyes. "I have some, but I don't expect it will do much good. I can't imagine why a ghost would come back younger than when she died. Virginia lived another twenty years after this portrait was painted. She was very white-headed and wrinkled when she passed away."

Jessa's head nodded in understanding and she fell silent again. Then, as an experiment (and because she felt braver by far with Mitch sitting so close) she raised her voice so she was almost shouting, "Hey Maria! Where are you?"

Mitch winced visibly at the strident question, and looked around the room. His eyes stopped at the doorway to the hall beside the kitchen. "Could you be a little louder please?" he hissed sarcastically. "You startled me!"

She started to lip off with her own brand of sarcasm, but stopped mid-breath. From the direction of the kitchen, she could hear a far-off clanking sound. It was as if someone was moving around... in the cellar? If there was no one down there, where was the sound coming from? Outside?

"Shhh," she laid a hand on Mitch's arm. "Listen." Her words were spoken just barely above a whisper, but it was as if the person in the cellar could hear what she'd said. It was suddenly quiet. Maybe too quiet.

They strained to hear any sounds again. The harder Jessa listened, the more she couldn't hear for the pumping of her heart and the strain on her ears. Then there was another sound, though this one was far different. Perhaps even more dangerous...

They could hear the unmistakable sound of footfalls

slowly coming up the cellar steps. They turned to stare at each other with such a look of surprise that had it been another time, it might have been comical. Now all she could think was: if Mitch didn't know who was in the cellar, then no one should be in the cellar. Which meant whoever it was, was up to no good.

Mitch rose suddenly, motioning for Jessa to stay back, but she rolled her eyes and gave him a dirty look. She fell in step behind him, and tiptoed toward the kitchen. The kitchen was empty, as they expected, but they were headed to the pantry where the hidden cellar door was. Each gentle step that caused the floorboards to squeak made her pull her foot up immediately from the floor. Jessa felt as though she was doing a jig, sidestepping boards and weaving a tapestry of fancy footwork to keep from announcing their approach.

The tall shelf doorway that led down didn't look any different than it had the other day, but she didn't know what it was supposed to look like. Did it lock? Was it ajar? Did it just require a shove from the other side to open? She waited until Mitch got into position at the opening. She stood back so when the door swung open, she would be out of its way. The footfalls were still slowly making their way to the main floor.

Mitch held up his fingers and counted off: one… two… three… He pulled the door open swiftly at the same time that Jessa leaned forward and looked down the dark stairwell. It was empty. The sound of stepping feet went suddenly silent. Again, they looked at each other with suspicious surprise.

Just when they were about to shut the door, from deep in the cellar they could hear the whispery chuckle of a husky-voiced man. Jessa swallowed hard; Mitch was in no better shape.

"Was that…?" Jessa began.

"The house is settling. Again. It just sounds like…"

There was another scraping sound, as if a box had

been suddenly moved, then the almost inaudible chuckle again. Mitch made a face and determinedly closed the cellar door. Jessa backed away from the pantry, watching Mitch run his hand along the side of the shelf, and flip a latch that locked the cellar from the main floor. As they backed away from the pantry, Jessa spoke quietly, "That did not sound like Maria, or any other woman I know."

Mitch looked up at the ceiling as if he could see through all of the timber and plaster to his own apartment on the third floor. Jessa walked away from him, giving him time to think alone. This was no ordinary house. Something was definitely going on here. He broke the silent truce, finally, and asked, "Jessa, you said you saw a man in your photos. Was it in the cellar?"

"No. It wasn't. Well yes, I had a vision of him there in the photos I'd taken when we were in the cellar together, but the first time I saw him in a photo was one I'd taken in your apartment." Immediately, she clamped her hand over her mouth and dropped her gaze to the floor. *Damn*, she thought. *Busted. Again.*

He cocked an eyebrow up and glared at her. Then, he mumbled under his breath, "I don't know why I'm not surprised to hear that!" However, while he didn't seem as angry as she'd expected, she hurried to explain.

"Okay, we both know I shouldn't have been in there, but there was nothing to stop me from having a look around. It was a tour day... anyway, I saw the stairs in the master bedroom and I was curious... Oh, don't give me that look, Mitch Connor; you'd've done the same thing. I won't think for a minute you'd let a good opportunity to explore get away from you!"

By then they were nose to nose with voices raised in anger. He hissed, "This is my home! I wouldn't go snooping in your home!"

"And how was I supposed to know it was your home? There were no signs that read: don't go up to the third floor, it's *his* home!"

Mitch rolled his eyes, turned away from her, then turned back. "It didn't even occur to you that you had no business up there? You couldn't tell it was lived in?"

Jessa shrugged her shoulders, but didn't back off from the glare she pinned him with. "Well, yeah! I knew when I got up there it was where you lived. I'm not a complete moron."

"Then why were you taking pictures there?"

She tapped her foot nervously and lowered her voice. "When I got there and I realized you lived up there, at least part of the time, I almost panicked. I hadn't been there very long. Later, I really did panic because when I started to leave, I could hear you in the stairway coming up…slowly. So I hid in the kitchen. Under the bar."

Mitch stared at her with his mouth open. "You were in my apartment when I thought I was alone? Are you some kind of pervert?"

That stung and Jessa had a hard time keeping the hurt from showing in her face. "I wasn't spying on you, stupid, I saw you lived there and took a quick peek at your CD collection, and then I got ready to leave. You stopped me, so to speak. Anyway, as I had been trying to tell you, I heard you on the stairway, but you only came partway up and back down. I thought you would come back up again, so from the floor of the kitchen I took a picture toward the doorway so I'd remember not to get myself in that position again."

"Okay," he said skeptically. "And?"

"And after you left, you did come back again, except this time you ascended a lot faster. And may I say you're lucky you didn't break your face that second time, you were going so fast? When I got my camera home, there was a man standing in my photo between me and the door." She finished simply and waited for his reaction.

It wasn't what she expected. "I take those stairs three at a time. Always." He frowned, puzzled.

She shook her head. "Obviously, but I don't get it.

What do you mean by always?"

Mitch scratched his head and looked quizzically at her. "You said you heard me on the steps, but I didn't come the rest of the way up?" She nodded. "I don't do that. Ever. If you hadn't noticed, those stairs are tiny. I take them three at a time. Usually at a run. It wasn't me you heard."

Jessa let that information settle. "That's insane. If it wasn't you on the steps, then who was it?"

They continued to look at each other, then turned their heads at the same time, slowly, toward the pantry. Jessa gulped in a quick, harsh breath. She couldn't believe what she was looking at. The cellar door in the pantry stood wide open.

With a little squeal, Jessa turned away from the pantry and ran into the front hall. She stopped and looked back, but Mitch had not followed. She was worried, but no way was she going back in there. A few minutes later, he came into the room. When he reached her, she grabbed his shirt with both hands. "Where were you?"

He put his hands gently on her shoulders and shook her slightly. "Jessa, calm down. I just went to the pantry door. The cellar is still empty. I must not have set the lock correctly. It came undone."

The look on his face was so earnest that she found herself willing her brain to believe him. "Are you sure?"

He tried to smile, and nodded. "Absolutely. You want some fresh coffee? I think you know the way to the kitchen upstairs…"

She laughed at his peevish expression and patted his cheek as she walked by, understanding how violated he must feel, knowing she had been there uninvited. "Poor baby. Okay, I'll lead the way."

Upstairs in his apartment, Jessa could almost believe they weren't in the old house. With its ultra modern décor and updated appliances, there was little about the place that spoke of age. The smell of brewed coffee filled the room, and she sniffed appreciatively. This was a world away from the ghosts that seemed to linger downstairs.

"So where, exactly, were you when you took the picture of the man?" Mitch asked, once they were sipping at the hot coffee.

"Over there," Jessa pointed to the kitchen bar nearest the door. She walked over to the spot and crouched down. As she did so, a cool spot of air washed over her and she shivered. Just thinking about it gave her the chills. "Can we try an experiment some time?"

He shrugged. "What do you have in mind?"

"I could come up here some night, late, and bring my camera. It feels like the ghosts have noticed me. I could see if I can get some more photos. You could come, too, and then you'll know what I mean. Do you have a photo of Maria?" She saw him wince when the girl's name was mentioned.

In answer, he stood and walked into the bedroom. When he returned, he had a framed photo of a beautiful young woman. He handed the frame to her, and she held it close to her chest as she examined it. Her mouth dropped open and the breath was sucked out of her lungs. The beautiful face that stared at her from the framed photo was the same one that had floated transparently in her camera viewfinder.

It was one thing to suspect the young lady was the missing Maria; it was another entirely to know that Maria was most certainly dead. Jessa was at a loss as what to say to the Eschers, though she wasn't sure it was her place. She had only the photos, if the images didn't disappear as they had with the heavy-set man, and she didn't know if that was proof of any kind, anyway. She slid her gaze to Mitch and wondered, again, if he had anything to do with Maria's death.

"Well, what have you decided, Jessa Bennett?" Mitch's voice startled her, making her flinch.

"About what?"

He laughed slightly, and then nodded toward the framed photograph that was still in Jessa's hands. "About who is in your photos? Anyone I know?"

Jessa sighed and handed the photo back to him. "It is Maria. Sorry, Mitch. I know you said you don't know what happened to her, but seriously, you don't have *any* ideas?"

Mitch turned his face so he was looking out the window. Jessa couldn't see his face to read his expression, but she could hear his uneven breathing. "Are you certain it's her?"

"Yes."

When he turned back to her, his eyes were wet but his face was dark and angry. "Damn it! Honestly, I don't know what happened to her. To know, for a fact, that she is dead... it's very disturbing. She had no idea what she was doing..."

Suddenly alert, Jessa sat beside him and leaned her elbows on her knees. "What was she doing?"

Defeated, he just shook his head and sighed. It was a shaky, sad sound. "Will you go now? I need to be alone. I have to think."

She stood and slowly started for the door. Looking back at him, she said softly, "If you want to talk, you have my number. Really, anything you want to say..." Her voice trailed off.

His manners confused her. He seemed genuinely upset to hear her say the ghost was his Maria. Perhaps, if he really didn't have anything to do with her death, he honestly didn't know. He didn't act like someone who was putting on a performance.

Jessa left the apartment wishing she could do something to comfort Mitch. Even knowing it was still possible he had something to do with Maria's disappearance, she couldn't quell the need to go back and console him.

She drove slowly back to her apartment, stopping briefly at Trader Joe's to pick up some of her favorite coffee. By the time she reached her apartment, she was so deep in thought that she didn't see the shiny black BMW parked in front of her building until it was almost under her bumper.

Her heart thumped loudly as she peered over her steering wheel at the little convertible. Mitch was still in the driver's seat, slumped down with his head resting against the back of the seat. He was staring up into the sky, watching the birds and squirrels flit from tree to tree.

How did he know where she lived? Probably the same way he found her phone number! She was most likely not that hard to find, though it gave her a start to think he might be stalking her… then she laughed softly. He was stalking her? No more than she had been stalking him.

She got out of her car and quietly walked up to his. The top was down but she wasn't certain he saw her coming until she leaned against his open window with her elbows. "What gives?" she asked softly.

He turned his head to look at her. His eyes were strangely bright. His voice was soft, almost inaudible, but fiercely intense. He whispered, "I don't know what happened to Maria. I don't know if she's dead or not, but I want to see this proof of yours. I have to know."

"If you didn't do anything to Maria," she countered in the same soft tone, "why is she still at your house? What is the attraction?"

Mitch sighed, and reached up to put his hand over Jessa's. "There are some secrets about Maria that would surprise everyone. Maybe it's time to let her secrets out in the open. I let go of her a long time ago. I would like her to let go of me."

Jessa tugged on his hand to get him out of the car, and motioned with her head toward the building. "Come inside, Mitch. Let's have some lunch and talk, okay?"

He didn't say anything, but he got out of his car and followed her up to the sidewalk. Jessa couldn't figure out his odd expression and quiet mood. The thoughts in her head were jumbled and her heart tumbled around inside her chest. She prayed, as they walked toward her home, that he was sincerely interested in proving his innocence. Inviting him into her home was either a brilliant move on her part or a really stupid one. Surely he wasn't there to make a ghost of her!

Even with all this on her mind, one thing weighed on her most of all: what kind of girl was she that she felt herself falling in love with this man who might be guilty of murder?

CHAPTER THIRTEEN
JESSA'S CAMERA

She led Mitch timidly into her apartment, hoping she hadn't forgotten to make the bed or throw her dirty underwear into the clothes hamper. When they neared the kitchen, Jessa looked up at the postcard of Bristol House on the shelf and, for an instant, wondered if it was going to go fluttering to the floor by her feet. It didn't. In relief, Jessa turned to Mitch and smiled brightly.

"This isn't as grand as your place." She felt like she was apologizing, but then, she'd never had someone like Mitch anywhere near her home.

He grinned. "I admire this place. It's very… charming. You have a nice eye." He squeezed her hand and added, "You must know that the people I come from almost always hire their decorating done. Yours comes from your heart. It's beautiful. It really is."

Jessa blushed with pleasure and looked away from him. To cover her discomfiture, she busied herself dragging out the bread from the breadbox and shaved ham from the refrigerator. Then, with chips and soda rounding out the spread on the table, they put their sandwiches together.

It was still a little early for lunch, and, distracted by their desire to look at the photos, neither of them was too interested in the food. Pushing the sandwiches aside, she set her laptop up on the table. As the photos loaded, she turned to Mitch.

"I am really nervous to show you these pictures, Mitch. I mean, what if the girl disappears from them? It happened with the man ghost. I just want you to know I'm not making this up."

He grinned shortly, but his eyes didn't smile with his lips. "I would bet that I'm more nervous than you are. My biggest fear is that it is Maria. My next biggest fear is that it isn't Maria. I almost hope there isn't anything to look at. That would be the best for me." He shook his head as if to clear these thoughts. "Damned if it is and damned if it isn't. I can't win."

Jessa nodded in sympathy. She wanted it to be Maria, but then again she didn't. How could that be? So, with a determined mindset, she set the photos in slideshow mode in a continuous loop. In slow motion, she reached over the computer keyboard and clicked the PLAY button. After the first picture showed the young woman (clearly blue and transparent) was still there, Jessa instead watched the emotions play across Mitch's face.

Mitch watched in horrified fascination. The pale blue ghost floated around the screen of Jessa's viewfinder, trying to keep within Jessa's sight, moving her mouth around as if she wanted to say something. Around and around the kitchen Jessa had turned, and over and over, the young woman kept up with the movement of the camera. Floating. Swimming. Whatever.

Mitch was so absolutely mesmerized that his eyes lost focus. She could see his expression as he left her and went back to another time and place with the lovely Maria. She could almost feel the two of them as they had been over three years ago. Mitch was with Maria there. Jessa felt a stab of resentment and annoyance. Where did this jealousy come from?

When she couldn't stand it any longer, she put a hand on Mitch's arm, gently, so as to pull him away from Maria's allure. His wide, tear-filled eyes swung from the ghostly visage to Jessa's concerned face." His mouth shaped an "o" of surprise and disbelief. Then he looked back at the computer screen, and shook his head slowly.

"I can't believe it is Maria. She's so… so lovely, even like this. Even as a ghost, she is a beautiful woman. Don't you agree?" Mitch looked at her imploringly.

Jessa smiled, though her heart was not in it. "Yes,

Mitch, she was a lovely woman. You do realize she's dead, right?" She hoped her question didn't come off as sarcastic. She hadn't meant it that way. He nodded, but she wasn't entirely convinced. So she said, "What do you think happened to her, Mitch? She wasn't sick, was she? She had no enemies, right? Why is she dead? Did she commit suicide?"

Mitch wagged his head, still trying to assimilate the remarkable photos. "Can we go for a walk or something? I need some air."

Jessa nodded in agreement, and slipped on her jacket. The fresh air would be good… and they both needed to get away from Maria's ghost. When they were outside walking side by side on the sidewalk, Mitch took Jessa's hand and threaded his fingers through hers. She smiled as they walked.

The lull in their conversation was peaceful. Fall foliage was in full bloom, creating a canvas of yellows, oranges, and brilliant reds. Evergreens wove a splash of green between the colors and the sun set them all on fire.

With regret, Jessa knew there were things that needed to be said. "So, what really did happen to Maria? You really don't know?"

She could feel him mentally pull away a little. He shrugged. "I guess like everyone else, I have my own theories. But if what you're really asking is: did I have anything to do with her disappearance or death, then the answer is no. I wasn't messing around when I said that."

"Then what's her story?" Jessa believed him… to a point. He seemed honest when he said he had nothing to do with her death, but she had the feeling there was more to the story. There was something he wasn't saying.

As Mitch thought about her question, his steps slowed. She stayed with him step for step, wondering what could have been so intense, so disturbing, that it would cause this kind of trauma in a man like him. He shook his head as if that could make the thoughts go away. He raked his fingers through his dark hair. "Oh, it all sounds so silly here in the open. It's a beautiful day. So bright and colorful.... so full life." He looked up at Jessa. "She believed in life after death. It isn't like she was alone about that, but she felt like the souls of her ancestors talked to her through a diviner, or a medium. They helped her make decisions about things important to her."

Jessa stopped in her tracks. As she stared into Mitch's eyes, she gulped like a fish. "You mean like *I talk to dead people*? That's creepy."

Mitch smiled slightly. "Sort of, but the whole thing was creepy. I still don't understand why she did what she did. Why did she believe she needed the ancestors to help her run her life? The money she spent on the medium was outrageous."

Quietly considering for a moment, Jessa finally asked, "How often did she... spend that kind of money?"

He shrugged with resignation. "It started about once every couple of months. Then, every month. By a year into our relationship, it was pretty erratic, but usually once or twice a week. Sometimes more. Sometimes less."

"Was she okay? You know, mentally?"

Another shrug. "At first she was. She was also very good at pretending. Near the end, she stopped pretending. She had become depressed and afraid of her own shadow. She wanted to drag me in on her séances, but I would have none of it. Sometimes I think if I had, she'd be alive right now."

Jessa was silent as she let this information digest. She knew almost nothing about the dark world of the dead, or what toll it would take on an otherwise mentally healthy, stable person. Talking to dead people seemed crazy to her. What could possibly have happened that lured Maria to this end? And still, why was she dead?

Mitch was speaking again, "In the beginning, it was a lark. I never realized for the longest time she was serious. But it kept going on and on. Jesus, I would come home late at night and find a circle of melted candles on my dining room table. She would be holding hands with the medium, who would be chanting. Maria would have her eyes shut and I could hear her chanting too, but I didn't understand what she was saying. When the session was over, she'd come to me and her eyes had a strange brightness to them." Mitch took a shaky breath. "I tried to get her to stop, to tell me what she was doing, but I never got a straight answer from her. It was always: *Mitchell, there are some things you just have to take my word for. This is one of them.*"

Jessa watched the torment and pain play across Mitch's face as he spoke, and she hurt for him. It must have been dreadful for him to see someone he loved turn to something so unorthodox for comfort. "Mitch, did she really think she could talk to her ancestors? What exactly did she hope to accomplish?"

He shook his head. "She knew I didn't like it. It got so bad that she would only let the diviner in when she thought I wasn't going to be home overnight. She started hiding the signs that they'd been at it. And when I caught her—" he choked back a cough "—she would come to me all soft and warm and her hands would…" Mitch looked at Jessa with eyes that pleaded for understanding.

Jessa dropped her gaze, embarrassed at the scenario that Mitch suggested. Maria used sex for his approval and silence. No doubt it was his money she used for the diviner. Perhaps it was not love that had brought them together at all; perhaps the answer was in the zeros that belonged to Mitch.

This investigation that she started was taking a strange turn. What happened to the simple snoop job she was hired for? And how did it turn into an investigation of the paranormal? This was a serious turn of events, and Jessa was not sure she wanted to be or should be involved. She suddenly wanted to wash her hands of the whole thing.

"Mitch, I… I…" she searched for the right words. "I think I need to step away from this. This is so far outside my knowledge or interest. I'm sorry that Maria is missing. I'm sorry that she is stuck inside my camera. I don't know how to help you."

Mitch smiled slightly and took her hand again. When he started walking, he pulled her with him. "It isn't your problem, Jessa," he spoke so quietly that she could hardly make out the words.

They walked a full block without saying anything at all, both alone with their own thoughts. For a man who many thought to have murdered his fiancé, Mitch was wrapped in self-reproach and blame. He took responsibility, but Jessa was starting to think the weight of it was not his to bear. What if... what if he truly had nothing to do with Maria's death? What if her disappearance was as much a mystery to him as it was to her parents?

Her heart reached out to him. Finally, she tugged on his arm, pulling him back from whatever memory he was pondering. "Are you up to seeing the rest of the pictures I've taken? You haven't seen the mysterious see-through man!" She made her tone light and teasing, though the subject was serious enough. Her manner and her accompanying smile earned her a return smile and affectionate squeeze of the hand before he turned with her back to her apartment.

While Jessa loaded up more pictures on her computer, they finally had the stomach to dig into the sandwiches that had been hastily covered and set in the refrigerator. As they munched, they examined the photo in question. This time, no amount of discussion between them could find a logical explanation for the transparent image of the man.

"This is weird, Jessa, so don't get creeped out about it, but I am looking at that man's suit and for some reason it looks familiar. I wonder if S. J. had a suit like that?" Mitch chewed thoughtfully, his melancholy from earlier had lifted slightly now that Maria was not the subject of their perusal. "But that's a dumb idea."

"Why?" Jessa was excited about the prospect. "It

would make sense. S. J. lived in the house and maybe he's still there guarding it, so to speak. Maybe he has unfinished business or he doesn't like all the tourists tromping around and he's trying to protect it."

Even as she spoke, Mitch was shaking his head. "Sounds good and all, but S. J. was not a heavy man. You saw his picture. He was thin. Why would a thin man come back as a fat ghost?"

Jessa arched an eyebrow while she considered that. "Good point. Did he get fatter later in life?" She grinned, teasing, but was hoping that the answer would be yes.

There was no answer from Mitch. He squinted his eyes and studied the suit. Something tickled the fringes of his memory. That suit was familiar. At last he gave up and then looked at Jessa thoughtfully. "Could I see the photos from the closet? Didn't you say there were some strange pictures there?"

Jessa nodded and opened that folder. "There seemed to be a ghost-like man in the shadows, but honestly, he probably isn't there now. The longer I looked at the photos, the less man-like it became. It ended up being just shadows. I'm sure my imagination had been kicked up several notches. With the smell and the sounds…" Jessa's voice trailed off to silence when she looked at the bemused expression on Mitch's face. "What?" she demanded.

"Smell?" he questioned. "Sounds?"

Jessa laughed self-consciously. "That's what took me to the second floor to begin with. First, I could hear a man laughing in the room underneath me and I thought it was you, though I have to be honest, the voice was much too low and husky and I remember thinking that at the time. Then, it smelled like the floor was covered with something rotten and I went to investigate. That led me to the bedroom on the second floor. And by the way, I think you have cobwebs floating all around; your hallway is swamped with them." She knew she was rambling, but she couldn't shake the feeling that

Mitch was about to get angry. She lifted her nose a fraction and glared back at him.

"Let me get this straight: you thought there was someone in a room *below* you, so you went *down* to investigate. Does this mean you were up on the third floor again? In my apartment? Other than when you took a photo of this would-be-transparent man?"

Jessa dropped her gaze immediately. *Damn!* Then, she raised her eyes again and, with a slight smile, responded, "Would you have let me up there if I'd asked... nicely?"

To her complete surprise, he laughed out loud. "Oh my god, Jessa, you have more daring than anyone I know. What were you taking pictures of this time?"

She chewed on her lip, not wanting to confess she'd been photographing the contents of his desk. She suspected he wouldn't think that was quite so funny. She tried to grin, but the quiver to her lip was incongruent. "Would you believe me if I told you I had to have another look at your fantastic CD collection? You have the most eclectic taste in music that I ever..."

Then, he interrupted her harshly. "You were snooping around my desk, weren't you?"

She had thought about denying it, but that would make her look even more foolish than she looked right now, so she let her shrugging shoulders answer for her. "I promise I'll ask permission next time."

Mitch snorted with disgust. "Did you find anything useful?"

With a genuine grin, Jessa could feel her spirits bouncing back. "Only the pictures from the closet. And if it makes you feel any better, I'll show you all the pictures I took that evening. Nothing incriminating, I promise."

He only shrugged his shoulders, but she could see the relief in them. Perhaps he really did have something to hide and she hadn't found it yet. Or perhaps he just felt his space had been violated. The more she thought about it, the more certain she thought that was probably the case. If it'd been her, that's exactly how she'd feel.

He confirmed her conclusion when he asked quietly, "What was I doing when you were snapping photos of my personal documents? Why didn't I know you were at my desk?"

A long moment of silence followed his questions. At long last, Jessa sighed. "You had just left. You looked like you were in a hurry. I hadn't planned on going inside, but once I couldn't see your taillights, I went up to the veranda and found the front door was left unlocked. It was like an open invitation."

Mitch shook his head and glared at her. "That's the night we searched the cellar, the same as the evening on the Terrace. I locked the door on my way out. I even checked to be sure it was locked. Be honest, did you pick the lock?"

Jessa shook her head vigorously in denial. "Honest, Mitch. It was unlocked." The sick nausea of panic started to constrict her chest. "This just doesn't add up."

Looking at her with a measured stare, Mitch said at last, "Jessa, nothing we're saying adds up. Either one of us isn't being honest, or there is something terribly wrong. We have to be completely honest from here on out if we want to figure out all these inconsistencies."

She nodded briskly. "Absolutely!" she agreed. Then she loaded a slideshow with all the closet pictures. For good measure, she added the photos from the cellar.

CHAPTER FOURTEEN
VIRGINIA'S DIARY

The rest of the photos were anticlimactic. Shadows were just that. With eyes squinted, a shape could barely be made out. Otherwise, there were no telltale signs of a ghostly presence. Though the showing was disappointing, the time spent was not.

No one was more surprised than Jessa when she found herself once again holding hands with Mitch. It was dark this time: pleasantly and anonymously late in the evening. The afternoon hours had sped by so quickly that when Jessa's stomach growled with hunger, they looked up with surprise to see that the day was almost over.

It was also a surprise to find that Mitch wasn't the evil presence that she'd imagined him to be. True, he could be putting on a performance, but his surprised reactions to her photos appeared too sudden to be practiced. She now doubted her first impression that Mitch was in some way responsible for Maria's murder or disappearance. If he were responsible at all, it would be for allowing her to use his money contrary to his own desires.

Jessa was cautious with this new discovery: that perhaps she had jumped to a premature conclusion about Mitch Connor. His character indicated he was incapable of Maria's murder, but how much did she really know about the circumstances? Did he have a Jekyll and Hyde personality? Selective amnesia? Those were questions that weighed heavily on her mind. However, after watching the raw emotion on his face when he saw the lovely appearance of Maria in the kitchen photos, Jessa had to wonder: was he still in love with her?

He left late: long after the photos were studied, long after Chinese take-out, long after a silly chick-flick movie. When Jessa slid into bed, alone, she grinned sleepily and wondered what it would be like to slide into bed and into the waiting arms of Mitch. A ghost of a smile played on her lips as she drifted off to sleep.

Later, her night was alive with terror. Maria's frightened face always floated directly in front of her, always struggling to tell her something, always frantically looking over her shoulder in apprehension. Jessa ran away from Maria's looming face, only to find her waiting just around the corner. Nowhere was she safe from the young woman's ghost, but Jessa wasn't afraid of the phantom. She was afraid of what Maria was trying to tell her and of what made Maria fearful. What would a ghost be fearful of? The question made Jessa dizzy with foreboding and hysteria.

In her dream, Jessa backed into a corner. It was dark with shadows, and prickly fingers brushed against her hair. Cold breaths grazed her neck and cheeks. A foul stench assaulted her, and she put the back of her hand against her nose as much to stop the smell as to defend herself. Maria strode purposefully up to Jessa, knowing that she was trapped by her own physical limitations and paralyzed by fear.

Maria's cool fingers gently cupped Jessa's face. Jessa closed her eyes, sweating with alarm, despite the cold, dead grip. Then, when the grip didn't go away and Maria didn't eat her face, Jessa opened her eyes experimentally. The dead girl's eyes looked straight into Jessa's until there was no doubt that she was "listening". Maria mouthed one word, but Jessa couldn't understand what it was. She wanted to scream in frustration. She started shaking in aggravation. What did Maria want? The ghostly image kept mouthing the same word over and over, willing Jessa to understand, but she didn't.

Unexpectedly, the tempo of Maria's non-verbalization changed. Her eyes widened with alarm and she continuously looked over her shoulder. Her mouth frantically formed the single word again and again as her hands tried to shake Jessa's face. Jessa could almost feel the wispy fingers dig into her skin. And then... Maria stopped struggling as a huge tear dripped fearfully down her face.

Jessa stared in fascination as the tear ran and dropped off the ghostly chin. She held her finger out and the single tear pooled on the tip like a buoyant bead of mercury. Her eyes rose again to catch Maria's gaze. Understanding passed between them. Then, Maria screamed silently as she looked one last time over her shoulder. An instant later, Maria was gone.

Jessa bolted upright in her bed with a loud cry. It was still in the dark, early morning hours. She looked down at the index finger she held out. On the end, still balanced precariously, was a single teardrop.

Jessa's heart pounded furiously. She felt dizzy and nauseated. This single teardrop was blue, just as blue as Maria's face had been. Its swirling iridescence was mesmerizing. Then, without thinking about what she was doing, Jessa stuck out her tongue and let the tear roll into her mouth.

For one second, Jessa's world remained silent. In the next second, a whispery voice hammered through her head in a sweeping rush: *Vernon!*

Jessa froze, stunned. Vernon? Who the hell was Vernon? The clock on her bedside table told her it was only 5 o'clock, but she knew with certainty she would not be able to go back to sleep with this new discovery. As she showered and dressed, she wondered: had this been a dream, or had Maria really visited her?

Later, cautiously, she walked toward her kitchen. With some trepidation, she eyed the postcard of Bristol House. One step at a time, she approached the shelf and when the card expectedly leaped from the shelf, Jessa not only made a mental note of where she was standing, but also tried to reach out and catch the card. She was not quick enough, and it fluttered to the floor at her feet. In that same instant, her gaze flew to the open window. She could not remember whether or not she had closed it the night before, but as that thought was forming, she whispered to herself, "Robin…" and then she watched as the bird flitted by.

Without moving, her eyes traveled to the kitchen table where she had put her camera. For the briefest instant, the robin's window visit was captured in the LCD viewer of the camera. She gasped in stunned surprise.

Leaving the card on the floor, she picked up her camera, turned it on, and pressed the PLAY button. The robin's image was there just as if Jessa herself had snapped the photo.

Her heart fluttered wildly. With fumbling hands, she opened her laptop, and then the folder with all the photos she'd taken. Her mouth dried and she gulped for air. For every day that she'd taken photos for the Eschers, there was a robin photo. How could she not have noticed before? That in itself was weird, but there was something even stranger: every robin photo was identical. Not just similar: but identical in every leaf, feather, and shadow.

Jessa hastily put the camera down and shut her laptop with a snap. She picked up the postcard of Bristol House and returned it to its spot on the shelf. She started brewing her usual pot of coffee and was in the middle of preparing her accustomed bowl of oatmeal before she realized that her mornings were abnormally déjà vu-ish.

She dumped the oatmeal down the sink and followed it by the fresh pot of coffee. Grabbing her camera and laptop, she headed to her favorite coffee bar for breakfast and to do a little Internet searching on a hunch that had been rolling around in her head.

With a tall, dark coffee and a gooey sweet roll smeared with chocolate frosting sitting beside her computer, she clicked on the Internet icon and began her search: Vernon Hubert.

With the aid of modern technology, the name popped up almost instantly on her computer screen: Vernon Hubert, brother of S. J. Hubert from Madison, Wisconsin. Jessa stared at the name, amazed at finding the information she wanted right off the bat.

The search, however, didn't produce as much information as she would have liked. He was older than S. J. by almost five years. He died under mysterious circumstances long before S. J. and Virginia, and shortly after Bristol House was completed. He was the wild card of the family, literally, as his main vice was gambling.

Jessa was disappointed to find no photographs or drawings of the man. She had hoped to match a known photo with the photo that haunted her from Mitch's kitchen. She sat for a while and let her mind wander as she aimlessly looked through the moment's news that came across her computer search engine.

Poor Maria... what had happened to her? Jessa could feel her lingering presence even here in the crowded coffeehouse. There was no doubt in Jessa's mind that the girl had been trying to get her attention in the photos... could she have crept into her dreams and haunted her there? Then, with a rush of excitement, Jessa opened the folder with the photos of Maria's face. Shortening the timing of the slides, she selected all of the photos and ran them as a slide show.

Heart pumping, she squinted and leaned in close to her computer screen. Concentrating on Maria's mouth, she studied the movement of her lips. Could it be... yes! So plainly that she was ashamed she had not understood it yesterday, Maria mouthed the word *Vernon* over and over. *Vernon. Vernon. Vernon.*

Vernon Hubert.

She shut her computer and left the coffeehouse. As she swung her car onto the Beltline, she dialed Mitch's number on her cell phone, but all she came up with was his voicemail. Frustrated, she snapped her phone shut and headed toward Bristol House.

Surely, she reasoned, some of those ancient documents in the second floor bedroom would have some information on the owner's brother.

She finally pulled in the driveway and then drove on to the very back of the property. Though the yard was huge, it was heavily wooded on one side. Near the lake, she could see a small boathouse and a rickety wooden pier. When she got out of her car, she leaned against the hood and stared at the lake.

It was another warm, sunny day. The lake looked inviting and Jessa wondered how many times Maria had stood in this very spot and admired the natural beauty of the lake and trees. She could see the Capitol across the water and the campus power plant with its white smoke stacks, as well as the construction cranes that were always on campus. Autumn was in full bloom and the whole area was awash with vibrant colors.

Turning her attention away from the riotous foliage, Jessa headed to the house with her camera bumping familiarly against her hip. Hoping the house would let her in, she stepped quietly up to the veranda and walked to the front door. The house was quiet. She held her breath as she tried the doorknob, but she was disappointed. It was locked.

Circumnavigating the house, she tried every window she could reach, but to no avail. Discouraged and irritated, she dialed Mitch's number again, but once again she got his voicemail. She frowned her annoyance at the back of the house where she stood.

A small sound clicked near her. Her eyes darted to the closed and locked cellar door. Then, gasping, her hand flew to her mouth to stifle any noise. Her unbelieving eyes watched the padlock slowly unclasp and fall off the lock hinge. The sound of the heavy padlock as it hit the ground was like a gunshot.

As she approached the cellar door, she couldn't help but wonder if this invitation was at the behest of Maria, or of the unknown, heavy-set man on her computer.

Keeping her eyes firmly on the lock, Jessa reached

down and pulled on the cellar door. It swung open with a loud creaking sound. She jumped back and let the door slam down. Then she laughed nervously and looked around her. The closest neighbors were far enough away that she didn't think anyone would have noticed the sharp clang.

She pulled at the door again, this time prepared for the creaky hinges. A foul odor wafted up from the darkness. Jessa fought the desire to hold her nose, instead pulling the neck of her t-shirt up over her nostrils. Though she was clean, she couldn't help but think that dirty armpit smell was preferable to the rank stink in the cellar. She descended the steps slowly, noticing as she did so the faint crackle of static electricity running along her arm hair and scalp.

Closing her eyes to get an accurate mental picture, she imagined where the steps leading up to the first story would be located. She crossed her fingers in hopes that the pantry entryway was not locked. If it was, perhaps if she was *very* lucky, the lock would spontaneously come undone as it had when she was here yesterday with Mitch.

The trek across the length of the cellar seemed interminable in the dark. Leaving the outside door open, she had at least a little light as she fumbled, nearly blind. Numerous times she tripped over an odd box or piece of broken furniture or toy. Once, she nearly did a face-plant when a marble rolled under her shoe. By the time her toe stubbed on the first of the steps leading to the rest of the house, she felt as if she was crawling with spider webs and loathsome insects.

It was with giddy relief that the pantry door, indeed, opened with a soft swish and she was finally standing in the kitchen. For as bright as the day was outside, the inside of the kitchen seemed dull and pensive. Sunlight filtered in through sheer curtains. Dancing dust motes played in the air. Jessa held her breath with anticipation, but the house remained deathly still.

Experimentally, she stood in the middle of the kitchen

floor, and as she turned a three-sixty, she snapped multiple pictures, in hopes of getting some of Maria's ghost again. Then, she walked slowly through the inner hall and up the back steps to the second floor. Here, the light was even more diffused than downstairs. Some doors were shut; heavy curtains, making the hallway extra dark, covered other windows. Only the room where Jessa knew the documents to be was brightly lit. When she entered the room, she saw that the heavy curtains had been pulled aside to allow the sun in.

The closet door was open invitingly. She quickly pushed aside the thought that someone, or some thing, had contrived to maneuver her here. She took a deep breath and pulled the chain to the light switch inside the closet.

She pulled two fruit crates out of the tiny room, then made herself comfortable sitting on the bed. She saw Virginia Hubert's name and signature over and over on the various legal papers, and soon she recognized the old-fashioned handwriting that belonged to her. She briefly examined several documents, then set them aside when nothing piqued her curiosity. She didn't know what she was looking for, but she knew she would find something of interest in here.

Normally, there was a lot of history in the documents that would have kept her interest for months. She was at the bottom of the first crate without finding anything that looked promising. With a fearful sigh that she might not find anything of value, Jessa pulled the second crate over to her to examine the contents of it. Lying on the top of all the jumble of papers was a thick, leather bound book with a broken lock around its middle.

Gently, Jessa pulled the volume onto her lap and opened it. She gasped in delight as the significance of this find dawned on her: it was Virginia's personal diary.

She scooted farther on the bed, resting her back against the old-fashioned headboard and pulled the diary into her lap. Skimming the first few pages, she searched for the name of S. J.'s brother, Vernon. Finally, the older brother was mentioned. He was not trusted, it seemed, by S. J. or Virginia.

Jessa read the faded handwriting:

June 15, 1863

The house is nearly complete but I fear the pleasure of the conclusion of construction is somewhat tempered by Vernon. Only because he's my husband's brother keeps me from saying anything. That man makes me so nervous I fear a breakdown.

June 23, 1863

The shutters are finished and were hung up today. Our house is now complete. We have decided on the name Bristol in honor of my parents. I do hope to have them for a visit soon. I miss them so very much. Vernon stopped by to see the finished house. His visit has taken some of the pleasure from this momentous occasion. Joey seems to take some comfort in Vernon's presence. I do hope his evil ways do not transfer themselves to my son!

Her next entry was not for another month. Jessa frowned in concentration as she read the entry. Virginia was obviously upset.

August 16, 1863

I have had just about all I can take of Vernon. I realize we are all the family he has, but he has tried my patience and good nature on more than one occasion. Today I caught him at my desk, going through my correspondence. I know he was looking at our finances. He has no business doing that. Yesterday I caught him telling Joey that S. J. intentionally stole Vernon's inheritance from Joey's grandfather.

I interrupted immediately and called him a liar. I believe I wasn't even nice about it, but Vernon must learn that he can't tell my son vicious lies… especially about his father! Then I told him he was not welcome at our house any longer. I spoke to S. J. about this problem and he certainly agrees with me, though it is difficult to turn away flesh and blood. But my parents are due to arrive within a month's time. I want my household as calm as possible. They weren't in favor of S. J. bringing me out here in the first place.

October 1, 1863

Why is this happening to us? Poor Joey, he was just a little boy! How could this happen? S. J. has been drinking again and I blame his brother. This has put such a smear on the Hubert name and I fear for my husband's heart. I don't know how long he will be able to bear the shame. My parents have been warned and will not entertain the notion of visiting here any more.

Jessa looked for an entry between the August date and the October date, but discovered several pages had been torn from the book, both before and after October 1. Scooting to the edge of the bed, she began to rifle through the box for the missing pages. As she searched, she wondered why these pages were gone and who had torn them from the diary.

CHAPTER FIFTEEN
VERNON

It was well after noon before Jessa stopped searching for the missing diary pages. She pushed the two fruit crates, minus Virginia's diary, back inside the closet. Before shutting the door, she took a couple of pictures of the closet's interior, just as she had the other day. It would be a curious occurrence if the strange shadow showed up again.

She straightened up the bed where the weight of her body had messed up the covers, then slipped the diary into the waistband of her jeans. It was bulky there, but she wanted to read more about the Hubert family.

As she was about to tiptoe out of the door, she turned to look over her shoulder, back at the bed, to assure herself the room appeared undisturbed. In a flash, the instant her eyes hit the bed, the room was inverted to the blackness of a negative. Just as quickly, it flashed back to normal, but not before Jessa got the barest glimpse of a man in a dark three-piece suit leaning casually on the bedpost... staring right at her.

She jumped back with a startled yelp, and scanned the brightly lit room. Had she finally cracked? Walking to the bedpost where she was sure the man had been standing, she waved her hand through the air. A sudden stench of rot burned through her nostrils. She gagged and choked, staggering backward toward the door. Blinding tears blurred her vision as she reached a hand out to grab the doorframe.

Her eyes could see the room lengthening abnormally until the harder she lunged and the closer her fingers came to the door, the farther away the door was from her. She could not reach it. Looking back over her shoulder, she tripped and fell onto her stomach. Unseen hands pulled her by the ankles, away from her escape.

She clawed at the floor, leaving scratchy marks on the

hardwood. Panic stole the breath from her lungs, and she didn't recognize the raspy noises coming from her throat. Finally freeing one foot from the invisible iron grip, she turned over on her back and, propped up by her elbows, started kicking viciously. She couldn't tell if her attacks met her target until she felt the sole of her shoe thud softly, but firmly, into heavy, thick air. A whisper of expelled air breathed near her.

She was stunned, but didn't take the time to reflect. She was at last free of the grip. In an instant, she scrambled to her feet and finally reached the door. Flinging her body through, she dashed down the hallway, into the stairway, descending two and three steps at a time.

No way was she going to traipse through the dark cellar, fearful of what was down there that might possibly be aware of her. She sprinted across the parlor and into the front hall. By the time she got out the front door to the veranda, she was in such a blind panic that she couldn't see anything. Tears of frustration and fear overwhelmed her.

The end of the veranda was a short sprint from the front door, but in her haste, she miscalculated the distance. Her foot slipped on the edge of the step and she fell hard on her bottom, skidding to an ugly heap at the bottom of the veranda steps. She had pushed her elbows out to stop her descent, but she was unable to stop and jarred her shoulders on her way down. As pain shot through her joints, she rolled awkwardly in the grass, and then tried to force her body to stand.

As she thrashed painfully about, two expensive man-shoes stopped her short. For a moment, her stinging aches were forgotten. Her nose, only an inch from the shoes, pointed upward, and she groaned in mortifying embarrassment at the perplexed expression on Mitch's face.

His tone was even when he spoke, "Breaking and entering again?"

Jessa groaned again and sat up in the grass. She knew

she must look frightful: grass in her hair, face flushed, clothes tousled, spider webs clinging to her t-shirt. She shook her head slowly and lowered her eyes. "Busted," she whispered, more to herself than him. "Again!"

The tears that welled up in her eyes were wiped angrily away. Mitch reached a hand down to her, and when she put hers in his, he gently helped her to her feet. She examined her injuries—scrapes on her elbows, a bruised knee, soreness in her back and shoulders. However, the strangest injury of all was the wide finger impressions around her ankles where she'd been held against her will.

Jessa felt almost faint with relief with Mitch beside her. She leaned into him as he put his arms around her, and pulled her into a tight hug. Her arms wrapped around his waist and, with her head against his chest, she could feel the slow, steady beat of his heart. It was comforting, somehow, to hear the rush of life that flowed through him. Jessa closed her eyes and sighed, willing the panic to lessen and her heart to beat normally.

When her breathing finally returned to normal and her eyes were dry of tears, Mitch asked, "Want to come inside? You look like you've seen a ghost." He smiled at first, then dropped the corners of his lips at the alarmed expression on her face. "Jessa? You didn't really see a ghost, did you?"

Tears filled her eyes again and she blinked them hurriedly away. Not trusting her voice, Jessa nodded vigorously, then turned to look at the second story windows. Hoping it was her imagination that allowed her to see the curtain suddenly drop over a bedroom window, she looked back at Mitch and said, "I don't want to go in there. I'm… I'm scared." She blinked rapidly once more.

He flashed her another quick smile, but she caught a hint of concern in his expression as he turned away from the house with her in tow. He pulled her hand to rest in the crook of his elbow, then covered it with his own hand. His voice was gentle when he spoke to her again. "I think we just about have time to stop by your apartment for you to freshen up before a walk through the zoo. Then, if we still have some daylight, we can take a look at the Olbrich Botanical Garden. After that, I suggest a quiet dinner at this superb Italian restaurant I have discovered. They have an excellent Chardonnay, or if I remember correctly, a pinot noir for you."

MITCH LISTENED CAREFULLY as Jessa retold the story yet again. It was the same each time she told it, but as she listened to her own voice, it seemed more and more incredulous. Jessa had to shake her head with excitement, mixed with bemusement to find herself in this situation, which bubbled up every time she looked across the table at Mitch. She had been so certain that he was guilty of a heinous crime against Maria Escher, and now she was happily having a romantic dinner with him. What was wrong with her?

Mitch had convincingly nudged her over to a different way of thinking. Where only days ago she had thought he was a murderer, now she had only compassion for him. She ignored the little voice inside her head that told her there might be more than compassion involved. Love... love was such a strong word.

However, in a lonely corner of her mind was the look on Mitch's face when he saw Maria's pictures. Jessa felt certain he must still love her. If her competition was a real woman, she could deal with it, but how did one compete against a ghost?

Jessa sat quietly and stared at Mitch for several long minutes before she realized he was waiting for her to say something. "I'm sorry... what? I was daydreaming."

Mitch chuckled; it was a warm rumble that came from his chest. With a hint of sarcasm, he said, "Oh, I see how you are. Am I really that interesting?"

She had the grace to blush slightly and grin. "I was just thinking about Maria. You two made a very nice couple."

A long minute passed before he answered, but his

voice was still pleasantly agreeable. He shrugged. "I'm sure most people would agree with you, but I get the feeling there was a question in there somewhere. Like, am I still in love with her?"

Jessa's blush deepened, and she looked down at her wine glass. "I wouldn't be human if I didn't wonder about it." She wasn't about to tell him it had never crossed her mind.

"I did love Maria. A part of me will always love her, but we were not the couple everyone thought we were. My folks and her folks had always hoped we'd get married. In some ways, it seems like I've been engaged my whole life. We were raised in similar households. Our parents' beliefs are the same. It just seemed like the natural course of events." He picked up a fork and toyed with the spaghetti still on his plate. "I loved Maria, I did, but I didn't always like her. I hated her constant dabbling with the dark nature. It's wrong and it made me unhappy. And because of that, I never could give her my whole heart. Sometimes…" he hesitated and frowned as he concentrated on his words, "sometimes I don't think I would have gone through with the wedding. I didn't love her enough to ignore that part of her life." He sat back in his seat and gulped the rest of his wine in only seconds. When he looked back at Jessa, his mood had darkened considerably. "Now you know what a rotten wretch I am. I have never told anyone that. I don't know why I told you. Jesus, you could crucify me with what you know."

Jessa gently put her hand on top of his. "I'm not out to crucify you. On the contrary, I just want to know what happened to her. Do you happen to know the name of the psychic medium she used?" Her face was an agreeable mask of serenity, but her inner woman was jumping for joy… had their wedding plans soured before she disappeared?

Mitch gave her a name: Madeline Hester, a woman whom Maria had been seeing for her necromantic rendezvous with her ancestors. Jessa recognized the name, but only from whispered conversations. She didn't know if this woman was legitimately knowledgeable, or if she was a charlatan interested only in money and gifts.

With this information tucked neatly into her memory, Jessa grinned and leaned on her elbows across the table. "I have some really cool, yet I'll admit it's freaky, news." She waited for Mitch's brows to rise questioningly. "I think I've figured out what Maria was trying to say. In fact, I'm certain of it."

As she expected, Mitch responded, "No kidding? How did you figure it out? What was she saying?"

She put a hand in front of her as if to stop him. "First, hear me out. It sounds crazy, but for some reason it worked out. Last night I had this really weird dream, you know, really scary. Maria was chasing me all around trying to say something to me and I just didn't get it. There was no sound that I could hear. But the craziest thing of all was that she started crying; tears were dripping down her face. So I held out my finger and caught a tear on the tip. And when I woke up and sat up in bed, the tear was still balanced on the end of my finger."

Mitch's mouth dropped into an "o" of surprise. "Impossible..." he stammered.

Jessa nodded her head in agreement. "I thought so, too. It was blue, just like Maria in the photos. But when I tasted the tear, it was salty like ours would be. And just as it spread on my tongue, a word rushed through my head... a lot like a whisper."

Mitch raised an eyebrow in doubt. "And what would that word be?"

Taking a deep breath, and hoping she didn't sound insane, she replied, "Vernon."

Sputtering and choking on a sip of wine he'd just poured, Mitch set his glass down hastily and put a napkin up to his mouth. When he stopped coughing, he stared at her incredulously. "S. J. had a brother named Vernon. He was no good."

This time Jessa grinned and nodded. "I do know, now, he had a brother Vernon. I don't know much about him. I know Virginia didn't like him much. That's what I was doing at Bristol House. And in my defense, I tried to call you several times to let me in, but you didn't answer. Anyway, when I had been in the second floor closet, I saw some boxes with old documents; you know the ones I'm talking about. Well, in there, I found Virginia's diary, but there were a few pages missing. I think they contained something about Vernon because in the next entry, she was really upset. Do you know what happened?"

"I do indeed." He shrugged. "At least, I know part of it. Vernon was a heavy drinker. As the older brother, their father was to give him the greater part of his wealth. But the old man, wise to the ways of his eldest son, decided to give all of his money to S. J., the younger son, because he didn't want all his hard work gambled away. Vernon was understandably bitter about it and when S. J. and Virginia built Bristol House, he felt it rightly belonged to him, because it was funded from what he considered his inheritance money. Vernon never got over the humiliation of having his inheritance stripped from him."

"Wow, that's awful. It would have been a lose-lose situation. Poor S. J. couldn't very well give it to Vernon either. I'm sure he didn't want it gambled away any more than his father did." Jessa tried to imagine the dynamics of the situation as it happened.

"I'm sure it was pretty bad for a long time," Mitch agreed.

"So what happened? To Vernon, I mean."

Shrugging again, he said, "Vernon died. There was some kind of scandal at the time. All of the records say he had a heart attack or something, but the scuttlebutt is that he committed suicide. Either way, S. J. and Virginia lived in the house long after Vernon had passed on."

Jessa was quiet for a moment, then asked, "If Vernon

was dead, what was to stop Virginia's folks from coming to visit? Your tour guide said they never saw the house and she never went back to Boston to visit."

"Well, that's a mystery. Again, this is just hearsay: before he died, Vernon said a lot of vile things and made a lot of threats about how the house really belonged to him. He said they'd live to regret taking his inheritance and pride from him. Virginia took it to mean her family, too, so she told them never to come. She felt she was saving their lives by keeping them away." Mitch sipped silently on his wine and watched as the emotion played out on Jessa's face.

"I still have Virginia's diary. I'd like to read it before I give it back, if that's okay."

To her surprise, Mitch laughed out loud. She couldn't help the smile that spread across her own face. Her heart flipped as she studied his handsome face; she had fallen for this man... hard. "I think this is a turning point in our relationship, Jessa. You actually asked me if something that was already mine was okay to keep. I think we're getting somewhere." He shook his head and chuckled again. "You may keep it for as long as you like."

Jessa grinned with an attractive blush covering her face. "Jeez, Mitch. I'm getting soft. What's wrong with me?"

His face stilled and he continued to gaze at her. "From where I'm sitting, I see very little wrong with you. Though, one thing I could mention right off the bat..." A teasing light jumped into his eyes. "I'd sure like another chance to kiss you."

Jessa's blush deepened and she looked down at her plate in embarrassment. She tried not to grin, but she wasn't able to stop. "Maybe tonight is your lucky night." Finally she met his gaze. Something was there between them, she was sure of it. Then, to be certain she was not keeping anything from him, she had to confess, "I'm going to call Madeline Hester tomorrow. I think that's a good place to start. I have to know what happened to Maria. This isn't just about my curiosity. I've been drawn into this. Unwillingly, at first. But now for myself, and for Maria, who I feel has asked me for help. I hope I have your blessing on this, but either way, this is something I need to do."

There was a thoughtful pause before Mitch finally spoke. "First, I have a question for you, and I'd like you to be honest with me." Jessa nodded hesitantly. "Who hired you to snoop on me? Was it Maria's parents?"

Surprised, Jessa nodded again. "How did you know? I thought you suspected the tabloids."

Mitch grinned at her, though it was a little sad. "Part of me was hoping it was. I suspected at the time you weren't being completely honest with me, or at least not telling the entire truth of it. I guess I wasn't being honest with you either. If we're going to do this, Jessa, we have to be totally honest. Totally."

"Absolutely!" she agreed. "That's why I wanted your blessing. I knew I'd do it anyway. I'd just rather do it with your knowledge."

There was a long, silent pause. Clearing his throat nervously, he said, "I want to help. Tell me what you want to do, what you want *me* to do."

"I need to know more about Vernon."

"I'll see what I can find out. I'll call my mom and see if she knows anything or has read any journals. I'll ask my housekeeper that I had as a child. She didn't think I could do anything wrong." He grinned sheepishly.

His grin turned into a surprised gape when Jessa responded, "Olivia Weller. Wonderful woman. Very sweet, too."

Mitch rolled his eyes and said, "I don't even want to know. She made the best lemon meringue pie. This one time..." his voice lowered and he leaned his head toward hers, making her smile conspiratorially.

The flickering candle caused lights and shadows to dance on Mitch's face. Tonight, she only wanted to be a woman on a date. She could wait until tomorrow to worry about dealing with the psychic.

AS JESSA WOKE the following morning, she tried to figure out how she was going to get up and around without going into the kitchen. The memory of the silly postcard of Bristol House dropping at her feet made her approach the kitchen with dread.

After showering and dressing, she had managed to avoid the kitchen altogether until she remembered suddenly that she'd left her cell phone on the table. Without thinking about it, she approached the kitchen table, and as she did so, she could see the postcard wobble and nosedive to a fluttering landing by her feet. Heart pounding suddenly, her eyes instantly flew to the window where, as if on cue, a bright orange-breasted robin fluttered past. Her eyes traveled to the table where her camera sat and, sure enough, for an instant the image of the robin could be seen.

As much as she could have used a cup of fresh, hot coffee, and as much as she desired her habitual bowl of oatmeal, she took only enough time to set the postcard back on the shelf, shut the kitchen window, and grab her cell phone. Today all those zeros in her bank account would be buying her breakfast.

CHAPTER SIXTEEN
SÉANCE

Jessa carefully dialed the phone number belonging to Madeline Hester. She knew very little about the woman other than that those who had a strong belief in the supernatural sought her out. There had been some talk about helping the police detectives as a psychic investigator with some cases they hadn't cracked, but it had been hearsay and Jessa hadn't paid too much attention to it. She let the phone ring against her ear.

It was obvious, through the photos, that Maria was trying to tell them something, and it seemed to have something to do with Vernon Hubert. But what? There seemed to be no possible connection, and yet, Jessa felt certain that if she searched long enough, she'd find it.

Her conversation with Madeline Hester was short. Almost as if she already knew Jessa wanted to speak to her, the older woman agreed to meet her at Bristol House later in the afternoon. So, pushing her fears aside, Jessa headed for the mansion.

With a giddy smile, she tapped Mitch's number in her cell phone. A rush of delight warmed her to the core when she heard his affectionate greeting. In a breathy voice, she informed him, "I'm on my way to Bristol House." They had decided the evening before that he would not stay there; instead he would live from his downtown apartment until they came to some kind of conclusion, whether it was a matter of their imaginations, or they discovered the real truth about what happened to Maria.

"Be careful... partner. I don't want to lose you."

Jessa heard the hesitation in his voice and wondered for a thrilling moment if he had wanted to use an endearment, but she tossed away the idea immediately. She didn't need to feed her imagination any more fuel than it already consumed, but she couldn't seem to lose her smile.

By the time she reached the driveway leading to Bristol House, she could already feel her heart palpitate. There was nothing malevolent about the structure today, but her response to it was as strong as if it growled at her. Though her first reaction was to turn and run, she lifted her nose and scowled in the direction of the veranda. Today, it was not going to scare her off.

After parking her car, she got out and leaned against the fender to study each of the upper story windows. Her imagination made the curtains flutter, and if she listened hard enough, she could hear the creak of doors from this distance. Then, she reached inside her jeans pocket for a large old-fashioned brass skeleton key. Mitch had given it to her so she could come and go as she needed instead of searching for an unlocked window to crawl through. She took a deep breath, and headed for the house.

The big key fitted neatly in the keyhole and she could feel the tug and click as the tumblers gave way. The door popped open a little as the latch released. Knowing she was returning to the house alone after the scare she had yesterday just about sent her over the edge. So, with a deep breath, she mustered up all the bravery she had in reserve and pulled the door the rest of the way open.

She had gotten as far as the parlor before she sensed she was not alone. No one stood near her, yet the feeling persisted. At one end of the room sat a small, round table. Madeline had said there would be a table like that here. It must have been the same one Maria used three years ago. She rested her palm gently on the top and moved it along slowly to the edge. As she did so, she could feel the tiny droplets of wax from the candles that had been used.

The sound of a mouthful of air inhaled near her ear, making her scalp prickle. She looked up quickly, but tried to mask the frightened expression from her face as she looked around the empty room. Like a cool breath, the hair at her temple swayed for a moment as the air was slowly exhaled. Though she froze as still as a statue, every cell, every fiber in her body jumped immediately to red alert. There was no indication whether this action was male or female, and Jessa had no idea what to do or expect.

She had brought a bag of items with her that Madeline had suggested would bring a satisfactory result. Very much aware of the breath that occasionally blew across her temple, she slowly set three candles on the table, followed by a bowl of perfumed potpourri. Beside the potpourri, she set a small loaf of freshly baked bread that she'd gotten earlier at a bakery. Once Madeline arrived, she'd unwrap the bread as an offering.

Jessa stepped away from the table. She wandered into the kitchen, peeking for a moment into the pantry to be sure the door to the cellar was closed. She discovered it was, then realized that if a spirit wanted to go anyplace in the house, the locked cellar door would probably not stop it.

As she returned to the parlor, she looked up at the portraits of S. J. and Virginia that hung above the love seat. The stares of the two were so intense that Jessa found herself needing to look away. Was it her imagination that made them seem as if they, too, were nervous and waiting?

She decided to wait by the little round table. Madeline would be here before long and she wanted to have everything ready. This was not exactly something she'd discussed with Mitch. Yes, he knew she was meeting Madeline at Bristol House, but when the medium had suggested a séance, Jessa had decided to see how it went before telling Mitch what she'd done. What harm could be done in so short a time?

She sat in a chair by the little table in a posture of waiting. The spirit that blew air on her hair earlier was not present that she could tell... until one of the candles fell over, knocking another down, then the third like a row of dominoes. With shaking hands, she stood them up again, but the instant they were propped upright, they fell again.

"Screw this!" Jessa whispered to herself. Carefully, as she stood the candles up for a third time, she used an old lighter to light each one. This time the candles remained standing. She opened the bread bag and tore a chunk off the fragrant loaf. Then, she went around the room closing the drapes and forcing the room into premature dusk.

At last, because there was no one with her, she clasped her hands together, closed her eyes, and spoke words that she thought sounded right: "Dear Maria, I have gifts for you that will cross over from life into death. Please speak to me, Maria, and be here with me."

Jessa held her breath and waited. Her ears strained to hear the tiniest sound. Was there a faint inhale of breath? Footsteps treading nearby? Did the wispy fingers of a spirit graze her arm?

She sat silently for several minutes without moving and without opening her eyes. Her ears picked up numerous wayward sounds, but nothing she could tell that was definitively Maria, or anyone else, for that matter.

Opening her eyes, she looked around the still empty room, almost afraid that she actually would see Maria standing there. Still, she was alone.

Then she noticed… the bread chunk she offered as a crossover gift, was gone. She ducked her head around the table, thinking perhaps she'd dropped it. It wasn't in her lap either, nor was it in the bag with the rest of the bread. Jessa's heart pounded furiously and her head started to ache.

She quickly stood and backed away from the table. Surely, she reasoned, there was a logical explanation. She would think really hard about it and see if she could come up with something rational. The problem was, she had no coherent thoughts at all. She only wished Madeline would hurry over so she wouldn't be alone in the house.

Jessa tiptoed back into the kitchen and stood by the old claw sink, looking out the back window. To her amazement, the chunk of bread dropped from somewhere above and landed in the sink. She yelped in surprise. Stepping away and looking up, she tried to see what caused the bread to drop there. She could see nothing out of place.

That is, until she looked in the pantry doorway. The door to the cellar was open a crack.

She sucked in a lungful of air, ready to scream. Before the sound escaped her lips, however, the doorbell echoed across the house. Without a backward glance, she raced for the front door, relieved that Madeline Hester had arrived.

In fact, the front door stood open, but there was no one there. Jessa's mouth dropped. Fear swirled through her veins and turned her stomach sour. Behind her, she could hear the door to the cellar slam. She whirled around toward the kitchen, but couldn't make herself go back in there. Then, turning back to the open front door, she gasped, startled to see an older woman standing there. She had a pleasant appearance, but her eyes had a look that made Jessa think she knew things…

"Madeline?" Jessa asked tentatively.

"You must be Jessa. It's been a while since I've been in this house." Madeline looked around. Jessa followed her into the parlor.

The instant the older woman saw the arrangement of items on the little, round table, she whirled around and caught Jessa by the shoulders. There was true fear in her eyes as they searched Jessa's for an answer. "What have you done?"

Madeline was stronger than she looked, and Jessa could feel her fingers digging into the flesh of her shoulders. She shook her head and whispered fearfully, "Nothing!"

"You're lying!" Madeline let her go, making Jessa stumble backward. She walked quickly over to the table where the candles were still burning and the bread bag was opened slightly. An instant later, Madeline had all three candles extinguished and the bread bag twisted tightly shut. In her nervous haste, she dumped the bowl of potpourri across the floor, scattering the fragrant confetti like the path of a tiny tornado. Her eyes looked as if she might cry as she helplessly surveyed the mishap. Then she strong-armed Jessa to the couch and forced her to sit beside her. "Tell me everything you did. Exactly. Don't leave anything out. Don't exaggerate."

For an instant, Jessa was transported back to elementary school to the only time she was sent to the principal's office for pulling another girl's hair. She'd spent more than an hour trying to justify her actions. Now, she found herself in the same situation. She tried to remember everything she'd done, and said, and exactly how she'd done it.

Madeline bit her lips in worry as Jessa began to tell her what had taken place. The older woman stood and scanned the room. She put her hands together and fretted. "Oh, this isn't good. Not at all. Did you state a request?"

Jessa squinted her eyes and tried to think over the pounding of her heart, and the panic, that threatened to stop her brain from thinking. "Yes, I offered the bread and asked if Maria would come speak to me. Was that wrong?"

"Depends," Madeline walked fearfully across the room and peeked nervously into the stairwell hallway between the parlor and kitchen, "on what Maria was doing at the time. If she is a free spirit, then we're probably okay. But before, there was another spirit that was not so gentle. She was terrified of him at the time. If she's under his spell, even as a spirit, the consequences could be disastrous."

Jessa's attention was now completely on Madeline's words. "What spirit? Did she know the spirit she was trying to contact?"

Madeline looked back over her shoulder at Jessa. "Why yes, of course. She knew exactly who she was looking for. And found."

"And who was this spirit?" Jessa held her breath for the answer.

"Vernon. Vernon Hubert."

"S. J.'s brother? Are you certain?" Jessa's mind reeled

at this information. Her hunch about S. J.'s brother was correct, then. Her memory took her back to everything she had learned about Maria and Vernon. A thought came to her that was so unreal, so sinister, that she almost could not comprehend it: could it be possible, *would* it be possible, that the person responsible for Maria's death wasn't a person at all? Was, in fact, a ghost? Could Vernon Hubert be responsible for Maria Escher's death? But how? "If Maria asked for Vernon Hubert by name, how did she find out about him?" Mumbling to herself, Jessa didn't look at Madeline as she asked the question.

When she finally looked up, she saw that Madeline had edged toward the front door. The older woman's face had become ashen and her eyes darted around nervously. "I have to go," she declared, though the statement sounded more like a question as her voice trailed off to nothing.

Jessa didn't want to stay here alone, but she knew she couldn't leave just yet. The house held her just as if she was anchored to the wall. "Please, Madeline. You promised to show me how you contacted the spirits for Maria. If we can recreate it, then perhaps we can discover what happened to her." Jessa reached for Madeline's hand. "And I need to know, truly, if this is a gift you have. I don't care about your need to make money; I'm not interested in spilling my guts to the world if you are not what you are advertised to be. I just need to know the truth about Maria: did you contact Vernon Hubert, truly?"

Jessa thought, at first, that Madeline was going to get angry, but the fear in her eyes as they met Jessa's was very real. She pulled away from the younger girl and stepped back to put some distance between them. "I have always been able to speak to spirits since I was a little girl. It scared my mama something awful. But honey, the things I saw here at Bristol House scared even me. It's usually like remembering a dream; thoughts come to me, visions, feelings... but that man, Vernon Hubert, was real. Solid. Angry. And he was glad to come into this world. Maria invited him. I told her to take it slowly, but she paid me no attention. She had to speak to Vernon. From the beginning I could feel his darkness, but Maria was so insistent. I thought if I could guide her, use simple precautions, then we could control the situation... him."

"Do you know what happened to her?" Jessa found herself holding her breath.

Madeline's eyes glazed over as she remembered. Her mouth slackened and her breath quickened. At first, it didn't look like she was going to answer the question, but finally, she said, "I don't know what happened to her. When Maria disappeared, I could feel the spirit backing off."

"Getting weaker?" Jessa said, trying to help, to understand.

"No, child. Just backing away. He was stronger than ever, but he seemed to have gotten what he had wanted. Maria ended up contacting him on her own; without me, she could proceed as quickly as she wanted. And Vernon wanted to be contacted, that's why it was so easy for her."

Leaning toward the older woman, Jessa lowered her voice to just above a whisper. "I have seen Maria. I took some pictures in the kitchen and I saw Maria's face. She was trying to tell me something. Finally, I figured it out it was the name *Vernon*."

Madeline gasped and quickly covered her hands over her mouth. "Was she... happy?" It wasn't the idea of the photograph that had surprised her; it was the name the young woman had uttered.

Jessa shook her head and frowned worriedly. "No, quite the contrary. She was terrified. And then I had a dream about her. She kept looking over her shoulder as if she was afraid of being caught, but I don't know what she was doing that would have frightened her so."

Suddenly old and defeated, Madeline sat down heavily on the sofa. She rested her face in her hands for such a long time that the cacophonic silence in the room drilled into Jessa's eardrums. "Madeline," she said finally, "tell me what's going on. I've obviously done something wrong, and I can't correct it if I don't know what it is."

The reaction from the older woman was not what she expected. When she sat up suddenly, her face was hard and emotionless. There was anger and irritation in her voice as she spoke: "You kids! You think you know everything. You think the world revolves around you." She flung her hand out towards Jessa in a gesture of dismissal. "You wear the cloak of immortality and you think nothing can hurt you. You think the world is yours, but I can tell you, little girl, there are far worse things in this life than you can imagine and your pitiful existence is nothing! Maria thought she was impervious to danger and harm. Now she's gone and it's her own damn fault. You! You are just like her. Could you wait for me? No!"

The venom in her voice was frightening, and Jessa backed away from the older woman as if she'd suddenly gone mad. "I… I … I didn't think…" she didn't know what to say.

Madeline practically spit at her, "I have to agree; you're right! You *didn't* think. All this could have been avoided if Maria could have waited and used the precautions I wanted her to use, but she wouldn't listen. Now, here you are doing the *exact same thing!* I wash my hands of it all. And if you end up missing, do not think I'll help." Without another word, Madeline turned away from Jessa and left the house with no uncertain slam of the door.

Jessa watched her go. Her heart thumped furiously in her chest and terror made her faint. She ran to the door blindly, but stopped just short of the doorframe. "Madeline! Wait!"

Madeline Hester gave no indication that she heard Jessa's desperate plea. Only when she was racing down the narrow driveway, did she look back to watch Jessa's anxious face crumple to tears as it receded in her rearview mirror.

"This is insane!" Jessa whispered to herself almost

silently, tears trailing a salty path down her face. She sighed and closed her eyes, trying to gather some strength. When she straightened, she had already decided she'd seen enough of Bristol House to last a lifetime. She was in danger of falling desperately in love with Mitch, but even that paled in comparison to the fear she felt in the house. She wanted nothing more to do with it.

She left the parlor in a mess. The fragrant scatter of potpourri wafted across the room as she looked back at the table. The bread bag was closed tightly, but she could still smell the hint of fresh bread mixed with the scent of flowers. The short candles still smoked slightly from having been lit, but they didn't look as if they'd come to life and burn the house down, so Jessa decided to leave them there.

Sighing deeply, she turned to step out of the front door. Her hand grasped the doorframe as she passed under it; otherwise, she didn't pay any particular attention to where she was going. Once she stepped through the open front door, she looked up, expecting to see the wide lawn just beyond the veranda.

But the lawn wasn't what she saw. Instead, she found herself looking at the tall wooden cabinets of the old fashioned kitchen. Her heart seemed to stop painfully before thundering uproariously in her chest. *Dear God!* She gulped an excruciating lungful of air. Tears pricked at her eyes once again, legs and arms became weak, and her head swirled with dizzy awareness. The front door, through the entire length of the house, could be seen open and inviting her to the front lawn.

In a blind panic, she ran for the open door, her eyes never leaving it. She burst through the front doorway onto the veranda, gasping oxygen like she'd been under water... and tumbled headlong down the cellar steps.

CHAPTER SEVENTEEN
LOST PAGES

Jessa held herself very still at the bottom of the cellar steps to take stock of the situation. Her arms and legs hurt; there would definitely be bruises where her body bumped and thrashed against the steps as she fell, but she didn't think anything was broken. Though it was dark, she didn't see any blood, either.

The rush of panic coursed through her silent body, on adrenalin-saturated blood, as her heart pumped furiously. The roar of her own arteries made her deaf to any sounds around her. She sniffed the air carefully, but the rot-drenched odor she'd smelled before was faint.

Then, she tried to justify to her sane mind what had just happened. Had she accidentally run to the back of the house after Madeline left? Was she that upset? Had she mistaken the cellar door for the front door and taken a tumble, thinking she was stepping onto the veranda?

Sitting up gingerly, she groaned almost silently as she tried to work her stiff limbs and muscles. Then, she peered furtively into the dark recesses of the cellar, fearing the worst, but praying for the best. Nothing, that she could see, was any more out of place than it had been the last time she was down here. Chairs were still upturned and broken, papers were still scattered about, and marbles still littered the floor.

She turned her head stiffly and looked up the steps to the door that led to the kitchen pantry. Today it seemed abnormally far to the door, but she rationalized that she'd been frightened and she wanted nothing more than to get out onto the lawn and into the daylight. She sighed.

Taking one last look around, she turned to pull herself up the first step, then froze in alarm. Very slowly, her eyes stopped short on the marbles scattered about the floor. Blinking heavily, she watched, horrified, as the round orbs of rainbow glass, cat's eyes, aggies, and commies rolled slowly along the uneven cement floor of the cellar, sometimes uphill. Jessa could do nothing but watch, eyes wide and jaw slack, with the thunder of blood roaring in her ears making her deaf.

When the marbles stopped moving, she squinted hard through her fear, daring the words they formed to disappear: *lost pages*. But the meaning escaped her. Lost pages? However, the instant her brain registered the words, the marbles rolled suddenly to the cracked depressions of the rough floor and laid there mindlessly still and motionless.

She turned back to the stairway with nothing on her mind, other than to escape this hellhole. As fast as her abused legs would carry her, she skipped up the steps toward the pantry. She ran. She ran more. Looking up into the lighted pantry doorway, she kept her eyes hungrily on the daylight.

After a full minute of running up the steps, she discovered she was no nearer to the top than she had been before. Looking back at where the marbles were lying on the floor, she was still only a scant half dozen steps from where she started and the kitchen was still a full flight of steps away. She was tired and out of breath from the exertion of running on the stairs. Panic took control; there was not enough oxygen. Gulping air, she suddenly went weak and doubled over. Nausea pushed and squeezed her until she vomited on the step by her feet. She shut her eyes tightly against the painful burning.

Please, please! Please! She whimpered helplessly. Great sobs wracked her small frame, shaking her sore shoulders and causing pain to shoot through her head. Then, her ears picked up the faintest sound… she didn't like it at all.

Involuntarily, she opened her eyes just a slit; long enough to see the marbles start to conform into position with military precision. For just an instant, Jessa could once more see the words *lost pages* appear, and then yet again, they rolled to where gravity pulled them.

Jessa looked upward to the daylight and freedom.

Tears streamed down her face. "Okay!" she screamed. "I got it! Lost pages! Now leave me alone!" She could hear the hysteria in her voice, but she didn't care. She'd never been so frightened; she'd never felt so powerless.

With a great, loud heave, she pulled herself to standing and willed the strength to return to her legs and arms. Grabbing onto the railing, she used the last of her might to hoist herself up from the bottom step. She could feel that she was finally rising from the cellar—from the prison that had held her captive.

At last, she was able to shove her body through the doorway and into the pantry. She turned and hastily pushed the cellar door shut and locked it, then ran into the kitchen. The air was heavy and humid, but even that was sweet compared to the dank rotten smell of the cellar. At the sink, she pumped water from the old-fashioned water pump, splashing it on her face. Then she gripped the front of the sink and closed her eyes. Tears ran together with the wetness on her face. She tried very hard not to cry out, her terror was so great.

Finally, she rubbed her face dry with the hem of her t-shirt and scrubbed at her puffy eyes with the back of her hand. She reasoned that she had not been able to get outside because she'd tried too hard to run. Now, she'd try walking purposefully. Though she held her head up bravely, she couldn't breathe with the effort it took to maintain this posture and found herself holding her breath.

Jessa finally reached the hallway beside the parlor. She hesitated for a moment to grab some air into her lungs. The air here was sluggish; she felt as if she was walking through water waist-high. When she started toward the door again, with eyes focused on her destination, she began to feel little fingers running along the hem of her shirt.

Her focus was broken and she stumbled slightly. Looking down, she could see the hem undulating as if a hand was running along the inside. Then, inhaling sharply, she watched in disbelief as her shirttail was pulled, tugged viciously away from her body. Shaking, Jessa yanked it away from the invisible hands. For an instant, she saw a tiny face, so small that at first she had trouble comprehending it.

Hysteria choked her and the air in her lungs wouldn't move. It was not a human face, but instead a tiny, bald faced, wrinkled monster with sharp talon-like teeth protruding from a bizarre grinning mouth. Before she could realize that it was gone, she could feel a tug on the other side of her body. A panicked scream erupted from her chest as she whirled around, yanking her t-shirt as she moved. Another little, tiny face was visible for just an instant before it, too, disappeared. She forced her eyes away from the hem of her shirt and looked with unrequited longing at the open front door.

Gasping for air that wasn't there for her, she could feel the oxygen deprivation burn and hear the screams welling up and disgorging involuntarily from her throat. The door was close, but too far. She tried not to let herself run; but her body didn't want to listen. The harder she tried to run, the slower she moved. The slower she moved, the more panic seized control. Nausea pounded through her. She was afraid she was going to be sick again. Still, little fingers tugged and pulled on the hem of her shirt. And again, she refused to look down and let her brain acknowledge that there were little creatures that wanted something from her.

"Leave me the hell alone!" she screamed with the last of her breath as she lunged for the door. An audible snap rent the air, and Jessa tumbled face first onto the hard floor. She didn't take the time to examine the bump that had begun to swell above her eye. The spell, or whatever creature had tried to keep her from the door, had suddenly let go. She scrambled on her knees in fast-forward motion to the opening.

Jessa tumbled out onto the veranda in a heap, arms and legs unattractively in the air. She sat dazed for a moment to gather her bearings. Before she could stand, she could hear the wind rising from across Lake Mendota. The trees near the house were still; not a leaf was moving, but across the lake, Jessa could see a gray, rolling mist heading angrily toward the house… and her!

She stood, looking around wildly for her car. She stepped off the porch just as the mist reached her, and pushed her down to the wet grass. She stood clumsily, legs shaking, and made another leap toward her car. The wind tugged and pushed her violently, slapping her against the ground.

She was rolled onto her back where she panted heavily, staring into the gray sky. Strident thunder boomed overhead, followed by angry fingers of lightning that crawled across the sky, bright in sharp contrast to the dark clouds.

Thunder bellowed and blustered, calling to her: *Leave us! Leave this house!* The answering lightning shrieked and howled, forming bright, split-second words: *Help me!*

The tug and pull of the wind, the angry roiling of the clouds, and the fierce, blustery bickering between the thunder and lightning made Jessa's world spin out of control. She fought for consciousness.

Crawling on her hands and knees, she slowly crept closer by inches to her car. When the mist tried to pull her back toward the house, she dug her fingernails into the ground and held on with all the strength she had left.

At last, she reached her car, but it took several long, grueling moments to open her door against the push of the raging wind brought in by the mist. Jumbled thoughts and shaking fingers made hard work of finding her car keys and getting them inserted into the steering column. At last, she finally was able to bring life to the engine. She stomped carelessly down on the accelerator, but the engine wasn't engaged, and it roared angrily. Finally, she jerked the lever to DRIVE and stomped on the accelerator once again.

Her car swung wildly straight for the house. The lawn was wet with recent rain, so her tires left deep scars in the lawn as she wrenched the steering wheel toward the narrow driveway. She fought for control, swinging the car violently from one side of the lawn to the other, only just missing the Bristol House sign by inches. The length of the driveway slipped and skidded under her tires, swaying drunkenly as she escaped.

Her tires left a rubber path on the street when she turned sharply, and up the road for half a block. The drive to her apartment was a blur of unshed tears, fear, and a dead fatigue that she could feel through her bones. She had no idea what route she drove and no memory of the ride.

Jessa stumbled into her apartment. She ran to her bedroom, shedding clothing as she went, before she realized she had not used a key to enter. Suddenly, she froze. The lock on the door had been broken!

Down to her underwear, she watched with bemusement as Mitch sat up from where he'd fallen asleep on her bed. Heart triphammering, she curled her arms close to her chest, using her shed jeans to cover herself.

"Mitch!" she whispered hoarsely, "What are you doing here?"

The next instant, Mitch was against her with his arms wrapped tightly around her body. He buried his face in the side of her neck. It almost sounded like he'd been crying. "Where the hell have you been, Jessa? I've been worried sick."

She pulled her face away from him so she could see his eyes. "What are you talking about? I called you this morning. You knew I was going to Bristol House."

Mitch held her head still with his hands, kissing her forehead and cheeks, grazing his lips across hers, and finally meeting her eyes. He held her gaze for a moment, then pulled back as he realized she was nearly naked. Stepping away from her, he sat heavily on her bed.

He sighed deeply. "Look, if you don't want to talk about it, that's okay. I'm just glad you are here and unharmed."

Jessa could feel her heart thrum rapidly in her chest. Dread nearly choked her. In a voice just above a whisper, she answered him, "But Mitch, I told you. I called you a couple of hours ago. You knew I was going to Bristol House. I met Madeline Hester there."

For a minute, she didn't think he was going to answer her. He stared long and hard. "You're kidding, right?" His voice was incredulous.

Tears and panic made her face hot and her throat sting. "Would you tell me what the flippin' hell is going on?"

"Jessa," he spoke ominously quiet, "that was *three days* ago."

THE HOT SHOWER did wonders for her tired, sore muscles. Nothing, however, could relieve the disoriented feeling of the missing days. As traumatic as her experience was, Jessa found herself quite literally starving to death. She sat with Mitch at a quiet restaurant in a dark corner away from the hub of the dining room. He pushed and picked at his food as she shoveled in mashed potatoes and green beans as fast as she could swallow.

When she could finally stop eating, she sat back in her chair and studied Mitch's face. His eyes and mouth were etched with worry and his face still had three days of beard growth. She dropped her eyes and shook her head in disbelief.

"Has it really been three days? I... I just can't believe it. Seriously, for me it was no more than a couple of hours." Jessa toyed with her fork, then tossed it to the table.

A rumble rattled Mitch's chest. "This borders on insane. I think we can learn something from this, but I'm not sure what it is. The crazy thing is that I was in Bristol House looking for you. I went all through the house including the cellar. And what you tell me happened... it sounds like some kook making up a story. If it was anyone else, I'd probably call them a liar."

Jessa shook her head. "I can't believe it either. Did you talk to Madeline?"

He shrugged his shoulders. "I tried to. She didn't

answer her phone, so I drove by her house. She's gone. All her stuff is gone and her landline phone has been turned off. She must've been scared pretty bad to run off like that."

"She's gone?" Jessa's mouth dropped open in shock. "She was furious when she saw what I'd done. I don't know if she didn't think she would get paid or if she was truly afraid."

Again, the shrug. "I don't think she's too worried about the money. She comes from one of the wealthiest families in Wisconsin. Something has her spooked. I wish we knew what it was."

"But how can we find out what it was if she's gone? Maria used and trusted her. How will we be able to retrace Maria's steps without her help?"

Mitch sat up straight in his chair and leaned across the table to take Jessa's hands. "For what it's worth, this is what I think: long ago, Madeline helped Maria open a door that had been long shut. For some reason, Maria got caught up with whatever spirit haunts Bristol House and she was killed for it. Murdered. Now you are here trying to do the same thing Maria did, but the door is weakened and you were able to give it a push. Madeline recognized that. You don't need her help, and I'm not sure she wants to help. Something in that house has frightened her so badly that she has gone." Mitch dropped Jessa's hands and motioned for the check to be brought to the table. "If you want to continue to figure out what happened to Maria, it'll be up to us. I don't think there's any help to be had."

"I'm scared, Mitch." Jessa could hear the whining plea in her voice.

"Then we'll stop. I'll close up Bristol House and we won't go there again," he said matter-of-factly.

Jessa considered that for a moment. To have this torment behind her was a wonderful thought. Never to return to that horrid place appealed to her. Finally, she grinned. "Okay. I would like to know, but not bad enough to go there again. Do you mind terribly?"

He grinned back at her. "I wish I'd never heard of Bristol House. The only person who may care is my mother. But if she wants to open the house, she'll have to come do it herself. I'm done with it."

With that decision made, the rest of the evening was restful and peaceful. Jessa marveled at the way Mitch held her hand and never left her sight, almost as if he was afraid she'd disappear again. When the day darkened to night, Jessa found herself loathe to have Mitch leave. She had become fearful of the dark, and even the shadows had become suspect.

They stood just inside her apartment door, wrapped in each other's arms, lips melting against lips. Without conscious decision, Jessa heard her voice, whispery and soft, say, "Mitch, don't leave. I'm so afraid of being alone."

In answer, he scooped her up and took her to the bedroom, laying her gently on top of the covers. There was little room for conversation as their bodies met and their needs were taken care of. Jessa felt the last reservation fall away as she surrendered her heart to Mitch. She was hopelessly, permanently, head-over-heels in love with him.

Hours later, when the daylight had barely crept up over the horizon, Jessa slipped out of bed, carefully, so as not to jostle Mitch's sleeping form. She padded softly into the kitchen, surprised for a moment when the postcard of Bristol House leaped from the shelf and landed in a flutter at her feet.

Her breath caught suddenly in her throat as this same memory pounded into her head. She leaned over and gingerly picked it up off the floor. Her fingers shook as she studied the house in the photograph. Almost all the color had leached out of the photo. In the second floor window, Jessa saw the unmistakable face of a young woman staring at her, but the horror of it was that this young woman had her mouth open in a silent scream.

Jessa dropped the card in a terrified gasp. *Oh dear God,* she hissed silently, *this is not over!* When she picked up the card

170

from the floor to place it on the shelf once again, the young woman's face was no longer visible. Even so, Jessa could still almost hear a screaming sound screeching through her brain.

She turned her back on the shelf to ready the coffee pot for her morning brew. Only then, did she realize the kitchen window was wide open. In horror, she saw the robin flit by the window and heard the unmistakable click of her camera from on the kitchen table. Without making coffee, and without shutting the window, Jessa ran back to her bedroom. Her heart plummeted with disappointment, and fresh tears welled suddenly in her eyes, as she looked at her now empty bed. Mitch was gone.

CHAPTER EIGHTEEN
SPIRALING ANGER

Jessa dressed quickly and took the time to brew her coffee and eat her traditional bowl of oatmeal. She didn't really taste her food, but kept her eyes on the window as if it would spontaneously open. She had tried several times to call Mitch, but each time got his voicemail.

The walls of her small apartment began to close in on her, so she swung her purse over her shoulder and headed for the mall. She sauntered blindly along the walkway, pretending to study the window displays, but her mind was elsewhere. What in the world had happened during the time she'd been in Bristol House?

For about the millionth time, she pulled her cell phone from her purse and punched in Mitch's phone number. Finally, on the fourth ring, he answered. "Mitch!" she breathed in relief.

There was a moment of silence before he answered her. "Jessa?"

She couldn't quite place the intonation of his voice. "Is something wrong?"

There was a small, humorless laugh on the other end. "I was about to ask you the same thing."

Though there was nothing sinister in his words, something about what he said made her heart suddenly race. "Oh, my god, Mitch, what is it?"

"Hell!" he said quietly. "Do you have any idea what day this is?"

Jessa swallowed hard. She could feel the adrenalin course through her veins and her hands began to shake. Sudden tears shook her voice. "The next morning?" she asked in a small, tentative voice.

"Jessa," Mitch sighed, "when I woke up, you were gone. I yelled into every room of your apartment, but you weren't there. Your car was there. Your purse was there. Even your camera was there. But *you* weren't."

A cry strangled her throat. "Oh, god, this isn't happening to me! I left you in the bed and I went into the kitchen to make some coffee. I have this postcard of Bristol House on the shelf in the kitchen and, I swear to you, there was a girl in one of the windows screaming. But then she was gone. I was so scared, and when I got back to the bedroom, you weren't there. I swear, Mitch!"

"That was yesterday," he said quietly, "and I thought you didn't want to see me again." He sighed, then said more to himself than her, "What the hell is going on?"

"Mitch? C-c-can I come see you? I'm..." she swallowed her tears. "I feel so ungrounded. I need something solid. I'm so frightened."

"Where are you?" he asked immediately.

"The mall. I'll meet you anywhere you say."

Minutes later, Jessa was headed to the Arboretum to meet Mitch, hoping against hope that her days would not suddenly shift again. What if they lost their alignment and she never got to see him again? Panic and anxiety forced her to urge the accelerator of her car to far beyond the legal speed limit.

To her infinite relief, he was there waiting for her. She yanked her door open and ran to him, throwing herself into his arms and relishing the solid feel of his body against hers.

"I'm so pissed!" she spit fiercely when she could finally breathe. "All these tears and being afraid... it isn't like me. Days ago, I'd have smacked anyone who would have described me like this and now, here I am, first class wimp. I suck!"

Mitch laughed against her hair. "That's my girl! You ready to kick ass and take names?"

Jessa laughed with him, though it was strangled by a childish cry. "Sorta. I'd rather kick ass than get mine kicked."

They picked a path and walked wordlessly for several

minutes. Finally, Mitch spoke, "I don't want you to go back, Jessa. I still think the best thing to do is to close Bristol House for good."

"I'd be lying if I didn't agree with you. Only," she bit her lip, trying to figure out how to explain what was going on inside her brain, "I don't think it's over. Maria is in trouble; she needs my help. I know how it sounds. Like I'm a lunatic. But dead or not, I need to help her. I need to stop this... thing... that is happening to me. And I may need your help."

Mitch's face darkened perceptibly. "This doesn't need to be your concern, Jessa. You should never have been involved."

She shrugged. "Maybe not at first, but now I don't think I have a choice. I've been noticed and now I can't get unnoticed. Do you remember the diary of Virginia's that I found in the closet on the second floor bedroom?" She waited for him to nod. "It was missing some pages. I think it would be a good idea to find them. I think Maria is trying to tell me about something that happened in the past before she came along. I think, since pages were missing from Virginia's diary, if I can find the missing pages, it will shed some light on why Maria was murdered."

"I don't like it." As his anger mounted, he began to walk faster. Jessa had to stretch her legs to keep up with him.

With a gentle yank on his arm, Jessa stopped and turned him to face her. "I don't like it either, but I don't think the house will leave me alone until Maria can rest peacefully. I think it's Maria's turn."

Mitch studied her face, then pulled her arm through his. He led her slowly back to their cars. Jessa felt a moment of anxiety when Mitch left her for his own car, but he had promised to lead her to his private apartment, and she drove on his bumper the whole way. They made plans to spend the evening at the Terrace again, but the weather had turned quite cool and rainy. So, after shivering over beer and pretzels for less than an hour, they returned to his apartment to watch a movie.

Jessa fought sleep as she curled up against Mitch's warm chest. Finally dozing, her subconscious thoughts abruptly whirred into action.

She floated effortlessly into the front door of Bristol House. She was aware that she was dreaming, but in her dream, her mind discarded that thought, and all others, until all she could feel, think, smell, and taste was of this house. She knew she was being drawn somewhere that she needed to go.

The walls of the old house slipped by her and she could feel the resistance in her own mind as she approached the pantry. She wanted to resist, but could only watch impotently as she saw her own hand reach out and unhook the latch on the cellar door inside the pantry. The door slid open with a smooth *whoosh* along the floor.

Rather than stepping down, she instead glided, descending the steps in a fluid motion, continuing past the boxes and chairs and toys to the back corner of the cellar where she'd not been before. She stopped beside a stained wooden crate, weakened with age and damaged from many years spent in the damp cellar.

Then, she felt the sudden zoom of movement as she rushed downward to the level of the crate. She became infinitely smaller, drifting between the slats and sliding between the sheaves of hundreds of papers kept there. She was looking for something specific. What was it? She wasn't sure, but she'd know when she saw it. Searching... searching... The words *lost pages* whirled in and out of focus.

Her unseen body tensed when she found a dark brown leather satchel. It was small and dainty, like the kind used a hundred years ago to keep special papers in, such as marriage certificates or birth documents. Concealed hands tried to wrest the satchel from deep inside the crate, but it wasn't to be moved. She wanted to cry in frustration, but she had no voice.

She retreated and zoomed fearlessly out of the crate, backing to the stairway, to the pantry, still with the crate in her sights. Dizzily, she spiraled up the steps and out the pantry, in backwards motion like an amusement park ride, reeling with nausea.

In one silent *pop*, she gasped and sat up suddenly on Mitch's couch. Her breath raged in her ears; her heart pounded heavily in her chest.

He looked at her fearfully. "You okay?"

Jessa smiled tremulously, but it didn't reach her eyes. "I think I know where the missing pages of Virginia's diary are." The dream-trip ran through her mind again, clearly, as if it had really happened to her. She should be afraid, she supposed, but the bit of information about the missing pages of Virginia's diary tantalized her and made her willing to forget her horror and fright. It all seemed so calm, here, sitting safely beside Mitch, that she could almost convince herself that her fright had been of her own making. But what of the missing time? Had she been knocked in the head and dreamed the horrors that had happened? It would explain much. However, it would not explain why Madeline Hester suddenly left town. Were the ghosts of Bristol House responsible?

"How would you know where to look?" Mitch eyed Jessa through half-closed lids.

His expression didn't give away any emotion he might be feeling. Jessa wondered if he would continue to believe her story if she now told him of the strange dream-trip that she had just taken while she was snuggled safely in his embrace. She was not sure she would believe it herself, had it not just happened to her. "Let's just call it a hunch, Mitch. I need to try." She kept thinking about the cellar and how she hadn't been able to leave until she screamed the words formed by the marbles… and then this strange dream trip… perhaps she could be brave enough to make one last trip to the cellar. Could she be that brave?

Mitch returned his gaze to the movie in front of them,

but Jessa suspected he wasn't watching it any more than she was. Perhaps she'd prove to be too crazy even for him: the man who had put up with his former fiancé talking to the spirits of her dead ancestors.

However, just as she made up her mind to leave for her own apartment, his arm around her tightened, and she once again laid her head against his chest, enjoying the warmth of his embrace for at least a little while longer.

JESSA STARED at the ceiling of her bedroom in self-loathing and boredom. Two days had passed since she had had the dream-trip into the cellar and she still couldn't work up the nerve to head back to Bristol House. It wasn't just a case of nerves that kept her away from the old house. It was Mitch.

With legs and arms like lead weights, Jessa struggled to sit up on the edge of her bed, trying to convince herself that she needed to shower and present her mirrored reflection self with something positive to look at, but she couldn't bring herself to care. She knew she was slipping into depression and every day she didn't meet the challenge offered to her by Bristol House, she felt herself being consumed by melancholy and despair. Mitch hadn't commented on her desire to return to the house to look for Virginia's diary. It had been obvious to her that he wanted her to stay away from the danger there, though she suspected he would do nothing to stop her. It was not a high-handed issue of control, but an emotional plea for her safety.

However, convincing herself that Mitch was partly responsible for her decision to stay away from Bristol House was wearing thin. She knew that inside her somewhere a coward was rearing her ugly head. This was a side of herself that she wasn't accustomed to seeing, one she hadn't really known existed. One she hated.

After an hour of energy-depleting preparation to meet the world with her usual effervescent grace, she finally gave up and stomped angrily out of her apartment. She purposefully skirted the kitchen along with its open window and little postcard with a mind of its own, preferring to find her breakfast and morning coffee at a Starbucks counter somewhere.

At some point between Starbucks and lunch, Jessa got a text message to meet Norma Escher at the restaurant. Letting her car idle in the parking lot, Jessa stared darkly, blindly, at her steering wheel. She had nothing to offer Norma about Maria. Sure, if she wanted to share the harrowing experience of a séance gone badly wrong, doors of a haunted house that kept a person inside its grip, and cellar steps that climbed forever to nowhere, then sure, there'd be something to talk about, but Jessa knew those were things that would get her locked up tight in a padded room with sweet nurses all dressed in white coats for company. With a deliberate punch, she deleted the message and snapped her phone shut. She couldn't face Maria's mother today.

She brooded as she drove aimlessly around the streets of Madison. There was no particular destination in her mind and the longer she weaved in and out of residential and business areas, the darker her spirits became. Bleak depression weighed down her every thought. She became angry.

Even Mitch was not safe from her furious, venomous mind. What if he really *had* murdered Maria? He shouldn't have done it! If he hadn't murdered poor Maria, there would be no cause for this hopeless misery. If Maria had not been so insane as to think she could gain insight and direction from her ancestors, then Mitch wouldn't have had to murder her. And Maria's parents… what were they thinking when they raised a daughter with such a warped sense of perspective? What kind of people did that, anyway?

Angry tears dripped down her cheeks and off her chin. She wanted nothing to do with anyone. Not Mitch. Not David and Norma Escher. Certainly not Maria. *Maria can go to hell;* Jessa thought cruelly, *she is probably already there anyway.*

As she got angrier, she mashed down hard on the accelerator, leaping the car across streets and lanes made for slower traffic. Even if the tears in her eyes weren't blurring her vision, the anger in her mind would still have prevented her from watching or caring how carelessly she was driving.

She was aware of a metallic crunch against her car door. Whipping her head around, she glared out of the car window to see pieces of metal and plastic tumble off the side of a parked car. Jessa sucked in a lungful of air and jammed her foot down on the brake. In an instant, the car spun around in a tight circle as the street and buildings whirled in a kaleidoscopic tunnel. Darkness tinged the edges of her vision.

Jessa knew she was going to faint. Her car seemed to spin very slowly, yet infinitely fast as colors and shapes blurred. Nausea roiled up in her stomach, made worse by the rage nesting inside her. She didn't care! *Die,* she screamed in silent agony, *die now!*

She finally came to an abrupt, silent halt. The absence of sound, after the screeching sound of metal breaking and tires squealing, was eerie. Too dazed to think clearly, Jessa looked around, puzzled by the silence. Something had jostled in her head because her vision was still blurry. She felt numb.

Holding her hand in front of her face, she splayed her fingers, watching with detachment at the runnels of blood hurrying from her fingers to her wrists, but the blood didn't seem to be coming from her fingers. She touched her forehead and winced, pulling her fingers away. Ah, that was where the blood was coming from! Then, her eyes rolled back and she succumbed to darkness.

DISTANTLY, JESSA COULD HEAR a burbling drip near her arm. Its steady cadence was comforting, lulling her breathing to the same constant tempo. In, drip. Out, drip. In, drip. Out, drip... Occasionally, a tinny voice would break through the monotony over the intercom, but then die down moments later.

She was so tired, she couldn't move. Couldn't even open her eyes. If she tried to think too hard, there was a spot on her brain that throbbed painfully, so instead, she let her mind wander where it wanted to go, as long as it didn't go to the dark place that plagued her.

The dark place was made of stone and mist. For a moment, she couldn't remember what it was that had made it so dark; it was a beautiful place. It had been loved, once upon a time. Now, it was... What was it?

Her head began to ache with remembering, and she turned sharply away from those thoughts. There was something she should remember, but it was too painful both inside and out. She let go, preferring to be cocooned in the safety of oblivion.

Though sealed tight, she became aware of a bright light penetrating her eyelids. She blinked and squinted, but the pain stabbed through her optic nerve like a scalpel. She wanted to shut her eyes and bow her back and writhe away from the light, but she was still immobile, drenched in sweat.

After a time, though, she became used to the light. It was less harsh and even inviting. It called to her; wanted something from her. Its power consumed her. Putting her elbows on the table in front of her, she leaned into the light, peering closely as if it was telling her secrets. Surprised, she sat back suddenly. The tiny room where she was sitting was stark and bare, dark except for the light shining down on the plain square table.

She shivered in her thin, white hospital gown, and wondered for a terrified moment if it was open at the back. Then her mind wandered again, and she became consumed once more by the bright light shining down on her and the table.

Besides the light, she realized she wasn't alone, and that the room wasn't completely empty. Across from her sat a young woman, beautiful, staring at her and waiting to be noticed. Jessa squinted, though it was hard to see much through the bright beam of light.

When she did finally recognize the woman, she realized it was someone she'd never seen before, but she knew the face. Intimately. She also knew, with certainty, that this woman, here with her now, was dead.

CHAPTER NINETEEN
STRANGE VISITOR

"You're dead," Jessa stated bluntly. "Aren't you?" She squinted through the haze of the harsh, white light bearing down on them from somewhere directly overhead.

Maria smiled warmly, making Jessa smile in return. Opening her mouth to speak, an annoyed frustration flitted across her fine features when no sound came out of her throat. Then gently, Maria reached across the table and picked up one of Jessa's hands, holding it firmly as if she knew Jessa wanted to escape the touch. Jessa tried not to flinch and hoped her fear didn't show in her eyes.

With her other hand, Maria wrapped her long fingers around her own throat, digging the tips into her skin in what looked to be a painful grip, but her smile only widened. This time, as she opened her mouth to speak, her voice came out as whispery as a butterfly's wings, but with the gentle hum of a bellows.

In a monotone, she said, *"I have tried so many ways to meet with you."* The young ghostly woman waited expectantly, still smiling brightly. When Jessa didn't respond, she continued, *"I... I know this must be frightening for you. To be honest, I feel fortunate it's working..."*

Jessa's hand trembled within Maria's grip. "Am I dead?"

"No, Jessa. If you were dead, it wouldn't be this difficult to speak to you." Maria smiled again, but her eyes became bright with moisture. Jessa recognized the difficulty it took for the other girl to speak to her, but at the same time, she knew she couldn't really be sitting at this table with the ghost of Maria. Could she?

She looked at Maria skeptically. "How do you know my name?"

For a moment, Maria started to laugh, waving her

hand in front of her in a congenial gesture. At that moment, the contact was lost and the room fell into absolute silence. Panicked, Maria quickly grasped her throat again and the distant hum of the bellows once again filled the room. *"Oh jeez,"* she said as in a very modern conversation, *"I was afraid I'd lost you! We can't break this contact again; I don't know how long it will last anyway. I could sense your name because it's in your mind. One of the perks, if there are any, of being on this side."*

"What happened to you? Are you dead?" Jessa could feel the hurried panic in Maria's voice, despite the monotone delivery.

Maria's voice trembled a little as she continued, *"Jessa, listen, please! I don't have much time, I'm afraid. I don't know how to answer your questions; I'm not dead, nor am I alive. But I can't stay here and I can't move on. My fate depends on you."*

Jessa pulled back, surprised, but stopped herself an instant before their hand contact was broken. She could feel the alarmed pumping of her heart. "I don't know if I can help you." She wanted to run far away from the ghostly girl. She wished she'd never heard of Maria or Bristol House.

"I saw you the first day you came to Bristol House. From the beginning, I knew you were different. Mother sent you, didn't she?" There was so much hope in her voice that Jessa felt the sting of her loss, and was engulfed with compassion and sympathy.

"Yes, that's right. How could you know that?" Holding Maria's hand, Jessa endured Maria's depth of longing, so emotionally painful and intense, that she had to steel herself against retreating.

Maria smiled again, her features more beautiful than ever. *"You were open to suggestion, to the idea that there is more to this world than meets the eye. I've always been that way, to a fault, I guess. My mother can be very persuasive when she wants something done. Please don't tell her where I am. I don't want to worry her if something goes wrong."*

She was talking to a dead girl: a ghost. Who was crazy here? Jessa couldn't decide. "What could possibly go wrong,

Maria? You're dead." *I think*, she added silently. "Besides, she is worried sick already. She just wants to know who murdered you."

Maria gasped suddenly, with so much emotion, that Jessa was thrown against the back of her chair. This news, apparently, was a huge surprise. *"I was murdered?"* Tears welled up in her eyes and threatened to spill onto her pale cheeks. *"Oh, my god, there is so much I can't remember clearly. Do you know what happened?"*

"No, I was hoping you'd tell me. No ones knows what happened to you. There was no body. Nothing to tell them anything at all."

"How long ago was I murdered?"

"Three years," was her reluctant reply. "Your folks hired me to take pictures and snoop on Mitch. They think he's the one." Jessa bit her bottom lip in frustration, feeling terrible about speaking so badly of Mitch, though she had to concede it was a possibility.

A wistful, sad look settled into Maria's face. *"Daddy, too? I miss them so much. Why would Mitch want to hurt me? He loves me."* Too much time was being wasted on idle conversation and her image began to flicker. When she realized this, she sat up straighter, gripped Jessa's hand a little tighter and spoke in a hurried voice. *"I need to move on. I can't stay here. But there are nasty spirits here who want me to stay and be one of them. They're harmless enough, I guess, but Vernon terrifies me. If I stay he'll…"* she choked back a sob and her image flickered again.

"Vernon Hubert?" Jessa questioned. "What… why…?"

Maria interrupted her with a tug of her hand. *"The door is open. It needs to be shut and locked. I can't do it, and at this time, Vernon has no control over the door. There is a key on a gold medallion that will open and shut the door. You have to find the key and close the door for good. If he finds it first, he'll ruin everyone and everything he comes into contact with on your side of the door."*

Jessa processed this information very quickly. "Is this

how he got here to begin with?"

"*Oh,*" Maria wailed, "*I was so stupid. He had the key. But he couldn't find the door. When I called him through Madeline Hester...*" Jessa nodded as she recognized the name "*...he finally found the door. I helped him open it. But then, he lost the key. It was my fault and he is so insane, so angry. He'll...*" again she sobbed and tears dripped off her eyelashes and onto pale blue cheeks. "*He'll hurt me. I run from him, but I can't run forever and he'll catch me. And then he'll hurt me.*" Maria's image flickered once again, but this time didn't regain its original brightness. She was fading from sight. Then, she looked over her shoulder to something that only she could see. Her eyes went wide and a humming gasp rushed between the girls. When she looked back at Jessa, there was real fear pooled there. Maria was frightened, terribly so. She leaned in toward Jessa and spoke hurriedly. "*Oh, dear God, I think he found me!*" Scanning the darkness on either side of her, Maria flickered and evaporated a little more.

"Maria, wait!" Jessa stood up from her chair, leaning over the table and trying to get a better grip on Maria's hand, but the slender fingers were slowly turning to the consistency of butter. "I need to know what to do!" She was practically screaming.

Maria's fading eyes were intent on Jessa's. "*My diary! Find my diary. It's hidden. I couldn't let Mitch see it.*" As she said his name, her features softened. "*Please, Jessa, find my diary in the... bureau, look... back... floor...*" Maria's voice was fading, dropping words, and becoming scratchy and indistinct.

"No! Don't go!" Jessa squeezed Maria's hand tighter, but the fingers slipped away, melting and vanishing like mist over the lake. "Maria! Wait! I don't know what to do! How do I close the door? Stay and talk to me!" Her voice was high-pitched in hysteria. "No, no, nooooo...!"

The light above the table brightened like a small sun, making Jessa close her eyes painfully. A sudden constriction clamped down on her chest. Trying to move her arms, she discovered they, too, were fastened securely at her sides, along with her legs. She fought against the constriction, trying to move from her prone position on the bed, but she could feel gentle hands hindering the movement of her limbs and holding her head still. She writhed and bucked, choking on a thin slice of wood clamped between her teeth.

Coated with a film of sweat, her energy evaporated with the last remnants of Maria's image in her mind. She lay still, except for the rapid rise and fall of her chest as she breathed hard. She could feel the light was still there behind blood red eyelids. Opening them a crack, her gaze swept the sides of the bed quickly before shutting again. White lab coats surrounded her. Had she finally jumped off the deep end and into the dreaded padded room?

Her tongue pushed the wooden depressor out of her mouth and then she licked her dry lips. Immediately, there was a glass of water against her mouth. She drank thirstily, then relaxed against her sweat-dampened pillow. Opening her eyes again, she surveyed the blurry room until the white shapes began to clear, and she lifted her gaze to the concerned faces of hospital staff. Then, her eyes stopped sharply on the only person not dressed in white: Mitch.

She studied his concerned face and smiled. It seemed to lift some of the worry from him, but not all, and she thought that she must look pretty pitiful lying here. A frown creased her forehead as she remembered the depression, the anger, and the spinning car. There had been a wreck, and this was the result. Her eyes became heavy, and shut tightly.

She opened her eyes again, realizing suddenly that she must have fallen asleep. The room was dark except for a yellow lamp on the bedside table. A shadowy figure was huddled up on a chair in the corner beside her bed. She cleared her throat, saying in a rough voice, "Mitch?"

The dark silhouette immediately unwrapped itself from the chair and scooted up against her bed. "Hey, girl. You okay?"

"Yeah, actually I feel pretty good. Can I go home? Am I hurt?"

"You got a good thumping from your steering wheel, but I don't think there's any permanent damage." She could hear the smile in his voice. "You scared me. Please don't do that again."

She looked down at her toes. "I was so angry. I guess I was scared, too." She paused, then asked quietly, "Is my dad here? Does he know?"

He shook his head, but she wasn't certain which question he was answering. "Your parents know and they were all set to drive up here from their home in the Texas. But your dad has been having trouble with his vision and your step-mom—"

"—doesn't like to fly, I know." She sighed. "So they aren't coming?"

Surprisingly, he chuckled softly. "I told them I was taking very good care of you. They seemed to be impressed, and surprised I might add, to hear we are... involved. I hope it's okay that I took a little liberty on that. They plan to come when you're well. They were very worried about you."

She sighed again. She loved her dad and step-mom very much, but it was she who had always been the strong one, always independent, and had kept them at arms length. "What now?"

"I've closed Bristol House. There won't be any more tours. Not for a long time." Mitch took her hand in his and she could feel its warmth travel up her arm. It was comforting and exciting. How could she think about that when she'd just been through such a horrifying ordeal?

"I have to go back," she said simply. His fingers tightened around hers. Inside the darkness of the room, she could sense his frown of disapproval.

"Do you think that's wise? After all, the last time you went there, you lost three days. What if you leave and you can't get back?" Mitch's thumb caressed little circles on the sensitive skin inside her wrist, sending fingers of electricity up her arms. For a moment, she closed her eyes and savored the feeling.

"I don't want to go, but I have to. I had a wonderful conversation with Maria. Did you know she kept a diary?" Jessa couldn't take her eyes away from Mitch's. It was because she was trying to gauge his reaction, she told herself firmly, not because he was so terribly handsome. She tried to keep the longing out of her gaze.

He became visibly upset at the mention of Maria's name and had not seen her expression. "A diary? She didn't have one that I'm aware of. How would you know this?"

She tried to remember as much detail as she could about her "meeting" with Maria, but as she told Mitch about it, it sounded strange and phony even to her; it was just a dream, right? She could see his doubt, but she pressed her belief just as strongly as she could. Finally, she reassured herself by assuring him, "I know how this sounds, but before you go calling for the psycho doctor, let me check it out. It's worth a look and can't do any harm. You can come with me. Please."

He shrugged, but she smiled because she knew he had conceded. She lay back against her pillow, exhausted, and closed her eyes. The memory of Maria's face flared briefly as Jessa drifted toward sleep. A ghost? Maria had seemed entirely un-ghost-like, but what did she know? Perhaps it was usual for ghosts to be emotional about the way they died. Perhaps that knowledge, or the lack of it, was what was keeping her from moving on. Or, perhaps there was something in her diary that would lend a clue as to why Vernon Hubert was still holding onto her.

JESSA WAS RELEASED from the hospital the next morning. She fretted anxiously as she waited for Jeanette to drive her home. Contrary to her last visit to Bristol House, or perhaps because of it, she could scarcely wait to search the entire house for a bureau or dresser (maybe one that was low or close to the floor?) that might contain Maria's diary. Had she gotten confused by thinking *lost pages* referred to Virginia's diary? Only, she didn't know if Maria's diary had any lost pages at all... or maybe that's what it meant because all the pages were lost...

Jessa decided not to think, and dropped her head back against the headrest in Jeanette's car. She gave her friend a grateful smile as the car pulled out into traffic and toward her apartment. When she was a little steadier on her feet, she'd have to look into replacing her destroyed Honda. Pity, that. She had loved that car!

Though her original intention was to return to Bristol House that same day, she found that she was sore and drained by the time Jeanette had her settled into bed. Before Jeanette left, she warmed up some soup for Jessa, but Jessa discovered that even sipping soup was almost more than she could deal with, and after a few tries, pushed it away. Letting fatigue take over, she turned on her side and promptly fell asleep.

Far from being a restful slumber, dreams pervaded her sleep. She stood on top of a mountain of old dusty, dirty boxes filled with all manners of legal papers and other documents. Box after box after box, she worked for hours squinting at the nearly illegible handwriting, old-fashioned and faded. She frantically searched for any sign of a diary, or paper from it, but it was so hard to tell one document from another. Was this it? No, it was a dinner guest list. Then perhaps this one? No, that was a recipe handed down from Grandmama.

The harder she looked, the larger the mountain of boxes became. At last, she realized she was not alone; someone else was looking through the boxes with her. She smiled in relief, but when she looked up to see who was standing near her, she gasped in horror: she was completely surrounded by the little shadow monsters that had tugged on her t-shirt days ago. Their little, bald faces could scarcely hold the wide, hostile mouths as they chortled with malevolent glee. They weren't looking through the boxes though; they were tearing and ripping papers with their sharp teeth as fast as they could manage.

No! Jessa tried to make her way to the nearest little monster, but the mountain of boxes shifted, threatening to spill her down its side. Off into the distance, Jessa could see a shadowy figure of a heavy-set man, dressed impeccably in a three-piece suit, watching the search with interest. Vernon: she'd recognize that character anywhere. As he walked, Vernon dragged a tearful Maria behind him, holding her wrists prisoner with the watch chain that dropped from his vest pocket.

Morning came long before Jessa was ready for it. She needed sleep, but she feared sleeping. She doubted there would be any real rest for her until this whole issue concerning Maria was at an end.

The hot shower did wonders to soothe her tired and aching muscles, though not the turmoil inside her head. Her dream-talk with Maria was still so fresh in her mind that it was as if a movie reel was playing its continuous loop inside her brain. The scene she kept coming back to most was Maria's shocked: *"I was murdered?"*

Not knowing what Virginia's diary had to do with Maria's murder and disappearance was frustrating to Jessa, but she still couldn't shake the feeling that that was where she needed to start. Virginia had something to share: whether or not it would shed some light on Maria's plight was up for grabs, but she was going to find out.

Dressing warmly against the chilly, dark day, Jessa moved slowly toward the kitchen, knowing as she did so what was likely to happen. She stopped at the point where the card of Bristol House had fallen to her feet before and stared at the shelf. As she leaned closer, though without moving her feet, she could see the card teetering. Backing away, the card settled still. Silently, she slid her foot forward a few inches. It was not a surprise when the card flinched. As her foot crept closer still, the card began to lose its balance. By the time her weight settled on that foot, the card appeared to leap off the shelf, then, before she could take another step, it had settled on the floor.

It was hard to look at the card as she picked it up; she feared what she might see. Indeed, her heart pounded a little faster and her breath came a little quicker as the woman in the upper story more clearly resembled Maria. The real clincher was the dark shadow developing in the window beside Maria's.

There was no time to lose. Maria's fate, whatever it was, was becoming firmer and less pliant by the day. How long would it be before all of Maria's fears were realized? Jessa shuddered. Unless she could understand what she needed to do, it looked very grave for poor Maria, indeed.

Jessa set the card back on the shelf and shut the kitchen window, turning away from it immediately to avoid the robin that was sure to appear. She could hear the soft flutter of wings as it flitted by the window, but she refused to look. Only when she heard the mechanical click of her camera's shutter, did she glance that way to see the bird's likeness show up on the camera's LCD screen. What she saw wasn't comforting.

The robin was there, but its bright orange breast was a dark blood red. The rest of the bird was almost black. Its normally black, beady eyes turned bright gold, and this time its head was turned. It was looking directly at her!

CHAPTER TWENTY
REVISITED...AGAIN

One look at the dark, water-laden clouds in the sky confirmed what Jessa was thinking: no matter what the distance, it would not be wise to hike to Bristol House today. As she chewed her oatmeal and sipped her coffee, she contemplated the problem.

Finally, she sighed deeply and dialed Mitch's number. She hated to ask him for a ride, but she was short on choices. He was at her door in a matter of minutes, making her wonder if he'd been expecting her call.

Once in her apartment, Mitch scooped Jessa up in an embrace that was tight and hungry. She could feel his worry and smiled against his neck. Without a doubt, she knew she could spend the rest of her life with these warm arms around her.

When he pulled away from her, it was only enough to look in her eyes and kiss her lips gently. "I'm okay, Mitch," she said softly.

He shook his head ruefully and smiled slightly. "I know. You are a strong woman. But I still worry about you."

Jessa went back into the kitchen to grab her camera, hesitating only slightly, knowing the disturbing picture of the dark robin was still in it, then slipped on a warm jacket and returned to Mitch. When she was buckled securely in the BMW, Mitch steered the car away from the curb with a firm push on the accelerator.

When he didn't head for Bristol House, like she expected, she raised her eyebrows in question. "What's up?"

"Business," he replied. "I have to go out of town for a while. I'll be flying out of the airport here in Madison; I'm leaving the car with you."

She sucked in a lungful of air. "I wrecked the Honda, so you're letting me use the BMW... doesn't make much sense." But she smiled as she watched the buildings slip silently by, outside the window.

Mitch took her concern seriously. "You didn't wreck your car because you're a bad driver. Besides, it's just a car. Cars can be replaced. You can't."

Jessa's smile sobered at his words. Though she wasn't looking at him, she wondered if he was thinking about Maria. Perhaps in her mind, she was hoping that Mitch no longer loved the murdered woman; she wanted Mitch to fall in love with *her*. Was he telling her that Maria couldn't be replaced? Her thoughts whirred into chaotic action. Overthinking, she knew in her mind that Mitch was not so shallow as to "replace" Maria in his life with her, she was nothing like Maria, but there was a bit of self-preservation rearing its protective head. She didn't want to be Maria's replacement; she wanted to be at the forefront of Mitch's life as Jessa.

"Where are you going?" Jessa changed the subject, preferring not to think about Maria at all. "Do you know when you'll get back to town?"

"I'm going to Florida to see my folks. I'll be back in a couple of days."

Jessa frowned as she let this information digest. Could this visit have anything to do with Bristol House? "Are you going to tell them about the ghosts?"

He snorted loudly, then laughed without much humor. "I'll tell them only enough so that they'll agree to keep Bristol House shut for a while. I wasn't going to tell them at all, but Mother has her connections that have wasted no time in telling her that I shut it down. One of the stipulations of ownership is that I agreed to live there for five years. That time period won't be up until the first of the year. I'm not staying there and haven't been for over a week; to Mother, that isn't living there."

"Doesn't she care that it isn't safe?"

Again, Mitch laughed. "I never liked living there; I've always hated that house. But honestly, sweetheart, you are the only one who has ever felt threatened there. I've never felt in danger and I've never encountered a ghost. Mother's claim is that the ghosts are a fantasy. By having my residence there, she can dispel that rumor and it becomes just a lovely old house. That's what she's always wanted, but you want to know a secret?"

Jessa nodded, smiling slightly, and pleased that he would trust her with this secret. "Certainly."

"Mother didn't want to live there herself. She's scared to death of the house. When she was a girl, she told her own mother that she wanted to live in the house when she was old enough to take it over, so Grandma thought that was a good idea. All Mother had to do was move in, but she lasted only part of one night. She was so terrified that she hasn't set foot in there since then; not since long before I was born."

"Oh my gosh, you're kidding! What happened?"

"She'd never say, but Grandma told me she came home about midnight that first day so terrified that they had to call the doctor to give her some medicine to calm her down. Since then she's ruled it with an iron fist, but from a distance."

A picture of a young woman leaped into Jessa's mind as she tried to imagine what could have happened. "Well, Mitch, then why would she insist you live there? Her son?"

"That is an excellent question, but I suspect it has something to do with the fact that I never believed in the supernatural and I was never afraid of the house. Actually, that isn't exactly true either. I never believed in the supernatural such as ghosts and spirits and such, but I've always hated the house. The house feels sick to me. I hate living there, but I've never been afraid." Mitch stared at the road as he drove, and Jessa knew he was seeing something that she couldn't.

Silence settled on them like a sleep that was hard to wake from. A thousand questions batted around inside Jessa's head, but Mitch's expression was so far away that she hated to interrupt him. They finally reached the airfield north of town and pulled into a parking lot. She rolled down her window and studied the planes there. There were few commercial planes and Jessa wondered which one he'd be on.

He noticed her perusal, and then pointed to a white Cessna set apart from the others. "Mine," he stated simply.

She rolled her eyes, but grinned to soften the gesture. "Sure. What else did I expect?" Her sarcasm was not lost on him, but he just grinned back at her and winked. She was glad he didn't apologize for being wealthy. It wasn't like he chose this family, and a few perks just came with the territory.

Moments later, his suitcase was pulled from the car's trunk and they were standing a couple hundred feet from the Cessna. He leaned over to give her a quick, awkward hug, then nodded to her before he turned and jogged the last few feet to hoist himself inside the plane. The plane's pilot was already warming up the engine. Before shutting the door, Mitch turned his face back to her and blew a kiss in her direction. Then suddenly, the door was shut and he was gone from her sight. "Be safe," she whispered in his direction.

As she watched the plane taxi down the runway, she wondered if she had told him that her plan was to go back to Bristol House. For now it was closed to the public, but in her pocket, she still had the large, ornate skeleton key that opened the front door.

Inside the BMW, she adjusted the seat and mirrors to fit her much smaller body. It purred silently under her touch, like a giant predatory cat on its best behavior. So unlike her little Honda, she was afraid this cat would throw her in the backseat and hunt and eat other little cars all over the streets of Madison. This was a lot of power... and she could quite get used to it! Her eager smile bumped into lowered eyebrows of excitement.

For her safety, and everyone else's, she drove more slowly than was absolutely necessary. Besides, she was lost in the feeling of unaccustomed luxury. Before she was aware of the route she took, or the time it took to get there, she found herself sitting quietly in the parking lot at Bristol House, staring up at the dark windows. Her cat had gone home.

Every thought left her mind, except one: find the missing pages of Virginia's diary. What could it possibly tell her? Certainly nothing about Maria as Virginia had been gone decades before Maria was born. The only thing that was certain was that she needed to see what was on those missing pages.

As she approached the veranda, she realized it would take every ounce of strength she had to go inside the house once again.

Since the day was dark with clouds that threatened rain, the house looked nearly black. Gray, diffused light filtered weakly through the sheer curtains on the windows in the parlor. Silence greeted her oppressively as if the house itself held its breath. Jessa squinted into dark corners, and strained her ears to listen for the tiniest sound. Her nose silently sniffed the air for the all-telling scent of rot that she now associated with the appearance of the specters.

And for all that the house was in living color, it certainly appeared shades of gray and taupe as in an old photograph. Even the portraits of S. J. and Virginia seemed to hold their breaths expectantly. Were they afraid of what would happen? Had they been forced to watch what went on as the decades spun by?

With leaden feet, Jessa knew she was headed for the cellar. The missing pages she searched for would not be in the second story bedroom closet where she'd found the actual diary. She knew, with certainty, she would find them in the cellar.

As she approached the pantry off the kitchen, she could hear the *whoosh* of the cellar door brush the floor and knew it had been opened for her. Vernon or Maria, someone wanted her down there. Before she ducked through the opening, she found a heavy cast iron Dutch oven to prop the door open with, and hoped it wouldn't disappear or let the door lock her in.

A foul stink rose up from the darkness. Jessa shook her head wearily, now convinced she wasn't alone, but also confident that she would not be leaving here today without Virginia's diary. As she stepped down to the last of the stairs, she reached for the electric light swinging nearby. The yellow light, though bright, couldn't reach the dark recesses of the cellar.

As she looked down to the floor, marbles scattered like cockroaches heading for cover. The sudden sound as they moved startled her, and she caught her throat in her hand, willing her heart to beat properly. Looking furtively to the shadows for the man-shape she dreaded, she made her way carefully to the back of the room, dark beyond description, to the box she'd seen in her dream.

There it was! She almost smiled as she hurried the last couple of steps and leaned down. The contents were old, so much older than she'd expected. The papers on the top were damp and smelled musty. It was an old basement smell.

Layer after layer, she peeled off papers and correspondence. She found the guest list for a party, the one she'd seen in her dream, and felt strangely euphoric. She also discovered the old recipe from Grandmama. It was a recipe for apple cobbler and was Grandmama's favorite.

Finally, she found what she'd come for: an old leather satchel, thin and small, that should be filled with legal documents of all kinds. With shaking hands, she tugged on the rusty clasp. It gave way easily and popped apart. Then she lifted the flap and peered inside. *Bingo!* She could see that it was filled with documents, yes, but also the edges of pages torn from a book—Virginia's diary!

Jessa was almost faint with relief. As badly as she wanted to read it, she wanted that much more to get out of the house. No way would she stay and read it here if she could be safely in her own apartment doing the same thing, but would she be able to escape?

She stood on shaky legs, clutching the satchel close to her chest, and inspected the length of stairs like a runner would contemplate the finish line. Could she make it? Was it possible?

She took a deep breath and forced her legs to move. At every pace, she found a box in her way, or a toy under her foot. Twice, she discovered her way blocked and had to retrace her steps. Every step back into the shadows made her bite back a scream.

Eventually, she reached the steps. Those, she took two at a time, until she reached the pantry. She shoved the Dutch oven away from the door and shut it forcefully. Heart pounding furiously, she leaned her back against the locked cellar door and tried to quiet her breathing. With a sense of elation, she allowed herself a small smile of satisfaction at the prize she still clutched to her breast.

The house silently watched her go. She felt it brood moodily, but at least there was no anger. Her eyes met the vacant stares of S. J. and Virginia from the portraits. As she watched, S. J.'s eyes seemed to take on an expectant look, but Virginia's appeared wide with relief. Carefully, she averted her own eyes, preferring to stare at the front door, and escape.

The purr of Mitch's car was so silent and soothing that Jessa could hear only the steady, quick pounding of her heart as she contemplated the contents of the little satchel. In there, she felt sure, were some of the answers she was looking for. Answers for questions she didn't even know to ask…

Before she got to her apartment, a light, steady rain began to fall. The dark day deepened its color, and though it was in the middle of the day, streetlights came on and houses glowed from the inside. Wearily, she trudged up the steps and let herself into her apartment.

As dark as it was, she didn't turn any lights on until she got to her bedroom. The single light on her nightstand gave the room its homey glow and she smiled in appreciation.

Then, sitting on her bed, she opened the satchel and spread its contents on her bedspread. *Oh lord! Would you look at that!* She gasped.

Between several sheets of paper, yellowed with age, a set of old cardboard photographs poked out. Photos were her passion, and besides being old and interesting, they looked to be in excellent shape… and valuable! She carefully pulled them the rest of the way out of the papers that had protected them for so long.

On top was one of a much younger S. J. and Virginia on what could have been their wedding day. It was a formal portrait, and the young couple wasn't smiling, but Jessa could immediately sense their happiness. One thing she knew about photos from so long ago was that the exposure time had been insanely long. She grinned. Virginia didn't look a day older than sixteen. S. J. looked well established, but probably wasn't more than twenty-five. She set it aside.

The next photograph was of Bristol House, though here it was only partially constructed. Jessa recognized the stonework around the veranda and the wooden beams that would soon be the tower that jutted from the upper floor. Grainy workmen dotted the grounds and she realized that not as much care went into this photo as in the wedding portrait. She flipped the photo over. In old, spidery handwriting was scrawled: *Bristol House as it was in early 1863.* There was some kind of emotion tied up in that simple statement, and Jessa wondered if it was taken before, but written after, whatever it was that had happened there. Yes, she decided firmly, something *did* happen there. She could feel it every time she entered the front door. Something awful had happened at Bristol House.

Picking up the first photo again, she flipped it over. She read: *S. J. and Virginia Hubert wedded July 16, 1857.* So they must've lived somewhere else and had son Joey, then in 1863 built Bristol House. Whatever had happened there, would have happened in the late summer or early fall of 1863.

Jessa set the photos aside to look at later. Separating the documents and newspaper articles from the rest, she picked up a sheaf of papers that had obviously been torn from a book, to examine them. Just as she expected, they were marked by dates with Virginia's distinctive handwriting. She settled comfortably on her bed to read the entries.

August 19, 1863

Vernon scares me. I fear for my safety as well as my son's. Little Joey is very impressionable, especially for a 5 year old. He soaks up everything Vernon says and I don't like it. Today Joey had something, a token that Vernon had given him, and when I asked him to see it, he refused me... his mother! I can't believe a man in good conscience would turn a little boy away from his mother. He said that Uncle Vernon told him "a real man needs to have some privacy from women". A man! Joey is only 5! I believe Vernon means to turn Joey away from me. Well, he will have a fight on his hands.

August 22, 1863

Last night I went into Joey's room to check on him; he's so sweet when he sleeps and I can forget the worries I carry around with me these days. But to my surprise, Joey was not in his bed. He wasn't even in his room! My first thought was that Vernon had kidnapped him and I was terrified. I turned to go downstairs and demand S. J. do something about it, but just as I turned from Joey's bed, I could see my son outside by the barn standing in his nightshirt. He was listening to something Vernon was saying, for I'm sure the shadowy figure in black was S. J.'s brother. Then, as I watched, Joey ran back for the house. I was so confused and frightened. Maybe it's wrong, but I can't depend on S. J. for help against his own brother and I need to take matters in my own hands. I haven't spoken to S. J. or to Joey about what happened and all is as if normal today. But I feel terrible inside and I have renewed fear.

August 28, 1863

I believe my son is becoming frightened of his Uncle Vernon. Vernon's behavior the last couple of days has been erratic and he swings from a very proper gentleman to a maniac. This morning Joey came in from playing outside and he had a red welt on his arm. I asked him where he got the welt; there are some older boys living down the street that can be quite rambunctious. But just as Joey was about to answer me, Vernon walked in and immediately Joey looked up at Vernon and he shut his mouth and not another word was uttered about the incident. I can't help but think Vernon was responsible, but I have no way of proving it, short of Joey telling me the truth, but the boy won't talk about it. I know he is afraid; he spent the rest of the afternoon only inches from my apron. What kind of boy would rather stay inside with his mother than go out and enjoy the sunshine?

Jessa shifted herself into a more comfortable position. She could feel Virginia's worry and fear. What was Vernon trying to accomplish by scaring Joey? Various scenarios ran through her head. None of them were good. She lifted the stack of photos from the bed and peered again at the wedding photo, wondering if Virginia had any idea what was in store for her. Had she had a sense of foreboding when she'd married into this family? Or had her love for S. J. overshadowed any doubts she might have had?

She slipped the wedding photo and the partially constructed Bristol House photo to the back of the bundle. As she set her eyes on the next photo, she sucked in her breath and dropped the entire stack to the bed. Then, cursing herself that she was startled so easily, she picked up the photo that had upset her. Though she'd never seen the face, she knew without a doubt that the man staring back at her, through years long gone, was Vernon Hubert.

CHAPTER TWENTY-ONE
THE TROUBLE WITH JOEY

He could have been a handsome man, but there was something unsettling in his eyes. They weren't just dark—they were piercingly black. In life, they no doubt had some color to them, but the old cardboard photo captured only the darkness and gave the man a hint of unpleasant depravity. Jessa could feel the emotion as she studied the photo.

She laid it carefully on the bed and reached for the next photo, but the disturbing stare continued to unnerve her, so she slipped it beneath the wedding photo. The next photo was a formal picture taken of S. J. and Virginia with a little boy sitting quietly on Virginia's lap. Assuming this was their son Joey, Jessa couldn't keep the smile from her face at his little expression. He didn't look more than three or four years old; holding still for such a long exposure would have tried the patience of many adults she knew. Little Joey was sweet-faced, but clearly unhappy as he remained still.

As she scanned the next two or three photos, it seemed to Jessa that Virginia was a woman after her own heart. She obviously loved photos, which were such a new fangled thing at that time. These were photos of Joey standing beside a wagon in which he'd piled rocks and a beloved stuffed bear; another of him smiling over his shoulder as he clung to the side of a wooden slatted fence; one more of him sitting proudly atop a horse. Virginia had to have spent a fortune for a photographer to capture these daily activities.

The next photo that Jessa picked up shocked her. It was little Joey, but there was a change in his exuberant demeanor. Sitting between his parents, he frowned up at the photographer in anger and frustration. His eyes were ringed with dark circles and his little body was bony with weight loss. Clothing covered his legs and arms, but there was a telltale bruise on his hand, peeking out from underneath his shirtsleeve. Jessa was beginning to suspect the boy suffered from Vernon's cruelty, and that pulling back more material might reveal more bruises. Both S. J. and Virginia looked unhappy.

It was the following picture that broke her heart. It was of Joey by himself, standing on the veranda of the newly finished Bristol House. The weight loss was astounding; the boy was nothing but skin and bones. The most terrifying thing about him, though, was the way his mouth was slack and his eyes were vacant of any emotion. This was a little boy with so much emotional trauma that just the image of it was unbearable.

Jessa dropped the picture beside the others. She couldn't normalize her anxious breathing, or her heart that was pounding painfully inside her chest. She knew, with agonizing certainty, that Vernon Hubert was responsible for Joey Hubert's heartbreaking condition.

She turned back to the diary and put a shaky finger on the next entry, trying to hold the papers still enough to read.

> September 1, 1863
> *Dear God!* Joey hasn't eaten for several days. He is nothing but bones and he sports more bruises than I can count. S. J. has finally ejected Vernon from our property, but I fear it's too late. Joey is terrified of his uncle, but because of his fear, goes willingly to him. I hear him cry at night, but my son will not tell me what is in his heart.

> September 2, 1863
> I cannot say how much I fear Vernon! He has ruined life for me and I will write immediately to my parents and tell them they mustn't come visit. I cannot offer them any explanation save for the fact that things are unsettled here. I

have almost given up any hope that they will be able to visit at all. I want to take Joey and run to my mother, but after what happened last night, I don't think it would be wise. Not only do I loathe leaving S. J. to the devices of his brother, but also now I cannot trust my son!

Jessa frowned as she let this information digest. She didn't realize she gripped the papers so tightly until a piece of the old stationery tore off in her fingers. She took a deep breath then riveted her gaze back to the writing:

Long after Joey should have been in bed, I was in the kitchen, checking to see that the crystal had been cleaned properly. Just as I was finished, and I was straightening the towels for drying, I heard a noise behind me. Quick as a wink, I turned to see Joey standing not three feet from where I stood. His face was red and puffy as if he had been crying, but his expression was mad… yes, mad as a lunatic! He had a long butcher knife in his hand; it was so big for him to wield, yet he held it steady as if he'd been taught how. I screamed in fright, but Joey didn't flinch. He came toward me, slashing that big knife out in front of him as if he wanted to cut me. Joey is a good-sized boy for his age, and I fear if he'd been any older, that would have been the end of me! But S. J. heard my screams and came running. Joey's strength was amazing, but we were able to wrestle the knife away from him. The things he was yelling, it was shameful and heartbreaking. Then, after a bit, when it was obvious to my son the knife was truly gone, he went limp and fainted. I carried him up to bed; he'd lost so much weight it was terrifying. I sat with him for a spell and he mumbled as if plagued by nightmares. Finally, he slept and I left. I wanted to speak to S. J. but my husband was indisposed. Well, he had emptied the brandy carafe!

Jessa sat back against her headboard and closed her eyes. How horrifying! Poor Virginia! Poor little Joey! S. J. was unable to cope, so he had gotten drunk to avoid what was happening right under his nose! Was it Vernon who taught Joey to hold the knife? Why would a little boy try to cut his mother?

Rain continued to patter against the bedroom window. It was still dark enough outside to be mistaken for late evening, and now the wind began to blow, causing tree branches to scrape against the glass. Jessa headed for the kitchen to make some coffee to ward off the chill of the day. As it brewed, she stared out of her kitchen window and watched the apartment courtyard fill with rainwater.

She was suddenly overcome with sadness, first for the little boy emotionally and physically abused so long ago by an insane uncle, and second because she unexpectedly missed Mitch's warm presence. She mused, miserably, that what had started as a simple snoop job had turned her whole world upside down. Never in her wildest fantasies would she have thought she'd be chasing phantoms and trying to solve a hundred and fifty year old mystery, as well as a fairly recent missing persons—or quite possibly a murder! These things were strangely related, and it was as if she would not be able to rest until these puzzles were solved.

Just as she had begun to turn away from the window, a dark bird flapped against the glass, startling her suddenly. She gasped and stepped back, recognizing as she did so, the dark robin with the blood red breast. Its head turned toward her, and Jessa could feel the intensity of the beady stare. It banged its beak against the glass so hard that she was afraid the glass would break.

As quickly as she could move, she whirled away from the counter and ran back to her bedroom. There, she pulled the window curtains shut and then curled up in a frightened ball on her bed. With the contents of the satchel spread across her bedspread, she squeezed her eyes tightly shut and tried to avoid the tears that threatened to pour from her eyes and throat.

It was noticeably later when Jessa woke. The rain had stopped, but she could hear the wind still howling outside. Hungry, she headed for the kitchen once again. The coffee she'd made earlier was cold in the pot, having turned itself off, so she dumped the contents down the sink and started over again.

A cup of coffee and bowl of soup later, Jessa finally returned to her room to finish reading Virginia's diary.

September 5, 1863

I have had to send for the physician to help me tend to Joey. He still doesn't eat much and his mood has deteriorated drastically. I caught him once in the wee hours of the morning leaving the house and I was so worried that I left the house myself to call for him. I couldn't find him anywhere, but when I went up to his room, he was already there fast asleep. I can only ascertain that he heard me and shimmied up the rose trellis and crawled into his window. I don't know what he was doing outside and when I asked him about it, all I got was a blank stare. My biggest fear is that he was meeting someone... perhaps Vernon, who has been banished from these premises. Still, I don't trust him and Joey isn't getting any better. Other than this one time, Joey has not been outside that I am aware of. If I catch him again, I shall insist that S. J. put bars on his window and a lock on his door!

September 9, 1863
Joey is bedridden now, as he has lost much strength due to his weight. He refuses to eat, but only drinks warm goat's milk and occasionally a cordial. The doctor can't find any reason for this illness and I suspect he won't! I think the cause of this is S. J.'s brother, Vernon. I am afraid to leave the house to go to church because I can't take Joey with me any longer. I don't trust Vernon to stay away and S. J. has not been himself and often locks himself in his study. My household is falling apart in front of my eyes and I have no power to do anything about it.

The next entry was dated nearly two weeks later. Tears filled Jessa's eyes as she read the handwriting that was hardly legible:

September 21, 1863
We buried my son today. I'm so sad I can hardly speak. I watched as his little body wasted away until there was almost nothing left to bury. God may punish me, but I hate Vernon Hubert, for I hold him to blame for Joey's death. That man had the everlasting gall to smile at me during the funeral. If I were a man, I would have killed him where he stood. My life is over.

September 25, 1863
Vernon will not leave us alone. He comes at

every hour of the day and night and yells up into our windows. The man is insane. He claims the money and house we have rightly, belong to him. S. J. and I have lost our son, and though I would trade all the money we have and the house to have him back, we have lost enough and will not lose our wealth, too. That man means to send us to the poorhouse, and I fear that is exactly what will happen.

September 29, 1863
God has granted us my most fervent wish. After a visit with the doctor, I have been told that I am pregnant again. I hardly know what to make of this news except that Vernon will not be part of this child's life. Oh, Joey would have loved to have had a younger brother or sister! Perhaps now that there will once again be an heir, Vernon will finally realize that his desire for the Hubert fortunes is out of his reach.

September 30, 1863
Vernon was found dead early this morning. He hung himself in the cellar of my home. He wrote a note, which was found in his breast pocket, that stated he would never leave this house. I suppose by killing himself here he thinks to stay. I shall have the cellar scrubbed from floor to ceiling and, God forgive me, I'm not sad to see Vernon gone.

October 10, 1863
I feel fear as the child within my womb grows. Good as promised, I feel Vernon's presence daily. Rarely an hour goes by without

something, a sound or an odd movement, distracting me. Sometimes I think I smell something awful, but S. J. thinks I am making up stories. I shall be on alert at all times. I still don't trust Vernon.

That was the last entry Jessa could find. She tried to understand what this meant: Vernon had threatened not to leave the house because he felt his inheritance was unjustly taken from him. Had he tried to turn Joey away from his parents in some warped manner that would allow him to assume the Hubert property? Could it be that he was still there trying to claim Bristol House?

Jessa returned the torn pages from the diary back to where they belonged. There were no other pages gone that she could see and she wondered why Virginia had not written anything else in it. She turned her attention to the newspaper articles folded neatly inside a large yellow envelope. As she had expected, there was a small obituary about Joseph Bristol Hubert. It was a small article with little actual information, but Jessa knew the heartbreaking story behind the death. Another obituary was about Vernon Tindle Hubert. There was no mention of his suicide; instead, it intimated he'd been the victim of an untimely accident.

Another article announced the birth of the second baby boy born to S. J. and Virginia. He was named Franklin Thomas Hubert. He weighed seven pounds, one ounce and was born February 23, 1864. This little boy would grow up to be the heir of the Hubert fortune and so continue the Hubert legacy.

Mitch's ancestor. Was he much like Mitch?

Jessa's phone danced to life with a song at odds with the somber mood inside her apartment. She grinned when she recognized Mitch's number on the caller ID. "Hey!" she breathed, smiling happily.

"Hey yourself, gorgeous!" Though she knew he

couldn't see her face, she blushed furiously at the endearment. Then he continued, "I'm almost at Mother's house. Taxi is slow. Traffic is slow. How are you holding up?"

She shrugged, then said aloud, "Good. I found Virginia's diary."

"What?" he questioned in surprise. "I thought you were looking for Maria's diary. Don't you already have Virginia's?"

"There were some pages gone. I found them in the cellar along with some photos and old newspaper articles. It's a very sad story." She told him what Virginia had written, things he hadn't known about his family. He was quiet and thoughtful as he listened. "I wonder how much of this was known, even at the time. Does your mother know?"

"Doubt it," he rejected that suggestion, "those things you found have been buried in that cellar for… I don't know how long. And there's no way Mother would have gone looking. But I'll ask her."

Jessa told him her theory about Vernon still trying to obtain the house. She was certain he'd think she was out of her mind, but he appeared to be keeping his mind open and taking her thoughts seriously. Then he asked, "What now?"

"I think this is only part of the story, Mitch. It tells us what kind of person Vernon was… hateful and vindictive. He cared nothing for anything but his own skin. Now we have to figure out how Maria fit into this. What was the connection? What did she have that he needed?"

Mitch was quiet for a moment, then spoke carefully, "For that matter, we have to consider what is the connection with you? What do you have that he needs? Why are you important to him, because it's clear to me that you are involved up to your eyeballs."

Jessa tried to laugh, but it sounded like a strangled cry. "I know what I have to do. I just don't know if I have the guts to do it."

"What's that?" Jessa could feel the tension in his

words.

"I have to find Maria's diary."

SHE WAS SO NERVOUS she couldn't think straight. She wished she'd waited for another day to go back to Bristol House, but she didn't. She was too anxious to look for Maria's diary. Normally, at this time of day, it would still have been light, but there was little light left in the day, and little cheer in the dark.

Mitch was not pleased with her. He had asked, nicely, if she would wait and return to Bristol House when he was back in town. Just a couple of days away, he said, but Maria's plight was weighing heavily on her mind. A couple of days in fear and terror would seem like an eternity. Or longer. Fear didn't seem to use the same rules about time as pleasure did.

For the time being, she was thankful that he was in Florida taking care of business with his parents. She had his car to use and a key to the house. What else could she ask for?

With a slight amount of guilt, she thought suddenly about David and Norma Escher. She suspected Norma would be sitting right next to her phone in hopes that she would get a phone call or visit from Jessa. Nevertheless, Jessa couldn't face the other woman yet... not without more solid information. Certainly she could not even begin to explain where Maria was and what she was doing. Norma would just have to wait until Jessa could explain this to herself; only then she would she be able to explain it to Norma.

Standing silently, alone, on the veranda, Jessa had to use both hands to steady the huge key as she inserted it into the old-fashioned lock on Bristol House's front door. As usual, the tumblers clicked easily and the door opened with a faint creak. She stepped quickly in and shut the door behind her.

She stood still just inside the front door, her gaze sweeping the darkened room. She had the uneasy feeling she wasn't alone, yet she could see no one. A quick peek down at her fingertips quelled the sudden notion that the little shadow monsters surrounded her, but still…

Then, silent and faded as an old movie reel, she could see the wavering figure of a heavy-set man, dressed all in black, flicker into being. Had she been struck with the notion, she could have reached out and touched him.

CHAPTER TWENTY-TWO
HIDDEN

Suddenly the whole world tilted sideways: gravity flowed one way and darkness gathered in the other. Jessa could hear her breath as it ebbed and flowed in and out of her lungs, but she felt nothing as she tried to make sense of what was happening. Between breaths, her heart beat a heavy, erratic rhythm. Her vision, which had darkened, finally began to clear, and she felt the tips of her fingers tingle as if they had fallen asleep.

When the world finally straightened, Jessa found herself on the floor. Realizing she must have fainted, she pushed herself shakily to her feet to get her bearings. The apparition, looking on in malicious amusement, was still there, only a few feet from where she had fallen.

Her mind reeled. Whereas Maria had looked solid, so life-like and detailed, Vernon's likeness had all the qualities of the old photograph she'd been studying only hours before. Was this because it was the only picture in her mind she had of him? Was he, indeed, a flight of fancy? A real ghost? Or just a ghostly image?

She brooded and frowned. What now? After all this time of trying to get a little information, she was still cut short at every turn—and she was getting pretty damn tired of it!

It wasn't clear to her where, exactly, she needed to look for Maria's diary, but she sure as hell wasn't going to let a see-through man stop her from looking. Though he was standing between her and the second floor where all the bedrooms were, she decided on an impulse that she'd go *through* him if necessary.

She gathered a deep breath and kept her eyes on the stair railing. Bracing herself, she meant to push her shoulder into the old man's belly and shove him aside. In reality, she breezed straight to the stairway, slipping through the specter as if he was no more substantial than mist. There was an audible gasp of surprise, but she didn't know if it came from her or from him.

She exhaled. With the breath fully purged, another inhale nearly choked her when she found herself not on the stairway, but surrounded by the tall pines of a night-blackened forest. Ahead, faintly shimmering in the distance, she could see the glow of the waning daylight through an upstairs window.

The distance between her and the light was lengthening as she stood staring with disbelief and fright. She began to jog without taking her eyes away from the second floor. The forest was damp, and the ground was covered with a heavy blanket of dead pine needles, masking the sounds of her steps. She struggled as the wet, marshy ground sucked at her sneakers, causing her to sink farther and farther into the forest floor.

Black limbs, coated in sticky pinesap, reached out to tangle in her jacket and jeans as she brushed by the trees. Unseen voices, disjointed and garbled, flitted through the breeze around her head and feet, swirling angrily to arrest her attention from her destination.

Strain filled her eyes with tears as she kept them trained hungrily on the light. Finally, her attention was broken when strange, wet fingers slipped inside the ankle of her jeans and began a caressing journey up her calf. She stumbled and whirled, stepping her feet high to shake off the offending fingers, and looked down in time to see a decaying, skeletal hand sink back into the mushy, inky pine floor.

She squealed and pranced away from the hidden hand. As she backed up against a tree, the pinesap oozed onto the back of her jacket, and for a moment, Jessa was stuck tight. She strained away from the tree, but just as she was about to discard the jacket, she came loose with a sick, slurping sound. She glanced hastily back to where the hand had disappeared and was alarmed to see the fingers break the surface of the spongy floor and beckon to her.

Quickly, she turned away from the withering hand and ran blindly, pushing away branches filled with curious pine needles that would have snatched pieces of her clothes. As she looked up at the light, it disappeared, throwing her into sudden darkness, before reappearing farther away. Her heart beat in frantic fury as she ran for this new light, hoping beyond words that this pallid beam still came from the upstairs window.

Her steps grew heavy and slow as she approached the light. Jessa could just make out the doorframe at the top of the stairs and she grunted with tremendous exertion at each stride. A voice coughed near her ear, making her flinch away from the sound, removing her attention from the doorway. Then the light moved slightly farther off. More tears filled her eyes, though now from frustration. She now knew the way out was to concentrate on her destination, but there was too much in this place that would keep her here.

Heavy, black shadows rolled in like mist on each side of her. With her eyes on the door, she couldn't afford to look away from the light, but the shadows pressed in on her as insistent friends that annoyingly wanted to steer her away from what she knew was right. They teased her and coaxed her, demanded and enticed. They slipped misty, wet arms around her waist and pulled. They yanked playfully at her hair and stuck their cold fingers in her ears. All the while, Jessa's tears spilled from her eyes as she kept a tight reign on the sobs that screamed inside her chest.

She finally reached the door, pulling herself through it with a painfully tight squeeze. Panting with the effort, she leaned her back against the doorframe and looked hungrily as the last dregs of daylight shifted out of view through the window. In the stairwell, dark now with the coming night, she could hear the disappointed "Ooooooooh!" as the shadows and voices shifted away from her. Not trusting them to stay on their side of the door, she hurried into the hallway.

She didn't dare look back over her shoulder, but as she stomped through the hallway and wiped the tears from her cheeks, she felt as if she'd been lingering around an open-air crematorium. The foul stench that clung to her clothes like a smoky haze burned her throat and sinuses, forcing her to stop and gag before she could move on. She was irritated at this show of strength, so with some effort, she kept a tight grip on her anger, waxing it until it was a firm state in her mind. It was her only defense against the terror that would otherwise have overwhelmed her.

Her best plan would be to hurry before Vernon could follow her here. Starting in the master bedroom, a quick glance told her there was no real place to look. The room was empty except for a small, ornate canopied bed and an equally small chest of drawers that sported a pink glass lamp. Before starting her search, she flipped the switch for the lamp, thankful the house had been converted to electricity long ago, and hoped that the light would dispel some of the gloom. She couldn't resist one quick glance at the door to assure herself she was still alone.

Of course she was, that she could see. Finally, with all the grit that she could muster, she turned her attention to the chest of drawers. There was so little to go on from the information Maria had tried to give to her: *bureau... back... floor...* Not much information at all, but the bureau was the logical place to start.

Each of the drawers was empty. Though this was the master, no one lived in this room. All this furniture was for show, but just for good measure, she tipped the chest back slightly and looked under it to see if anything had been fastened to the bottom. Nothing. Next, she examined the small bed and the opening of the fireplace. From what she could see, there was nothing unusual or any place to hide anything as large as a diary. Her heart, her breath, her shaking fingers kept up a frantic tempo of urgency as she searched.

She felt along the walls from the floorboards to as high

as she could reach. Still nothing: no secret cubbyholes, no safes behind pictures, no loose brick or floorboard that would indicate a hiding place.

Leaving the light on in the master, she stepped out in the hallway to examine the next bedroom on the floor. Just as she'd seen in the master, there was a tiny bureau and a day bed and nothing else. This was a very small room; probably at one time it had been a nursery due to the size and proximity to the master. However, this room, like the master, yielded nothing, and Jessa could feel the disappointment weigh heavily on her.

Bureau... back... floor... bureau... back... floor... This house had three floors, but it was unlikely Maria would have used the third floor to hide a diary that she was keeping a secret from Mitch. Again, it seemed to Jessa, doubtful that somewhere on the first floor would be a likely hiding place; tourists and tour guides were bound to be anywhere. Logically, the second floor had to be the right one. Bureau, that was obvious. Only, which one? Each bedroom had a bureau.

Before she could enter the next bedroom across the hall, Jessa stopped in her tracks, suddenly assaulted with a memory-triggered thought: she had seen/felt what she assumed was the ghost of Vernon Hubert in the bedroom where she found Virginia's diary. If Virginia's diary was in that room, then why not Maria's? If Jessa had found and read Virginia's diary there, then why couldn't she assume Maria had done the exact same thing?

Suddenly the door at the end of the hallway slammed shut, demanding her attention. She was not aware that it had been open, but as soon as her eyes were riveted to the small bedroom at the far end, the door slowly opened invitingly. It was the same room she'd decided to investigate next, so she slowly walked that way, trying to convince herself that it was Maria, not Vernon, who summoned her.

At the end of the hallway, Jessa reached in and flipped

on the light before she entered the little room. She knew it was only cosmetic; no light would stop a ghost if it was inclined to do some mischief, but it made her feel better and it was, after all, quite dark, now, inside the house.

A faintest hint of rotten meat pervaded the room. It wasn't strong enough to be alarming, but just the same, Jessa was wary as she ignored the box-filled closet and went straight to the bureau. Just like the last two rooms she'd examined, these drawers were also empty. She sighed in frustration and leaned her back against it as she examined the rest of the room for signs of a hiding hole.

She could see nothing but the stacks of papers within the boxes inside the closet. She didn't want to go there again, but her determination to find the diary, if it existed at all, overshadowed her fear of the ghost of Vernon Hubert. Then on an impulse, she tipped back the bureau to examine its underside for any signs that something was or had been attached to it. Again, she came up empty-handed.

Then, she thought: if I really wanted to hide something, it would have to be in a place easy to get to, but not easy to find. Easy to write… and easy to run from… easy come… easy go…

One by one, starting at the top, she pulled the drawer out and away from the base and set it gently on the wooden floor. She ran her hands on all sides of it but found nothing unusual about it at all. Leaving it there, she pulled the second drawer out and examined it also. It, too, was just a drawer.

But when she pulled out the third drawer, she immediately gasped in delight. Such a good match that it would have been almost undetectable to the casual eye, someone had fitted a false back at the end of this drawer, leaving a two-inch space where something, like a diary, could be hidden from anyone who cared to look, yet it would be easy to get to and easy to hide.

She tipped the drawer upside down and was rewarded with a small "thunk". There, to her infinite satisfaction, was a small, well-used journal. Jessa pulled the diary close to her chest as if it were a trophy won. She was so dizzy with relief that she had to wait for the world to settle before she could return the drawers to the bureau and leave.

However, leaving would prove to be more difficult than she had anticipated. As she turned off the last of the upper floor's electric lights, she hastily started for the steps with her eyes intently on the hall at the end of the stairway. Before she reached the stairs, though, the stench she now associated with the appearance of the specters that frequented this house, almost knocked her breath away with its potency.

She was immediately on guard. Her eyes twitched this way and that in an effort to locate the source. He was there! Standing at the top of the steps, between her and the safety of the outside, was Vernon Hubert. He wore the black, three-piece suit she'd seen in the photo from Mitch's kitchen. His countenance was stern, angry, and if he'd had substance, he might have stomped his feet in rage.

For a panicked moment, Jessa was afraid he would grasp her hand and then his own throat to talk to her the way Maria had done. Before that thought was fully matured, though, he spoke in a whispery voice, no more substantial than the wind, but full of rage and anger: *"Do not come back!"*

Jessa blanched at the fury in those soft words. Never had she wished more than now that she had *not* come back. She put her fist against her mouth and swallowed a scream that would have filled the room.

Again, the eyes of the ghost blazed, first appearing like dark holes, then glowing red... back and forth... black and red. *"Mine!"* he roared.

But Jessa's own anger was a growing seed inside her. This was Mitch's house. Vernon Hubert was dead! Without conscious decision, her sarcasm, like a weapon, came thundering to the surface. "Well, if this is *your* place, why do *I* have the key?" She pulled the big skeleton key from her jeans pocket and dangled it in front of him just out of his reach.

The fury on Vernon's face would have been comical had Jessa not been so mortified at what she was doing. Her heart crashed inside her chest until she was afraid it would crawl out of her throat and run away. The old man scowled and his eyes turned black, his arms lifted, and a great cyclonic wind whirled around them, whipping Jessa's short hair around her face. She held tight to the diary and key, fearing they would be lost in the maelstrom. The more afraid she became, the harder the wind circled around her. As it whirled ever faster, bits and pieces of the forest became visible. She was terrified of being thrown into the blackened forest with no light to guide her to the safety of the parlor.

In spite of this, her own anger had not died. With great effort, she pocketed the key and lowered her head and shoulders against the furor. Then she headed directly for Vernon.

The rot-stench clung to her like overgrown ivy, and though it was more difficult this time, she managed to mow a path through him to finally reach the steps. He bellowed in rage and the wind picked up its furious pace. Forest and stairs swirled in a dizzying, twisting tunnel. Praying to hit the stairs and not the spongy floor of wet pine needles, she continued into the wind. At last, with the steps firmly under her feet, she ran down two steps at a time, hesitating only long enough to steal a glance over her shoulder to see Vernon thrashing himself against the wall on one side of the hall to the other and back again. His voice, though still carried on the wind, boomed and crashed unintelligibly.

Outside, the darkness was eerily quiet. The house, tonight, would keep its secrets. Its tormentor might still be in the grip of his own storm, but it did not spill out into the night.

JESSA FOUGHT THE RAGGED EDGES of sleep as she wove her way through the streets of Madison. The dark evening turned even darker as it grew old, but the rain that blew in cleaned and shined the streets and cars, bouncing lights and colors on everything it touched. This had been an eventful day; she was dead tired.

As she entered her apartment, she turned on every light she passed until the rooms were as bright as mid-summer. The lights seemed to ward off the chill, as well as keeping the night firmly away from her.

Later, as she showered, she felt the anticipation of discovering the secrets of Maria's diary. Tired or not, there was no way she would be able to wait until morning to start reading what Maria had written. It wasn't until she'd toweled her hair and body dry that she wondered: what if this isn't Maria's diary? It's true, she hadn't looked inside the book, but it was a journal, and how many people would have hidden their journal there in that house? Tamping down her misgivings, she pulled away the elastic binding that kept the book shut and opened it carefully to the first page.

The journal was incredibly organized and written in exceptionally neat handwriting. Across the top of the introductory page was written: Maria Rose Escher, with the date. This journal had been conceived only months before she'd disappeared. Each entry was dated, and though these were not the dates Jessa was particularly interested in, she decided to peruse them to discover what might have led up to the events that took her life.

With only the lights in her bedroom remaining on, a soft music station played soothingly in the background. A hot cup of cocoa warmed her hand as she made herself comfortable on her bed, leaning contentedly against the headboard. The journal rested open on the first page and Jessa began to read:

Dear Journal,

I am not much of a writer, and I don't feel like writing either. I'm more of a talker. No offense, please. I am talking to you like a friend because I think that is the only way I will be able to continue this journey of mine. It's a journey I feel I must take.

I have been plagued my whole life with thoughts and feelings that I don't think are normal. The way my brain works, well, it is disturbing to say the least. I had gone to see my family doctor and he put me on some antidepressants, but they didn't do anything but make me want to eat chocolate all the time. That sucked. Frankly, he tried several different ones, but nothing changed the way I felt. Then he gave me the name of a psychiatrist he knew. And I thought: oh great, he thinks I'm a nut!

But, I have to say, Doctor P, who I will now begin to address as DP, is wonderful! She doesn't think I'm a nut, I guess, or else she thinks I'm worth rescuing because she keeps telling me that I'm making progress. Today she suggested I start this journal because by writing down what I'm feeling, I might be able to make sense of my strange thoughts.

I sincerely hope, Journal, I will not continue to be crazy. It's just that with every day that goes by, my deepest wish is to understand and talk to the people who have come before me and who make me who I am. The thing is, the ones I most want to talk to... are dead.

Jessa sucked in a deep breath as she tried to understand Maria's strange passion. Could Maria actually be crazy, or was this something that many people dealt with? Was it possible to talk to the dead like a friend? Even with these questions burning in her brain, she had to admit that there were many things that had happened to her the last few weeks that she would never have believed a month before. Despite the hot cocoa and the warm blankets around her, she shivered.

Like the seductive song of a siren, Jessa had no choice but to read on. Maria, it turned out, was very good... and very bad.

CHAPTER TWENTY-THREE
DEAR JOURNAL

Dear Journal,

So many things are happening to me that sometimes I want to scream. These longings and desires I have to reach out to my ancestors are becoming unbearable. I know exactly what has put these ideas into my head: my mother! Your grandmother this... your great Aunt Nettie that... She makes me want to talk to them; they seem so wise.

Sometimes I think I'll just burst if I don't get to ask them questions. It's almost as if, with their guidance, my own life will go much more smoothly. Today, when I was visiting with DP, she suggested that maybe I could talk to them. Of course, I was skeptical, but interested. She thought if Mother had photos or a diary or even stories about them that it would help me with my life to see how they led theirs. I thought it was a very good idea... oh, how I wish I could just ask them some questions.

***

Mother was just full of information! I was so excited. Besides Aunt Nettie and Grandmother, I've discovered a whole set of relatives that just beg to be part of my life. Mother knew a lot about them, and she and I had a really nice chat. There were pictures and everything! Oh, the second and third cousins, great-aunts and uncles, who were actually friends, distantly related, at one time or another. This one picture of Aunt Nettie, though, had her eyes so lively and bright that I am quite sure she was looking through the ages right into my eyes. I know we have a perfect understanding. Oh, how I wish I could meet her!

Almost a week has gone by since I've seen DP. I can hardly wait to see her again. She'll be so excited for me, and when I show her the pictures, she'll understand why I've needed these people in my life for just ages. All my energy is aimed at these people and even though I know they're dead, they aren't really. Not to me!

***

Oh I forgot, Mitch proposed to me the other day. I've always known he was going to. It was romantic, though I would have said yes even if he proposed while I was bathing. I will make a good wife and he will make a good husband. Mother and I have most of the plans done, as we have been expecting this day for most of my life. Now we have to set the date. I'll ask Mother what she thinks. But I really would love to talk to Aunt Nettie. Aunt Nettie would know when the right time would be; I just know she would.

Jessa stopped for a moment, wondering why Maria would not have consulted Mitch for an appropriate day to get married. Wasn't it his wedding, too? She was amazed that the other woman would be so energized about her dead ancestors, yet almost forget about her wedding in the real world. Then, Maria's mood changed drastically:

DP makes me so mad I could spit! At first she was happy I'd found some of my ancestors. I showed her the pictures and told her the stories and she was really pleased... at first. But she just doesn't understand. I told her my goal was to actually talk to Aunt Nettie. Then she smiled and was terribly condescending when I told her that. I don't think she believes me! She talked to me about them being dead and all... doesn't she think I know that? But it doesn't seem right to me that that should stop me. There must be a way. And let me tell you, Journal, when I want something, I usually get it. I will not take <u>no</u> for an answer.

***

I have just had some information that is so exciting! First, Journal, I have to say that Mitch doesn't know I've been writing. It isn't that he'd care so much as I don't think he'd understand. Actually, I know he wouldn't understand. I told him about my ancestor obsession years ago and he thought I was crazy then. So I haven't said anything about it since. Besides, I want to keep this to myself for a little bit longer, then if it works, I'll tell him about it, and we can both explore our pasts together. Ok, here it is: I just met someone, who knows someone, whose first cousin goes to a psychic medium who performs séances for people who want to talk the their dearly departed. Yes, I know it sounds a little crazy, but what if... what if I really get to speak to Aunt Nettie? I know she'll help me make decisions about my life that will make everything better.

I love Mitch, I really do! Jessa paused for a moment, reflecting how odd this statement seemed. *I want to make him proud. I want to be a good wife. We look good together. That's what Mother tells me. I just wish that he'd been willing to move to Birmingham to be with me instead of me moving back to Wisconsin. It's so cold here.*

***

Since I moved in with Mitch, I have had to find another psychic medium. The first one didn't work out so well. It was a young man out to make a buck, I suspect. But I have new information that will hopefully bring about better results. Birmingham seems so far away, and though I'll miss it, I can see so much possibility here. There is a whole network of people who believe in necromancy just as I do. In fact, Wisconsin is just infested with ghosts, they say. Is it the area that makes it easier to talk to the old relatives? I don't know, but I look forward to talking to Aunt Nettie. Anyway, this new woman is coming by today at two. Her name is Madeline Hester. I hope she's good, because she's costing me a lot of money. Well, she's costing Mitch a lot of money. It's our money, right?

***

Yesterday was my first meeting with Madeline. She was very nice and a lot younger than I imagined. Still, she is old. Maybe fifty. I wanted to get started right away, but she said she had to have a round table. When I asked her why, she just said that it made the spirits of the ancestors easier to contact, so before we actually get started, I have to find a round table. I think I'll get a small one. She wanted at least three people to attend the séance, but I told her I wouldn't be asking Mitch just yet. I don't think she was too happy about it, but who's paying her anyway? Me! She said she'd come back on Friday. That's two days away, but I guess that will have to do. I hope Aunt Nettie isn't busy. I sure would like to talk to her.

I missed my appointment with DP. I feel really bad about it, but I've been so busy setting up this meeting with Madeline that DP just slipped my mind. Oh well, I'm sure people do that all the time. I'll make the appointment next time. Wow, she'll freak when I tell her what I've done!

***

Cool, Madeline was awesome! We closed all the drapes in the parlor and she made me light three candles and put them in a certain arrangement. She also had me put some fragrant potpourri in a bowl on the table, a fresh slice of cake on a plate for an offering, and then we held hands and began to concentrate. I can't believe it; I'm shaking just thinking about it! Aunt Nettie came through just as clear as a bell! I had all kinds of questions to ask her, but by the time we spoke the initial chants and asked for an audience, the time had gotten away and I only had a little left to actually talk. But I'm ecstatic with the results. I think I'll have Madeline over for another session soon. I haven't said anything to Mitch, but he's got so much money, why would he care? He'll never know. Should I tell DP? I wonder what she'd say…

***

We set the date for June 4th. Mother was not too happy with it as she and Father had planned on a cruise, but Aunt Nettie said the 4th and so I'm going with that. After all, she has all the years of living as experience and she is so wise. Mitch said he didn't care. He doesn't seem to care about anything but his political meetings. I guess that's the life of a politician's wife.

I forgot another appointment with DP, but I have a hard time worrying about that. I don't think she'd believe that Madeline is a real psychic medium. But there is so much going on that I can't explain. Besides, Madeline doesn't doubt what I'm trying to do even if DP does. She's very encouraging. I hope Mitch will be when he finds out. I've spent a terrible sum of money on this endeavor, but if he loves me, he'd want to see me happy. Right?

***

I dumped DP. I know that sounds harsh but when I talked to her briefly on the phone, she discouraged me from seeing Madeline. DP called her a quack. But as far as I can see, she's done me more good than going to a counselor, so that is my decision. I've had Madeline back a couple of times since I last journaled, and I have discovered ancestors I knew nothing about wanting to talk to me. I asked Mother about them, as I'd never heard of them, and to my astonishment, they're real! Let's see: I've met Janice, who was a distant cousin that was killed in a car crash when she was twenty; Beatrice, who is Nettie's youngest sister; and a sweet, young man named Aaron. I will see Madeline again soon. I can hardly wait!

***

I'm sorry it's been more than two months since I last wrote, but things here have just been terrific. I have gotten to speak to Aunt Nettie several times, and she knows the most wonderful things. Some things I ask her, well, they are of a personal nature and it quite embarrasses me to have Madeline Hester listen in to all my insecurities, but I don't think she minds, especially considering all the money I'm paying her. Mitch hasn't noticed yet, that I'm aware of, but I suppose it's only a matter of time. After all, he is the one who oversees the bookkeeping. But why would he care? He has lots of money and I'm the one who he has chosen to help spend it. Still, it would be easier on my conscience if he knew. Speaking of Mitch, the wedding plans are almost finished. Mother and I laugh sometimes because these are plans that have been in the works for so long that all we needed was a groom who could afford me! Ha! Anyway, Mitch is a lucky guy. And I'm a lucky girl. We were made for each other.

***

Well, damn! Mitch found out how much money I was spending on having Madeline out to the house so much. He was really furious at first, but it didn't take long to change his mind. That's why I'm here, right? To make him happy? And I know just what to do to ease his... mind! Besides, he needs a wife who will be able to present herself as an asset for him. That's why I had to spend all that time in Birmingham. Charm schools are not as outdated as you might think. Must go, Journal. Madeline should be here any time, and Mitch just left the house. I can't wait to talk to Aunt Nettie!

***

Tonight as I sat at the table, I felt so nervous. Looking around the dark room I felt as if something was different. Only three candles lit the room, as usual, but it was also darker since it was nighttime. Madeline was holding my hand so tightly that I was afraid she would cut off the blood circulation, but I just closed my eyes and mumbled the words she'd taught me. My heart was pumping so loudly that I could hear nothing else. I know I was grinning like a fool. But it wasn't Aunt Nettie who tried to get through. It was someone else. Someone I didn't know. I was thrilled! Who wanted to meet me? Madeline didn't say right off who it was, but she did say it was a man. I had to laugh; I always have trouble keeping men away. I guess they like the way I look. Anyway, I still don't know who the man was, but I'm terribly excited to meet him. I told Madeline she must come next week. I don't think I could wait two weeks!

***

I have been doing plenty of homework. My sessions have been going so well, and I've grown to love dear old Aunt Nettie. But I can't help but be intrigued by the man who tried to get through to me. Madeline says he has been near a time or two since then, but has never tried to make contact with us again. It made me wonder: who is he and why me? Then I thought... what if this wasn't my ancestor, but Mitch's? The idea of it sent thrills up and down my spine. How awesome would it be to present Mitch with one of his ancestors? So I asked his mother if he had any male ancestors with strong personalities, and she didn't really know much (or wasn't willing to say), so I dug a little. It seems that the original owner of the house had a brother who, as it turned out, was quite naughty. The man's name was Vernon, so when Madeline comes next time, I'll ask her to ask for Vernon and see if that gets any results. I'm so excited! I know this will help my relationship with Mitch. Sometimes, though we've known each other for more years than I can remember... sometimes it seems like we have nothing in common.

***

I love Mitch, I really do! That said; I hope he remembers that when I introduce him to his very own predecessor!! I had the feeling that tonight would be my lucky night. Everything went as planned. Every cent I've spent has been worth it. Aunt Nettie was great, but to have ancestors on both sides of our family to draw strength from will bind us together like nothing else will! So instead of asking for Aunt Nettie, I asked if Vernon would please come to see me. I nearly fainted when I heard the door open and the faint steps that surely belonged to him. And then, suddenly, there he was... wavering before me like a dream. I wanted to reach out and touch him, but I was way too afraid. I don't think

Madeline had really believed it could happen. I couldn't help but smile at her triumphantly. He was there only a few seconds. I will find him again and then I hope to convince him to stay longer. We can be such great friends. He looked so strong and vital. I know he has lots of things to teach me. Finally, I will be able to understand the past to get the edge on my future. My future with Mitch is now secure.

***

Madeline comes tonight! Yay! I told her not to come to the door until Mitch's car is gone.

***

Good news and bad news. Bad first: Aunt Nettie didn't show up tonight, and I'm very disappointed because I wanted to show her the fabric for the gift table. I can't decide on eggshell white or antique white, linen or silk crepe. I'll wait and ask her another time, I guess. But now good news: Vernon showed up and, wow, he's kind of scary. But so full of life, pardon the expression. He was so realistic that Madeline looked truly frightened. Even though I was also, it would do no good to let her see that in me. That is something that a good politician's wife will need to remember: never show fear! Anyway, he came through an invisible door that, I swear to you, sounded as if it had rusty hinges. He laughed loudly when he looked around the room, but when he did that, I got the feeling that he knew the house intimately. He touched his own chest and laughed again as if he was surprised how solid he felt. It was almost as if he had won a prize or a game. Funny. "You seek me and I have come," his voice spoke inside my head. Honestly, it almost seemed like a threat, but I'm sure he didn't mean it like that. "I am not a puppet for you to command. Your beauty does not sway me. But you have invited me here and now that I have come, I will do as I wish… as will you." Very ominous, but only moments later, he was gone again. I don't think he meant to go so quickly. I'm sure there are many rules on both sides of life that must be followed.

***

The strangest thing happened today. Madeline was here for our afternoon appointment, and we were able to call up Vernon again. I've almost given up on Aunt Nettie, as I haven't seen her for ages. If I didn't know better, I'd think she was afraid of Vernon. Anyway, it's obvious to me that Madeline is afraid of him because the way he came barreling through the door today made her shake in her chair. He seemed somehow more solid than he really should. If it weren't for his eyes, I'd think he was just a nice old man, but his eyes are particularly scary. As soon as he was here, he pointed his finger right at me and said, "This is my house. Leave it at once." Well, Madeline had enough of his attitude and she sent him back. That's what she thought she did. I knew better. I could still feel his presence. But I didn't say anything because I was curious. And when Madeline left a few minutes later, I relit the candles and said, "Vernon, are you still here?" I almost fainted when he answered me. Then he showed up again! So I said, "We can be such good friends, can't we?" and then all he did was laugh. I didn't particularly care for the way he laughed, but I'm willing to give him the benefit of the doubt. So when I asked him what it was like on the other side, he just laughed again and said the house was his and that he wasn't going to leave it. I feel sorry for him. Poor man thinks the house belongs to him when it belongs to Mitch and soon, me, too. Well, I'll invite him back and maybe if he spends some time here with me, he'll be good with that. Oh, I can't wait for him to meet Mitch! (and oh my god what is that awful smell?)

CHAPTER TWENTY-FOUR
MARIA'S MADNESS

Dear Journal,

The wedding is two months away, and my life is falling apart. I've been having some conversations with Vernon without Madeline's attendance. At first this was great; it saved me a ton of money. Madeline had told me once that no soul from the other side had power over anyone from this side. I'm glad, but Madeline was very upset about my dabbling alone, not because of the money, she said, but because now she says it is risky. Seriously, I couldn't imagine what she meant. But I think I'm beginning to see. I wanted to talk to Vernon again so I tried to find him on my own. Then a faint whiff of decay wafted across the room. I was tense with terror, and the bright sunlight was abruptly gone. A thin crack of lightning splintered across the sky just outside the window. I knew I wasn't alone any longer. I felt sick at my stomach and I was afraid I was going to throw up; the stench was so harsh. I ran upstairs to mist some body spray on a cloth, and then as I held it to my nose, I breathed the faint scent of the lilac water I'd sprayed on it. It helped to mask the stink, but not entirely, not nearly enough. But it was better. The idea today was to understand why Vernon looked so solid and Aunt Nettie wasn't any more substantial than a watercolor. He never really answered my questions, but I can't actually tell how much of what I say he understands. He looks very determined about something. Finally, I was able to understand something about a key that he had made before he died. I think this key was supposed to allow him to enter this world of the living, but he couldn't find the door. I think I'll take a break from Madeline's séances for a bit, and I don't feel like trying it alone again. I've had just about all I need for a while. Besides, there are wedding things to buy…

***

Jessa sat back and closed her eyes. The contents of Maria's journal set her mind and heart to racing. The poor girl was troubled. Was she insane or did these things truly happen to her? Just as that thought nestled into her brain, she realized that the same could be said of her! If Maria was insane, so was she. If Maria was truly experiencing these things, then so was she!

Jessa looked at the closed journal for a moment, noted where her finger held her place and decided she didn't have time to read each page like she wanted to. If she were to discover what happened to the other woman, she'd have to search for important passages.

***

Oh dear God, my hands are shaking! I haven't called Madeline for nearly two weeks and it has been quite peaceful. I miss Aunt Nettie, and though it would really be nice to chat with her, I don't want to risk calling up Vernon. But tonight while I was soaking in a bubble bath, I heard the bathroom doorknob jiggle. I thought Mitch wanted to join me. I said, "Come in," but when the door opened, it wasn't Mitch who stood there: it was Vernon. I was embarrassed and mortified; I screamed and splattered soapy water everywhere, and moments later, Mitch was there. He tried to soothe me, but I was too terrified to be placated. Vernon was gone, at least from my bathroom, but I didn't know how gone he was. I wanted to talk to Mitch, to explain what had frightened me so, but because I was so incoherent, I don't think he believed me. I don't blame him at all. Now I have a true mystery: was Vernon serious about a key? Can he open the Door without consent?

***

Skimming the next few pages, Jessa put into place what must have been going through Maria's mind. Maria hadn't known anything about Vernon, or what had happened to him, so that he'd remain between the life and death worlds. There was only one thing she was completely clear about: ever since she and Madeline had opened the door, Vernon wouldn't stay away. In the beginning, Maria was thrilled, but the excitement had worn thin with each subsequent visit. Not only had the ghostly specter felt as if the house was his, he'd also treated Maria as if she was an intruder. Part of Maria had obviously been intrigued with him, but when he wasn't there, it seemed she often found herself wishing he were.

***

The thing about the Door, I've decided, is now that it is open, it has remained so… at least to Vernon. He sports a long chain around his neck with a bright golden medallion hanging from it. At first, when he spoke of a "key", I thought he meant a key like the big skeleton one I carry for the house. But the medallion doesn't look like a key, and if I hadn't known to look for it, I might have missed it. From the golden center of the medallion, a tiny fat key, no longer than an inch, snaps out. With this, somehow, Vernon is now able to open the Door from his side any time he pleases. It is a magic key that I don't understand. I desperately wish the medallion were mine. The longer I look at it, the more I want it.

***

I have just had the last fitting for my wedding dress. What a disaster. I have lost so much weight that I no longer look beautiful in it. I have lost a lot of my curves. I can't seem to think of anything but the key. I want it so bad! Sometimes I sit for hours just brooding about it. On the occasion that Vernon appears, he seems pleased with my moodiness. I think he means to drive me away. But not without the key! It will be mine!

***

Today my worse fears have been realized. At the mere thought of Vernon, I could hear the creak of the Door, and he was standing before me with the key stretched out in his hand. I thought he meant to give it to me, so I grinned and reached for it. But the hand that he gripped my wrist with was so solid it hurt, and I fear I will be wearing a bruise by evening. Even so, I could not keep the hunger out of my eyes as I stared at the beautiful key. He didn't speak out loud, but just the same, I heard his voice inside my head: "Don't tempt me; leave the house before I hurt you. I will have no problem doing that. There is nothing for you here but misery and truth. I don't think you can handle either." That man has a lot of nerve. Bastard!

***

I need the key. Every cell in my body yearns for it. I will call Vernon to me and try to trick him into giving me the key. He is so solid and real that I wonder if he still has the urges live men have… Today I shall flirt shamelessly with him, and make him feel like the important man he thinks he is. I disgust myself with the knowledge of how low I'll stoop to obtain the key, but I have to remind myself why I do it: to keep him on the other side of the Door and prevent him from returning here!

***

I know my mind is dipping dangerously toward darkness and insanity. I have offered myself up to a ghost. I'm so ashamed, yet if I could be honest with myself, I'd do it again. When I walked into the parlor, I could see Vernon there. I was prepared for the worst. I slipped out of my knit top and then my jeans. I beckoned him to me, and he came willingly. His shoulders felt solid under my fingers. And though I wanted to cry, I didn't even flinch when he slipped his cold fingers inside my panties. So when I had him where I thought I could bargain with him, I told him I'd make him feel like a man again if he would give me the key. I was not prepared for his roar of madness. It vibrated the windows and shook the house. Something was terribly wrong. I raced for a chair to hide behind; fear enveloped me like a swarm of gnats. Vernon tore around the room in a mad rage. I knew he was beyond angry. I don't know if he was angry that I asked for the key or that he couldn't perform that manly act. The gold medallion was so close to being mine, but in the end, it belongs to him. I still want it. I will keep working on a way to get it from him... again. He controls the Door.

***

At long last, I possess the key! I had an idea that if I lit the candles and put out the bowl of potpourri, he might come through without me asking for him. When he entered the room without even a creak of sound from the Door, I was startled but tried to keep him from seeing my rising fear. I just said, "Hello, Vernon. Come to call?" I knew he was perplexed and I was counting on that. My plan was to keep him off guard. He said nothing but I could see he was intrigued. So then I told him (as I planned very carefully): "I won't leave. You won't go. So I guess we're at an impasse. But I have a suggestion... I wish to see what's on the other side of the Door." So he took the medallion from his neck and removed the key. After the door was open and the key was returned to the medallion, he turned back toward me and motioned me to follow. But he was not wearing the medallion and when his attention wasn't on me, I snatched the chain from his grip and pushed him back through the Door and locked it! I know he must be furious. Then I had to drop it on the table. I know it was created with dark, demonic forces. I can feel how alive it is. But I can't stop myself from coveting it. It's mine! It's mine! It's mine!

***

I can't eat. I can't sleep. Hell, I'm afraid to sleep. I'm deathly afraid Vernon will find a way through the Door without the key. It has become so easy for him to travel through worlds—what if the locked Door fails to hold him?

***

I fell asleep. I was so exhausted. I was startled awake when I felt an icy breath against my neck. Vernon's misty body was hovering above me with the medallion dangling in his fingers. He found it! I tried to grab for it but he pinned my arms against the pillow. His eyes bore into me like a drill. And the vile things he said to me… but what he meant was that if I ever take the key again, he'll hurt me like I've never been hurt before. And then he was gone with the key. I could do nothing but cry and ache.

Jessa leaned back against her bed and closed her eyes. Her heart ached for Maria, but she desperately wanted to shake some sense into her. What the hell was she thinking? How could this have gotten so out of control in Maria's weak mind? She changed positions to a more comfortable one and read on:

***

This evening was quiet as I walked through the first floor of the house. I could feel the faint static of electricity and I knew I wasn't alone. I dashed into the parlor and saw the flames rise suddenly from all the candles on the little round table. All I could feel was the fear that Vernon would come through the Door and make me suffer. Instead, I heard the sweet voice of Aunt Nettie. I hadn't seen her in so long that I rushed up to the old woman and embraced her before I realized her transparent body was not solid enough for that. Not like Vernon's had become. Aunt Nettie said nothing to me, but looked fearfully over her shoulder. She held her hand out to me and I to her. Then she dropped a heavy object into my hands, and turned, quickly disappearing through the wall again. I stared after her, knowing that the only thing that would make the Door work was… Aunt Nettie had given me the key. I couldn't believe it! How had the old woman gotten the medallion? She must've been terribly afraid. And as much as I wanted the key, too, I am also afraid. The key is heavy in my hands, and I can see the intricate design that makes the key work. It must have been forged in Hell. I will go see what the fuss is all about. I will go through the Door.

The thought was so frightening that Jessa dropped the journal onto the bed and stepped away from it. Leaning against the wall, she closed her eyes against the thundering inside her chest. It was hard to imagine the mental strength it would take to make such a decision. But surely… surely Maria survived the trip. Is this what had become of her?

Jessa returned to her bed and forced herself into a comfortable position again. The wind outside had picked up, and she could hear the swaying of branches as they danced. The darkness of night seemed to seep into the room and collect some of the meager light from her nightstand. Almost without her own presence of mind, she picked up the journal and turned the page. It was a relief to see that Maria's hand had once again written in her journal, although now the handwriting had changed. In a frantic, untidy way, she continued her story.

***

I'm so sorry, please forgive me! There are things that living people should just not know. I wish now I'd never heard of the Door or had taken a fancy to see what was on the other side. There are things so hurtful… Jessa could not read the words smeared there. It was almost as if Maria's tears had soaked up the ink and made it illegible. *I have attended parties for friends who are also getting married, but it means nothing to me. Mitch… how will he ever forgive me for what I have done? I'm not sure the Door can be closed now. I'll never be able to forgive myself! I blame myself for Mitch's drinking. I know he is worried about me, but I can't be bothered with that just now. There are too many things on my mind. Too many worries about the safety of my world. Today I am supposed to go to a party in honor of my best friend. I have a new white dress and everything, but I have this fear that I will not make it. Mitch is out in the boats with his friends. We had such a fight that I'm afraid he'll start drinking before the party. Oh God, this can't be happening!*

Then there was nothing. The rest of the journal pages were empty. What had happened to Maria? Jessa could only wonder that Vernon had somehow lured or taken Maria to the other side of the Door and had somehow trapped her there. How awful! Jessa felt sick at the prospect.

CHAPTER TWENTY-FIVE
PLEA FOR HELP

It was late and Jessa was tired. However, her mind refused to rest and, instead, conjured up visions of Maria as she slowly turned to depression and madness. How could any mind stay rational in such an insane situation? Still, there must be some remnant of reason left in the beautiful woman if she had the coherency to want the Door locked. But... was this now Jessa's task?

She thumbed through the rest of the empty journal pages, hoping that she would find some indication of what happened next or what she needed to do to help lock the Door. Where was the key? Did Maria still have it? No, that much was obvious. If Maria had the key, she would lock it herself. The Door was still open, which allowed Vernon to pass through. In the last journal entry, though, Maria was still in possession. Something happened that Maria and Vernon both lost possession of the key. But what?

Idly thumbing through the pages, Jessa let her mind ponder the questions. It seemed as if there were so many more questions than answers. If any answer came to her, it only seemed to add more questions to the list. She felt like she was gunning in neutral.

With her thumb, she riffled the pages absently. With each pass of her thumb, Jessa could feel the puff of air as the pages closed, then she would catch the edges and flip through the pages again. It made a small, fluttering sound. Again. And again. And again.

Finally, Jessa's eyes began to close sleepily. Inside, her mind was still on overload, but, except for the shuffling pages of the journal, her body refused to be drawn into any action at all. Her ears didn't want to hear, but a sound kept persisting in her consciousness. It almost sounded like someone calling her name: *Jessa! Jessa! Jessa!*

With eyes still shut, Jessa stilled her hands and the whispered name stopped. She almost smiled in relief and began to riffle the journal pages again. *Jessa! Jessa! Jessa!* Then her heart bolted wildly, throbbing violently inside her chest. Her eyes went wide, and she stared at the innocuous-looking journal. Maria?

Gently, Jessa let her thumb caress the edges of the journal pages, then in a quick movement, riffled them to hear the whir of air as the pages closed... and to her amazement, her name came out as soft as a baby's sigh. *Jessa!*

Maria was trying to contact her.

Her fear was a wild thing to be tamed. It was too late and she was too tired to go to Bristol House tonight. Plus, she was far too terrified. Without changing into her nightclothes, and without removing the items she retrieved from the cellar, she wiggled herself into a comfortable position and closed her eyes again. Maria could wait.

But Maria couldn't wait. As soon as Jessa succumbed to the dark nethers of slumber, Maria's face was there, anxiously coaxing her into sleep-sheltered coherency. The beautiful blue visage entreated Jessa with tear-filled eyes. *"Jessa, can you understand me?"*

The voice warbled almost unintelligibly, but in her dream-mind, Jessa nodded her weary head. She squinted to concentrate on Maria's mouth as the other woman spoke; the sync didn't entirely match up. *"You need to lock the Door. Do you understand?"*

Again Jessa nodded with fatigue. "How can I lock the Door?" Even to her, the words sounded slurred and faded. She tried again, "How does it lock?"

For a moment, Maria stared, sifting for understanding. Then she moved her mouth to speak and her words followed soon after. *"The key. You must get the key!"*

"I don't have the key! In your journal, *you* had the key. What did you do with it?" Jessa's chest tightened as she railed.

"You read my journal!" These words Maria whispered to

herself, her voice rising in excitement. *"Then you understand how the key works."*

"Where is the key?" Her mind threatened to wander, so she frowned in concentration, staring hard at Maria's face.

The question seemed to stump Maria's ethereal spirit and for a moment she faded slightly. Jessa reached out to touch her, but in her dream-state she was unable to do more than feel a cool mist stroke her fingers. *"The key? I don't have the key. I... I dropped the key a long time ago. Will you look for it?"*

Suspended consciousness began to make Maria fade gradually in and out of visibility. Jessa scrubbed her eyes, but she was losing her fight with sleep. "I have no idea where to look..."

"Come to Bristol House and talk to me. Come, Jessa! The Door needs to be locked for good."

If Maria said anything else, Jessa was not aware of it as she drifted away from the conversation. The rest of the night was spent running away from wispy, curious spirits that darted in and around Jessa, never staying long enough to make contact, but always within reaching distance.

Morning came as a dreary, foggy day. Dark and moist, no sun pierced the heavy bank of clouds that hung overhead. The face that peered back at Jessa in the mirror was puffy and looked pale. Her eyes were red-rimmed from inadequate sleep. She yawned hugely and stepped into the stinging, hot shower.

Closing her eyes, she let the hot water run down her body and wash away the wispy webs of slumber. Her arms were stretched out, hands splayed against the shower stall to catch her balance. She sighed contentedly.

She felt a muscle twitch in her calf and she blindly reached down to rub the spot, but as she did so, the muscle stopped twitching and another twitched on her other leg. In an instant, she felt unreasonably apprehensive and opened her eyes a crack. The great, wide mouths of two shadow monsters grinned up at her, one on each leg.

Little bald faces, little hairy fingers… they tugged on her skin as if they wanted to eat it. Jessa jolted back suddenly and screamed, throwing herself against the shower door. Another little monster squealed behind her as she pinned him, but she screamed again and threw herself across to the other side to get away from it. Then her foot slipped on the slick surface of the stall, and she flailed her arms around to catch herself. She completely lost her balance and slipped headlong onto the shower floor. As she fought for consciousness, a tiny shadow monster opened its mouth wide around her big toe. As it crunched down, she was thrown into a black, terrifying void.

A cool spray of water splashed onto her face. She surfaced from a dark place abruptly, sputtering and coughing water from her nose and mouth. She looked around her, amazed to find that she was still lying on the shower floor. Then she drew up her limbs immediately, remembering the shadow monsters, and looked fearfully around. She was alone. Her toe was untouched. How much time had passed?

She had been lying there long enough for the hot water to become cool, so she turned off the spigot and stepped gingerly out of the stall. The mirror showed her a reflection that was even less appealing than the one she'd seen earlier. Her puffy eyes did not sparkle, and the pallid color of her skin stretched over a bony face. Already, purplish bruises started to show up on her arms and legs where she'd fallen. She averted her eyes as she dried off and dressed.

In anticipation, panic started to pound inside her chest as she made her way to the kitchen. Step by step, she inched closer to the postcard of Bristol House, knowing precisely at what step it would suddenly leap from the shelf to fall to the floor. Her breath was shallow and fast as the card did fall, and she swore she could hear the telltale sound of a far-off scream as it did so. The fingers that picked up the card shook uncontrollably.

When she looked at the card, she gasped to see the

tiny image of Maria in a wide mouth scream as she leaned out of an upper story window. Behind her, in the shadows of the room, was the unmistakable black silhouette of a heavy-set man.

Again, Jessa averted her eyes from the photo as she set it back on the shelf. She couldn't even begin to assimilate the task she knew she must ultimately complete. Reaching to close the kitchen window, she braced herself for the appearance of the dark robin. Unlike before, she leaned close to the window and looked out to see its dark body dive toward her, but its suicidal plunge toward her caused her to yelp and slam the window shut. The bird banked in the last moment, avoiding certain death, but then turned to peck mercilessly at the glass. The bright amber eyes glowed alarmingly. The dark robin became a scarlet-breasted crow, fluttering frantically at the glass to get inside.

Was the terrified mewling coming from her? She reached over the sink and flipped down the blinds to cover the window and the image of the crow. Immediately, the sound of flapping wings stopped. Timidly, she lifted the blinds and peeked outside. The robin/crow was nowhere to be seen.

Somewhere between the blinds and the coffee pot, Jessa decided firmly not to allow the spirits of Bristol House scare her out of her apartment again. She was not the same girl she was a month ago. She'd seen things…

Though she wanted to be curled up in front of a fireplace anywhere except here or Bristol House, the smell of the hot coffee brewing was more comforting than she could have imagined. Just to be on the safe side, however, Jessa poured herself a bowl of cold cereal in lieu of her customary oatmeal. A few minutes later, as she was sipping her coffee and chewing thoughtfully on her cereal, she cringed as a particularly hot spoonful of oatmeal burnt her lip.

Immediately she threw down her spoon, slopping globs of the steaming cereal over the table. Oatmeal? Her heart raced and her head pounded. She couldn't finish it, but instead set the hot bowl in the sink and ran cold water in it. Tears pricked at her eyes. What the hell happened to her cold cereal?

Find the key. Find the key. The words kept thrumming inside her head. With Mitch's steering wheel under the palms of her hands, she eased the beast into the street and headed to the only place that would hopefully end the Door's free passageway. Even knowing what she must do didn't ease the actual task.

The streets of Madison were strangely empty, making the trip to Bristol House seem more like something out of a horror movie set. Heavy fog puffed ahead of her, curling tendrils of mist around the windows and doors. When the entrance to Bristol House came into view, she eased the car into the driveway. Thunder rumbled overhead and the sky darkened with an imminent storm.

Jessa's heart beat rapidly inside her chest. Everything inside her objected to returning to the old mansion, but Jessa knew this was something she had to do because, if not her, then who? In the seat beside her were the bowl of potpourri and a loaf of fragrant bread to use as an offering... and hopefully, a meeting with Maria. All too soon she was standing, quaking in fear, on the veranda of Bristol House.

As she had when Madeline Hester was supposed to meet her, Jessa lit the three candles that still sat on top of the little, round table in the parlor. Next, she sat the bowl of potpourri beside the candles. Last, she opened the fresh bread, tore off a chunk, and set it near the potpourri. Taking a deep breath, she spoke in a clear voice, "I would like to speak to Maria Escher. Please take this gift of fresh bread as a token of friendship so that we can communicate between the worlds of life and death. Please speak to me, Maria, and be here with me." Then she held her breath and waited.

The room was dark. Though the curtains had not been closed, little daylight seeped into the house. Almost continual thunder rumbled outside. Inside, all the color seemed to be leached out of the furniture, walls, and woodwork. Chill permeated the air. As she waited, she began to smell the heavy, gut-wrenching scent of rot. The Door was opening.

Jessa put a hand up against her nostrils to fend off the powerful smell. Finally, as if superimposed on the parlor wall, blackness emerged, taking on the shape of a human being. Maria, looking as if she was painted in watercolor, stepped into the room. Her entire body was transparent, like looking through blue cellophane paper of uneven thickness. Jessa stared, not quite daring to believe that Maria's ghost actually stood in front of her.

When she spoke, her voice was tinny and warbled. *"Jessa!"* she whispered, looking fearfully over her shoulder at something Jessa couldn't see. Returning her attention to Jessa, she smiled a little tearfully.

Jessa was immediately empathetic with the other woman. She rushed up to her and in the same hushed whisper, took her hands and replied, "Yes, Maria. I want to help you. Where is the key?" Maria's hands, though icy cold, were not like mist as Jessa had been afraid they would be. She could feel the contours as soft as gelatin, but solid enough to hold.

The look on Maria's face was heartbreaking. Was it possible for a ghost to yearn for the living world in a desperate and continuous state of longing? Was this young woman homesick for those who had loved her in life?

"I lost the key. I was running from Vernon. I had the key. But as he caught up with me, I didn't have it any longer. I don't remember exactly what happened. You said I was murdered?" Maria started to cry and choked back tears.

"Your parents think Mitch murdered you. They wanted me to find any evidence that he might have wanted to harm you. Could it have been Mitch?" As Jessa spoke, she couldn't admit to herself how important Maria's answer was to her. Please, please, please, don't let it be Mitch, she prayed.

Immediately, Maria shook her head. *"No, Mitch wasn't even here that day. He was on the boat. He was very fond of me."*

Jessa frowned at Maria's description. Fond? "What happened?"

"I don't know!" Maria wailed, tears dripping down to her chin. *"All I remember is Vernon. He will hurt me; I know he will. He's hurt others. He'll hurt me. But worse, when he has the key back, he can find the Door and it will be so dreadful. No one who comes into the house will be safe from him... You must find the key and lock the Door."*

"If I lock the Door, will it keep Vernon from coming through to this side? Will the living world be safe from him?" Jessa's voice quivered as she fought tears herself. She imagined what tragedy would result if Vernon came through and set his anger upon the innocent. The tours would have to stop permanently. What if he could somehow leave Bristol House? How could she make them believe her and understand?

"If Vernon gets the key, he'll be able to do as he pleases. With the key and the location of the Door, he'll become solid: as solid as you are but unbelievably strong. Bristol House will no longer hold him. With the key destroyed, he'll remain just as he is now: insubstantial: a ghostly fright. He might be able to go through the Door, but he won't be able to hurt you."

"What will happen to you? Will he still hurt you?"

Maria slumped in defeat, looking small and vulnerable. *"It doesn't matter what happens to me as long as the Door is locked and the living world is safe. After you lock it, destroy the key. Don't let it lure you into keeping it. It's alive and dangerous, and it wants to wreak havoc. Please!"*

Jessa's eyes lowered to the floor as she pictured the horrific eternity Maria would endure, running from Vernon so he wouldn't hurt her. It would be unimaginably hideous. "I don't know where the key is," she whispered.

Maria shrugged. *"I was running from Vernon."*

"Where?"

"In the driveway. I was trying to escape."

Jessa hesitated as Maria looked tearfully over her shoulder again. "Maria, do you think it was Vernon? Can a ghost murder a human?"

At first Maria looked startled, but then a look of great sadness came into her eyes. *"Maybe he did. I don't remember. But he's capable."*

Moments later, the spirit of Maria was yanked forcefully toward the blackened Door. She yelped in surprise and a long keen of agony sliced the air, fading until nothing was left but an empty room and a feeling that someone had died… again.

CHAPTER TWENTY-SIX
THE KEY

Jessa stared at the smooth wall. Her brain was almost numb as she watched Maria being jerked back through to the other side. Even knowing she could prevent calamity in the world of the living, could she doom Maria to endless days of torture from a man-spirit so utterly malevolent? What choice did she have, really?

Close to madness herself, she turned away from Maria's plight inside the Door and left the parlor. She didn't want to catch Vernon's attention: she needed to find the key. It was fortunate she had someplace to start looking. The last place Maria knew she still had the key was in the driveway as she was trying to escape to her car.

Jessa tiptoed outside, making as little noise as possible. She began to walk the length of the driveway, examining the smooth surface of the blacktop. If she had dropped it here, how could it have escaped notice for the last three years? Rain, snow, wind... and Mitch would have seen it.

At the end of the driveway, Jessa turned back toward the house. Obviously, it would not be on the surface: time would have swept it away. In fact, it was probably never there because it would not have gone unnoticed as investigator after investigator came here to find any trace of the missing young woman.

She examined the grass edges that had been neatly mowed on each side of the driveway. Who did the lawn maintenance anyway? Perhaps the key had been in the grass and was now a jumble of unrecognizable metal? Not likely, she deduced, if Maria was still worried about locking the Door. If the key was destroyed, it was reasonable to assume that she would know it.

As Jessa traipsed back to the house, she could feel the heavy fog thicken. Droplets of moisture gathered on her jacket and in her hair. Visibility was barely ten feet, yet she refused to give up her frantic search. In her heart, she knew Mitch would not want her to be searching for anything so close to the house, so she had to finish her investigation before he returned from Florida.

At the veranda, she stared off toward the end of the driveway as Maria might have once done. Though she couldn't see it for the fog, she would have thought that Maria's car would be near the parking lot; that if Maria were indeed running from Vernon to escape, she would have kept to the left side of the driveway as she ran from the house since it was likely her car was parked on the right side as she faced the house. So, she'd examine it first. She dropped to her knees and spread her fingers into the wet grass to push the blades to one side and then the other, examining down to the dirt. The driveway seemed immensely long, but Jessa couldn't afford to be careless with her exploration.

Her search was tiresome. Her knees ached; her fingers were sore; her eyes were strained. Maybe she had it all wrong. Perhaps she, herself, had dipped into psychosis to join Maria and this was all an exercise in madness.

Near the end of the driveway, where she'd imagined Maria's car to be, Jessa sighed and dropped down to lie on the smooth driveway. She rolled to her back, and stared into the heavy, dark sky. She could feel the tears that threatened to spill out of her eyes. What had become of her? She was not the same person she had been before this investigation had robbed her of her innocence.

Lying on her back, knees up, arms splayed wide, she let the tears roll down past her ears. This was hopeless and fruitless. She felt both responsible and idiotic. She lay there and sobbed into the sky.

When her tears finally dried up, she cast her gaze back at the house. It was barely visible in the mist, and for a mad moment, she felt as if it was taunting her—laughing that she'd given up the search for the key. What sane woman let a house ridicule her? As that thought congealed, something hot seared the fingers on her right hand. She turned her eyes there and noticed something shiny just inside her reach. She caught her breath and propped herself up on an elbow. The key!

Jessa laughed as she plucked it from the grass. Over the years, it had become entrenched deep into the soil, avoiding notice. While she could only assume it had rolled from Maria's hand, she celebrated the fact that she was, indeed, *not* mad and that she had a real chance to lock the Door.

With the shiny medallion in her hand, she examined the intricate design along the edge and ran her fingers across the top of the small key that rose from the medallion's smooth center. It was attached to a long, heavy chain and could have been worn around the neck. As she stared, it warmed to her and winked enticingly. A deep, powerful longing took root in her mind. *The key was hers!*

But the key *wasn't* hers... a flitting image of Maria's anguished face arrested her desire for the gold for a mere instant. That was all she needed to turn her eyes and heart away from the commanding presence of the key. She had to ignore its control and influence that would turn her away from the vital task of locking the Door. It seemed to be an interminable walk to Bristol House as the pull and tug of the key cried out to her.

Hours, or seconds, later she stood in the parlor facing the blank wall where the Door was located. What would it look like if she stepped up to it with the key in her outstretched hand? Would the key know its business and lock the Door of its own volition? Or would she have to find the lock and insert the key into it?

Her frightened heart thrashed inside her ribs like the angry pounding of the dark robin/crow at her kitchen window. Nausea bubbled up from her stomach and soured the taste inside her mouth. Her mind asked the forbidden question: what was on the other side of the Door?

Her strength to resist was fading. She clasped the medallion so tightly in her hand that its design left its imprint in her skin. She took no notice of the pain it inflicted. Just as she thought she would be able to defend against it no longer, she pulled the little key from its place in the medallion and thrust it toward the parlor wall.

Immediately, a black doorway opened, yawning, like a huge offensive mouth. A fetid breath blew across Jessa's face, causing her to gag. With her outstretched arm disappearing into blackness, she could feel the key connect with the locking mechanism: the Door was locked!

Almost.

In the last instants of the locking action, Jessa felt an iron-tight grip on her wrist. The key wobbled in her grasp, and for a second, she was afraid she was going to drop it. She couldn't pull her arm back and away; the only direction she could go was in. As she struggled, the blackness seemed to swallow her up, inch by inch.

She was too frightened to cry. As she struggled, she dropped the medallion into her pocket to free her other hand, but even then she couldn't pull her arm away without letting go of the key. Something had hold of her and there was no letting go. Something, someone, wanted her inside the Door.

Digging her heels in, she used the last of her strength in resisting the pull inside the Door. In the end, however, she wasn't successful, and the last thing to leave the world of the living was her face. When the blackness of the Door enveloped her face, she scrunched her eyes shut and held her breath. Terrified beyond measure, anxiety and panic imprisoned her in a claustrophobic web.

She fell to the floor and curled her knees up against her chest. She was aware that the ground was level and that she was backed up against a wall. She fingered the key lightly, then dropped it in her pocket beside the medallion, but did not bother to snap it back onto the medallion's smooth front. When she opened her eyes, she could see nothing but blackness.

It wasn't long until her eyes adjusted to the dimness inside the Door. There were many noises, too. Despite her desperate situation, she was still curious. Finally, she ventured a whispered, "*Maria?*"

After a time, Jessa could hear the soft footsteps belonging to a lightweight person. At last, she could see Maria stepping nimbly toward her. This was not the *same* Maria she'd seen in her camera and visions. This Maria was tall and willowy, solid, and very real.

Jessa stood suddenly, glad for Maria's friendly smile. She reached out to embrace the other woman, but was stopped short when her arms went completely through Maria like a breath through mist. She was not prepared for Maria's abrupt expression of grief and fright, or for her gasp of sudden surprise.

When Jessa looked down at herself to see what had caused such a reaction, she realized that it was she, not Maria, who was no more substantial than the mist outside. Her joyful face fell. Was *she* dead now?

Maria's voice was quiet when she spoke. "I was like that once. When I first came to the world of the dead, I was as transparent as you. The longer I'm here, the more solid I become. I'm not sure which one is better, but the more solid I get, the more hopeless I become."

"*Am I dead?*" Jessa asked in a shaky, tear-filled voice.

"Honestly, I don't know. I have trouble remembering the past when I'm in here. The more solid I become, the harder it is to remember. I didn't remember that I wasn't always solid until I saw that you weren't. Then I remembered." Experimentally, Maria waved a hand across Jessa's arm and through it. Chills ran in electric rivulets up and down her skin.

"*I brought the key. I thought I had the Door locked, but at the last moment, I got pulled inside. Do you know what happened?*" Jessa wanted desperately to embrace Maria, if only to feel a sense of reality, however bizarre.

Maria laughed slightly, though without real humor. "No, but I'm sure it had something to do with Vernon. He always seems to know where the key is, but there are things here that even he can't control. He is at odds with other spirits, and sometimes they keep him busy enough that he stops noticing me and I can hide. If he pulled you in, then something has distracted his attention away from you, because he wouldn't go willingly."

"Why is it so dark?"

"It's dark?" Maria questioned. Then, "Hmmm, I guess it was dark once. That's another thing I forgot: the darkness. It lightens as time passes. I can see more than I once could."

"Is there any way out of here?" Jessa wanted to cry as a wave of panic hit her again.

Finally Maria grinned, brightening up her entire face. However, Jessa could feel a sense of sadness too. Maria could never go home. "If you still have the key, I think you can. That is, as long as you leave before Vernon gets back. If he finds you, he'll try to keep you."

Jessa grinned back at her, at long last feeling that there might be a little hope after all. *"Can I ask you a question before I go?"*

"Certainly."

"Once you were on this side, have you been able to see your Aunt Nettie and the others?" Jessa questioned.

Maria smiled and spoke quietly, "Yes. Aunt Nettie is a lovely person, though not the answer to my prayers that I once thought she would be. I had thought she would be strong and decisive having lived a long time, but she is as she was in life: full of doubt and troubled just like the rest of us. I have learned so much about life and about myself. I wish I had a chance to use what I've learned, but it's too late for me. And I regret it."

"Is there no way to come back with me?" Even as she asked, Jessa wasn't certain she wanted the answer to be yes. Did

Maria still love Mitch? And did he still love her?

Maria's sad smile haunted Jessa. "Everyone says I was murdered, remember? Your world is for the living. I belong here, in the land of the dead."

"But…" she had wanted to argue with the other woman, but how could one argue against death? Just then, a strident bellow reverberated across the dark space. Maria cringed and whimpered. Jessa knew she should be afraid, but she wasn't sure what she was afraid of. *"What is it?"*

"Quickly, you must get on the other side of the Door. Lock it. Don't look back! Please hurry!" Maria motioned for Jessa to follow her to a destination only she could see.

"But Maria, the Door is just here. I haven't moved since being pulled through." She pointed behind her, though her eyes were still too weak to see clearly.

"Oh," Maria wailed, "it's so hard to explain. It isn't that the Door moved, but things don't work here like they do there. It's like, have you ever worked with chalk or charcoal?" She waited for Jessa's nod. "If you draw something with a heavy hand and what you've drawn is really dark and thick, then you smear it with the palm of your hand?" Again she waited for Jessa's nod. "Essentially, what you drew has moved because your hand pushed the charcoal across your paper. To touch the outline of your drawing, you would touch a different spot on the paper. Does that make any sense to you?"

"Sort of. I get what you're saying… the Door is there?" She pointed to where Maria had indicated.

"Yes! Go!" Maria said quickly.

Not quickly enough, though, for as Jessa geared up to sprint across the short space, Vernon's very solid, very big body came into view. Maria squealed suddenly and dashed off, disappearing into the darkness away from them. Vernon stood indomitably between Jessa and the Door.

"Where is the medallion?" he boomed. He sniffed the air around him. "It is close. Where did you put it?"

Jessa dropped to her knees and cowered away from him. She could feel the hot metal scorch her skin through the material of her jeans. As she sat there hovering in fear, though, a seed of anger began to grow inside her. She did *not* belong here!

Despite the transparent wispiness of her body, Vernon was somehow able to yank her to her feet. This surprised Jessa and she yelped in pain. An instant later, he shoved her up against the wall, which she could only guess must be inside the parlor, and imprisoned her there. Her shackles were not physical, but something otherworldly. She could not move from where she stood. Her anger waxed. She had a feeling it was a good thing she didn't know what he was capable of or she might have been a lot more frightened than she was. She would not give up the key easily.

Then she was alone in the waning darkness, for as time passed, her eyes began to penetrate the gloom. She could make out some parts of the house, though never clearly, and always backward, a little like a warped mirror. Chitters in the distance kept her on edge, and she was fearful of seeing the little shadow monsters with their great grins full of sharp teeth.

She was neither hungry nor thirsty. How long had she been here? Was it day or night? There was no way of telling, and perhaps, time evolved differently here than it did on the outside. Did spirits die here too? Or was this an endless cycle of domination and pain?

After a time, a sound, far away, tickled her ears and caused her attention to perk up. The sound was not coming from the inside of the Door, but instead from the outside. Someone was in Bristol House!

Sudden tears pricked Jessa's eyes. Logically, there was only one person who would have access to the house and that person was Mitch! Jessa tried to pull her body around so she could see behind her inside the house. Concentrating until her head hurt, she could see Mitch wandering through the parlor.

He was, at times, clear as if she were looking through a mirror, and at other times, he was a charcoal drawing that someone had smeared with their palm. Strange, warped sounds surrounded him as he whispered to himself or as he had a particularly strong thought.

Taking a chance that she would not attract Vernon's attention, she called to Mitch, *"Hey! I've been pulled inside the Door. Mitch! Can you hear me?"* She knew her voice was shaking and frantic, but she was so terrified that he wouldn't be able to hear her.

As soon as she stopped speaking, he looked up and around. He had heard her! "Jessa?"

Her breath became ragged with longing and excitement. *"Mitch! Help me!"*

But time, or rather the passage of time, wasn't on her side. As if in an old movie reel, Mitch was suddenly pushed into fast-forward. He moved in quick, choppy steps through the parlor, the kitchen, and throughout the cellar. Then he was gone. Jessa screamed and screamed, but in his triple-time movement, he didn't respond to her words or screams. Ultimately, she sagged against her restraints into despair and melancholy.

Time crawled. And sped quickly. She could see the passage of time as a tangible thing as the parlor became clearer and the days blinked off and on like a child playing with a light switch. Did Mitch think she disappeared from his life like Maria had? He must be going through hell.

CHAPTER TWENTY-SEVEN
MITCH'S DREAM

Mitch returned to the house several times. It was difficult for Jessa to determine the amount of time that passed, but she had tried to count off the times that the parlor was bright enough to be a day against the darkness that must be night. A week, that was her best guess.

At the end of her week, Jessa was surprised to see someone enter the house with Mitch. In their smudged, blemished way, she guessed the other person to be someone in a uniform such as a policeman or a contractor. Would there be an investigation? Was he boarding up or tearing down Bristol House? So much tragedy was connected with it. What would happen to her if the house were destroyed?

Then time slowed. When night arrived, Jessa worried that it would be interminable. Vernon had yet to return to her and she'd, thankfully, been left alone. Besides the noises she'd grown accustomed to hearing, there was no particular activity from Maria or any of the other spirits here. Looking down at her legs and arms, she could see that she was becoming less transparent, but she refused to forget. She told herself her own story over and over until it was a set pattern in her mind.

Once, when she was retelling the part of her story when Maria had come to her in a dream, she was immediately startled into absolute awareness. This long, interminable night would be the perfect opportunity to talk to Mitch! He would dream her.

So she closed her eyes and concentrated on him: his eyes; his smiling, talking mouth; the way he combed his hands through his hair. She imagined his every expression from joy and laughter to anger and silence. She heard the way his voice sounded when he talked to her. She imagined the exact pitch and timbre when he laughed, chatted, and his mumble of agreement or argument. She could see the way his body moved as he walked or sat down. She observed the way his arm rose to push a button on the TV remote when he changed a channel.

She said aloud, *"Mitch?"*

There was no particular answer, but Jessa could see him raise his head as he became aware of her inquiry. Just as she understood this, she knew he was asleep and that his dream-self was attentive to her. "Where are you, Jessa? I have been trying to find you."

The need to cry burned her throat. *"I know, Mitch. I have been here all the time. I'm stuck inside Bristol House."*

"But you aren't!" She could hear the anguish in his voice. "I looked there. I've looked everywhere. I can't find you."

"Oh, it's so hard to explain! Vernon Hubert has taken me here. I am shackled to the wall somehow and I can't escape. Please don't give up on me. I need you to do something for me." As she spoke, though, she could tell Mitch's mind was wandering in his sleep.

"What? What did you say? Your voice, it fades in and out." He tried hard to concentrate on what she was saying, but her voice sounded tinny and far away.

Jessa tried again, *"I need your help. Can you go into the parlor and light the candles for me? If I can see them, then maybe I can find my way home."*

"Candles? What candles?" Mitch's dream-mind faded and left for a moment. Jessa held her breath in panic, but then finally, he returned. "Candles? What candles?"

"Mitch! Listen to me and concentrate. In the parlor, there are three candles on the little round table. Light them and keep them lit. If they melt down, light another one. Please!"

Jessa closed her eyes in concentration, willing him to understand. She knew he would have trouble believing his own mind when he woke up and she was desperate for that not to happen. Think, think, think! At last, she imagined a match lighting a candle. In her mind, she kept lighting her imaginary candle with the lone match until it became a reality: solid and hot. When she opened her eyes, she knew that an unbelievable thing had happened: Mitch would wake now with a single wooden match clasped in his fingers. *"Remember,"* she whispered.

Mitch left her, then, for the netherworld of dreams and desires. For an endless time afterward, she waited for the long night to conclude. It was fortunate that before the night was over, Jessa could see that Mitch, in his fast-forward, jerking movements, finally lit the candles in the parlor. She celebrated silently and joyfully.

Her joy was short lived, however. The burning of the candles attracted Vernon's attention. He came to her in a fury, rolling through the dead world like a black blizzard. "Give me the medallion!" he bellowed. He grabbed her by the arm and jerked her from the wall. She was nothing more than a rag doll in his grasp. He had been here for a long time and had learned things… yet Jessa suspected he was only guessing where the key was. Otherwise, he would already have it.

Anger and confidence coursed through her unexpectedly. Perhaps she did have some power over him after all. Now that she was loose from the wall, all she needed was to distract him so she could make her escape into the parlor.

"Want the medallion?" she taunted. *"I have it. Want it?"*

For a moment of absolute silence, he stared at her. His fierce whisper made the hairs on the back of her neck stand up, "Give me the medallion!"

Slowly, she pulled the medallion by the chain from inside her pocket and dangled it tantalizingly in front of her. The bright gold swung back and forth before him like a shiny pendulum, catching his eyes and forcing his face to swing in tandem. *"Then take it!"* With a great heave, she imagined it flying long and far as she catapulted it with all her strength into the black void of darkness. She listened for the metallic "clink" of its landing, but there was nothing except silence.

Vernon roared as he turned and lumbered after it. He seemed like a great dog hounding after a bone as he disappeared, forgetting that Jessa was there. He thought he finally had the key and the Door was his, but Jessa knew better.

She had the key. It had never been returned to its place in the smooth center of the medallion. Then reaching into her pocket for the key, she turned to the parlor and watched as the candles burned low and then were replaced and burned and replaced. Time was going too fast.

With the key leading the way, she made to step through the Door when a singular sound stopped her. Maria stood several feet away, her eyes tearful. *"Maria?"* Jessa questioned.

"Lock the Door behind you," she mumbled.

"What will happen to you?" Jessa's heart ached at Maria's plight. Vernon would be livid when he found the medallion did not contain the key. Would he still be able to pass through the Door as a specter, though, without the power the key provided? Would Maria suffer for her duplicity?

Maria sobbed. "Just lock the Door."

"Come with me!" Jessa said suddenly.

"I can't. I'm dead." Maria turned her face away from Jessa. "Go, Jessa. I'm sorry I opened the Door. Thanks for doing what I was unable to and locking the Door."

There was no time to lose; Vernon would soon discover that Jessa had deceived him. With her physical state becoming more solid, she made a grab at Maria's arm. She was not firm enough to hold on to the other woman, but she did get her attention. *"Please?"* Jessa pleaded. *"It won't hurt to try…"*

Tears poured from Maria's eyes as she faced Jessa. "I miss my mother so much! And Daddy."

Anguish twisted Jessa's heart. She whispered frantically, *"Then come."*

Though not dense enough for an actual embrace,

Maria hurried to Jessa and looped her arms around her waist. Jessa shoved the key in front of her and together they began to make their way through the Door.

They knew the instant Vernon discovered the key was missing as his bellow of anger shook the entire building. With her attention focused on the lighted candles, they popped through the Door and tumbled to the hardwood floor. Jessa didn't take the time to check for scrapes and bruises, but instead turned to thrust her hand inside the black Door. She could feel the locking mechanism turn firmly, and as she pulled her hand back, she could sense a solid body hitting the Door. Vernon!

The house held its breath and time stopped. Jessa's eyes flew to the still second hand of an old clock. She waited. There was a faint "pop", and the second hand of the clock began to slowly tick off the seconds again.

So many things assaulted Jessa at once: it was dark, most likely night. Mitch was gone. Though time seemed to finally march on, the house itself still appeared to be holding its breath. The Door was closed, locked, but Jessa could feel the almost indiscernible vibrations of Vernon's body as he hit the Door over and over, trying to break the spectral gate between worlds. She fell back to sit in a heap on the floor and stared at the wall where the Door was located, praying that the lock would hold.

Long seconds ticked anxiously by. The lock held the Door. Jessa breathed with a little relief, but was unwilling to relax completely as she knew Vernon would not give up so easily. Besides, she didn't know if Maria could be trusted not to return the key to him… Maria!

She twirled her head around the room looking for the other woman. Maria was gone! Frantically, Jessa jumped up from the floor and ran her palm over the smooth wall of the parlor. She checked her pocket for the key and could feel the warm, glowing heat and the intricate design of its edges. Maria had not taken the key from her.

A quick perusal of the parlor turned up empty, so Jessa dashed into the kitchen. She gasped suddenly when she saw that the cellar door was wide open inside the pantry. Could Maria have gone down there? For a moment, Jessa couldn't imagine forcing herself to descend those dark stairs, but only for that moment. How could those stairs contain anything worse than what she'd just experienced?

As she stepped down slowly, she realized that Vernon and his spectral world had no power over her. The fear he'd instilled in her was hers alone. She let him scare her. Well, she vowed, not any more.

At the bottom of the stairs, she pulled on the electric light chain and watched the shadows bend and sway as the bulb swung on its wire. Everything looked as it did the last time she'd been down here; there was no sign of Maria.

She ascended again, but when she reached up to push the lock into place, she hesitated. If Maria was down here, she wanted her to be able to come up to the main part of the house. She shut the door gently without hooking the lock.

Jessa wandered throughout the downstairs of Bristol House looking for Maria. It was because she couldn't find her that Jessa began to worry about what she'd done. Maria had been gone these past three years, most likely murdered at a young age. What was Maria now that she was trapped on this side of the Door? Would she forever be that blue ghost, yearning for something that she would never be able to have? Would she, could she, be visited by the mother she missed so much? If she couldn't be sustained here, would the Door have to be opened again, risking entry by Vernon, to travel back to the dark world of the dead and be forever fearful of being hurt?

Jessa sank down on the loveseat in the parlor and put her head in the palms of her hands. A moment later, she was startled when she felt a tender arm slip around her shoulders. She inhaled suddenly and sat straight. Maria was sitting beside her with an expression of sadness and pain.

There was nothing that could keep the wide grin from Jessa's face as she stared in awe at the other woman. Even Maria pulled back somewhat, surprised at her reaction. "Oh my gosh, Maria, look at you!"

"What are you talking about?" Maria returned, puzzled.

Tears threatened to bump into Jessa's wide grin. She didn't trust her voice to speak, so instead, she pulled Maria's hands into her lap and squeezed them fondly. Maria didn't understand and she shook her head in bewilderment. "What?" she whispered.

"On this side of the Door, you have always been blue... a specter that haunts these rooms. But look at yourself! You are as solid here as I am!" Jessa gave her arm a playful yank.

Immediately, Maria looked down. Her dress, shredded beyond recognition, hung like dirty rags from her shoulders... but she was as substantial and dimensional as Jessa! "Wow!" There were no words that came into her mind to express the unexpected astonishment of this discovery. "Wow!"

Opening her mouth and then closing it in absolute perplexity, Jessa took a mental step back to gather her thoughts. "Okay, so why do you suppose you look like me?" She rubbed Maria's arms gently.

The other woman shook her head and said nothing. Then she spoke in a whisper, "I have a thought, but it's ridiculous. It's just a theory."

"Shoot. I'm willing to believe almost anything." Jessa grinned in encouragement.

"It's so insane. But... it's almost like I wasn't dead at all. That's silly, I know." The look on her face was so infused with hope and longing that Jessa almost couldn't respond.

Finally, she found some words and whispered them carefully. "Oh, my gosh! You weren't murdered! You had been missing for so long that everyone thought Mitch did you in. But he convinced me that he had nothing to do with your disappearance. I believed him, after a while. Then I thought that Vernon… but maybe it's true that a ghost can't actually murder a human: he can only pull them to the other side and make them a miserable part of his world. Do you think that is possible?"

Maria giggled and shrugged her thin shoulders. "I'm starving. Does Mitch keep food in here any more?"

Jessa laughed out loud. "When have you ever heard of a hungry ghost? I think there is a fridge stocked very nicely up in the apartment."

The two women left the parlor and headed up the stairs to the third floor. It was not until they were almost in the master bedroom that Jessa felt the sting of dread. There would have to be a confrontation with Mitch. When he learned that Maria was alive and well, where would that leave her? She smiled sadly to herself. She would not stand in the way of Maria and Mitch. If they belonged together, then at least she knew she'd done the right thing by bringing her back to this world.

An angry ghost would forever haunt Bristol House. Vernon. The key burned inside her pocket.

MITCH WAS NOT THERE. His bed was neatly made, though, and the fridge was stocked full of the basic ingredients for almost anything. Maria opened the door and let the cool air waft over her. Sitting on the floor, she began to rummage through the contents, pulling cheese, pickles, hot dogs, and various fruits and veggies out with abandon and stuffing them into her mouth. She barely tasted or chewed, so great was her hunger.

Jessa went to the sink and filled a glass with water and kneeled down to hand it to Maria. Maria looked at her in surprise, then gratefully took it and gulped the water until the glass was completely empty.

A moment later, Maria looked distressed and slapped a hand over her mouth. She got up quickly and ran into

Mitch's bathroom, heaving up everything that she'd stuffed into her mouth. Feeling sorry for her, Jessa helped her wipe up her face and told her to take a shower. There were no clothes of Maria's left to wear, so Jessa found a big t-shirt and some boxers for her to put on after the shower. In the meantime, she pulled eggs and ham, peppers and onions from the fridge and began to make an omelet. That would do for starters.

Maria ate the omelet hungrily, but slowly this time so she wouldn't vomit. Long before her plate was empty, she was full and nodding sleepily. A moment later, the young woman ambled over to the bed and, in seconds, was fast asleep.

As tired as she was, Jessa stayed to clean the kitchen and return everything to the fridge. She tried not to think about anything, but Mitch's face kept intruding into her thoughts. What now?

She needed to call him, but it was late and she didn't know what to say to explain what had happened. Hell, she couldn't even explain it to herself. Even so, she left Bristol House a few minutes later, after checking on Maria, and in her mind laughed humorlessly at the turn of events. She was driving Mitch's car... obviously that would have to stop. She sighed with a sadness that touched her very core.

The instant she opened the door to her apartment, she knew she wasn't alone. Her heart skipped with dread, fearing that the shadow monsters had somehow taken over, but there were no monsters anywhere. Carefully, she stuck her head inside her bedroom door...

Mitch slept peacefully in her bed. He'd obviously been in a posture of hopeful waiting as in his hands was the pillow she'd made in eighth grade home-ec class with her name embroidered on it. He hugged the pillow tightly.

Her heart ached with this discovery. She loved him so much, but he belonged to another woman. Very quietly, she slipped out of her shoes and slid into bed behind him, pushing her body right up against him, and put her arm around his waist. Tears spilled onto her cheeks as she slowly succumbed to the sleep she so desperately needed.

CHAPTER TWENTY-EIGHT
LETTING GO

It was a dream she'd had often of late: one moment she was asleep, the next moment she was being awakened by small, hungry kisses across her cheeks and lips. In her dream, she was in love with the charming man kissing her and it seemed only natural to wind her arms around his neck and pull him closer to her. She heard her own sigh of longing when his lips seared a hot trail of kisses on her neck, enflaming the skin there and burning her to her bones. When she felt the weight of his body cover hers...

She realized she had to pee.

Only when she roused herself enough to get off the bed, did she become conscious of the fact that she was still pinned under the weight of his body. Mitch! Her eyes flew open and met his frank and relieved gaze.

"I'm glad you're home," he said in a husky voice that shook with suppressed relief.

"I am, too. How long was I gone?" She spoke softly, not wanting to break the enchanting ambience of the moment.

"Ten long, excruciatingly horrible days." He tightened his grip on her. "What happened? Where were you?"

"It's such a strange story. I'm afraid it will be hard to believe. I'm not sure I believe it myself and it happened to me!" Jessa knew she was deliberately delaying the announcement that Maria was back, but she desperately wanted Mitch for herself for just a bit longer.

A quick glance at the clock said it was still very early; in fact, Jessa had only slept for a couple of hours. Mitch must have discovered her there and couldn't resist a kiss or two. She knew her first priority should be to go check on Maria; in fact she should have brought her back to this apartment because, after all, it was hard to imagine the damage three years in the dark world would have caused, but she had resisted.

Then she gave Mitch a strange, puzzled look. "If you'd been back for ten days, why was your car still at Bristol House? I drove it here from there."

He looked at her for a moment as if he didn't understand the question, but then grinned sheepishly and replied, "That isn't my only car."

"Oh," she snorted in a very unladylike manner, "silly me."

"Besides," he leaned close to her neck again and took tender bites of her skin between words, "I had the title transferred to your name. The convertible is yours."

She pulled away from him, the kisses forgotten. "What! Are you insane? Why?"

"You don't like it? You don't want it?" Mitch sat up so that Jessa could climb off the bed. She stood, arms akimbo, and glared at him.

"I can't *afford* it!" Her chest heaved angrily. She glared.

"You can if I *give* it to you. What's wrong? What happened that you are so defensive? If you don't want the car, then fine. But if you don't want the car because of something that has happened to make you change your mind about me, about us, then I want to know about it. What gives?" He wanted to put an arm around her, but she moved away from him, turned her back, and stared out the window.

Jessa didn't answer for such a long time. She didn't trust her voice to speak without Mitch hearing the cries and hurt in her throat. Finally, she had composed herself enough to say, "Mitch, there is something you need to know."

Then it was his turn for a bout of silence. He tried a laugh as he spoke, but the worry was evident. "Let me guess, you met Vernon Hubert, and he's an ass, and you don't want to be involved with my family any more because you don't want to raise children who will also turn out to be asses."

At that, Jessa grinned. Strangely, a part of that

suggestion was true. "Okay, the Vernon Hubert being an ass part is true, but the rest of it… no. The day you left I went back to Bristol House to get Virginia's diary and the things written there would break your heart. Did you know that they had two sons? The oldest, Joey, died of some strange illness and Virginia blamed Vernon. I don't know if there was physical foul play or if he'd set the boy against his parents and broke his heart. You should read the diary. It's very sad."

Mitch sat heavily on the edge of the bed and rested his head in his hands. "I didn't know that. And then?"

"And then, I made *another* trip back to the house and found Maria's diary…"

"Quite a sleuth, aren't you?"

For a moment, Jessa couldn't tell if the question was made in jest, but she ignored his tone and continued. "I had a dream and a good idea where it was. You know what I'm talking about, don't you? A dream that comes true?" He started to deny it, but before he could speak, she continued, "Don't even go there. You woke up the other morning with a wooden match in your hand after dreaming that I talked to you. And you went to Bristol House to light the candles. Right? That's how I was able to find my way back." She waited until Mitch sighed heavily before she continued. "Maria's diary was full of information, mostly about why things had gotten so out of control. Then she came to me in a dream and wanted me to return to Bristol House to find the key to the Door. And after I found it, well…"

"So, it's true. You were on the other side of the Door." The statement was spoken with sadness and fear.

"The Door has a lock which Vernon had possession of. Thing is, he couldn't come through the Door for all these years because he couldn't find it. But when Maria had her séances, she opened the Door for him. By the time he understood how to use it, she'd stolen the key from him. And then he came after it… and her."

"She was murdered by a ghost?" Mitch looked up at

Jessa with pleading eyes, hardly daring to believe what she was saying. "How can any sane person believe this?"

"Well, that's the thing, isn't it? When Vernon came after Maria, she dropped the key and now he knew where the Door was, but didn't have the key. Neither did she. So their spirits could use the Door and go back and forth, but on this side, their bodies are spectral, not solid. And, Mitch, I found the key. I locked the Door."

"Thank God. Did you ever discover what actually did happen to Maria? Can her ghost be put to rest?"

Jessa tried to smile, but it felt awkward on her face. "I suppose some day. But not today. Maria is not dead. I brought her back with me and locked the Door behind us. She's still at Bristol House in your apartment."

Nothing prepared Jessa for the tears that welled up in Mitch's eyes. Or for the cloudy anger that gathered in his face. "You are kidding me. Damn it to hell, Jessa!"

"No, Mitch, I'm not. Your lives can resume as usual, if that's what you want. I'm going to tell Norma this morning." Jessa tried to keep the heartache out of her voice. She was not Mitch's fiancée, and she refused to stand in his way. Maria would still make a good wife if Mitch wanted it to be so.

"What…" Mitch's voice cracked until he had to stop and clear his throat. "What does she look like? Three years… are you certain she isn't dead? Are you certain she hasn't been infected with Vernon's hatred?"

"Mitch, I was on the dark side of the Door. Just like Maria. Vernon didn't infect her any more than he infected me. When I got ready to return, she was crying that she missed her mother so much; I couldn't bring myself to leave her there. I'm solid and real, see? Maria doesn't look any different than I do. Except maybe she was hungrier. Much hungrier, actually. She made a mess in your fridge." Jessa looked down at her feet as she spoke. She didn't want Mitch to see the anguish she knew would show in her eyes.

He wasn't even looking at her. He stood up from the bed and leaned his forehead against the dark window. His warm breath frosted the cold glass. "Can I see her?" His voice was so soft, Jessa could hardly hear the request.

"Of course. Let's go right now." She stood directly behind Mitch and leaned her forehead against his back, wishing for the millionth time that there had never been a Maria and that she'd met him under different circumstances. Finally, she stepped away from him and pulled on her jacket against the chill of the early morning hours. "Get dressed," she suggested.

While Mitch dressed, Jessa went into the kitchen to make some coffee to drink on the way. She decided she needed the caffeine to stay awake and thought Mitch could use some as well. However, as she stepped up to the kitchen doorway, the postcard of Bristol House leaped off the shelf and landed with a strangely loud thud by her feet. Her jaw dropped open in surprise, though the scream she could hear did not come from her own throat, but from the tiny woman now leaning out of the second floor window in Bristol House's photo. Nearly simultaneously, her eyes flew to the window, which slammed shut with a loud bang just as the black crow, now a powerful raven, fluttered against the glass. Her camera, sitting on the table, snapped a sudden photo of the black bird, its mouth open in a furious scream. This was not over!

Without giving the postcard another glance, all Jessa's thoughts for coffee vanished as she ran back to the bedroom. Though the bed was still mussed from recent occupancy, Mitch was nowhere to be found. An instant later, she grabbed her purse and flew out the door. Not until she was in the BMW did she wonder what Mitch had been driving.

Even with the top up, the convertible was quite chilly. Jessa suspected it would be some time before she would be good and warm. The drive to Bristol House seemed extraordinarily long and was made in anxious silence. It was a lot of information to take in all at once, Jessa knew, especially given the paranormal circumstances of recent events. Would she have believed if these astonishing experiences belonged to someone else?

Where was Mitch now? Had time slipped again?

As she drove up to Bristol House, it abruptly occurred to her: perhaps Mitch wanted to see Maria alone. She was an outsider, after all, to their personal lives from that earlier time.

There was a light on in the attic apartment. Jessa walked as silently as she was able to the house. The big skeleton key was almost hidden in her tight fist. She didn't know if Mitch was here, but it would be a good place to start looking. When she stepped onto the veranda, she could see his dark form sitting noiselessly on a wooden porch swing. She moved to sit beside him. "Mitch?"

"It happened again, didn't it?" Mitch's voice was soft, but full of frustration and dismay.

"I just went in to make coffee. How long was I gone?"

"It's been a couple of hours. You weren't anywhere. I figured you would head here so I have been waiting. I haven't had the nerve to go inside. I'm glad you showed up." Mitch's face reflected the turmoil within. He had no reason to think that Jessa was being anything but honest with him. She did not seem to be given to exaggeration… sarcasm, yes, but not exaggeration. Yet, how could he believe what she was asking him to believe? If Maria was actually at the house waiting for him, where was she these last three years if not just where Jessa said she was? Maria would have contacted her mother if she'd been able; that was a certainty.

"I'm sorry. I don't know what's happening. I thought by locking the Door it might be over, but as soon as I stepped into the kitchen, I knew it wasn't. I don't know what to do, but I know there is something." Jessa swallowed her fear, scooting closer to Mitch to let his warm body feed her the courage she needed. "I'm ready to go inside. I hope Maria is okay."

He nodded silently and stood, pulling Jessa with him. The door creaked softly as they unlocked and opened it. The house inside was silent. They stood, hand in hand, and looked around, then finally faced each other. Then in soundless agreement, they headed for the third story apartment.

It wasn't until Jessa was halfway up the stairs to the second story did she remember the terrifying trip through the dark forest when she had gone to fetch Maria's diary. With that in her mind, she sprinted the rest of the way up and waited for Mitch there. He gave her a puzzled frown, but didn't ask about it as they continued on up into the master bedroom and the apartment above that.

The moment Mitch's eyes landed on Maria, Jessa knew she'd done the right thing. His eyes softened and his shoulders sagged with relief from the heavy load he had carried with him for so long. He looked infinitely tired and strangely old.

The other woman was not in bed where Jessa had left her; she was sitting daintily on the couch with the television on, but with no sound. There was no indication she knew they were there until Maria, without her eyes straying from the program on the television, spoke softly. "So much has changed."

Mitch nodded in agreement, and though he'd made no sound, Jessa had the distinct feeling that Maria had "heard" him. As it seemed often to be with people who knew each other so intimately, there was an undeniable connection between them. Jessa was jealous at once, but she schooled her features into a placid mask and watched the silent couple with interest.

When he sat beside her, Maria, still without looking at him, reached over to pat his knee as if consoling a child. Finally, she raised her eyes to meet his. Still, she was a beautiful woman. "It's alright, darling. I missed you."

A sob threatened to push through Mitch's chest. With difficulty, he worked through it and finally said in a husky voice, "I missed you, too. I thought you were dead. We all did."

Maria smiled slightly, though it was tinged with sadness. "I did, too. Everything is so muddled in my head. I'm so sorry I put you through this, Mitch. I never wanted to hurt you."

"I know you didn't. I never intended to ignore you. If I could go back…"

Maria reached up and put her hand over Mitch's lips. "No!" she said forcefully. "Don't speak of the past. What's done is done. If I've learned anything, it's to let the past go. That is a road I never intend to travel again. I know things are different now. Things change. Some good and some bad. But you aren't the same man, and I'm not the same woman. I don't ever want to be that woman again."

A tear slid down Mitch's cheek, which he wiped angrily away. "I never stopped loving you, Maria, in spite of what your mother says. I would appreciate it if you remember that when you go to her."

Maria smiled again, but this time with joy. "Yes, I suspect Mother was quite put out with you. Jessa tells me that Mother hired her to snoop on you."

Then to Jessa's embarrassment, they both turned to look at her. Suddenly self-conscious, Jessa turned her gaze from them and backed away toward the kitchen. When she bumped into the counter, she turned and made a show of examining the contents of a bowl of fruit. When she peeked back at them, they had once again turned their attention to each other.

Maria had a soft hand on Mitch's cheek as she spoke, "How long have we loved each other, Mitch? I don't remember life without you in it."

The words Maria spoke were like hot knives thrown into her skin. As Jessa listened, she could feel the contents of her stomach sour and rise. Maria and Mitch were still in love. And that left her exactly… nowhere.

As silently as possible, she turned away from the couple on the couch and slipped out of the apartment. She prayed feverishly that no spectral nonsense would impede her flight from Bristol House. Just once, more than she could have imagined, she wanted to get away from the house: not to escape the ghosts, but to escape the ache that threatened to destroy her heart.

CHAPTER TWENTY-NINE
THE POSTCARD

Even knowing she would wake up Norma Escher, Jessa determinedly stopped by the woman's home just before daylight and knocked loudly on the front door. For several long minutes, the house remained silent, and Jessa wondered if the Eschers were home. Just as she was about to leave, she could hear the sound of movement and the unmistakable whispers of questions. They were trying to decide whether or not to open the door.

Jessa smiled crossly and pounded on the door again. Then, just for good measure, she pushed in the doorbell several times, listening with satisfaction to the echoes of musical notes.

Finally, the heavy door opened only as far as the safety chain would reach, and she could see David's single eye peer through the crack. When he realized it was Jessa, the eye went wide and the door went shut. A moment later, the door was opened all the way. David and Norma both stood in terry robes, worried expressions, and welcomed her into their home.

As soon as they shut the door behind her, she grinned at them and said, "Sit down."

A WEARY HOUR LATER, Jessa returned to her apartment. She felt beat up physically and drained emotionally. The meeting with the Eschers went very well, all things considered. Norma, usually dressed to kill and artfully made up, flew into a pair of well-worn jeans and a wrinkled t-shirt and yanked on her poor husband until he was also dressed. Before they headed out to Bristol House to meet their daughter, though, Norma insisted on listening to Jessa's story not once, but twice, asking her question after question until the facts were firm in her head. How much of the strange and extraordinary, bizarre and fantastic story they believed or understood, Jessa couldn't tell. Their hearts were hungry for any information, no matter how outlandish. In regards to their daughter, they were willing to believe anything that would bring her back to them. Though for as much as Norma was anxious and excited to see her estranged daughter, there was some hesitation and trepidation in her manner. At last, when all her questions were answered satisfactorily, they were finally in their car, driving away from Jessa with a grateful wave of their hands.

At her apartment, Jessa bypassed the lure of her bed for the unwelcome seduction of her kitchen. The postcard still lay on the floor where she'd left it. She hesitated to pick it up, but knew she had to see what was going on with the picture of Bristol House. Dread coiled in her stomach like a snake getting ready to strike.

In the photo, the tiny woman in the upper story window that Jessa thought to be Maria, was now gone. Every window except one was dark, and in that one the black silhouette of a heavy-set man leaned against the sash. The eyes glowed red and black and she could almost hear the rumbling of anger in the man's chest. The strangest thing about the photo was, except for the red angry eyes, all color had been leached out of the postcard and was beginning to resemble the aged photos that she had seen from Virginia's diary. Vernon was still very angry and he still lusted after the key. That thought made the very object he wanted burn hotly in her pocket.

What now? She set the postcard back on the shelf and sighed. Picking the camera up from the table, she pressed the play button to study the image of the angry raven. Even knowing what it would look like, she couldn't stop the sudden gasp of surprise at its raging expression: beak open wide, talons fully extended as if to rip a gash through the glass. She turned the camera off quickly to get away from the image.

Later, showered and dressed in a comfy pair of sweats

and big sweatshirt, she lay down on her bed to sleep, but sleep didn't come. Even as tired as she was, she was unable to forget the conversation between Mitch and his beloved Maria. They had, in front of her, confessed their continued love for each other. Jessa tried not to let the hurt envelope her, and she rolled to her side, curling up into a fetal position. The tears that threatened finally broke loose and spilled down her face and onto her pillow. Great sobs soon followed.

Sleep finally claimed her.

Much later, a persistent pounding, followed by a deep-voice shouting her name, yanked her back to the conscious world. She tried to muffle the noise by putting her pillow over her head, but that only stopped the noise for a few fleeting moments. Then, an angry sound of wood splintering shot through her pillow barrier, and she sat up quickly and looked around her in a daze. She could feel her face was puffy and red from crying.

When Mitch's face materialized at her bedroom door, she couldn't decide if she was ecstatic or furious. All she could do was open and close her lips with the gulping motion of a fish out of water. Finally, she settled with a sarcastic, "If you wanted a key, all you had to do was ask."

Mitch leaned against the doorframe of her bedroom, out of breath after breaking the wood around the lock on the apartment door with the heel of his boot. He looked chagrined for only a moment before folding his arms across his chest angrily. He glared with one eyebrow cocked up. "I thought you disappeared again."

Jessa rubbed her face with her palms and sighed. Then she glared fiercely back at him, annoyed that he would think she wanted to be a witness to their amorous declarations. "Of course I left. Did you expect that I wanted to watch you and Maria proclaim your everlasting love for one another?"

Mitch snorted and sat down on the edge of the bed near Jessa. She pulled her arm and leg away from him as if she were afraid he was crawling with lice. "If you had stayed, you might have learned something."

"I learned everything I needed to know. The rest is just junk as far as I'm concerned." She pushed the covers away from her and slipped out of the bed. "I'm assuming you and Maria are picking up where you left off. Did you see Norma? She was anxious, I think."

Mitch nodded but continued to stare at Jessa strangely. "Norma was very emotional. I think she still holds me responsible for everything. I guess I don't blame her. If I had a daughter... I guess it doesn't matter. David didn't say much. Maria and I have had a long time apart. We have both changed. I have moved to a place in my life that stopped involving her. I had started to like where I was. Now she has returned and—."

"And," Jessa interrupted, "now that she is back in your life, you both have some adjustments to make. I imagine Maria will be more careful with her activities from now on. Lucky you, though. She is lovely." Imagining them together sliced a fresh gash in her heart.

"I do love her," Mitch didn't lose the puzzled expression as he spoke, "but I'm not *in love* with her. Sometimes I'm not sure I ever really was in love with her. I thought I was. Everyone thought I was. But now, I know it isn't true. I am in love with someone else."

Jessa's eyes narrowed sharply at the possibilities. A sudden, comical picture of Lucille Ball and Ricky Ricardo came into her head. "'Splain yourself, Lucy!" she said in a terrible Cuban accent.

"I love *you*, Jessa. You're the most irritating, sarcastic woman I've ever known... and I wouldn't change a thing about you!"

His words refused to congeal in her head. What was he talking about? He was in love with her? Had he flipped? Dare she hope he was telling the truth? She wanted to pinch herself to be sure she wasn't dreaming. "You can't love me."

"You can't stop me," he retorted.

"But guys like you love girls like Maria. Not me. I'm just a regular girl."

She was startled by his sudden laugh. "If by regular you mean normal, then you've got it all wrong. There's nothing normal about you. In fact, I'd wager there's little about you that is ordinary in any way. I have my work cut out for me just to keep up with you. You have more impudence than anyone I've ever known. You're brave. You are truly a good person. Your brain: it is irritating, annoying, sarcastic, and jumps from one place to another quicker than most people can think. I love your brain."

She grinned crookedly, sifting for the compliment in his words. "Thanks, I think." She wanted so much to believe he meant what he was saying, but what about Maria? She'd heard them confess their love. What about that? "Want to talk about it over coffee?" she asked tentatively. At his nod, she headed for the kitchen.

The sudden vision of the Bristol House postcard sitting precariously on the shelf in the kitchen made her stop short just outside the bedroom. She looked back at Mitch where he stood by the window, staring out into the street. She calculated for a moment, weighing her actions: the last couple of times she went to make coffee, Mitch disappeared. Or more likely, it was she who disappeared. Now, because she was so tired of fighting it, she was unwilling to take that chance. She turned back into the room.

"Mitch? Would you come to the kitchen with me? I don't want to slip away again. And to be honest, I'm scared. I'm not as brave as you think I am." Jessa lifted her eyes to meet his, but the expression on his face was unreadable. Sadness? Fear?

He looked like he wanted to respond, but no words came from his lips. So in answer, he turned away from the window and took her hand. Jessa led the way, but walked more slowly as she approached the kitchen.

"What's wrong?" Mitch asked quietly, sensing her

growing fear.

Jessa stopped and looked back at him. Then she nodded toward the shelf and whispered, "This is where you usually lose me. See that postcard? When I get a foot or so from the shelf, it falls off. I swear the photo looks different every time I look at it."

"What is in the photo?" He stared at the card as if it would spontaneously burst into flames.

"Bristol House. Watch carefully. The kitchen window is open, and a bird will fly into view. You can see the bird's image in my camera. It's creepy."

Mitch stared hard toward the kitchen without moving from his spot in the hall. "If anyone but you told me this, I'd call them a liar. But you have been honest with me... well, mostly." He grinned to soften his words.

She grinned back. "Self-preservation," she replied flippantly.

Then, as she turned back toward the kitchen, her fingers slipped very slowly away from Mitch's. As they lost their touch, Jessa could feel a cold void crowd in on her. She whirled around in excruciatingly slow motion. Mitch began to flicker like an old movie reel spinning to a stop. "Mitch...!" she screamed as she lunged for him.

"Jessa...!" His voice was low and sluggish. His body fell gently forward, toward her, with his arms extended. Her image flickered and wavered with the dying beat of a heart monitor. "Jessa! Jessa! Jessa!" There was pain and panic in his scream.

In the last moment of visualization, their outstretched hands finally made contact. The old movie reel sped up and straightened; the heart monitor picked up and maintained its steady pace; and Jessa and Mitch clung together in an embrace that stole their breaths away.

Minutes passed as they gripped each other in thankful awareness. So close... they were too close to losing each other in a bizarre slip of time... again. Jessa leaned her head back so she could see his face, but never let go of his fingers. She shook with the terror of what had almost happened.

"Together, okay?" Her voice wavered, but like an old friend, her brave resolve checked in, and with Mitch firmly in tow, she plunged straight for the kitchen shelf.

The postcard of Bristol House leaped from the shelf and fell with a loud, strangely metallic thud at her feet. She reached down with her free hand and picked up the card to examine the photo. What she saw there frightened her more than anything she'd ever seen or experienced.

The photo, dark in super-contrasted black and white, looked almost nothing like the postcard she'd purchased that day weeks ago. The house itself had become older and had fallen to disrepair. Wild, unkempt shrubs and trees littered the lawn and nearly covered the veranda. The most frightening thing of all, though, was the souls reaching out from the windows in utter terror. A man. A woman. A daughter. And a very gleeful silhouette of a heavy-set man with terrible red eyes.

Mitch stared in appalled fascination over her shoulder as she studied the card. "What the hell is that?" he croaked.

Jessa could only stare mutely up at him. Finally, she found enough voice to murmur, "Oh my dear lord! Vernon has them!"

Mitch was immediately tense, alerted by her words and tone. "Them who?"

"Maria and her parents! Oh lord, Mitch, they're in trouble! We need to get there!" Yanking on his arm, Jessa dashed into the kitchen in time to hear the slamming of the small window. The huge black raven flew its body heavily into the glass, cracking the surface from impact to edge. Broken shards fanned out from the blow, yet the bird stayed there flapping its wings frantically to get in. Jessa drew in a horrified breath as she watched the beak and talons hit the fragmented glass repeatedly. In contrast to the dark body, its bright eyes were the color of hot flames. She backed slowly away until the kitchen table stopped her.

Mitch pulled her close to him, away from the table, when he heard the disjointed click of her camera's shutter. In the instant that the photo was visible on the LCD screen, they could see the angry black bird filling the screen, beak open in a wild scream, orange and yellow flames leaping from its eyes. Terrified beyond words, Jessa silently turned and dashed from the room, jerking a willing Mitch behind her.

Without stopping to get embarrassed, she peeled off the sweats she was wearing and slipped into the pair of dirty jeans she'd thrown on the floor just before her shower. In the pocket of the jeans was the key to the Door where she knew she'd find Vernon Hubert.

MITCH DROVE, gripping the steering wheel with white-knuckled fingers. He stared straight ahead, silently, wishing they were already there and dreading when they would be. He had no love for Bristol House, now more than ever.

Jessa sat in likewise position, her mind a movie reel of alternate endings and possible outcomes. What would she find when they got there? Or was she just out of her mind with worry for no reason? In the worst-case scenario, would she be able to help save them?

When they pulled into the Bristol House driveway, Mitch unexpectedly stopped the car alongside the commemorative plaque on the signboard. Like a switch, the light was abruptly drained from a weak sun that had been trying to shine through heavy, autumn clouds. For a moment, they shared a look that was full of dread before Mitch rolled the car slowly toward the house.

The closer they got to the house, the more it resembled the photo on Jessa's shelf. In their absence, a wind had swept up and pulled a shutter from a window; limbs and branches lay strewn about as if it had seen little care lately; and in the dark, gray autumn afternoon, there was little color left in its façade.

Though David and Norma's car was still parked in the driveway, the house itself was deathly silent.

CHAPTER THIRTY
HAUNTED FOREST

There was a small comfort that she was not going to be walking into the house alone. As they headed for the veranda, Jessa checked in her pocket for the key to the Door. Certain she'd locked it yesterday, she was convinced the only way to keep it locked was to destroy the key itself. Her biggest concern now was to make sure Vernon stayed on his side of the Door while Maria and her parents remained on the other.

She was so deep in thought that she wasn't watching her steps until Mitch shouted in frustration. As she looked up, the walkway to the house had lengthened until the house was a small spot on the horizon.

She whispered a harsh expletive under her breath. Then she turned to Mitch and declared, "Vernon will try anything to keep us away. He knows I have the key. Keep your eyes on the door and don't look away no matter what happens. If we don't focus, the house's location may change. And hold my hand. If one of us has our attention diverted, we could be separated." She held her hand out to him.

He hesitated, puzzled, for only a moment, but his face smoothed in assent. Even without this miserable burden, he had come to trust her completely. Clasping her hand securely, he ran with her for the front door, eyes glued to their destination, minds focused on their task.

As they got closer to the house, the air became so thick that breathing turned painful. A fierce wind kicked up in their faces, swirling grit in their eyes and stinging their skin with tears. Their breathing labored under the strain; their movements became sluggish and difficult. Each step was demanding as they inched their way forward.

Time meant nothing as they neared the veranda. With all their focus on the front door, the house finally began to loom larger. Step by step, they struggled against the wind and the infernal sluggishness that slowed their pace to almost a crawl. At the edge of the wide porch, Jessa reached out to grab onto the railing several times before she could finally feel the smooth banister under her hand. It was so slippery that for a moment, her grip almost failed.

With effort, they launched their bodies up onto the veranda floor. At last, as they finally stood in front of the door, Jessa felt something sticky on her palms where she'd gripped the porch rail. Hundreds of tiny insects were smeared and plastered to the grooves of her hands. She stared in horror as the minuscule bug segments beaded together into whole beings and began to move up her wrist with a delicate clicking sound.

"Oooh, oooh," she shrieked in a panic, scraping her hands harshly against her jeans. The tiny insects fell off easily. She checked her arms and legs for any signs of the little creatures and when she was certain they were off of her, she looked up and grimaced at the appalled expression on Mitch's face. Was this Vernon's tactic to scare her? She cringed.

The front door was unlocked and standing slightly open. Jessa peeked inside timidly. She could feel Mitch's warm, uneven breath near her ear as he leaned in nervously beside her. The house was quiet and smelled stale. She listened for any sounds, hoping to hear some shuffling movement that might belong to the Eschers, but there was nothing except the awful silence.

Mitch scrambled into the room behind her in a protective hover. Inside, the room was dark and smelled of decay. She could only hear the rhythmic beating of her heart and the hollow sound of her own breathing as the air filled and vacated her lungs. Its intensity made her ears hurt.

"We need to check the wall in the parlor, and if the Door is open, then I'll make certain it's locked. But more than anything, we need to find Maria and her parents. If Vernon was somehow able to take them through the Door, then just locking it won't be enough." Jessa grabbed Mitch's shirtfront with both hands. "And don't let go of me!"

His eyes went wide with incredulity. "What can we do besides lock the door? What more is there? I'll do anything to help; just tell me what to do."

Feeling the weight of the world on her small shoulders, she sagged against him. Finally she looked up and whispered, "If we can find the Eschers and be certain they are on this side of the Door and Vernon is on the other where he belongs, we need to lock the Door and then destroy the key. Thing is, I don't know what destroys it."

Mitch was stunned, but determined. He took Jessa by the shoulders and turned her around, away from him, but kept a firm clasp on her hand. "Let's get this over with. Whatever it is that you need from me, I'll do it. What first?"

"We'll locate Maria and her parents first. Then we can figure out what destroys the key later." She turned enough to meet his eyes and almost smiled. Then, with her concentration on the stairway to the second floor, they started slowly across the wooden floor.

Their hand-in-hand search of the first floor revealed nothing noteworthy. The cellar door was locked tightly in the pantry. The kitchen was empty. The strange annex bedroom was untouched. All of the closets were bare. Jessa slid her hand across the smooth wall in the parlor where the Door was located. It appeared to be firmly locked and still, except for the faintest vibration that thumped against her palm like an errant heartbeat. Though evidence said the Eschers were still here at the house, they were nowhere on the first floor. Then they turned their attention to the stairway.

As they moved, their footsteps echoed strangely. They were both aware of it, but said nothing. Before they reached the steps, they realized that something had changed. Jessa almost touched the railing to the upstairs, but then a sound from Mitch distracted her. She turned, instead, to see what had troubled him. He was staring down at his feet. Her gaze followed his.

The smooth wooden floor was littered with dead, spongy pine needles. They had entered the forest where Jessa had found herself when she went for Maria's diary. It was black as pitch; the upper floor doorway was a bright light shining in the far distance.

"I knew you had… seen things. But it's so much worse than I could have imagined." Mitch's voice was cold and low, whispered as if he didn't believe what he was seeing. "I always believed you, but this… this is so much worse."

"Hang on to your hat, cowboy," she whispered back, "it's about to get serious. I was here before. One of us has to keep our eyes on the light at all times. When I was distracted, the light moved farther away. If we can stay together, linked physically, then maybe we have a better chance of not losing our focus. There are things here that you don't want to meet. Trust me."

The ground was a thick, spongy soup as their shoes made sucking sounds with every step. Gnarled branches, hard to see in the blackness, grabbed at their hair and clothes. Jessa stared at the light until her eyes burned, but the way was always twisting and rambling, and the light so far away.

She could feel Mitch holding her hand tightly; so tight, in fact, that she was afraid she was losing circulation in her hand. She glanced back at him, praying that his eyes were still focused on the second floor light, and screamed in surprise. Looking down at her fingers, she opened them quickly and dropped the strange skeletal hand she held, the same one she'd seen the other day. It flopped on the ground, shaking as if it were laughing, before digging itself into the piney floor.

Heart racing wildly, she looked around for Mitch, terrified of losing him in this mad, godforsaken forest and fearful of traveling this path alone. The darkness was so complete, though, that she couldn't make out anything more than the black, craggy pine trees, and the darkest blue sky beyond. When she closed her eyes, she discovered that the mad pine forest was not silent.

A quiet, weeping sailed through her mind; a woman or girl was crying, and the sadness was almost tangible. For a moment, she had to console herself or fall into crying, also. With a quick glance over her shoulder at the light, she gingerly walked away from it and toward the expression of grief.

Not far away, she could see the young woman sitting on a stump with her face buried in her hands. The woman's shoulders shook with each breath as she sobbed. Tears streamed through her fingers. The woman's white dress was in tatters, but once it must've been beautiful. Then Jessa, as she registered who the woman was, realized Maria wasn't alone. Kneeling beside her was Mitch.

They both looked up to her at the same time. Beside them, on the ground, was three candles partially burned down. They smoked as if they'd been recently lit. Then it hit her like a runaway truck: Maria had relit the candles. Maria had called to Vernon!

Anger was immediate and hot. A red, glowing resentment welled up suddenly and took complete control of Jessa's wits. "What the hell have you done?" she screamed.

Maria jumped up and ran to her, putting her arms around Jessa's shoulders. Jessa tried to shrug away, but Maria was strong and held on tightly. "Oh, Jessa, Jessa, forgive me! I should have run from Bristol House when I had the chance. Vernon came to me like he used to before he became so solid. I felt sorry for him. I wanted to give him the key. Mother tried to stop me. So did Daddy. What have I done? What have I done?"

With that, Maria turned away from Jessa and Mitch and leaned her forehead against a tree. Jessa's stomach tightened in a knot of nausea. Had Maria, teetering between sanity and insanity, forged an emotional bond with her captor? "Where are your parents now?" Jessa steeled herself against Maria's tears.

"Upstairs. Asleep. I gave them something. They're okay. I thought if I could help Vernon, then no one else would have to know what I'd done. I'd help him then I'd take my parents away. I didn't realize that once he had me, he'd want them, too. He doesn't have them yet, but he will if I can't save them. But I didn't think! I didn't remember what Vernon could do! And now I can't find my way out of this damned forest."

Maria spoke so softly that Jessa could barely hear her at all. "How can I believe anything you say?" Jessa asked. From the corner of her eye, she could see Mitch's frown. He didn't want to believe Maria wasn't telling the truth. "How do I know this isn't a trick to trap us all?"

Maria turned to face her, eyes shining bright and full of tears. "Be… because I have this for you. It's the only way to destroy the key." She held out her hand. In her palm rested the medallion, shining abnormally bright in the darkness. Jessa could see the recess where the key fitted into place.

Jessa took the medallion quietly, hoping it would be the means to the end, but that didn't include the fact that they needed to get out of the deadly dark forest first. "Okay, we'll take this thing one step at a time." She looked back toward the light. It was farther away now, but still close enough for a clinging hope. "Last time I held Mitch's hand, he still slipped away from me. We can't be so careless, not even for a moment. We need to talk, constantly. If you leave or think you need to veer off then we have to know. Understand? We can't afford any miscommunication."

Mitch nodded slowly. Maria agreed hastily and grabbed Jessa's hand. She gripped Mitch in her other hand and waited eagerly for Jessa's command. Jessa hesitated slightly, feeling the weight of many lives on her shoulders. Still, it seemed to be her decision, and she knew there was no one else who could make it for her.

With her eyes on the light, she headed to the meandering path again. There was a constant stream of babble between them as they traveled, to reassure each other that no one had dropped away. When Jessa's eyes glanced at the other two, their eyes were on their destination; when Mitch peeked at the women, they were looking straight ahead. No one was more vigilant than Maria. Her gaze never wavered from the light.

Minutes into their trek, they could hear the faint beating of drums. Not drums, Jessa thought with a panic, but the beating of a heart. It became loud, then soft as it wafted on the wind. She stumbled on a rock in the path. When she looked down, she was surprised to see there *was* a path. It was well worn enough to indicate that it had been traveled many times before, but who would be traveling such a path?

Up ahead, the path curved sharply to the right. They hesitated. It moved away from the second story, but Jessa was reluctant to veer off it: what was beyond it that needed avoiding? Carefully, she picked a stone up and tossed it into the black void beyond the trail. She could hear the "plop" into water, then something large broke the water's surface and growled. With a frightened yelp, the trio sprinted away, following the groove worn in the ground.

They were finally making some headway toward their destination. The light from the second story doorway was only yards away. It was all they could do not to break free of each other and make a run for it, but Jessa had the sudden suspicion that it would not be a wise move. She stopped abruptly and pulled Maria's hand until she and Mitch had also stopped.

"What?" Mitch whispered anxiously. "The door is right there. Why can't we just run?"

Jessa shrugged with eyes narrowed on the pathway between her and the door. "Because we'd never make it."

Immediately, on the path, the annoying skeletal hand crawled out of the springy pine needle floor. It wasn't alone. Foggy shadows, void of light and sound, crept in from beside and behind them. Maria screamed as she whirled her head around. She seemed to be familiar with these dark entities.

"This is bullshit," Mitch growled quietly, never taking

his eyes from the decaying hand as it crept closer.

Indecision hemmed them in as their foes inched closer. Finally, Maria turned slightly toward Mitch and spoke rapidly, softly, "Mitch, I'm really sorry. If I get out of this, I will never allow anyone but the living into my life. You are a wonderful man. I'm sorry it didn't work out between us, but it wouldn't have anyway. As I said before, I've changed and I don't want to be part of your life any longer. Jessa, if we make it out of here, thanks for saving my life. You will have my eternal gratefulness."

"You are leaving Mitch?" Jessa's throat hurt just to ask.

"I left him a long time ago. I chose the dead over the living. What does that say about our relationship?" Jessa could hear the hurt and sadness in her words. Her eyes searched for Mitch's.

He was not looking at her. At long last, he advised, in a tone that brooked no argument, "Together... I'll kick the hell out of the hand like I'm making a field goal. Then we duck and make a dash for the door. Count of three? One. Two. Three!"

Without stopping to think about the risks, they ran for the hand and Mitch aimed a ruthless boot directly in the palm. The bony fingers splayed in surprise, then met the boot in a scattering joints and cartilage in all directions. The shadows, slow to react, reached out fat arms to scoop up the humans, but they ducked and slipped beneath their grip.

They tumbled into the upstairs hallway and immediately looked back at the door. The stairway was dark, though not as dark as the forest, and the only thing left of the woodlands was the sad and distraught, "Oooh, oooh," of the shadows as they lumbered away empty-handed.

Jessa almost giggled as she rose from the floor. She dashed into the far bedroom, knowing somehow that the room where the diaries were found would be where she'd find Maria's parents. When she got there, they were sitting on the bed, dazed, but unharmed.

"Quick! Come with me!" She took Norma's hand and pulled her from the bed. Like obedient children, the Eschers stumbled quickly after Jessa. When she reached Mitch and Maria, she motioned for them. "Let's use the back stairway by the kitchen. I don't know about you, but I'd just as soon not take the chance that the forest will reappear."

With nods of agreement all around, they dashed to the back of the house where the stairs, narrower and steeper, led to the hallway between the dining room and the kitchen on the first floor. Running through the house, they hurried for the front door and the safety of the veranda. Only Jessa stopped when she heard and felt the faint pounding behind the parlor wall where the Door was located.

Timidly, she put her palm out flat against the flowered wallpaper and closed her eyes. Thump. Thump. She could feel the unceasing strikes as a massive body was propelled against the Door.

Vernon.

She reached into her pockets and held out the medallion in one palm and the key in the other. Apart they looked innocent enough, but together she knew they had a power that knew no bounds.

As she brought them together, the pounding beat on the other side quickened as if frantic. The faint click as the key and medallion locked together silenced the thrashing... but only for a moment. In the calm, Jessa walked to the middle of the room and looked all around her. Then in a flash, the heavy low beating started up again, this time from every direction as if the house itself suddenly had acquired a heartbeat. Breathing accompanied the steady rhythm... thump... thump...

Bristol House had become a living thing, brought together by the sinister man who always thought the house was his to control. High-pitched squeals of the tiny shadow monsters, with their big mouths and sharp teeth, echoed through the halls. The walls shook with dour emotion.

Unwanted, her heart began to beat in tandem with the house. She whirled around the room, searching with her eyes for the front door, but the walls all looked the same and there was no place to run. Little, scared noises escaped from her throat as she ran from wall to wall. The house was going to swallow her up because she couldn't find the way out of it.

CHAPTER THIRTY-ONE
GHOSTLY SOJOURN

The tempo of the house changed slowly. Jessa sank to her knees and put her hands over her ears. Thump thump... thump thump... Jes-sa... Jes-sa... it seemed to say. Terrified, she closed her eyes and curled up into a ball.

A scratching sound begged for her attention through all the loud wailing of the tiny shadow monsters and the thumping and bumping from the other side of the Door. Because it was such a distinct sound, so different from anything around her, she risked an open eye to locate the source. From her spot in the middle of the floor, she examined the walls along the baseboard, the corners, and the ceiling. Then, gasping with dread, she sensed rather than saw, the decaying skeletal hand crawl and scratch its way down the bottom step of the stairway. It had come out through the stairway/forest!

Crawling back on all fours like a spider, Jessa backed away from the hand until she was forced up against the far wall. "Go away!" she screamed, but the hand, with its clinging skin and knuckles clicking with every movement, kept its steady forward pace. When it was closer to her, she kicked out at it with her foot. She knew it was a futile gesture because it had regrouped after Mitch kicked it apart. What was this horrid beast? What did it want?

In a last-ditch effort, Jessa pulled the medallion from her pocket and swung it by the chain at the mutilated palm. She struck at it repeatedly, but nothing would stop it. At last, exhausted, Jessa hurtled the medallion once more, but this time the hand leaped up and caught the pendant in its fingers. With a fierce yank, the medallion was wholly in the hand's possession, and Jessa was staring after it dumbstruck. She scrambled after it, but the hand now scampered quickly away.

When it was inside the doorway that led upstairs/to

the forest, the fingers curled up and squashed the metal until it was an unrecognizable hunk of gold. The key, crushed inside the medallion, became useless. As the fingers continued to bear down, the mangled gold began to melt with great heat.

Jessa tore her eyes from the melting gold and looked fearfully around the room. The tempo of the thumping increased. The breathing became labored. Sweat poured from her face and arms. She peeled off her jacket and threw it aside.

By now the gold was a bright pool at the bottom of the stairs. The hand was gone, though it could have been burnt to cinders by the heat. The wallpaper on the parlor wall began to bubble and the walls themselves buckled. Jessa looked around desperately for a way out. At last, she could see the front door standing wide open. She was as far from it as she could be, while still remaining in the parlor. So close, but impossibly far.

The oxygen, coming in the door, caused the walls of the parlor to combust and burst into bright orange flame. The Door, a dark void, began to suck in the buckled, burning walls. Keeping low to the ground, Jessa started to crawl to the front door.

Smoke filled the air, replacing the oxygen. She coughed and tried to breathe normally, but the heat seared her throat and lungs. All she could think about was escaping from Bristol House. If she made it out alive, there was absolutely nothing in the world that would make her return to this place.

Her eyes stayed on the door and the light. Inch by inch, she crept closer. Flames leaped around her like dancers, nipping and touching, but always moving. Smoke tried to dull her vision, but she refused to give in to panic and terror.

At one point, she wasn't sure she would make it. She closed her eyes and rested her face against the wooden floor. Her hands, still outstretched, lay motionless. A moment later, though, she could feel the cool touch of a hand on hers, grabbing and pulling her toward the door. Two hands.

She was pulled clumsily, though with great relief, out into the cool, damp grass away from the house. Sitting up carefully, she stared into the worried eyes of Mitch and Maria. "Who...?" she began.

Maria grinned and picked up one of Jessa's hands. "We both did. Mitch took one and I took the other. I'm so glad you're safe!"

A loud rumble exploded behind them. They turned quickly around in time to see a magnificent fireball rise up from the roof of Bristol House. Glass exploded outward from the windows and soon flames licked hungrily at the sills. The neatly painted exterior bubbled and burned, and the intricate gingerbread soon dissolved into char.

Far down the street, they could hear the high-pitched wailing of a fire engine racing towards them. Bristol House was beyond saving. All five survivors huddled close to the old stables and waited for the bright red engines to speed up the narrow driveway, but nothing could be done except to watch it burn.

Mitch put his arms protectively around Jessa's shoulders as they stood, fascinated, and watched the house burn. The fire was infinitely bright in the dark sky. Even as the men from the fire truck scrambled to pull the hoses off the back of the truck, Jessa could see that there would not be much to cool off... the house was burning too quickly.

Fanned by spectral hands, the flames engulfed the house. The Door, destroyed now and beyond use, sucked in the burning timbers as they fell. In only a short time, and as the firemen and onlookers stared in fascination, there was soon nothing left of Bristol House except for a small amount of smoking rubble.

In the instants after the house was completely gone, Jessa looked into the smoke and, for a moment, thought she could see people in old-fashioned clothes walking through the remains. She squinted and concentrated on the figures. Then with a start, she recognized Virginia and S. J. Hubert. With them, shrunken and defeated, was the wispy form of Vernon. They were no more substantial than the smoke they walked through. Virginia and S. J. embraced Vernon, turning their backs on Jessa with an appreciative nod. Jessa knew this was the last anyone would see of these long-ago people. Just as she was about to follow the others to the cars, her eyes caught sight of a little boy who had been standing so still that she hadn't noticed him until now. Joey! He grinned and waved at her, then he, too, turned and ran quickly after his parents and uncle.

Tears pricked at her eyes, but she said nothing as the cars whisked them away from the Bristol House location.

IT TOOK JESSA DAYS to warm up despite almost burning in the fire. Mitch was a constant presence as she recuperated. She missed Maria, who had returned to her home in Birmingham. Wisconsin was too cold, she declared, but she loved Jessa and made her promise that she and Mitch would come for a visit soon.

"I love you!" Jessa's heart beat a little faster and unfamiliar electricity shot through her body. She'd never tire or get used to those words spoken to her by Mitch. He lay on the bed with her, arms around her tightly, as if he was afraid she'd disappear again.

Timidly, she replied, "I love you, too. You have no idea..."

Mitch grunted and ignored her statement. "I do have an idea!"

After a few days, Jessa finally crawled out of bed as her beloved photography called to her. David and Norma Escher had given her a scandalous amount of money for helping Maria return to them. She hadn't wanted to accept the money, but they insisted. Afterwards, they closed the restaurant and followed Maria down to Birmingham. It was, perhaps, their way of keeping an eye on their daughter or maybe they just couldn't bear to have her out of their sight.

Early one morning, Jessa woke up and watched Mitch sleep. The lines of exhaustion and worry that etched his face were finally clearing. The weight of the years had taken their toll, and he now slept harder than he had ever slept. Jessa carefully slipped out of bed, not wanting to disturb him.

She padded quietly into the kitchen. A few feet from the kitchen shelf, Jessa looked up to see the postcard of Bristol House. Her mind was on other things as she stepped closer. Just as she was within reach of the shelf, however, the card leaped off and fluttered toward Jessa.

Her heart leaped painfully in her chest. Oh no! Then her hands shot out and fumbled around trying to catch the card as it fluttered in the air. Finally, she snagged the card just before it landed on the floor. For the first time, she didn't feel the presence of dread.

She examined the photo and what she saw astonished her. This was not a photo of Bristol House, but of the ruins that were once the house. Burned to the stone foundation, the woods and lawn were green and dazzling. There was an inset of the house as it appeared before the fire, and it was bright and colorful—as it was intended to be.

Immediately her gaze flew to the kitchen window. It was shut and locked, just as she had fixed it the night before, and when she went to peer outside, there no birds to be seen. Even the broken glass had miraculously been mended with the disappearance of the malevolent figures that haunted Bristol House.

Jessa knew Mitch had plans to rebuild Bristol House, and it seemed the right thing to do, but this time *without* the ghosts. There would be no ancient, evil Door to invite unwanted guests from the dead world.

She and Mitch would be married soon, in a small, private ceremony at the courthouse. Her dad and step-mom drove up from Texas to join them for the service. There was no reason to worry them with the details of her frightening encounters at Bristol House. Her heart still ached with the experiences she'd had, but she suspected the scars would not last long. She and Mitch had a lifetime of joy ahead of them, and she would not use precious time brooding about the past.

ABOUT THE AUTHOR:

Donna Hawk has always believed that creativity is the spark that makes life magical. A retired teacher turned storyteller, she now pours her imagination into the written word crafting stories designed to inspire, entertain, and transport readers into new worlds.

When she isn't writing, Donna's creativity takes many forms: painting vivid landscapes, sketching playful designs, and crafting one-of-a-kind wooden jewelry boxes and resin art pieces. Each creation whether on canvas, in wood, or in words carries her signature blend of artistry and heart.

Donna writes with the same passion she once brought to her classroom: a belief that stories have the power to ignite curiosity, stir emotions, and remind us of the beauty hidden in everyday life. Her books are more than stories; they're invitations to dream.

Other books by Donna Hawk

Desert Gold

Of Stone & Mist

Where Darkness Walks

Tattered Heart

Shadowed Hands

Key to the Iron City

Mercy, Me

Bastet's Heart

Butterfly Totem

Seeded

Scorched

Stronger

www.ingramcontent.com/pod-product-compliance
Lightning Source LLC
Chambersburg PA
CBHW022141170626
46807CB00005B/2025